# THE BURNING SKY

## JACK LUDLOW

First published in Great Britain in 2011 by
Allison & Busby Limited
13 Charlotte Mews
London W1T 4EJ
*www.allisonandbusby.com*

A CIP catalogue record for this book is available from
the British Library.

10 9 8 7 6 5 4 3 2 1

13-ISBN 978-0-7490-0832-1

Typeset in 11/18 pt Sabon by
Allison & Busby Ltd.

Paper used in this publication is from sustainably managed sources.
All of the wood used is procured from legal sources and is fully traceable.
The producing mill uses schemes such as ISO 14001
to monitor environmental impact.

Printed and bound in the UK by
CPI Mackays, Chatham ME5 8TD

To Gregg & Christina Prisco

Sorry I missed
your wedding

Live long
Love much
Laugh lots

# HISTORICAL NOTE

Throughout the novel, the Empire of Ethiopia is also referred to by its historical name of Abyssinia. Having, it is claimed, lasted 2000 years, it has waxed and waned, and at times included parts of Eritrea, Saudi Arabia, Sudan and modern Somalia. The names in the context of the 1930s are interchangeable, and the land it occupied then was close to that which it holds now as a Democratic Republic.

# ETHIOPIA AND THE HORN OF AFRICA, 1930s

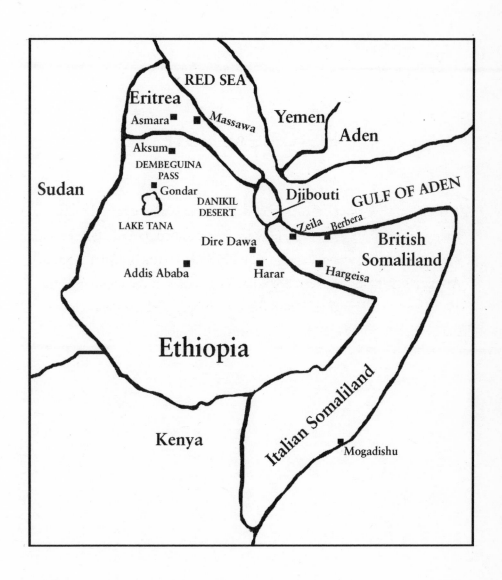

# CHAPTER ONE

If Peter Lanchester had any notion of appearing incongruous as he strode down the Reeperbahn, it did not show, while he was also self-possessed enough to ignore the looks he was getting from the inhabitants of the city of Hamburg. No strangers to eccentricity, they nevertheless rarely saw a man dressed in a bowler hat, let alone a thick beige overcoat called a 'British Warm', standard dress for off-duty British Army officers and perfect protection against a biting north-east wind.

The tightly rolled umbrella would be seen as sensible in a port that sat in the broad funnel of the River Elbe, which frequently brought in foul weather from the North Sea. If not that, a Baltic tempest could come racing across the flatlands of Holstein, either to drench the city or scar the flesh with a Siberian wind. As Lanchester made his way, a careful ear would have noted some symmetry in the tattoo of the brass ferrule striking the pavement in rhythm with the heels of his highly polished black Oxfords; sensed, perhaps, this fellow, wearing a striped military tie, was either a serving or an ex-soldier.

The bar he was seeking looked dingy from the outside, and entry into the dim interior did little to elevate the first impression. Hat off now – Lanchester was, after all, an officer and a gentleman – he ignored the slobbish fellow who sought to guide him to a table and made his way to a point where he could survey the far-from-spacious room, to peer through eyes stung by the smoke-laden atmosphere, the product of numerous cigarettes and too many cheap cigars.

Most of the tables were occupied, but having identified the man he was looking for, and observing he was in deep conversation with another, Lanchester chose a table for himself. He took the precaution of flapping a lazy hand across the chair before sitting down, and even more care not to put any part of him, including his calfskin gloves, on the little round table, much scratched and sticky with dried alcohol. His hat he placed on his upright brolly.

The champagne bottle, two glasses and a bill appeared before his bottom hit the velvet-covered, gilt-painted chair; the overweight and overmade-up whore was sitting opposite him a second after, leering with a mouth full of misshapen teeth, elbows on the table and her cavernous cleavage pushed forward, trying in German to sound seductive while wafting in his direction a mixture of bad breath and cheap perfume.

The temptation to rake his brolly across the table and remove the bottle and glasses was one he had to resist, but the presence of the prostitute he could not abide, being too fastidious a fellow for her type. So, sure she would understand a modicum of English in one of the world's busiest trading ports, he told her, in his very clipped tones, to 'fuck off!'.

That she reacted so badly was unfortunate, producing a stream of loud German invective, which drew unwelcome attention, in particular that of the man he had come to see. The eyes flicked over him and he knew he had been recognised: when you have fought in battle alongside a fellow his features never fade. But Lanchester was pleased Cal Jardine did not react in any special way; he looked over and then looked away with an unhurried turn of the head.

Picking up the open champagne bottle Lanchester perused the label, which told him it was a non-vintage Ruinart, which, if true, would indicate a decent brew. Curiosity, and a conviction it was false, had him pour a drop and hold it up to one of the dim wall lights, wondering if he would see any bubbles, his suspicions confirmed when none appeared. He waved to the man who had served it and he came waddling over, his hands clasped before him.

'*Sprechen Sie* English?'

'*Ja*, a leetle.'

'Good,' Lanchester said, lifting the champagne bottle. 'Take away this rubbish and bring me something decent to drink.'

'Is fine champagne, *mein Herr*.'

'It is shit, old boy, and most certainly not champagne. Now, be a good chap and do as I bid. Dish me up a Moselle of the quality Herr Jardine over there might drink. Oh, and when you bring it, make sure it is unopened, *verstehen Sie*?'

The waiter, who was either naturally greasy or inclined to excessive perspiration – Lanchester had mentally named him 'the slob' – looked him up and down; he was a fellow accustomed to a rougher clientele: merchant seamen, local riff-raff and the like, but it was impossible to equate the elegance of the man he was observing with them. Everything about him, from the toe of his gleaming shoes, through the sharp crease on his trousers, to the neat, swept-back and barbered black hair, marked him out as very different. The face, with its somewhat severe features – well-defined nose, high cheekbones and direct, black eyes – merely added to the overall impression of one who was accustomed to getting his way.

'And please do not try to cheat me, old son, or you'll find yourself occupying a cell in Davidstraße.'

The eyes of the slob narrowed, trying to figure out, Lanchester supposed, if in mentioning the St Pauli police station he was bluffing. The slight smile he wore was designed to hint at assurance and it worked; the man nodded and went to do as he was asked.

Cal Jardine, having finished his conversation, was now showing his companion out of the club, passing by Lanchester's table as he did so, but he avoided looking at him until the fellow was through the door and he was coming back, this coinciding with the arrival of a long-necked, brown wine bottle, taken from the slob by Jardine, who looked at the label. He rattled off a stream of German, sending the waiter scurrying away once more.

'I've ordered something better, Peter, something you will enjoy.'

'I have to say, Cal, the old German sounds very proper.'

'Just back in the groove, Peter; remember, I was partly raised in Germany.'

'As well as most other places on the bally Continent, I seem to recall. Happy to stay here, are we, with what is going on, Nazis and all that?'

'I have commitments that keep me here.'

'Are you going to sit down, Cal? I do so hate looking up at people, it makes me feel as if I'm back at school.'

Jardine sat down as the slob returned, with a bottle poking out of an ice bucket, two glasses, one of which was picked up to see if it was clean, that followed by a sharp nod which sent the man away. While that was happening, Peter Lanchester, in the way of a man who has not seen someone for years, examined Jardine, still a handsome bugger he thought, with the build of the rugby back row he had once been, a hard man who lived a testing life, the face lean, with the scars to prove it faintly evident on brow and jaw.

Then the piercing blue eyes, under those pale eyebrows and lashes, were on him. 'Let's leave it to chill, Peter, shall we, and while it does perhaps you will tell me what the hell you are doing here in Hamburg?'

'Why, Cal, old boy, I have come to find you. I was told this was where you did business and it seems I was correctly informed, though I have to say it is not the most salubrious emporium I have ever been in.'

'I prefer discretion to decor, Peter, and this is very discreet.'

'As is the whole area, Cal. Working out of the red-light district seems to suit you. Still smuggling out the Yids?'

'Don't you mean the Jews?'

'Same difference.'

'No, Peter, one is a race, the other an insult.'

'Odd, I thought it was halfway to being a language.'

'Peter, I don't have much time.'

'Business is brisk, then?'

'More truthful to say it is looming. So?'

'Simple, Cal. Certain worthy people at home require a disreputable character to do an honourable thing, and I advised them you rather fit the bill, you being a multilinguist and something of an adventurer. It also has to be a chap with certain military skills, which you also possess.'

'I no longer serve His Majesty's Government. I sent in my papers, remember, several years ago.'

'It's not HMG, Cal, which makes you perfect for what we have in mind. I believe the word is "deniable", which sounds like one of those dreadful new Americanisms to me. But you are still a soldier at heart.'

'I left the army a while back, Peter.'

'In a fit of pique I seem to recall.'

'I prefer to see it as righteous anger.'

'Do you think that wine is chilled yet?'

Jardine took a waiter's friend from his pocket and cut through the seal with the small blade, before inserting the corkscrew and easing out the cork, which he sniffed at, then nodded. A drop was poured into the glass closest to him to be swirled and examined before his nose went into the top and took several sniffs. He tasted it with a sort of sucking sound before swallowing. Satisfied, he filled Lanchester's glass, then his own.

'Cheers,' Lanchester said, lifting his glass high.

'*Slange.*'

'Still the model Caledonian, Cal.' Lanchester also sniffed the wine before swirling it once more to take a sip. 'I say, old boy, this is rather fine.'

'I have to tell you that, whatever you have come to see me about, I am very busy.'

'Too busy, old boy – I'm afraid Herr Hitler's minions are on to you.'

'I'm not doing anything illegal.'

'When did that ever matter in a fascist dictatorship? And, if my reading of these recently promulgated Nuremberg laws is correct, you are sailing very close to the wind.'

'All I am doing is helping Jews to get out of Germany.'

'With everything they possess, Callum, which will not please the Finance Ministry. They prefer that when the Yids . . . sorry, the Jews, decamp to safer climes, they leave behind most of their worldly goods. Also, the idea that you are making pots of money from it . . .'

'Who told you I was making pots of money?'

'Little birds twitter, old boy.'

Cal Jardine looked around the dingy club. 'Then why am I operating out of this dump? If I had any money, Peter, I would have a cavernous office overlooking the Binnenalster.'

'This wine was not cheap.'

'This wine was a gift from a grateful client. There are some things even I decline to get out of the country unseen.'

'So you're Robin Hood?'

'No, but neither am I the Sheriff of Nottingham. I do charge a fee out of principle, also because I have to live, and as well as that I have to make payments to certain people, like the fellow you saw me talking to when you came in.'

'Shipping agent or ship's captain?'

'None of your business, Peter, and if you don't mind me asking, what are you up to these days?'

'This and that, Cal, but I was asked to do this little errand because we are friends.'

'Never really friends, Peter.'

'Soldiers together, then, and fighting the good fight. It was felt that, since you know me, you might listen to what I have to say; not, I am sure you will agree, something for which you have a sterling reputation.'

'I always listen, Peter, it's just that I so often disagree with what is being proposed, like dropping bombs on women and children in undefended Arab villages to pacify them.'

'Let's not get into that, Cal,' Lanchester insisted wearily, as the phone behind the bar began to ring. 'It is now so sterile. Britannia has departed Iraq, so they are now happily murdering each other instead of engaging us to do it for them.'

'We left the Iraqis with a deep and justifiable bitterness.'

'You see everything as black and white – Manichean, in fact.'

'While you, Peter, and your like, don't see human when you see black, brown or anyone who does not ascribe to the thirty-nine articles of the Anglican faith.'

'Look, Cal, there are things about which you and I will never agree; let us just accept that, shall we? But I have come to tell you that you are in some danger, and also that I carry a proposal for a certain task, which given your well-known prejudices, or as you choose to call them, your principles, will be right up your street. Besides, your name and activities are so well known you are going to have to get out of Germany.'

The slob finally picked up the ringing phone.

'You think they are planning to deport me?'

'No, Cal, our information is that they are planning to arrest and incarcerate you.'

The phone was jammed down and the slob moved with surprising speed to whisper in Jardine's ear. If he had a sense of urgency, the man he communicated with showed none.

'That, Peter, was my contact at the local Nazi Party office.' That got a high-raised eyebrow. 'Money well spent.'

'And there's me thinking the Party members were pure and honest.'

'Purity and poverty find it hard to coexist, especially for a widow with three children.'

'An attractive widow, I suppose?'

'Ravishing! Apparently there is a squad of Brownshirts on their way to pick me up, though not, it seems, to hand me in to the authorities.'

'I have to say, old boy, I thought you had more time.'

'It wasn't you that put the Germans on to me, was it?'

'Perish the thought.'

'We have to leave, now.'

'Correction, Cal, it is you who has to leave. I have done nothing.'

'How little you know the country, Peter. There could be someone in this bar watching us, and since you were the last person to speak to the man who has now disappeared . . .'

'Are you going to disappear?'

'Without haste, yes. You coming, or are you going to wait to be interrogated?'

'Probably best, pity to leave the wine, though.'

'Let's take the bottle,' Jardine said, with that seductive, lopsided grin Lanchester remembered so well: the one, and he resented this, that seemed to weaken women's knees more readily than his own biting wit.

Jardine stood up in a way that ensured the bottle was hidden behind his back. Peter Lanchester, taking his pace from his fellow countryman, rose slowly, hat and brolly in hand, and followed Jardine as he sauntered towards the back of the room. As soon as he was seen to move in that direction, a brutish-looking type, with a square head and a flattened nose under a narrow forehead, rose to cut across his path.

Cal approached him in a casual manner and, as soon as he was close enough, he swung hard, hitting the thug with the bottle, taking him across the upper cheek, where it broke and cut him; then, bottle dropped, he kicked him in the groin before, as he fell forward, swiping him with a haymaker on the side of the ear to fell him. Behind the two Britons, the rest of the clientele was getting out fast.

'I say, old boy,' said Lanchester, this while Jardine put the boot in until the fellow lay bleeding and comatose. 'You have not lost your barbarian touch.'

'It a rough old town, Hamburg,' Callum said, as he stepped over the body, carrying on until they came to the foot of a set of steep stairs by a closed door.

'Just your sort of place, then.'

'Wait here, Peter, I have one or two things to collect.'

Callum Jardine took the stairs two at a time, with Lanchester calling after him, 'I hope it's not one of those ugly tarts that use the upstairs rooms, old boy.'

Lanchester opened the door and, bending forward, looked out before exiting into a narrow alleyway, where he donned his bowler. He was still there when Cal Jardine reappeared wearing a Burberry trench coat and carrying a large Gladstone bag. With a gesture he indicated that Lanchester should follow him and they made their way down the alley and out onto the wide avenue of the Reeperbahn.

'Cab rank, over there.'

'You armed?'

Jardine patted a bulging trench coat pocket. 'Just a precaution, Peter.'

They were crossing the street when the open-topped truck appeared, loaded with burly SA Brownshirts, the street-fighting thugs of the Third Reich. Cal turned his face away until they got into a cab, then with the door closed and a hand shielding his face, he watched as the Brownshirts jumped down and ran into the dingy bar, each one carrying a club or a cosh.

'Where are you staying, Peter?'

'Kaiserhof.'

'*Altona Bahnhof, bitte,*' Callum said to the driver. 'Might I suggest you ring and request them to send your luggage back to England? Ask how much the bill is, including carriage, and say you will send a cheque.'

'Why the train?'

Callum Jardine just smiled. 'So what is this honourable job?'

'Abyssinia. The Italians are gearing themselves up to invade and the poor fuzzy-wuzzies will struggle to boot them out.'

'They did it before.'

'The Battle of Adowa was forty years ago, Cal, and Mussolini is a different kettle of fish altogether. Officially HMG's policy is to work through the League of Nations, and before you say what a lot of good that will do, I will say the folk I represent wholeheartedly agree with you. The League is a toothless tiger, but Stanley Baldwin knows the British electorate will not tolerate anything that smells of war, quite apart from the fact that challenging Italy might drive Il Duce into the arms of Hitler, which is inimical to British foreign policy.'

'I seem to remember the British Foreign Office to be a murderous beast, Peter.'

'They believe in realpolitik, Cal, as the Huns are wont to say, but there are others less concerned with that who are prepared to act. We need to get some modern weaponry into Abyssinia and damned quick, and we would like you to both buy it and deliver it.'

'You seem very sure I can do this.'

'Don't be modest, Cal, you've run guns in the past.'

The taxi pulled up outside the railway station and they both got out, Jardine paying the driver and giving him an overly lavish tip. Entering the concourse, walking quickly, he made straight for a side exit, calling to Lanchester to pass his bowler, which he did. Callum Jardine then dropped it into the first litter bin they passed.

'I say, Callum old boy, I bought that in Jermyn Street at no little cost.'

'Too distinctive and Messrs Bates and Company will happily sell you a replacement. That taxi driver, who I tipped excessively, will be questioned and he will not only recall two Englishmen, one of them wearing a very distinctive hat, but will tell them we came here. They, I hope, will then assume we have made for somewhere like Copenhagen, given the trains to there run from Altona.'

'And we're not.'

'No.'

'You have a safe route out?'

Jardine had opened his Gladstone bag to produce a woollen muffler, which he handed to a companion who did not have to be told to put it on. 'I wouldn't be much of a Scarlet Pimpernel if I had no way to save myself, Peter – more than one, in fact.' Jardine then put a couple of pfennigs into his hand and indicated a phone booth. 'Now, you have just time to make that call to your hotel.'

'And then?'

'Certain things have to be brought forward.'

'Your Jews?'

'That fellow you saw me talking to when you came in is, if all

20

goes to plan, going to take us all to Rotterdam. You might just get a chance to learn a little Yiddish in the next few days.'

Lanchester was on his way to the phone when he stopped and turned back, his look curious. 'What about your paramour, Cal, the widow, your contact in the party office – is she to be left to her own fate after tipping you off?'

'The call she made will have been from a public phone, Peter, and Lette always knew this was possible. She will find another man to comfort her, and if you'd ever seen her you would know it will not be long in the coming.'

'A little callous perhaps?'

'Make your call.'

# CHAPTER TWO

Hamburg was a great, bustling city and also an international trading port full of seamen from all over the world. It was therefore a perfect place to avoid detection: even if rendered curious, no one overreacted to a strange face, a different voice or odd clothing, so there was little risk in travelling to wherever Jardine was headed. He bought a newspaper, a copy of the *Völkischer Beobachter*, flicking quickly through the pages before handing it to Lanchester.

'It's unlikely anyone in Hamburg will trouble you if you're reading that rag. Old Adolf is not held in high esteem hereabouts.'

'And here we are in England, convinced the entire German nation adores him.'

'What you have to worry about, Peter, is all the idiots in England who admire him and his mode of governance.'

'Where are we going?'

'It would do no good for me to say, since you don't know the city, and let us stop speaking in English, shall we?'

They travelled by bus, crowded given it was the end of the working day, boarding separately and sitting apart. Lanchester was at the rear, the newspaper held open to hide his face, though he kept a watch out of the corner of his eye, while trying simultaneously to decipher the stories in the Nazi Party's daily house journal, the banner headlines screaming abuse at the 'International Jewish Conspiracy' being the easiest to unravel.

The bus wended its way through various streets of Altona – wide boulevards of tall buildings, deep pavements lined with trees – until Jardine stood up. Lanchester waited a few seconds before doing likewise and joining him on the step, staying separate still as they alighted, though heading in the same direction along an avenue lined with small shops. Jardine stopped by a public phone while Lanchester moved past to idly examine a pillar plastered with posters full of warnings and exhortations from the Propaganda Ministry, vaguely aware that his companion had dialled more than once; in fact he did so three times.

'Code was it?' he asked, once Jardine joined him.

'A simple method, using the stories in the newspaper. Pick one on a page, refer to it and that page number is the key to the meeting place, one of half a dozen. You have to assume every *Judenhaus* is being watched, even if only by a nosy neighbour. Maybe a phone is being tapped, so no names either. My contact will come to meet me at a coffee bar, which is the designated number.'

'Might he not be followed?'

'He's good at avoidance.'

The coffee house in question was cramped and had no chairs,

just a series of small, high, round tables at which a customer could stand, a commonplace in Germany, which Lanchester, in a whisper, condemned as comparing unfavourably with a Lyons Corner House.

'I agree, Peter, but the coffee is so much better.'

'Too strong for me, old boy, and no pretty Nippies to serve us and tickle our fancy with thoughts of illicit carnality, quite apart from the fact that I prefer tea.'

Two cups were consumed before Jardine's contact arrived, his appearance – slim, athletic, with blond, near-white hair and blue eyes – giving Lanchester cause to wonder, not helped by the loud and very obvious way he greeted Jardine, returned without the use of a name by either. Another round of coffee was procured and then the two heads came together over the top of the table while Lanchester made a show of once more trying to read his paper. After a few minutes the contact left and at a nod from Jardine they exited a few paces behind to follow him.

'Your chum looks the perfect Aryan, I must say.'

'One hundred per cent Jewish, Peter; they're not all ginger hair and ringlets.'

'And he is taking us to?'

'A safe house, where there is a family waiting to be helped to leave the country.'

'I assume they are Jews and filthy rich?'

'Wealthy, yes, but not as well off now as they ought to be. They are members of a family that have been in Germany for nearly three hundred years, since the time of Fredrick the Great; in fact, the Ephraims were his bankers during the Seven Years' War. If we were in Berlin I could show you the house they were allowed to build, the first of its kind in the city and quite famous. Over time the family have bred and spread. This branch owned the department store and several other businesses in Königsberg.'

'Owned?'

'The local Nazis kicked them out of it without so much as a pfennig in compensation, but that's East Prussia for you. The further east you go the worse the anti-Semitism gets.'

'It's the way of the world, Cal.'

'Is it? Papa Ephraim has an Iron Cross, First Class, which he got fighting us at Third Ypres. He was a major in the Imperial German Army and now he's a sort of non-person.'

'One is sorry for the Jews, of course, but they have brought some of it on themselves.'

'Have they? By being prudent when others were blind? By being strong families and good neighbours, a community who looked after each other when times were hard? Does it not occur to you they might have a superior way of living their lives than us?'

'Have you converted, old boy?'

'You know me, Peter, I don't believe in anybody's God. It's about the only thing I share with Adolf Hitler. Have you read *Mein Kampf*?'

'Good Lord, no!'

'I suggest you do, because it will tell you what the next twenty years are going to be like and, if we don't stop these bastards, the next thousand years. The Kaiser was bad enough but this bugger is worse. He's a criminal leader running a criminal government and they will kill anyone who they do not like. I am doing my little bit to thwart him.'

While listening to this Lanchester had been casting his eyes about, across to the other side of the street and behind, his attention being taken by two men in dark double-breasted suits and big hats whose pace and route matched theirs.

'You always were destined for sainthood, Cal, but I must tell you I think we are being followed, or maybe it's your blond chum.'

'We are and he is, Peter, by people who are there to make sure no one else is doing the same. If they speed up and pass us that is a signal to disperse, so we will take the next turning and make contact later.'

'And your blue-eyed boy up ahead?'

'Can take care of himself.'

'How organised is this?'

'Well enough to work, but they will need to find someone who is not Jewish to replace me.' Jardine grinned. 'Perhaps HMG will send someone.'

'No fear,' Lanchester replied, doing nothing to keep the distaste out of his voice. 'I hope your charges are not headed for Blighty.'

'Where else would they go but to the Mother of Democracy?'

'We've got quite enough bloody refugees already. I don't suppose you will take my advice to quit while you are still ahead, Cal. Don't hang about, just go.'

'No, when what you're saying, Peter, is leave these people to their fate.'

'Why did I say "sainthood" when I meant "martyrdom"?'

That made Jardine laugh, which he was still doing as the blue-eyed boy turned and entered a recessed doorway in a long mansion block, the front door open still when the two Brits got to the bottom step. Lanchester followed as his companion skipped up and into a dark oak-floored hallway, smelling strongly of polish.

He was then led towards the rear of the block to where a slightly ajar door took them into a well-appointed apartment full of good, heavy furniture, the seats of which were occupied by a middle-aged couple and four children of various ages. As they entered, the man stood up, his face carrying an anxious look of uncertainty, while the mother wrung her hands, clearly very frightened.

'Herr Jardine?' he enquired, in the way one does, Lanchester registered, when one is meeting someone for the first time.

The subsequent conversation, in rapid German, left him isolated, so he occupied himself in examining the furnishings, dark, ponderous and of the imperial age. He was aware that, on entering, there had not been that thing on the door lintel containing a prayer, the name of which he could not recall, which he had been told graced the home of every Jew.

This was not a Yiddish household, and as if to underline that, there was a large portrait on the wall of old Paul von Hindenburg, Reich Chancellor of Germany before Hitler, as usual in his medal-bedecked field marshall's uniform, and looking so bulge-eyed and ferocious it was as if someone had a tight hold on his ancient balls.

Interest turned to the family: the father, talking to Cal, was grey-haired, with soft eyes and pale skin, the rather plump, fair-haired woman and her handsome children listening intently. The eldest, a girl, was strikingly beautiful, with dark eyes, flawless skin, clad in an elegant grey suit, and he guessed her to be of marriageable age, which earned her a smile intended to be disarming. In reply he received a glare and a dismissive toss of her head. Then she looked back to Jardine and that look softened considerably.

Has a soft spot for the lad, Lanchester thought, and on first sight! That was not an entirely happy reflection, given he had always seemed to play second fiddle in the lady-chasing stakes to the bugger.

Of the three boys, two were in their mid teens, while the last looked about twelve. All were well dressed and groomed, with that carefully barbered look that comes from wealth and an abundance of servants, leaving Lanchester with the general impression that they did not look overtly Levantine. He was also aware he was being introduced into the conversation and his presence explained.

What followed was more disputative, and from what words could be picked up it had to do with what Jardine thought they could safely carry, the young girl entering the fray being especially upset at what she was being told, eyes flashing under pretty lashes and the long fingers of her pale white hands used to emphasise her disagreements, with one of her brothers telling her, in words and gestures Lanchester did comprehend, to cease being so selfish.

'Having a spot of bother, old boy?'

'I've told them we must cut down on what they can take with them,' Cal replied.

'I rather gathered the drift of that. What's the normal drill?'

'A small vanload is usual, but I have said anything except what can be carried has to be left and that does not run to trunks full of clothing. We dare not expose others to potential arrest, given we have no idea what the police or the Gestapo know.'

The word 'Gestapo' made the mother put a hand to her mouth. 'And it is not going down well?'

There was no need for Cal to answer that, while Lanchester was aware the girl was glaring at him as though he was the cause of the change, so he deliberately looked at her legs in a wolfish way that had her pushing her skirt forward to ensure the knees were fully covered.

'We are going to have to get into the docks without being seen,' Cal insisted, 'which means we can't go through the main gates as planned, pretending to be normal passengers.'

'False documents, I take it?'

'Yes, but if they are on a special alert they might not pass muster, and our friends, when seeking out Jews, have a very simple method of establishing their religion.'

The girl was still arguing with her father, though in a hushed, assertive tone, so Lanchester said, 'I should tell Bonny Lass what will happen to her if the Gestapo get their hands on her. Never mind them examining her father's cock, I doubt the interracial sex laws will hold when they see her in her smalls. I have to say I wouldn't mind interrogating her myself.'

'It's my job to help them, Peter, not terrify them.'

'I was thinking of getting the sods to behave, on the very good grounds that we, I suspect, will be going out by the same route as they.'

'Correct.'

The argument was not swift and it was not without raised voices, which reminded Callum Jardine of the aperçu that two Jews in an argument were always good for at least three opinions, but eventually what he was insisting on seemed to be reluctantly accepted. A time was arranged and he signalled to Lanchester they could leave by the mere act of lifting his Gladstone bag. They exited to the sound of raised voices.

'Now they can argue about who has to give up what!'

The next bus journey was longer and involved a change, taking them over the wide River Elbe to the endless warehouses and docks of Germany's premier port, running along a series of high walls that enclosed the whole area until they alighted at what looked like a set of main gates. As soon as the bus disappeared Jardine spun round and led Lanchester away, walking quickly.

'Even you can't get through those main gates without papers, Peter.'

'A British passport generally does the trick, old boy.'

'Not without a seaman's discharge book or a valid passenger ticket, and you must have realised by now how strict the Germans are about one having the right papers.'

'Bloody nightmare, they behave as if everyone is an enemy of the state.'

'In Hitler's world everyone is.'

They walked a fair distance, all the while keeping to the dockyard wall until they came to a long street, dead straight and full of muddled, grimy warehouses, with Jardine slipping into the doorway of one, dropping his Gladstone, telling Lanchester to wait as he went ahead.

'If anyone approaches me, whatever they are dressed in, take that bag and make yourself scarce.'

'And then?'

'British consulate's your best bet; I take it you know where that is?'

'I'll find it.'

'As I said before, I have no idea what the Gestapo know about me and my activities.' That was followed by a very direct look. 'You might know more about that than I do.'

'Bits and bobs, Cal, that's all I have.'

'You knew enough to warn me I was about to be raided and I am curious as to how you got that information.'

'A chap in the Berlin embassy, I was at school with him, passed on the stuff about you, but I hardly think this is the place to enquire about such things.'

'So?'

'As far as I know, you are under suspicion, Cal, but how deep that goes . . .' Lanchester shrugged. 'My chum did not expect you to be fingered so soon, but he intimated it would not be weeks before you were arrested and that I should warn you to scarper.'

'Perhaps you were the cause.'

'Can't think why.'

'Perhaps they thought you were a Jew, Peter.'

'*Me?*'

Amused by the shock, Jardine added, 'If I am not intercepted I will go in a doorway about fifty yards along. Wait a few minutes before following me and call out your name when you arrive.'

Jardine's shoes echoed off the street cobbles and the high buildings as he walked along the street. About a hundred yards on some people were still working, well past the usual hour, loading a lorry, while the other warehouses seemed to have shut up shop for the day, giving the street a deserted air.

He knew that could be false and mentally he was working out the odds: those Brownshirts in the Reeperbahn did not matter – they tended to be dense thugs – but if the Gestapo was on his trail, and it would be wise to assume they were, then they would not want to take just him, they would want to catch him in the act of smuggling out Jews. Cue a diplomatic protest to HMG about British nationals interfering in Germany's internal affairs and embarrassment all round.

The Ephraim family would be coming by car within the hour, and if this place were being watched, the Gestapo would wait and try to take them as well, giving them a banner headline locally about treacherous Jews being aided by outsiders. Common sense told Jardine that Peter Lanchester was right: he should walk away; the risk to him came from being here when they arrived. The Dutch captain he had already paid and he would not care if his passengers were two people or eight.

'Why is it,' he murmured to himself, as he pulled out a set of door keys, 'I have never had any common sense?'

It was an office of sorts, dirty walls in need of fresh whitewash, a ceiling with holes big enough to show the naked wooden laths, a desk and a chair set against the back wall alongside a battered wooden filing cabinet and an excessively large cupboard, all sitting on plain floorboards. Once inside he checked for signs of entry: an oil lamp just behind the door, so that if it was opened too wide oil would leak onto the boards to create a stain impossible to remove; little scraps of folded paper in odd places; a hair spat on, then stuck to a filing cabinet drawer, and inside that an open ink bottle, precariously balanced, that required his inserted fingers to keep in place.

Lanchester saw Jardine disappear, which made more acute his examination of the street: he too could see those loading that lorry in a desultory fashion, but they had not paused or looked in Jardine's direction. No one had emerged from any of the other buildings along the way, these observations being made as he was harbouring the same notions as the man he had come to Hamburg to find.

He could just go and leave Jardine to it, the danger to him if he left was minimal – how could he be arrested for merely talking to a fellow countryman? That was until he recalled this was Hitler's Germany, a country where the rule of law did not apply. Besides, he had a job to do, so after the required interval, he picked up the Gladstone bag and made his way to the doorway, heart in mouth, croaking his name at the panelling.

'What is this place?' he asked as soon as he was inside, the act of brushing his sleeves in such a grubby location an automatic one.

The smell was of musty and disturbed dust, made worse as Jardine lifted a worn blind to reveal a grimy window from which he could watch the street.

'The way out of Germany, Peter. There's a tunnel under the dockyard wall that we have kept as our exit in an emergency. Smugglers built it during the last war to get contraband in from Sweden and they brought it back into use when the Nazis banned certain imports. Being kindly disposed, they have given us the use of it as a one-off way out.'

'Black marketeers?' Jardine nodded. 'They would not be Jewish by any chance?'

'There are plenty of Aryans up to the same tricks.'

'Except Aryans, even criminal ones, are less likely to be watched.' Jardine looked at his watch. 'We have a little time to chat now, Peter, so why don't you tell me what it is you came to Hamburg to propose?'

'I told you.'

'You told me what you wanted, but not who wanted it done.'

'I think that is better left till we are safely out of here.'

'Don't prevaricate, Peter,' Jardine snapped, going to his Gladstone bag and, on opening it, producing a Mauser pistol, which he passed to Lanchester, followed by a clip of bullets. 'I take it you still know how to use one of these.'

'I do, but I have a strong disinclination to employ them in the situation in which we find ourselves.'

'Last resort, Peter; best to leave a couple of dead secret policemen behind us than end up in somewhere like Dachau.'

'Where and what is Dachau?'

'It's a special prison for enemies of the state, but just be satisfied it's not a place you would want to visit.' Jardine pushed the chair

33

towards Lanchester and sat on the edge of the desk. 'Now please answer my question.'

Lanchester clicked in the clip of bullets, having first checked the safety was on. 'The idea was that I would take you back to Blighty to meet a group of people who share your concerns.'

'And you, Peter?' That got a raised eyebrow. 'You don't strike me as a knight in shining armour. Quite the reverse, in fact.'

'I am a messenger, Cal, what I believe is irrelevant.'

'Funny that, Peter, I always had you down as someone who lacked beliefs.'

'It makes for a contented life.'

Jardine went to stand by the window, far enough back from it to not be observed. 'My question?'

'I represent a group of people who think that unchecked fascism is a danger to our national security.'

'Can't fault that.'

'But they are not in government.'

'Churchill?'

'Most folk think he's just a mad old warmonger.'

'That's not an answer.'

'It will do for now, old boy.'

'You said a group of people?'

'An eclectic mix who think if we back Ethiopia and put a stopper on Mussolini it will make Hitler think twice about disturbing the peace.'

'It won't, but I need names.'

'Not yet, Cal, just take my word for it they exist and that the funds are available to aid the world's underdogs.'

'Most people I know think Fatso Mussolini is a genius for making the Italian trains run on time, especially those with a few quid and no brains. They are the same ones who admire Adolf and think Britain would be better off with someone like him in charge. You know the type, shoot a few miners and the world will be safe.'

'Shall we leave politics out of it for now?'

'If you insist, but guns cost a lot of money and they are not easy to come by without everyone knowing about it, the arms trade being somewhat incestuous by nature.'

As he was speaking, Jardine went to the door and, opening it, peered out just enough to look along the street. When he looked back at Lanchester it was with a less than happy face.

'What's wrong?'

'That lorry, they are taking far too long to load it.'

# CHAPTER THREE

'**C**an you stop your Yids?'

Jardine, who now had his own pistol out, was, for the first time, really sharp. 'Peter, this is not the bloody golf club, will you stop calling them that.'

'Can you?'

'There's no telephone here.'

'Something of a flaw in the organisation, I hazard. I'm beginning to regret accepting this commission, all this danger is not my cup of tea at all.'

That laconic statement got Lanchester a look and a wry smile: Jardine had been right when he declined to accept that they were really friends, but they had served together as young subalterns in the last months of the Great War, and whatever else the man was he was no coward; he had been a damned fine officer with a mind sharp enough to know when it was foolish to be brave, as well as when it was necessary to employ just that quality to carry forward his men. They had both stayed on in the army after the war, Lanchester because he was open about not being fit for anything else, Jardine for his own personal reasons.

That he lacked convictions did not single Lanchester out from his fellow regimental officers: they were all racial bigots to a degree, with the concomitant drawback that some of them were certifiable dunderheads as well – not all the donkeys in the British army were generals. Lanchester was far from the exception: it had been Callum Jardine who was the outsider in his declarations that what they were doing in the Middle East on behalf of the British Government was utterly wrong and likely to produce the exact opposite result of what was intended.

You did not pacify the locals by dropping bombs on rebellious Iraqi villages, killing more women and children than the targeted fighters, acts carried out at the behest of government ministers like the aforementioned Winston Churchill, who had been Chancellor of the Exchequer at the time. These policies were something about which Peter Lanchester had been sanguine, and Callum Jardine furious enough to eventually resign his commission.

'Why we did not crush these Hun buggers when we had them on the floor, I still do not comprehend, Cal. Their army was totally beaten in 1918 and now they tell us they were stabbed in the back by their own bloody politicos.'

'You trying to remind me I was wrong about that, Peter?'

'Only in a roundabout way, old boy, but I do recall you saying that there was every reason to grant the Hun an armistice instead of killing several thousand more, whereas I was all for pushing on and burning Berlin. Come to think of it, I'd still happily go to Holland and shoot the Kaiser.'

'I was concerned about more of us dying for no purpose, not least myself, and I am sure you can remember the losses we suffered as well as I can. But I'm doing my best to make up for not agreeing with you here and now.'

'And to quote that fine comedian, Mr Oliver Hardy, this is another fine mess you have got me into.'

'Not that again!'

Iraq had been Mesopotamia when they first served there and it had been hell: hot enough to fry an egg on the toe of your boot, dusty, flyblown and deadly. The army of which they had been a part had artillery, trucks, armoured cars and aircraft; the Arabs old pattern rifles, guile and, sometimes, suicidal bravery, which made patrolling extremely risky.

Lanchester was of the opinion that shooting first and asking questions after was sound military sense; Jardine, marginally senior by date of his commission, was not, and in employing his tactics he had got two infantry half-companies trapped in an Iraqi village of mud huts and narrow streets, totally outnumbered and with no means of calling for support.

'I got you out, didn't I?'

'Only by my crawling on my belly for several hours along a dry watercourse! Christ, I am still picking the sand out of my teeth. If you'd heard some of the names my chaps were calling you . . .'

'Don't worry, Peter, my lads were using the same language and it was we who provided the rearguard and took the casualties.'

'Justice and no more, old fruit, and thank the Lord no one died. But the question is, if we are in the soup now, which I rather suspect you think the case, how are we to get out of it?'

That got a wave of the Jardine's Mauser. 'I don't think we can shoot our way out.'

'Nor, I suspect, will you think of sacrificing your . . .' Lanchester paused then to choose his word carefully '. . . refugees?'

Jardine went back to his bag and opened it again, taking out a folder of papers. 'These are their travel documents, Peter, tickets from the Hook of Holland to Harwich, as well as the names of their British sponsors, with supporting letters. Without someone to vouch for them and feed them they will be turned away.'

'Money?'

'They will have their own, at least in highly saleable commodities, which was what we were arguing about in that apartment. I was telling them to take those and abandon everything else.'

That got a loud and disapproving sniff, to which Jardine responded with a bored look. He moved to the large cupboard, opening both the doors and reaching inside. Unable to see, Lanchester heard a series of wooden clicks. Then his companion emerged, closed the doors and soundlessly moved the cupboard to one side, revealing a square hole in the floor.

'This is the tunnel. It takes you into the docks, and if you walk directly down to the quayside and turn left you can't miss the *Den Haag*.' There was no need to say that was the Dutch ship by which they were to depart. 'The captain has been paid.'

'Risky.'

'No, he has helped before and I trust him.'

'It does not strike you that the Hun have knowledge of this tunnel?'

'That depends on whether you have told me everything you know, Peter.'

'I would have to be stupid to hold back on anything now, would I not?'

'It's possible they know, but unlikely, Peter, because if they did, I would have been taken as I walked in here, as would my refugees. Germans are methodical, it is not in their nature to take chances, and the first thing I checked was that no one had been here since my last visit. Not even the most careful entrant could have passed by the precautions without leaving a trace.'

'Supposition, brother.'

'What else have I got? If the Gestapo knew this was the way out they would have been all over it to make sure they did not cock up, and they haven't. It is also true that if your chum in the Berlin embassy knew certain things, then Jerry knows too.'

'My man knew what you were up to but not how you go about it.'

'Did he tell you how he found out?'

'No, and I did not ask.'

'There's a lot of competition in intelligence-gathering in this neck of the woods, the new boys created by the Party treading on the toes of the old police and spy agencies, like the Abwehr. Your embassy contact wasn't the military attaché by any chance, was he?'

'Clever boy, Cal.'

'Rumour has it there's a turf war going on between the Abwehr and the SS, who want all counter-espionage to be in their hands, so the army boys might not be averse to queering their pitch by passing on certain bits and bobs, as you called them, to our embassy. What do you think?'

'It's a reasonable prognosis, but that does not explain the thugs we avoided earlier.'

'If relations are bad between the SS and the Abwehr, they are truly

40

diabolical between the SS and the SA. If my name and location came up as a suspect, the Brownshirts would jump at a chance to beat their rivals to it so they can claim to be the true guardians of the Nazi faith, and they spy on each other all the time. We will never know, but it is very possible that a party of Gestapo were on their way to the Reeperbahn when that truckful of club-carrying beauties alighted.'

'And here and now?'

'Why would the army intelligence boys tell the Berlin attaché half a tale? – which backs up my theory that this escape route is unknown to the Gestapo. They have only got part of the story and that is there is a cell in Hamburg, of which I am a part, queering their pitch of stripping the departing Jews of their wealth. They would deduce we are using the Elbe to get them out with their possessions, but that only allows you to block the obvious routes, like the main dockyard gates.'

'They could search the departing ships.'

'It would take too long and upset the ships' owners, who would divert their cargoes elsewhere. I would guess they have limited information about the where and when of any alternative exit, and it is obvious we must have one that does not involve normal tickets, so they would have to spread themselves around the whole area, which is huge. These docks are close to the size of Liverpool.'

'They might also be inside on the quays?'

'Perhaps, but again distributed very thinly and wondering what to cover, and we have to hope no idea of which vessel we will be heading for, given there are dozens of them sailing in and out of the port every day.'

'Have you asked yourself how they came by whatever knowledge they do have?'

'Of course, but I don't think there's a leak at the Jewish end. That could only come through interrogation and I am unaware of anyone being arrested who knows anything.'

'And you would know?'

'My Jewish contacts would know.'

'If I was running this show from the Hun end, they wouldn't.'

'Is that what you're in now, Peter, counter-intelligence?'

'Good God, no! You know me, Cal, I couldn't run the sock counter at Harrods.'

The absurdity of that would have made Jardine laugh at another time; now was too serious. 'Since I am making assumptions, I must give you a choice. If you wish to go, do so now, through the tunnel; give the captain my name and he will get you out of here even if me and my party don't manage to join you.'

'Have I ever told you how your bloody nobility gives me a pain in my posterior?'

'More than once.'

'One of these days you must tell me the real reason you engage in such asinine activities.'

Jardine pocketed his Mauser, picked up the Gladstone bag and went to the door, turning the handle. 'I would advise you not to hold your breath while waiting for a response.'

'Where are you going?'

'To see if I can draw off any watchers. Maybe if I move, so will they, because I am convinced they cannot know who is coming and from where, or if they are close to the real escape route. But for certain they know my identity, so they might tail me, which will leave the way clear for the Ephraims.'

'And if you're wrong?'

'Then you will hear gunshots. After that, you must decide how to act on your own.'

'Say they do follow you, I assume that leaves me to get these bloody people through the tunnel?'

'If you wouldn't mind.'

'And you, how do you get out?' Jardine just grinned and touched the side of his nose with an index finger, which exasperated Lanchester. 'If you do manage, Cal, for the sake of the Lord do not tell anyone I helped to rescue some Yids. I'll never live it down.'

'Army & Navy Club, Peter, two weeks from now and you can buy me luncheon. Oh, and by the way, don't be surprised by the way our party is dressed. Can I have my scarf back, I might need it?'

Lanchester was taking the muffler off when he too grinned. 'Does Bonny Lass speak Yiddish?'

'No idea.'

Lanchester ran a tidying hand over his glossy black hair. 'Might be prepared to learn if she does, don't you know. How long does it take to get to Rotterdam?'

'I saw the way she looked at you, Peter; for what you're thinking about Tokyo is not far enough.'

'And I saw the way she looked at you, Cal, but never underestimate the charm of a true Englishman.'

The sun is slow to fall near the Baltic, but it is low in the long evenings, so it cast deep shadows between the high warehouses that lined the deserted street. Approaching the lorry, with a couple of men seemingly working to load it, moving boxes about, it was hard to appear nonchalant, even harder not to look too directly at them to see if they had the kind of coarse appearance such labourers should have.

Gladstone bag swinging in one hand, the other in his trench coat pocket holding tight the now warm stock of his pistol, Jardine did flick a glance towards them as he passed close by, throwing them a crisp 'Guten Abend'.

His suspicions were heightened by the way they failed to respond, it being a mark of polite behaviour for Germans to do so, while the impression of faces too bland was fleeting, of hands a bit too white and teeth that seemed too even. Likewise the clothing had none of the wear that came from doing a lousy job for low pay. The hairs were standing on the back of his neck when he passed the cab, yet he dare not look back to see if they were watching him.

In such building-created canyons, sound travels, and though he could not see it, he heard the distant start of a car engine, as well as that particular whining noise one makes when reversing. As he came to the first junction, to a road running away from the dockside, he looked along it to observe it was empty; had the car been there and so obviously official-looking it had needed to be withdrawn? How many bodies did they have on this job?

His heart jumped when the lorry engine started, a deep throbbing note as it idled, then the pitch of the engine rising as it revved and moved, that mixing with the crack of his heels on the pavement. Gears and engine pitch changed twice, then the noise became a diminishing echo, fading eventually till his shoes were making the only audible sound. The combination of that car noise and a lorry, hitherto stationary too long, indicated they were either police or Gestapo. It made no odds which, they had moved because of him and that had to mean he was being tailed; good for his refugees, not so hot for him, given he had no idea of the resources they had employed for the task.

The street being long and straight, he saw the Auto Union coupé, hood up, coming towards him at quite a distance, moving slowly on the cobbles, which made it buck and sway, the jarring of its body as the springs failed to cushion it properly indicating the car was carrying too heavy a load. The first clue to it being the Ephraim family was the sight, in the driver's seat, of the man Lanchester had called his blue-eyed boy, both hands on the wheel, staring straight ahead, while alongside him sat the father with a worker's cap pulled well down, hiding his grey hair.

Jardine saw blue-eyed boy's lips move and guessed it was an admonishment not to look in his direction, the coincidence of their arriving as he was departing as good a way as any to let them know of possible danger. As the car passed, it being natural for him to glance in its direction, he saw five people crowded in the rear, the daughter and youngest son sat on laps, then the suitcases strapped onto the jump seat, too many to his mind, which produced a flash of irritation which grew as he crossed the road behind it, halting at a bus stop and able to look back the way he had come and see the vehicle drive on past the doorway from which he had emerged.

That luggage rankled: it was always a problem to get people to leave things behind, items they had probably not even noticed for years suddenly taking on huge sentimental importance. Valuables he could comprehend; it would be a fair bet that Papa Ephraim had stuff on his lap and all around his feet, old master and modern art paintings in leather tubes, a case of precious objects that had to include heirlooms and, inevitably, a solid-silver seven-branch candlestick for Friday night prayers. It did not matter what he made of the car and it being overloaded – it only mattered if those on his tail, and they had to be there even if he could not see them in the gathering gloom, were made curious.

Blue-eyed boy would not stop until he was out of sight: the ship was not due to sail until first light, so a way would have to be contrived to get the family into that tunnel entrance in the dark. It was no longer his problem; he just had to keep the watchers watching him and then he had to get clear and out of Hamburg and Germany by a different route, the first stage of that to get on the approaching bus.

Jardine knew with night coming his best chance was to return to St Pauli, though not to the bar in which Lanchester had found him – the red-light district was busy in the hours of darkness and there were streets there that would make it near impossible for anyone to follow. Once in his old stamping ground, his way out he already knew, the only problem he had was of being picked up before he could get there.

Many times throughout his life Callum Jardine had been in a position of danger in which he could do nothing to alleviate it; people now saw the last campaign of the Great War as a walkover, the German army retreating and the Allies dogging their heels. It was nothing like that: in retreat the Kaiser's army made the advancing Allies fight for every pre-prepared trench system and they had been constructed in advance and in depth.

The only way to take them, tanks rarely being available, was by infantry attack, and if the tactics had improved since the bloodbaths of Verdun and the Somme, it was still hard pounding, while to that was added the feeling, with things hopefully coming to the end, that no one wanted to be the last one to stop a bullet.

Sitting on the first bus, which took him to the Hauptbahnhof, followed by another from the main railway station to St Pauli, Jardine was aware that he was sat in well-lit seats and easily observed, a bit like a target in a shooting gallery. That feeling did not diminish when he was finally on foot and he had to remind himself of those times, the occasions when, as a soldier in battle, you come to terms with the possibility of death, allied to the knowledge it is not in your hands to avoid it. The hardest part was to keep his watchers feeling he was unaware of their presence: never spin round, don't do that stopping-to-look-in-a-window trick so you can see if anyone else halts too – let them think they are secure and potentially you are unknowingly leading them to something significant.

The Reeperbahn was, by the time he got there, its usual Friday night self, full of locals drinking in the bars, of sailors and visitors from more straight-laced communities come to sample the liberal streets of the famous red-light district. In the many iffy places Cal Jardine had been since he left the army he had learnt that setting up a way out was of paramount importance, one of the first things to be worked out before indulging in any activity, and Hamburg was no different – it was just easier than most.

He suspected his tail knew they were in trouble when, after talking to a streetwalker, he dived into the Herbertstraße: first they lost sight of him because of the high metal panels that shut off the street from public view. When they, too, pushed their way through the unlicensed whores who congregated at each end of the street, passing the big sign saying 'Women Prohibited', they entered a narrow, crowded and garishly lit alleyway, full of men either just staring, or bargaining with the scantily clad women sitting in the brightly lit windows.

The narrow alley Jardine made for had more than just a raised window beside a doorway; it was an apparent dead end, but a special one, and as he entered he spied Gretl, the woman who worked there, deep in discussion with a drunken, noisy quartet who, by their colouring and dress, looked to be seamen and Dutch. Jardine had passed several windows in which sat young and attractive women, scantily clad and available for business; this was a different kind of establishment altogether and the way Gretl was dressed underlined that.

A big lady in every respect, tall and far from young, she had on red lederhosen, a waistcoat of similar leather material which hardly managed, so tight was it laced, to contain her huge bosom, and on her head a horned helmet that barely contained her brassy fair hair. This outfit was set off with a pair of black, shiny thigh boots with spiked heels, while in her hand she held a riding whip.

Gretl had worked the Herbertstraße for decades to become a feature of the place. Most of the window girls came for a few years and many from country towns and villages, not Hamburg. They saved up the money they made from selling their bodies, overseen and kept medically clean by the municipality, then retired back to their locality, no doubt without their neighbours being aware of their past, to set up a shop or some kind of business, or merely to become a marriageable catch with their nest egg – in some senses a more morally upright bunch than those they served.

As he approached, walking at speed, Gretl turned to look at him and he was presented with quite a sight: her eyes were picked out in thick kohl, her cheeks caked with deep make-up and her lips a bright-red slash on her lined face. She was in the midst of a stream of German invective that told those with whom she was negotiating that the price they wanted to pay for her services was very far from sufficient. When Gretl looked like that, the customers who got into her inner sanctum paid a high price for their parsimonious temerity. It would be painful, but that was before she eased their soreness with the other skills she had honed over the years.

Sighting Jardine she smiled, exposing large, yellowing teeth, then enquired in a deep guttural voice if he had finally come for a treatment, which made the Dutchmen, for in their protested responses they established that was their nationality, look and act aggrieved. All she got was a quick peck on the cheeks, leaving Jardine with the taste of pancake on his lips as he slipped past her. The last thing he heard was Gretl reassuring her putative clients that he was only passing through.

There was no way of knowing if his tail had seen him come in to Gretl's little cul-de-sac. If they had, she would delay them and be damned ferocious with it, but all it would take to shut her up would be the production of an identity card: no one feared the police more than those who lived and worked the Reeperbahn; if a customer complained to the *Polizei*, they always took their side – the reputation of the district came before right and wrong. If it was the Gestapo, that was ten times worse.

The room Gretl used was lit in red, with *couchettes*, a bed and various instruments of torture on the walls, manacles and harness. Behind a curtain was a door to the back alley – every establishment had them, gloomily lit by the moon and barely wide enough for two people to pass, but, like the street it served, cut off by high barriers at both ends, these locked. Once through, Jardine dropped his bag and took out his Mauser, waiting: if they were coming they would do so immediately.

After half a minute, when nothing happened, he opened the bag, well aware he had a limited amount of time, trying to assess the probable actions of those pursuing him. If he worked it right, that would allow him to get clear; getting it wrong probably meant incarceration in somewhere like Dachau, being subjected to repeated beatings and torture as the SS sought information on his Jewish contacts so he would take some of them with him as he died to avoid that.

Since they did not follow they could not have seen him disappear and thus had no idea where he was: he could be in any number of the rooms behind an empty prostitute's window, so the only way to collar him was to shut off the Herbertstraße at either end and that would take time – time to get to a phone and get a message to whoever was overseeing the pursuit, time to get the manpower in place – and he calculated he had up to ten minutes before such precautions could be brought in to play, a period he cut in half for safety.

Off came his trench coat and out of the bag came a sailor's reefer jacket, a cap and a duffle bag, as well as the scarf he had taken from Lanchester and that was wrapped around his neck. The pistol was transferred, as well as a wallet containing his British passport, also the few possessions he wanted, a change of shirt and socks, his washbag and a money belt containing some US dollars, British pounds and a thick bundle of German marks, several of which he extracted before concealing the belt under his shirt. His German papers, bearing a false name, he kept handy, as well as the discharge book he had, which identified him as a Czech sailor.

The Gladstone he left by a wall in the middle of the alley so as to protect Gretl – they would question every whore in the street, and since none would admit to knowledge he had to suppose they could not finger anyone, which should lead to an impasse: not even the Gestapo could shut down the Herbertstraße without causing a riot in the city of Hamburg. He went back through Gretl's parlour to find her in full flow, beating on the bare buttocks of one of her Dutchmen while his three companions, bottles of very pricey beer in their hands, noisily egged her on.

Jardine didn't stop and neither did Gretl, she was too professional, even when in passing he stuck a rolled up bundle of marks into her ample cleavage. Within seconds he was out in the crowded street, heading for the barrier, his heart in his mouth as he joined the throng and slipped between the two overlapping metal plates, to be immediately accosted by one of the unlicensed street girls. Engaging in conversation with her allowed him to assess the risks he faced, relieved that all he could see was one anxious-looking fellow in a long leather coat and fedora, less at ease given the sound of approaching sirens, added to the attention he was getting from the whores.

To disappear was easy; all he had to do was walk off with his whore. Who was going to stop a man dressed like a sailor doing that?

# CHAPTER FOUR

'I hope you got your money's worth from the lady of the night, old boy.'

Peter Lanchester said that as he poured Jardine a small glass of Château d'Yquem, the wine with which he was washing down his bread-and-butter pudding. All around them was the buzz of conversations, the Army & Navy Club being full of lunching officers, both serving and retired, careful of their manners under the basilisk portrait gazes of senior commanders of the past, in red coats and blue, as well as great paintings of land and sea battles in which Britannia had been triumphant.

The mere fact of Lanchester being present testified to the success of getting the Ephraims out of danger and he had been decent enough to accompany them all the way to Harwich. They were now happily ensconced in St John's Wood, where they were to stay with their well-heeled fellow-Jewish sponsors.

'As they say in certain of our newspapers, Peter, having paid her I made my excuses and left. It is not a good idea to get into bed with the Hamburg streetwalkers.'

'Diseased are they?'

'Unregulated will do and that's before their pimps try to cosh and rob you. The window girls are not only pimp-free but are taken out of circulation if they have picked up anything untoward, which in itself is too commonplace in such a busy international port.'

'I shall remember that if I am ever again in Hamburg. I must say your girl Gretl sounds like a real card, not that I am much taken with the idea of the treatment she metes out.'

'I'd like to see her dealing with Goebbels – she hates the Nazis, as an awful lot of Germans do.'

'Then why did they vote for the buggers?' Lanchester snapped, in a rare flash of real passion.

That was said in too loud a manner and it attracted a degree of attention, especially from the older members: balding, grey-haired men with the broken-veined faces of the serious port drinker and the watery eyes of their years and endemic disapproval. They reminded Jardine of every officers' mess he had ever been in, both at home and abroad, which always had its quota of elderly majors going nowhere, men whose sole joy in life seemed to be making existence hell for the newly commissioned subalterns, while simultaneously blocking the road to promotion for everyone else.

'Hamburg didn't vote for Hitler, Peter, nor did Berlin and they loathe him in the Ruhr, but when you've been humiliated in war, had hyperinflation twice in twenty years, suffered massive unemployment and witnessed an old dodderer like Hindenburg running the show and favouring his fellow Prussian landowners with the few coins left in the coffers, anyone who promises you security, a bit of national pride, a job and change has a certain cachet. There are, of course, no elections anymore, just the Führer of the German *Volk*.'

'Apologies and thank you for the history lesson, Cal, but I seem to have sidetracked you when you were regaling me with how you got out of Hunland. Sharp thinking to head inwards rather than out when the borders were being watched. I take it you did not linger long in Berlin.'

'I went straight from the railway station to the passenger barges that run down to Prague.'

'And your forged papers stood up to scrutiny?'

There was no need to say they had been checked, and more than once, in a country in the grip of deep paranoia layered on top of an endemic and historic love of bureaucracy. Travelling without papers was impossible and you could not even stay with a relative in Germany for more than two weeks without registering your presence at the police station. Every mode of transport had roving officials checking documents and that included Elbe barges. It was thus a good job those he carried had been supplied by members of the Hamburg underworld and were of a high standard.

'Being foreign gets a lot of scrutiny, but I pretended to be a *Sudetenlander*.'

'And what, pray, is that when it's out and about?'

'German-speaking part of Czechoslovakia, one that Hitler wants to be incorporated back into the Reich, like all the bits that were hived off by the Treaty of Versailles. I said you should read *Mein Kampf*. Anyway, being an ethnic German, sadly cut off from my *Volk*, and I played that up a lot, got me a certain amount of sympathy. Accent's a bit tricky, mind, bit like speaking Welsh.'

'Welsh as an accent *and* German, so doubly damned, poor sods,' Lanchester opined, picking up the wine bottle to ensure it was empty. 'Is it not odd, though, the way we never think of other nations having accents? Port?'

'Not at luncheon, Peter, and not when I suspect I might need a very clear head.'

Lanchester signalled to the waiter, told him to serve them coffee in the library, a quiet place to which they retired, taking up seats in the far corner, away from the door. 'You know what we are after already, up to a point.'

'I do not know the "we", and while you said money was available, I would need to know how much and where it came from to be sure I can trade in the places I need to. That is one area in which all must be secure. Nothing is more likely to get one into trouble than trading for arms, then coming up short with the lolly. Then I would want to know precisely where you fit in.'

Lanchester looked around the book-lined room, empty except for one very old gent sound asleep in an armchair, probably a victim of an early luncheon, yet even then, in this bastion of the British upper crust, he spoke in a whisper.

'I did do a bit of intelligence work, in our old stamping ground, the Middle East, but I got the heave-ho when the budgets were cut because of the financial crisis. So now I am freelancing, though I have to say I still have good and valuable access to information through my old chums. That aided me in finding you.'

'Ask anyone else, Peter?'

'No I did not. Few have your unique combination of skills.'

Suspecting that to be a lie, Jardine asked who else was involved.

'Churchill is helping us in his fashion.'

'Not financially, I hope. I heard the old bugger lost all his loot on Wall Street and was living off his writing.'

'Another is Ernest Bevin.'

'What!' Jardine's surprised response was loud enough to penetrate the slumbers of the old gent, who snorted and shifted in his armchair, the next comment much softer. 'Surely those two are not in cahoots?'

'Necessity makes for strange bedfellows, Cal.'

'Warhorse Winnie and the leader of the Transport and General Workers' Union? Talk about chalk and cheese, and did I not read Churchill was praising Mussolini to the skies for his statesmanship at the Stresa Conference?'

'Think of the newspapers he writes for and his need to earn a crust. Winnie is more pragmatic than you give him credit for. He has the right contacts and Bevin has a hefty dose of the funds.'

'Which are?'

'Not far off the half-million mark – not all from union sources, of course.'

'I wonder if Bevin's members know what he is doing with their contributions?'

'Fighting the good fight, or planning to, for we can assume they are anti-fascists to a man. There are other contributors right across the spectrum: shipping, industry, even the arms trade, but they, especially, have to be very careful not to upset a government who provides a healthy part of their living.'

'Are not these the very same people who admire Hitler and tell me that Mussolini makes the trains run on time?'

'There are folk on both sides of the argument, Cal, but in the people I represent, the common view is that if we don't stop these bloody dictators we will be obliged to do a 1914-18 all over again, and that means national ruin.'

'The place to do that is in Europe, not Africa.'

'What if one of them fell?'

'Hitler is a very long shot, Peter. The Germans are efficient at everything, dictatorship included. Damn near every voice that could be raised against him has been either eliminated or incarcerated. If there's a communist left in a place like Hamburg, they are keeping their heads down and the population are doing likewise, because the only thing you get when you protest is either a visit at midnight or a bullet.'

Lanchester smiled. 'Which leaves old fatso. If Mussolini can be held up in Ethiopia, he's not that secure at home.'

'You sure about that?'

'Christ almighty, Cal, it's Italy – no one is ever secure there.'

'Italy,' Jardine, pointed out and with some emphasis, 'is at this moment more stable than our supposed main ally, France.'

'Never could rely on the Frogs, could we, really? Always moaning. Too damned sensitive, and as for those miserable *paysan* blighters who sought to rob us blind in the Pas de Calais . . .'

'I'm rather fond of the French.'

'Then, old boy, and not for the first time, you go against the grain.'

'So, Peter, do we have a plan?'

'Are you saying yes to the endeavour?'

'No, I am saying do we have a plan?'

'It would be more accurate to say we have an intention. As I intimated in Hamburg, and I am sure I have reiterated here, great caution must be taken to avoid contamination for certain people.

Their role is in discreet finance, extensive contacts and the provision of the necessary services.'

Jardine knew what that meant; right now there was nothing, and if there was ever going to be anything, he would have to create it, which was a far-from-attractive prospect. Against that he was now at a loose end and a man who had an abhorrence of inactivity. Being in London made him uncomfortable also: there were too many unhappy memories here.

'So tell me what you do have.'

Lanchester obliged and in doing so added some sobering thoughts to the mind of Callum Jardine. The Eyeties had completely rebuilt the port of Massawa in Eritrea, turning it from a wooden jetty into a modern facility, and they were using that to pour in troops, arms and vehicles to their main base at Asmara. They had built good roads both to their capital, as well as to the Ethiopian border and also constructed an airbase big enough to cater for their three-engined bombers.

Having been defeated by the Ethiopians some forty years previously at the Battle of Adowa – held in Italy to be a crushing national humiliation – it seemed they were taking no chances this time. It was going to be massive force and modern weaponry against what could only be an ill-equipped native army, with the aim of total conquest.

'There's no way enough arms can be smuggled in to face that, Peter, at least of the level required. You're talking about tanks and artillery. Only governments can do that.'

'True, what we are doing is tokenism, really.'

'Then why do it?'

The place was filling up with those who had finished their grub; the armchairs would now be occupied by old buffers in need of a postprandial nap, and this forced Lanchester to lower even his previous whisper – his head was now very close to that of his companion.

'It will help to save our blushes in the future and, who knows, the fuzzy-wuzzies might make the Italians pay a very high price for success, maybe even too high a price. Imagine if the buggers came unstuck . . . but even holding them up might do. I doubt Mussolini can either take his time or lose too many men, given the people he leads have no greater appetite for conflict than we do in Blighty.'

'An attitude they share for a very good reason. Their donkeys were far worse generals than even our lot. The Italian army lost more men on the Izonso river front than we did at the Somme. What are their forces like now?'

'Navy looks good, and I suspect the pilots are dashing johnnies. Ground troops are not the best, but they never were, given their officers are more interested in being well barbered than being well trained. Some good regiments, the Alpine chaps are top class, but there are also Blackshirt units in their bits of the Horn of Africa and I suspect they are rubbish, a bit like your Hun SA.'

'Then why use them?'

'Forget all that guff about Italy needing colonies, Cal, this is a political enterprise to bolster the regime, and it is my guess that whoever is in charge has instructions to put Mussolini's ex-street-fighting cadres at the front of the battle so he can claim it is Fascist willpower which has overcome the fuzzy-wuzzies—'

Jardine interrupted. 'Can we call them Ethiopians, please?'

Even hissed, that got them attention, so Lanchester rose. 'What about a walk in Green Park, oh sensitive one?'

He had to sign for his bill and don his new bowler before they exited, crossing Piccadilly to the park, with Lanchester resuming where he had left off, as they sauntered down paths filled with office workers out enjoying the sunshine, with the odd tourist admiring Buckingham Palace or the bas-reliefs on Decimus Burton's Hyde Park Corner arch.

'If we can get stuff in to augment the local weaponry, and they can kill enough Blackshirts, it might cause him big trouble at home. Bringing him down is probably asking for the moon, but if we can remind the Eyeties of the cost of conflict that can only be to the good. If it keeps them out of Hitler's embrace, then—'

'They will fall out over Austria when Hitler invades, which he will do if they don't agree to a political union, especially when the Ösis become part of the Greater German Reich and demand the Trentino region back.'

Lanchester sighed. 'They know not what they did at Versailles, do they, slicing up and parcelling out bits of the old German and Austrian empires?'

'I think they knew, Peter, but I don't think they had much choice.'

'If we have to fight the Hun again, I will personally shoot the first bugger to mention an armistice or peace terms. So, how do we feel about the job, which comes, by the way, and I have not mentioned it, with a very healthy stipend?'

With a private income, money was only of concern to Jardine because it was a bad idea to work for nothing; even in Hamburg he had taken a small amount in pay. 'I'll look at the salary when I've looked at everything else. What paperwork do you have, order of battle and that sort of stuff?'

'Quite a lot.'

'Maps too – what about arms?'

'That's your bailiwick, old boy, the only thing I will say for certain is they cannot be bought or shipped from these shores.'

'Then I need to see some people before I commit to anything, here and overseas.'

'Fair enough. How long?'

'Couple of weeks, Peter, but be warned, I might turn you down flat.' The look Lanchester gave him then was discomfiting, being too knowing: he knew his one-time fellow officer could not resist an underdog or a cause. 'I mean it, Peter.'

'Of course you do, Cal, old boy. Now where are you staying?'

'Across the park at The Goring.'

'Not with the ex-wife?'

'Hardly.'

'Still not forgiven you?'

Jardine shook his head fiercely, making it obvious that was not a subject he wanted to reprise and the forgiveness bit was a dig: who was to forgive whom? He had come back from the war to find his wife's lover in bed with her. Still carrying his service revolver he had immediately shot the fellow dead. It had been quite a cause célèbre at the time, especially when, at the subsequent Old Bailey trial, the jury had acquitted him of murder. Lizzie Jardine was one reason to stay out of London. With his wife, it was a case of make up for a bit then fall out again, and with her being a Catholic, even if she was not in the least bit moral, divorce was out of the question.

'Talk to you anon, then?' Lanchester said, tipping his bowler as he walked away, his brolly ferrule beating out a tattoo. 'I'll put in a decent cheque to cover your expenses.'

Jardine's first task was to order a new passport – his old one had some too-revealing stamps – and that required a visit to a photographer and an hour in the Victoria offices where they were issued, his excuse for a

61

replacement that he had lost his previous one. Back at The Goring he wrote to ask for an appointment with Geoffrey Amherst, and his next task was to book a train and ferry crossing back to the Continent, his destination Monaco.

Lanchester's papers, including a cheque for a hundred pounds, arrived before he ate dinner and he did not look at them till afterwards, thankful he had eaten little given his appreciation of the situation was likely to induce indigestion.

The Abyssinian invasion force was reported to consist of nearly seven hundred thousand men, two-thirds of them Italian, the rest made up of Somali and Eritrean levies, as well as units from Libya. But it was the equipment levels more than the numbers of bodies that were sobering. Six hundred tanks, two thousand pieces of artillery and close to four hundred aircraft were either in the region or on the way, and given they were not all yet in theatre, Jardine concluded Lanchester, or someone like him, had very good access to what should have been secret Italian information.

Some of the units could be discounted, like the so-called *Arditi*, Mussolini's Blackshirts, who would be made up of ex-street thugs and Fascist arrivistes, more boastful than brave. But as Lanchester had pointed out, there were units like the *Alpini*; in a mountainous country like Ethiopia they would be invaluable. Just as deadly would be the local askaris, troops able to fight in the terrain and climate because they were accustomed to both and, if they were anything like the ones the Germans had used in Tanganyika in the Great War, the most dangerous force of all, given they would take casualties in a way he doubted would apply to the regular Italian army. Worst of all for the Abyssinians was Italian air power: three hundred modern bombers and fighters against which the defenders could muster only some twenty-five old biplanes.

Studying the maps, it was clear the Italians would have to come from the lowlands of Eritrea and Somalia and ascend into the high country around Addis Ababa, their capital being the hub of resistance and the place the Ethiopians would be determined to defend. He let some tactics run through his mind but decided to let his notions lie fallow until he had talked to Amherst, who was, as a military strategist, very much his superior. Even then, the ringing of the bedside phone broke his train of thought.

'Mr Jardine, you have a visitor downstairs.'

'I do?' he replied, looking at his watch: ten o'clock was a late hour for anyone to call. 'I'll come down; ask them to wait.'

In a life of much risk, and even being in London, Callum Jardine never allowed himself to take a chance. If it was a habit that others might sneer at – a sort of showing off – it was one he stood by because you only got the chance to be wrong once. So when he went down to meet this visitor he did so by using the service stairs to the basement, past piles of fresh and dirty laundry and all the paraphernalia that hotel guests never see in the mass. There was a fire exit and he hit the bar, emerging into the street at the hotel rear.

Coming round to the main entrance his first look was at the cars parked nearby, to see if any of them had passengers or some sign, like a trail of smoke coming from a cigarette, to show someone waiting. Sure they were all unoccupied, he made his way to the well-lit doorway, eyes cast right and left to pick up anyone immobile in the shadows, then he had a long look through the glass of the revolving door before he pushed his way into the lobby.

He spotted who had come to see him immediately. If the clothes were different, a dark-blue suit instead of grey, she was as well dressed

63

and groomed as she had been the last time he had seen her clearly; the back of a car and dressed like a stevedore did not count.

'Fräulein Ephraim?' he said, softly.

She had been facing the lift and staircase, sat on the edge of a couch, and his surreptitious approach startled her so much she spun around in alarm, making him wonder if, in her mind, she was suddenly back in her own country worrying about a visit from the Gestapo. That faded quickly as she composed her features and stood up.

'Please Elsa call me,' she replied, in accented English.

'I didn't know you spoke our language.'

'I do not well, Herr Jardine.' The grin with which he responded was only partly to dismiss such a comment; the other part was a genuine feeling that he was with a very attractive girl. 'I ask Herr Lanchester to telephone me when you arrive in London, if you arrive in London, zhat is.'

'I'm sure he could not wait to place the call.'

She smiled herself then and that softened features he had thought to be somewhat stiff, the normal look a girl of her age would employ in the presence of anyone older. 'He is very push, your Herr Lanchester.'

'So he did not advance to Peter?'

That got a real smile. 'No.'

Seeing the night porter hovering he asked, 'Will you join me in a drink?'

'I came to thank you only.'

The way she said that struck a false note. 'Which does not debar you from accepting a glass of champagne, surely.' Seeing the hint of reserve, the tightening of the cheeks, he added quickly, 'To celebrate your deliverance and mine, of course.'

'That would be most kind, but—'

'Your father and mother are well?' Jardine interrupted, a ploy both to stop her refusal and to let her know that he understood that there were constraints on how she could behave. 'Not to mention your brothers.'

The toss of the head, which threw her long black hair to one side, was enchanting. The well-defined black eyebrows, plucked to a perfect arch, went up as well, to dismiss as pests her three male siblings. 'My brothers, phut!'

He took her elbow and led her deeper into the hotel lounge, to a pair of couches on either side of a low coffee table, guiding her to one side while he sat on the other, the night porter having followed at his signal. Jardine knew they had a Sekt on the wine list, but he suspected a German sparkling wine might not be welcome: better to stick to France and safety.

'Veuve Clicquot, please,' looking at her to ensure it was an acceptable choice. 'Now Fräulein, while I am delighted you have come to call upon me, I suspect that gratitude, which could have been expressed in a note, is not your sole reason for coming here.'

She knew how to sit, her back ramrod-straight, her knees slightly turned to one side, but she did not know how to dissimulate, so her response was blurted out, showing a loss of composure.

'I want to help.' A questioning look made her continue. 'I can not here sit in London while my fellow Jews are hunted animals in Germany.'

The waiter arrived, on his tray two glasses and the bottle sticking out of an ice bucket. Jardine told him to leave it then waited till he had gone. 'Does your father know you are here?'

'*Nein.*'

Jardine grinned, the lapse into her native tongue was telling. Was what she said the truth or just an excuse? He had seen the way she looked at him in Hamburg and, not being without a certain degree of vanity, there was the possibility that Elsa saw him as some kind of knight in shining armour, while he also had the distinct impression she was a wilful creature. Smiling in a way that made her uncomfortable, he lifted up the champagne and exposed the cork. Cloth in hand he then opened it expertly, holding tight the cork and turning the base of the bottle so that it opened with a soft plop. He picked and tipped each glass in turn so there was no overspill when he poured, before handing her one glass, raising his own.

'*Prost!*'

As they both sipped he wondered if she really knew what she was proposing to take part in. It was not some game, it was deadly, but against that her fellow Jews needed all the help they could get because Jardine had a very strong feeling things were going to get worse. Elsa Ephraim was very young, but she was also stunningly beautiful and that was always an asset in anything clandestine. Yet the truth was, such a decision did not lie with him.

'When you finish your drink, I will call for a cab to take you home.' Seeing her face fall, and wondering at the real reason, he added gently, 'But I will arrange for you to meet someone, and it is for him to decide if you can be of use.'

# CHAPTER FIVE

'Researching Abyssinia is not easy, young Jardine,' Geoffrey Amherst said, waving his pipe to emphasise the point, and also coughing, a regular feature of his conversation, given he had been gassed in the Great War. 'Little has been written about the place in a military sense, don't you know.'

'I found that out for myself, sir. There are books by intrepid travellers which tell us about the people and the culture, but the only operations which provided any enlightenment on tactics, Magdala and Adowa, went back to the last century.'

'Don't discount those, laddie, because they do provide a degree of illumination.'

Magdala had been the name given to a British punitive expedition undertaken in 1868 by Lieutenant General Robert Napier and units from the Indian army to rescue a number of hostages – missionaries and the two diplomats sent to arrange their release. That resulted not only in a comprehensive victory but also in the death of the then emperor, who took his own life rather than surrender.

The Italian campaign of the 1890s, which ended with total defeat at Adowa, had been a fiasco brought about by a distant, posturing politician, crowing about Italy's right to colonies, insisting on a battle the local commander did not want to fight. Out of twenty thousand Italians engaged, nearly two-thirds had become casualties, a humiliation which brought down the home government and for decades cured the nation of the idea of foreign adventures. It had also raised the Emperor Menelik, whose men had won the battle, to mythical status. It was that debacle Mussolini was looking to avenge.

'Napier bribed his way to victory,' Amherst said, as he rolled out a map on his table, 'and, of course, he made it obvious he had no desire for conquest, just for rescue, so he was able to split the tribes rather than unite them. Very tribal is Ethiopia, which needs to be borne in mind.'

Jardine was looking around the book-lined study at the endless volumes on military history, memoirs, campaign studies, plus the owner's own works on battlefield tactics and strategy, before turning back to the man himself: slim, balding, with a thin moustache – the pipe was a mistake given his afflicted chest. Introduced to him by a cousin many years past, Jardine had found him a rather pernickety fellow, very confident of his own opinions on matters military, with the caveat that he was a clever bugger and usually right. The man had one quality that made him valuable right now: he was always willing to share his view and to proffer advice.

'Did you know old Menelik had Russian advisors at Adowa?'

'No, sir.'

'Ignored them completely when they advised him to refuse battle. If he had not enjoyed such overwhelming numerical superiority the Italians might have won.'

Jardine referred to the Italian order of battle, which he had shown the older man earlier; tellingly, though he raised an eyebrow, he did not ask from where it had come. 'Mussolini is taking no chances now.'

'You going out to advise them, laddie?'

'No, sir,' Jardine replied with a wry smile, 'and I'm not sure I am capable, or if I were, if I would be welcome.'

'Interest just general, is it, then?' To respond to that was tricky because he did not want to lie if he could avoid it. The pause was enough for his host: he was a man of enormous discretion. 'None of my concern, of course, so don't bother with a reply.'

The finger was on the map now, pointing to the main Italian base at Asmara, then tracing the main route up past Lake Tana to the Abyssinian capital. 'Addis is the key for the invaders, and given what we suspect the locals have, to try and stop them in open battle could be suicidal. A native army can rarely fight a modern one as Britannia proved too often in the past. Much harder now, of course, and as you so rightly point out, equipment apart, the enemy is not going to allow itself to be overcome by numbers this time.'

'So the tactical advice would be to avoid contact?'

'Most definitely, young Jardine.' That way of addressing him had always made him curious, always made him wonder if Amherst knew an older Jardine; he had never had the audacity to ask. 'But those Russians were right forty years ago and Menelik was lucky. If they have someone giving that advice now and they ignore it they will be annihilated. Look here.'

Always brisk in his speech, that was given like a command.

'The Danakil Desert to the east, bad country to fight in for anyone, but open and thus ten times worse for an army without an air force. Any incursion south of there from Italian Somaliland will be as much a diversion as real, to draw off part of the defence in Tigray Province. The route from Asmara to the south is the way the Italian army will employ for their main advance, and here, on the Ethiopian west,' a finger jabbed down, 'the mountains and the Great Rift Valley – that is where they should seek to fight.'

'Let the Italians have Addis Ababa?'

'The Russians let Napoleon have Moscow, and look what happened to him. Attrition is the key to defeating Mussolini, a drawn-out war and mounting casualties that cause him trouble with his home population. Seek to use the cover provided by the mountains and forested valleys, hold off his forces till the weather changes and the rains come, which are torrential in the mountains. Low cloud means planes can't fly, which neuters the air force and time spent clambering about in wet weather will make his troops tired, miserable and sick of being away from home. Use ambuscade and stick to small-scale actions, that is what you should advise this Haile Selassie chappie.'

That was followed by a direct look and a rather toothy smile. 'But, of course, you are not advising him, are you, young Jardine?'

'Is there a flaw in that notion?'

'Well spotted, boy,' Amherst cried, like a pleased schoolmaster. 'You recall my saying the place is very tribal and the present Lion of Judah, as Selassie styles himself, is not loved by all. There has been much palace intrigue in old Ethiopia, don't you know. Had to manoeuvre his way to the top spot, so he might be in a jam if it comes to a long drawn-out war. Might need a quick victory just to

70

hold his position. If he tries it, he will lose. Tricky, what?'

'Surely the solution would be to offer battle once, with a pre-plan to break off the action quickly, retreat to prepared positions for stands of short duration, with a rearguard willing to make the necessary sacrifices as his forces disperse into the mountains. Thus he shows the folly of engagement in force and gets his tribes to agree to a new strategy. From what I have read, the one thing that unites them is the determination not to become just another subject African race.'

'It's damned difficult for a disciplined army to retreat in good order, laddie. For what is really a peasant force it might be impossible, and that means sacrificing his best troops to save the mass. Without those semi-professional levies he might find himself turfed out by one of his own, regardless. You'll stay to luncheon, of course. Be a bit basic, since my wife is away.'

That proved to be an understatement: Amherst was not a hearty trencherman and he was the type to keep the wine bottle safely out of reach behind his back, so it was sparse fare and careful sipping for Cal Jardine as they talked about Hitler's programme of rearmament, of the just-signed Anglo-German naval agreement – that had caused a rift between Britain and France – the woolliness of the League of Nations and the recent Stresa Conference, at which Mussolini had signed up to a limit on German expansion, to Amherst's way of thinking only as a ploy to get his own way in the Horn of Africa.

'He won't keep his word, young Jardine, but in the hope of keeping the ice cream vendor on our side we will refuse any request from Ethiopia for either aid or arms, and so will our prickly French chums, not that they are in any state to intervene, anyway.'

'Are *we*, sir?'

'No, laddie! The army is in a shocking state and the ordnance is out of date. We have too many officers who are ill-equipped to fight the last war, never mind the next, tactical stupidity at the heart of everything they do.'

Jardine had to nod at that: he had served with some real dunderheads and had dined with and been inspected by senior officers who made his regimental idiots look intelligent.

'What got us the breakthroughs in the last show? Tanks. Have we got enough armoured vehicles, as well as of the right kind, and methods of employing them properly? God, no! Government won't spend enough money on aircraft, so really and as usual, we only have the navy. They are not much use unless we tell Mussolini we will sail through the Suez Canal to the Red Sea and bombard Massawa. There's no chance of that while the Italians have a full battle-ready division on the Libyan border ready to close the canal completely if we try.'

'Germany?'

'Determined on war since the Treaty of Versailles, and don't be fooled that Hitler is the only one who wants it. His generals are just as eager and they have been planning it since they were forced to surrender. When it comes to grievances, he and they have a raft of them, given what we sliced off the sods. Half of Silesia, the Sudetenland and the blue touchpaper has to be Danzig and that damned piece of territorial stupidity called the Polish Corridor.'

'You should hear the Germans on that, sir, they become incandescent.'

'Can't say I blame them. If we are not at war again by 1945 I will eat my hat. As the wise Roman said, "If you wish for peace prepare for war", but no one in this land of ours is listening.' That was expounded with passion, leading to a bout of coughing, until he spluttered. 'Life is so much easier for dictators.'

'You're not suggesting we look for one, are you, sir?'

That comment made the older man laugh with real gusto. 'Only if it's me, young Jardine, only if it's me.'

The stopover in London was only to pick up a suitcase, then it was off to Victoria for the boat train, a run through the verdant county of Kent to Dover, and a bit of a rough crossing that had Jardine staying away from those passengers who lacked sea legs. On the afterdeck he let the wind blow him about as he watched the disappearing white cliffs and recalled the first time he had done this, as an eighteen-year-old newly commissioned officer. His stomach had been less stable then, due to a combination of excitement and anxiety.

Anxiety? To go to war, when so many had paid the ultimate sacrifice before you, was something that could not be avoided, and especially when the evidence of what was happening at the front abounded – the ever lengthening casualty lists, the badly wounded men in the streets, the black-clad widows or old men with funeral armbands. These concerns were reflected in his mother's sad eyes the day he joined up, but there was another reason: the fear of letting yourself, your peers or the regiment down by being shy in battle or going mad with shell shock.

Excitement was a common emotion for a youngster in such a situation, the chance to prove yourself a proper man quelling the fears of death or being maimed, that and the high spirits of your companions, all of whom seemed determined to arrive in France in a state of inebriation. After landing he had gone to the infantry training base at Etaples to find himself once more shouted at by unsympathetic sergeants as they sought to teach him what he would need to know to avoid the average death within two weeks of new subalterns on the Western Front.

The drinking did not abate: there had been gambling in nearby Le Touquet, or nights out in the fishing port of Etaples itself, a place of seedy bars and brothels catering to the carnal needs of the British army, with outrageous overcharging and ill-disguised resentment the norm from the locals. Being an officer he had been given leave to go to Paris, a city, even in wartime, so easy to fall in love with; that is, if you could stand the rudeness of the Parisians, even to a British officer who spoke their language. There he had steeled himself for his first paid encounter with the opposite sex, approaching many a Clichy doorway before shying away, the face of his young and beautiful wife intervening.

The Ludendorff offensive had put paid to that aim: every man was needed at the front to stem the great German bid to drive the British army into the sea. They were now the mainstay of the Allied fight, given the French had been bled dry at Verdun and the Russians had thrown in both the towel and their tsar. His baptism of fire had removed any trace of callow romanticism from Callum Jardine.

He was under the command of a grey-faced captain leading a hastily gathered force from at least ten different regiments, seeking to contain the flank of an ever-increasing bulge. Fighting was close, personal and mobile, not the trench warfare he had expected; at least any trenches he and his platoon occupied were the shallow ones they dug themselves in the hard earth for one night's occupation only.

Food was intermittent, washing or a change of clothes out of the question, and often ammunition was only acquired by begging from a neighbouring unit. They were pushed very slowly backwards by repeated German assaults, each time extracting more in the way of death than they suffered.

Battle comes down to that before your eyes, so it was only much later he found out what a close-run thing that last great German offensive of the war had been. Erich von Ludendorff had thrown in every man he had, only to be sucked into a giant salient, one he could not hold for lack of numbers and reserves still fit to do battle, so slowly, that sack started to deflate.

The Yanks had begun to arrive in force, part of the reason why the Germans had cast everything on that one throw, and panic had finally unified the Allied command under Marshal Foch. Now Jardine became part of his relentless drive that threw back the enemy and gave them no respite until they had pushed back past their start line, then on through the supposedly impenetrable Hindenburg Line.

When they took prisoners, the first noticeable thing was their obvious hunger – the German army was lacking in food and, when questioned, ammo and men, as well as the will to continue, while behind them their country was sliding inexorably towards a bloody communist revolution, which forced the abdication of the Kaiser and the advent of a civilian government that sought an armistice.

The young lieutenant who stood up on that early November day, when the guns went silent, to look over the shattered battlefield before him, was a very different sort from the near-boy who had stood on this deck. He had his own wounds to carry, none of them serious, and a memory of men he had led, dying under his command, this while he had seen four commanders come and go, one through cracked nerves, the rest in death, as had a dozen fellow lieutenants. Lanchester had been there that day, as filthy and mud-caked as he, carrying the same physical complaints, cursing the idiocy of granting the Germans a peaceful end to a bloodstained conflict.

It should have been enough, that war, but it was not.

\* \* \*

He decided on a night in Paris, and that meant dinner at Taillevent, one of the oldest restaurants in the city. After a sumptuous meal it was a taxi to the Gare de Lyon to catch up with *Le Train Bleu*, running south to the Côte d'Azur. Leaving behind the smoking industrial chimneys of outer Paris it was hard to imagine this country he was passing through, with night falling, as one in the grip of political turmoil, but it was, the left and right at riotous loggerheads, the Popular Front versus Action Française.

He went to sleep in his wagon-lit as it raced past grey stone buildings and woke when it was passing the red-tiled roofs and houses with sun-bleached walls that formed the outskirts of a city he knew well, teeming Marseilles. He had spent part of his childhood here and loved it: how much more romantic to read was *The Count of Monte Cristo* when you could actually look out and see the Château d'If from the Corniche?

Lunch was five wonderful courses as the luxury train followed the coast, the sky that deep Mediterranean blue, the landscape burnt scrub backed by high hills, with occasional fields of lavender on one side, beaches and sea opposite, on through what had been the playground of the rich until the Depression either wiped out the fortunes of the wealthy visitors – Churchill had been one – or so lowered the value of the pound that not even wealthy Brits could afford a four-month stay to avoid their national winter.

The home of Sir Basil Zaharoff was, like many dwellings in Monte Carlo, built into the side of a hill. He was not a man to call upon unannounced and Jardine had sent him a letter before going to see Amherst, though given he had dealt with the old man before, he was sure he need not wait for a reply. Reputedly the richest man in Europe, Zaharoff had many soubriquets, the least attractive that he was the original 'Merchant of Death'. Cal Jardine had always found the infamous arms dealer courteous, of lively mind and a person of wide interests and strong personal attachments.

He was shown into a large study overlooking the yacht-filled harbour to find his man sat behind an enormous desk, before open windows. 'Captain Jardine?'

'That, Sir Basil, is not a title I use, quite apart from the fact that my fellow officers, serving and retired, think it infra dig to use any army rank in civilian life below major.'

'Why would that be?'

'Captain is a naval rank and vastly superior to its army equivalent.'

'Ah, your English habits, so strange to we foreigners, regardless of how much time we spend in your country.'

God he's aged, Jardine thought: the moustache was dropping, the goatee beard straggly and the skin falling from his cheeks, but that was not a comment one would make to anyone, and certainly not to a person of his eminence.

'You will forgive me not standing to greet you, my legs are not what they once were.' An arm was waved to invite him to sit, to which Jardine agreed; he was offered an iced cocktail, which he accepted, and then engaged in twenty minutes of polite conversation, which he enjoyed. 'But you have not come to see me for the chit-chat, I venture.'

'No. I have been engaged to see if I can get some modern weaponry into Abyssinia.'

It was hard for such a wracked face to fall but his did. 'Oh dear, Jardine, that is not, I think, very wise.'

'When was what you and I do wise?'

'You hoist me, as you say, on the petard.' That was nonsense, of course, Zaharoff being one of the wisest men he had ever encountered: he might be an arms dealer, but he was knowledgeable and no hypocrite. 'You know I am no longer active, I have retired to this prison for the rich.'

'But I suspect you know who is.'

'I hear things, that is true, for I have kept many of my contacts; but I will say this, it will be hard to purchase modern weaponry for such a cause, and I suspect not easy to get it to where it is needed if you can.' He began to tick off the sources. 'Belgium and Czechoslovakia are the least scrupulous as of this moment, but you would require very deep pockets, especially without political clearance from your own government.'

'My government must know nothing of what I am doing.'

'Something I suspected must be the case, Jardine, or why come to see an old fellow like me, eh? Discreet purchase raises the cost – and substantially, my friend – quite apart from the fact the rascal Hitler is now being open about his rearmament programme instead of doing it in secret, as he and the General Staff have been doing for a decade and a half now. The two countries I mentioned will need to look to their own armouries in the face of his actions – they border Germany, after all.'

'I won't mention a figure, but I suspect money might be constrained.'

What Lanchester had mentioned did not go far in Zaharoff's world, but typically he did not ask him the source of any money, it being none of his concern.

'The Italians are pouring much treasure into the Abyssinian venture, more, in truth, than they can afford.'

'They are overextended?' The emphatic nod was good news: it meant that the tactics outlined by Amherst had an even better chance of success – nothing drains money like an open-ended conflict.

'I point out to you, Jardine, a number of things pertinent,' Zaharoff said, ticking them off on his fingers. 'A lack of money means a dearth of supply, while even if you were able to buy the most modern weaponry, your Abyssinians would not be able to use it without instructors. Even with such men to teach them you do not have time on your side. My information is that the Italian build-up of forces is near to complete. The only thing stopping them from moving is the lack of an aggressive commander, and Mussolini can alter that tomorrow.'

'I don't know this General De Bono.'

'Nearly seventy years of age, which is well past the time a man might be at his peak.'

That got a smile. 'I cannot recall if it is polite to remind a man of his age and when he was at his most active.'

'You were always a flatterer, Jardine.' Seeing his guest then frown, he added, as he rang a bell on his desk, 'But never a sycophant.' A sober-suited fellow answered the bell. 'Drouhin, bring me the files on Abyssinia and Rumania.'

Zaharoff was smiling at him now, but Jardine did not react, albeit the idea of a file on Rumania was intriguing: what purpose could that possibly have? Reaching into his pocket he pulled out the Italian order of battle and gave it to his host. 'Perhaps your man Drouhin would like to copy out this document.'

Zaharoff put a pince-nez on his stark, bony nose and looked at the document, nodding. He had always been a magpie when it came to intelligence; one of the reasons he had been so successful was his ability to outguess his opponents as well as governments through a network of well-placed informers.

'Interesting. Thank you.' Drouhin was back, carefully placing the files on the desk. The old man handed over the order of battle to Drouhin, who apparently needed no telling what to do, then opened the top folder and extracted a paper as the secretary left, handing that to Jardine.

'Here is an appreciation of Emilio De Bono. He's a long-serving soldier, successful as a young man, and now a member of the Fascist Grand Council. On the face of it he is a strong supporter of Mussolini, though my reports have him as a man who clings to the monarchy, and the King of Italy does not always see eye to eye with Il Duce. De Bono is a sentimental fellow, he cries readily and often, which argues he is no great warrior or a man who will see the blood of his troops spilt without conscience. I have also here his original plan for the invasion of Ethiopia, which involved nothing like the number of troops on this paper you have given me.'

That was a separate folder and, given to Jardine, one he examined with professional interest, because its nature indicated a cautious commander who had set out limited objectives to be captured over time with the emphasis on security at each stage of his advance. How the hell Zaharoff had come by it was a mystery and it made Jardine wonder if the order of battle he had handed over was quite as interesting as the old fellow had said – he probably had it already. Clearly he still spent a lot of money – and he had masses to disburse – on his own spies.

'Do you have the new plan?'

'Unfortunately no, Jardine, and you, of course, have not seen that which you have just looked at.'

Possibly untrue, but not something to question; the other file was. 'Rumania?'

'The Germans, as well as rearming, are also selling – they need the currency, after all – and one of their clients is Rumania. They are re-equipping their forces, and in that file is a list of what we suspect the Germans are supplying. Not tanks or field artillery, of course, for they have only just begun to manufacture those in quantity, but they had a surplus of small arms, given they have been secretly making them since the foundation of the Weimar Republic.'

Jardine took the list and examined it: Mauser rifles in the shortened K98 version, MG38 machine guns and 50 mm mortars.

'What that means, of course, is that the Rumanians have a lot of old equipment to dispose of. Austrian Mannlicher rifles and old-pattern Maxim machine guns, which I sold them myself.'

'Meaning?'

'If the Ethiopians have anything, it will be weapons of that vintage. They will be much more likely to use them wisely than anything they require to be instructed to use, but that is not the real point. Such items will also be cheap.'

# CHAPTER SIX

Train journeys are good for thinking and the return trip allowed Jardine plenty of time to ponder on what Basil Zaharoff had said, the primary conclusion being that it made sense, mostly in money terms. The old man had promised to check on matters for him and let him know what was going to be available and who to contact in the Rumanian War Ministry to facilitate matters. He had sent a preliminary telegram to Lanchester, telling him that Bucharest was the place to do business and arrangements should be made to bank funds there, and some early moves taken on transportation, with Zaharoff adding another bit of advice.

'At the risk of stating the obvious, Jardine, nothing will happen unless the wheels are oiled, and the Rumanians do not come cheap. I have had dealings there over many years and I know they expect to be bribed and that their preferred currency is Swiss francs.'

'Especially if I am in a hurry.'

'Try not to let it appear so, for if they suspect you are eager, the price of help will double, at least.'

Now he was speeding back through France weighing the alternatives. It was a case of supplying a decent amount of old equipment as against a small quantity of new, the cost of the alternative being prohibitive, even if it could be found. Striking was the simple fact that the most potent arms dealer in Europe, albeit he was no longer really active, had not offered him anything other than information – not even an old competitor who could help. Quite apart from the politics of standing aside in Abyssinia, the major manufacturing countries were looking to their own needs and, apart from Germany, they were keeping what they made at home.

That the Germans had been rearming for fifteen years was an open secret: Jardine moved in circles well aware of this, and any government with an intelligence set-up knew it too. They had opened secret factories in Russia, as well as in Germany itself, for the one thing the Great War had not done was to tame the ambitions or power of the Great General Staff. Even before Hitler, the now-defunct Weimar Republic had relied on the army, and the Nazis had been required to seduce and reassure the military in order to see them into power.

Back in his London hotel room, he laid out the bones of what he had discovered to Lanchester. 'So there we have it, Peter – not perfect, perhaps less than satisfactory, but given the time, maybe the best we can do.'

'What would be required if the answer is to go ahead?'

'Funds available as I have already outlined, to buy the goods and transport them to the Black Sea, a ship waiting at Constanta to take them to the Horn of Africa, and some way of assuring me that once that vessel is off Somaliland there is a way to get them to where they need to be. I presume that has been thought about in advance.'

'We have a representative out there, a district officer primed to do what is required.'

'Who?'

'Chap called Mason, who is also our link to those around Haile Selassie, and the idea is that once the weapons are on the way you go in and set up the operation overland with his aid.'

'Which has to be carried out in secret, Peter, because if the Italians even get a sniff they will scream blue murder.'

'He has assured us this can be done.'

'By road?'

'God no, that would be too obvious, seeing there's only one road in and out and it runs past the barracks of the Somali Camel Corps. The powers that be in British Somaliland would throw you in the clink if they caught you, and impound the goods. The Ethiopians will provide the men and transport to get them across a discreet part of the border.'

'That sounds very like camels.'

'Spot on, old boy. The main road, not much of one I am told, runs through Hargeisa, the administrative centre of British Somaliland, while the railway from Djibouti to Dire Dawa is under French control, given they built it. Neither is useable.'

'Would you be offended if I said this whole idea is a bit half-cocked? I have to buy a load of weapons and get them to the Horn of Africa, with no feeling of assurance that when I get there I will not be kyboshed by my own government, then sneak them overland across what might well be a bloody desert.'

'Using the old slave trade routes, Cal, which, I'll have you know, are not entirely redundant.'

'There are too many "ifs" in this, Peter.'

'Never knew any operation to be different, Cal. "If" number one! Will the backers agree to what is being proposed? "If" number two, can you get hold of what is available in the time we have? Three, can they be got, by ship, to the Somali coast? Four, can we get them ashore and across one of the least hospitable places on the planet to where they can do some good?' Lanchester leant over grinning and slapped him on the back. 'Bloody simple, really.'

'One step at a time in other words?'

'Precisely.'

'You could lose your shirt on this.'

'It's not my shirt.'

'How long before we know the funds are available for use in Rumania?'

'They are in place now, Cal, in a Swiss bank, three hundred thousand pounds sterling, with the reserve if you need more, which means that you and I should pack our bags for Bucharest.'

'You're coming too?'

'Old chum, I trust you, but not with that much lolly. I am there to sign the cheques.'

There were two people to see before heading east, the first being the man who had recruited him for the Hamburg operation. He took Elsa Ephraim with him to the huge heath-side house in Hampstead, though after the introductions, she was asked to wait outside.

'Now, that is a real looker,' said Sir Monty Redfern, as always, when using an 'r', making it sound as if there were several instead of just one. 'I didn't know you liked them so fresh.'

'I admit to temptation, Monty,' Jardine replied, 'and I was sorely tempted a few nights back, but I kept my buttons done up because she is young and naive.'

'So you are a fool.'

'How was New York?'

'Too many Jews, what do you think, and loud, so loud. Worse than Palestine, my God!'

Patron of several Jewish charities, Sir Monty was a self-made millionaire who had earned his money in chemicals, never boasting that he started with nothing as a fifth son of refugees selling such things as bicarbonate of soda door to door; such tales had to be dragged out of him. Money had not sophisticated him much: he dressed in clothes he had owned for years and his shoes were never polished, but if anyone in Britain was doing what they could for the Jews of Europe it was he, because, as he insisted, anti-Semitism was not confined to Germany, there was plenty of it in Britain.

'You raised some funds?'

'Not as much as those crooks could have contributed.' To Monty there were only crooks or good people; there was nothing in between. 'Of course, they have their own organisations who are pleading for lolly.'

Jardine laid the money belt he had brought from Hamburg on the desk. 'This will help.'

Monty picked it up and weighed it in a way that made Jardine think he could count the unseen contents; maybe he could.

'I took a lot of money off those Jews who could afford to pay and used it to get anyone too poor but under threat through the port.' The word 'Communist' hung in the air, but was unmentioned. Jardine had got several Reds out from under the threat of a National Socialist bullet, but it was not a thing to make public. Few countries wanted Jews, none wanted to import revolution and no one of that political persuasion had been sent on to England. 'That is what is left over.'

'Jardine, you I should employ to sell my chemicals, then I would be rich, no?' That was followed by a frown. 'You have taken care of your own needs.'

'I have.'

'Good.' Monty knew and approved of the Jardine rule: never work for nothing. As he had observed, there were not many rich Jews in his native Scotland, the competition was too stiff. 'Now, your young lady.'

'She wants to help.'

'You think perhaps she would consider to make an old man happy?'

'Your wife would kill you.'

'What do you think she does already? Spend, spend, spend!'

'She could act as some kind of secretary.'

'My wife sees that kind of secretary, I will be eating my own balls for dinner.'

'Talk to her, see what comes up.'

'Jardine, I know what will come up, it is what I will do then that counts. Now, what are you up to?'

'Who says I am up to anything?'

'When God gave me this big hooter, Jardine,' Monty said, grabbing his hooked nose, 'he did it so I could smell my fellow humans telling fibs. You will be up to something or you would have asked me if there was some job needing doing.'

Jardine grinned and explained: not one to trust easily, he trusted Monty Redfern absolutely.

'That is a good cause, those poor black people, even if they are misguided religious. There are many Jews in that land, but not that Haile Selassie. Lion of Judah, my arse. How can you be that and not be Jewish, eh? You know Bucharest?'

'I don't even know Rumania.'

'There are good people there, but many bad ones, too, and it is not the easiest place to be Jewish. It's hard to lay blame – forgive me saying this, but I know, 'cause deep down I am still Russian, the Bukovina Jews are dumb Hasidic bastards. But there are some good Ashkenazim and Sephardim in Bucharest. '

He went to the back of his desk and opened an address book, penning a quick name and address. 'Call on this fellow, tell him I sent you. If you need anything he will help. Now, show in that delightful young lady and let me dream the dream I can look forward to repeating when I try to get to sleep tonight.'

Jardine's next stop was in South London, at a gym down the Old Kent Road. He walked through the door to the smell of sweat and high-odour embrocation. The place needed a lick of paint, if not several, and the windows were missing several panes, with bits of cardboard where there should be glass, while the lights were bare bulbs hanging from the ceiling. Around the room lay the various things required to keep a boxer at his peak – hanging punchbags, weights, mats for floor exercises – while in the middle was a full-sized ring in which two young fellows were sparring.

Shouting at them from the ringside was Vince Castellano, a one-time soldier in Jardine's regiment and a useful welterweight boxer. A tap on the shoulder made him turn round, which revealed a flattened nose and the scarred eyebrows of a fighter, as well as a couple of proper bruises. The voice had the slight slur of badly fitting false teeth.

'Good God, guv, what are you doin' 'ere?'

'Come to see you, Vincenzo.'

'Keep sparring, you two,' Vince shouted, 'my old CO has come to call.'

'It's a long time since I was that.'

'Must be three years since I seen you last, Mr Jardine, when you'd just got back from South America.'

'I've still got the hangover and the bruises.'

'That was a right night out that was, eh? You should never have taken me to that posh club up west. Toffee-nosed gits.'

'And you should not have tried to fight everybody in there including the coppers who came to arrest us.'

'Shouldn't drink, should I, guv? But you knew that, so I always blamed you for that barney. That's why I let you pay the fines.'

'How's business?'

'Dire and don't it show? Fallin' down, this gaff is. I only keep the place goin' 'cause of the kids. If they wasn't 'ere 'alf of them would be in choky.'

'How's your Italian?'

'Bit rusty, I only really speak it wiv me mum. Took her home a couple of years back for a visit.'

'I remember you telling me.'

'Not a success, was it? Most of her family think the sun shines out of Mussolini's arse when I think he's a pot-bellied git.'

'Passport still valid?'

'Yeh.'

'I am going to do a job where I need someone to trust to mind my back. It might have a place for an Italian speaker too, and it pays well.'

Vince looked around his dump of a gym. 'I got to keep this place goin', guv, bad as it looks.'

'Could anyone take it over for six months?'

'Only if I could pay 'em.'

'That can be arranged, Vince, but let me say this before you think about it: the job could be dangerous.'

'Everythin' you do is dangerous, guv.' Jardine made a pistol with his finger and thumb. 'That dangerous?'

'Yup, but there's enough pay to keep this place open and you in beer for a year.'

'When d'you need to know?'

Jardine penned a number and handed it over. 'You been in the ring again, Vince?'

'Naw, feet are too slow now.'

'The bruises?'

Vince touched his upper cheek. 'Got them fightin' Mosley's mob, blackshirt bastards.'

'Politics, Vince?'

'Can't let them just walk about shouting abuse just 'cause someone's a Jew, ain't right.'

Jardine looked around the decrepit gym. 'You're probably doin' good work here, Vince – what if you had a benefactor?'

'He'd need deep pockets.'

'And if I could get you one?'

'When was the last time somebody kissed your arse?'

'Pay. Twenty quid a week and whatever it takes to get someone to replace you here. You can ring me tomorrow.'

'To hell with that, I'm in for twenty smackers a week. Lead on, Macduff.'

Jardine rang Monty Redfern that night to tell him about Vince's gym and how he got the bruises. It was a near-certain bet that the Jewish millionaire would back that.

'All I remember of Vince Castellano was that he was a bloody handful,' Lanchester remarked. 'Fine boxer, mind. Did the regiment proud.'

'I don't think he drinks anything like he used to, and who knows, those fists of his might come in handy.'

'So where are you off to in best bib and tucker?'

Jardine pulled a face. 'I'm taking Lizzie to dinner and dancing at the Café de Paris. Apparently "Hutch" is playing tonight, and no doubt there will be two idiots trying to convince us of some new dance craze that is going to sweep the universe.'

'Ah, the lovely Lizzie Jardine.'

'Don't you start, Peter.'

'You cut her too much slack, old boy.'

'I think you have that the wrong way round.'

'Would you divorce her if she agreed, Cal?'

'I would if that was what she wanted but I would have to get an annulment from the bloody Pope.'

'A gentleman to the last, but that's not what I asked.'

'Peter, it's none of your business. Now, if all our arrangements are in place Vince and I will meet you at Victoria tomorrow morning.' Picking up his shiny top hat, Callum Jardine, dressed in white tie and tails, bowed Lanchester out through his door. The Humber he had ordered was purring gently outside and that took him to Connaught Square to pick up his wife, who was, as usual, not ready.

'Fix yourself a drink, Cal, I shan't be long.'

'When have I heard that before?'

'What?'

'Nothing.'

Going into the drawing room he stared at the furniture with distaste; Lizzie had redecorated once more – it was a biannual event – and this time all the furniture was white, even the sideboard which had on it the bottles and glasses. He poured himself a malt whisky, pleased that his wife had left out a jug of water, a pinch of which was put in the glass to release the peat flavours. That he took to the long French windows overlooking the garden square.

How many times had he stood at these windows waiting? Too many, the record being an hour – that had led to a row about the time it took her to get made up and dressed, then to an even more furious altercation when she found out he had sent the taxi away on the very good grounds the poor bugger had to make a living, which he did not do idling outside their house. There was no point in being cross; in fact, if she took long enough they might give the table he had booked away. He would much rather go to the Bag O' Nails anytime.

'Now, you have to admit, Cal, that is a record.'

Turning slowly he looked her up and down, knowing Lizzie had quite deliberately posed under a tall standard lamp to be admired, and admirable she was. Blond, with a pixie face and that bloody pert nose, wearing a white dress overlaid with silver, she had been the most beautiful debutante of her year, and daft Callum Jardine, fresh from the wilds of Dumfriesshire, tall, handsome, golden-haired and soon to be a dashing officer, had been the one who won her hand. He had suffered nothing but trouble and heartache since.

'Well, are you going to say anything?'

'Is white this year's colour?'

Her tongue came out. 'You are a pig, Callum Jardine.'

'True,' he replied, damned if he was going to compliment her. 'Shall we go?'

The food at the Café de Paris was not inspiring, served as an adjunct to the entertainment, rather than on its own merits. They had danced a quick foxtrot right after cocktails, then had dinner to the sound of 'Melancholy Baby' and 'The Very Thought of You', with Lizzie mouthing along and making moon eyes at the singer, even more outrageously when 'Hutch' came on to play.

'Pity Edwina Mountbatten has got her claws into him, darling,' he whispered mischievously.

'Just make sure Dickie doesn't get his bits into you, Cal. He does so love a handsome man.'

'I wish he would try, I haven't killed anyone for a while.'

That made her frown deeply. 'Must you bring that up?'

'Sorry,' he replied insincerely. 'I thought it was proof I loved you.'

The eyes went dewy. 'Do you love me, Cal?'

Here we go again, Jardine thought. Why can I not stay away from her? What is the matter with me? He so wanted to not sleep with her but he knew he would weaken, even as he looked around the packed room and wondered who else had enjoyed the privilege. She would drink just a little too much and get all romantic; he would have lowered his resistance by exactly the same means and he would sashay her into that bedroom at Connaught Square, hoping he could avoid looking at the bedhead and remembering the face of the naked man sitting up, his eyes wide with fear, just before he put a bullet in the left one.

# CHAPTER SEVEN

'Our friend does not look in a good mood this fine morning,' said Peter Lanchester to Vince Castellano, as they watched Cal Jardine, a luggage porter alongside, heading towards the ticket barrier. His shout echoed as it always does in a railway station. 'Had a good night, did we?'

'Do shut up, Peter, and let's get out of this bloody country.'

'I sense domestic harmony has not reasserted itself.'

'When was the last time you 'ad a belt round the ear'ole, Mister Lanchester?' asked Vince, ''cause I can see one coming your way.'

'Long time since Cal and I exchanged blows.'

'Them mess dinners were a bit 'airy.'

Cal Jardine marched past them, his face still stiff: last night had conformed to the usual script, with much tender lovemaking, but so had the morning with its customary mutual recriminations. He needed some of that sea air to clear his head, and some action to salve his soul.

First stop was Belgium, a place where, in Vince's parlance, they could 'tool up'. Lanchester's Mauser had gone into the North Sea as soon as he and the Ephraims had cleared the Elbe, Jardine's pistol into the Danube at the Czech border, neither wishing to be caught bringing a gun into England. By the same token it was not an easy place to buy personal weapons, but Brussels was, and even if they were going to a country at peace, some kind of weaponry was a sensible precaution. They bought two ex-US Army Colt Automatics, while Vince got himself a vicious-looking hunting knife. In passing, Jardine took a shine to a rather natty leather attaché case.

'I'm going to have to get you a new suit, Vince,' Jardine insisted, looking at the light-brown pinstripe with very pronounced lapels.

'You don't like me togs?'

'You look like a bookie.'

'I wish I was a bookie, the robbin' bastards.'

They bought him something dark blue and discreet, with Vince insisting he now looked like a 'bleedin' undertaker'. The next train was a sleeper via Paris to Milan, then another to Vienna and finally on to Bucharest, the city they called Little Paris. Jardine could immediately see why, laid out as it was in wide boulevards and big open squares and parks in a way that mirrored the designs of Napoleon III's architect, Baron Haussmann.

It was the Austro-Hungarian Empire, at the height of its pomp, which had built most of Bucharest, turning it from a sleepy and desolate conurbation into a jewel on the Dambovita river, all of this explained to Vince by Peter Lanchester.

'The good baron tore down old Paris to rebuild it and apparently it was pretty grubby and smelly. As well as bringing light and air it provided very good fields of fire for artillery, given the city was prone to riot. If your lot got uppity he could mow you down and I daresay they can do that here too.'

'If the old git is still breathing send him to the Elephant & Castle, that could do wiv a clear-out – and not just the houses.'

They booked into the Hotel Palace Athénée – Jardine in a suite, given he needed to look well heeled, and a telegram went off to Zaharoff via his secretary Drouhin, to say where they were staying; you did not use the name of his employer in a public communication if you did not wish to immediately set off alarm bells. His contact name, Colonel Ion Dimitrescu, came by return, with Jardine putting in an immediate telephone call to his office, which had, of necessity, to be discreet and in German, which he had been told the man, like many of his countrymen, spoke fluently. It took ages and some insistence to get through.

'We have not met, Colonel, but we have a mutual acquaintance and he has kindly given me your name as someone who can advise me about certain aspects of a country I do not know at all.'

'This acquaintance is?'

'A resident of Monte Carlo and a man with whom you have done business in the past.'

That led to a pause: this was not a man to be rushed. 'Is he an elderly gentleman by any chance?'

'Newly into his eighth decade, Colonel.'

'And your purpose in being in Bucharest, Herr Jardine?'

'I am looking for business opportunities in a *general* sort of way.'

Jardine emphasised the word 'general' and he was not disappointed, given his hint seemed to be picked up. 'And how can I be of assistance?'

'Might I suggest we have dinner together at my hotel tomorrow night and I can outline my needs?'

'Allow me to consult my diary.'

That was just a holding tactic: Jardine suspected a man like Dimitrescu, even if he had never met him, would know precisely what commitments he had. 'Where are you staying?'

'The Athénée Palace.'

'Tomorrow evening?'

*No doubt after a day of making enquiries to find out who I am, one of which would be a telegram to Zaharoff.* 'Around nine perhaps, Colonel; I am informed you do not dine early in Rumania.'

Jardine and Vince spent the next day finding out about their surroundings, including a very quick way to get out of the hotel unseen, this while Lanchester saw to the banking. A wander round the city showed a mixture of the very new and the timeless, expensive cars many times required to use their horns to move aside horse-drawn transport, like the cabs called *trăsurăs*, with Vince sure he was able to recognise the swear words.

The language was akin to Italian, derived as it was from the Latin left behind by the Roman Empire, which had established a frontier in this part of the world to keep out the barbarians from further east, and one held onto by a population that refused to speak Turkish when ruled by the Ottomans. They hated the Austrians and Russians who had occupied the city several times with as much passion, but German was a second language, hardly surprising given the monarch was Carol von Hohenzollern-Sigmaringen, part of the same extended family as the exiled German kaiser.

Mentally, as he always did, Jardine was imagining ways to leave the country; while what he was involved in carried none of the dangers of Hamburg, the arms trade was inherently risky, peopled by shadowy types in whom it would be foolish to repose any trust. In reality there was only one way to move speedily and that was by car – public air travel was non-existent in this part of the world and the trains were too obvious.

Walking aimlessly, seeking to imprint the place on his mind, he and Vince came across a crowded flea market down by the Dambovita river, a sluggish and ugly watercourse, and there he bought a couple of flat caps and two old sets of overalls, which went into a battered old suitcase. His next task was to find a second-hand car.

They took a tram along one of the main boulevards leading to the suburbs, and sure enough, as the road left the quarter of big shops and offices, the businesses became smaller and more diverse. Vince spotted a forecourt of dust-covered cars and what followed was a farcical piece of haggling that went on for an hour and ended up with Jardine, thanks to Vince's inherited Italian skills, paying less than half the opening price demanded.

'How the British ever got an empire beats me,' Vince said.

'Easy, Vince, we just overpaid.'

'A Citroën, old boy,' Lanchester scoffed. 'Could you not find anything British?'

'The make doesn't matter, Peter, what matters is that we have it, that it is full of petrol with spare cans and that we all know where it is parked. We've bought some maps too.'

''Cepting I can't drive, guv,' Vince said.

'Then you have to learn on the job.'

That was too good to let by. 'Steady on, old chap, we're here to work?'

'It's not funny,' Jardine snapped. 'If we have to press the alarm button, it's get out as quick as we can and make for the Czech border.

Make sure you each have enough cash handy for bribes, in case passports are not enough.'

'That comes under the heading of teaching your grandmother to suck eggs, old boy.'

'Lorries?' Jardine asked.

'No one outfit is big enough for what we need so I will probably arrange for two or more to provide our transport once we are sure of what we require. Now, if you don't mind, I have to report back to London.'

Jardine opened his door to make sure the corridor was clear: they should not be seen together and he had told his Rumanian contact where he was resident. 'Now, Vince, tonight I am having dinner with this colonel. Take up a seat where you can see us together – I want you to know what he looks like.'


Colonel Dimitrescu was a handsome fellow, with olive skin and swept-back, thick, dark hair, a thin black moustache, well dressed in a grey suit, white shirt and dark tie. He reminded Jardine of the American film actor, Don Ameche. His handshake was dry and firm, while his dark-brown eyes looked steadily into those of the man greeting him.

'Colonel.'

'How is our mutual friend?'

'Looking his years, I'm afraid, but his mind is as sharp as ever. Shall we eat, or would you care for an aperitif first?'

'Perhaps a drink, yes. I have always found champagne the best, and since the hotel has a bar dedicated to that . . .'

'Then let us go there.'

Dimitrescu wanted to examine him before committing to a dinner table, which left Jardine wondering how much he had found out, because Zaharoff would be discreet. The champagne bar was dark-panelled and hushed, with few clients, so a perfect place for them to quietly talk. With two glasses of Mumm in their hands they clinked them, eyes locked, his enquiring, Jardine's without expression.

'You are an interesting man, Herr Jardine.'

'Am I?'

Dimitrescu nodded. 'You cannot act as you do without leaving a trail and it is the business of colleagues of mine to pick that up. Certain activities in South America, for instance, and then there is Palestine.' Jardine just nodded; there was no point in denying his previous gun-running exploits, but he was pleased at no mention of Hamburg. 'These perhaps tell me the nature of what you are seeking help to do?'

'They would indicate that, yes. I have been advised you are in a position to facilitate certain matters.'

'Perhaps. It is too early to say.'

'You are part of the War Ministry?'

'Yes, I am.'

'And at present engaged in the procurement of certain items for your army?'

Dimitrescu smiled, which, being lopsided and showing very good teeth, made him look even more like the film actor, but it was a false expression: his eyes said he was not pleased. 'That is supposed to be a secret.'

'Please be assured I will tell no one, not even those I represent.'

'And they are?'

'Please, Colonel, you would not expect me to answer that.' The Rumanian took a sip of his drink. 'But if you were in the act of procuring

100

certain items, that would surely mean they were replacements for equipment you already possess.'

'And that interests you?'

Jardine nodded, which brought another smile, this time genuine, a sudden emptying of the glass, then, 'Perhaps we could go to dinner now.'

Which was his way of saying 'perhaps we can do business'. Silently they made their way through to the dining room: large, with a high ceiling, hung with several glittering chandeliers, the decor heavy and rather Edwardian. Conversation stayed off the subject until they had ordered and he was good at inconsequential talk, using it, like his host, to form an impression of the man with whom he was dealing.

'As you will know, Herr Jardine, much of my poor country was occupied by the forces of the Triple Alliance during the Great War. To be under the thumb of the Austro-Hungarian Empire once more was terrible, but to let those shits of Bulgars into our fair land was an unparalleled crime . . .'

Cal Jardine was no prude – he could curse with the best of them – but the use of the word 'shit' and the vehemence of its use surprised him, coming as it did from such an urbane source. In the luggage he had brought to Victoria Station had been a Baedeker and several books on the country, second-hand jobs he had found in Charing Cross Road, so he knew of what the colonel spoke. A search of *The Times* newspapers at the London Library, with issues going back to before Rumania was a country, had told him just as much about the history and events since the end of the war.

Anthony Hope's fictional Ruritania of *The Prisoner of Zenda* had nothing on the place, with a king, Queen Victoria's grandson, sitting on the throne who had married once against the law, had that annulled, got wedded properly next to a Greek princess, only to come a cropper with a famous courtesan called Magda Lupescu, the pair of them scandalising Europe by their shenanigans. He had renounced his throne in favour of his son by the Greek, then came storming back to overturn and retake his crown, this before he started interfering with the government of the country and causing more problems than he solved.

Though *The Times* was careful, it was obvious that to fall out of favour with those in power was as deadly here as in Germany. Arrest was without habeas corpus and the old rubric of attempted escape was used to see off opponents of the regime, and there were many, particularly an outfit called the Iron Guard, violent and virulently anti-Semitic, which had already assassinated one prime minister and, more recently, a minister of the interior. Dimitrescu was still speaking and Jardine had to force himself to concentrate.

'. . . so what we have existed with these last years is an armoury made up of many weapons from many different sources. Naturally that means many different types of ammunition are required to be stocked.'

'I did some research, Colonel, naturally, so I know what you say is the case.'

Meant to deflect the man it failed: Dimitrescu was determined to list the contributors. 'Original German weapons, of course, some Russian rifles, but most of the ordnance are the gifts given to us by France and Britain, so that together we could fight the Central Powers.' His voice had risen at the end, as if he had led the charge to do that himself.

'Yet broken up into smaller parcels they could be passed on into other hands.' Dimitrescu's eyes narrowed as he digested what Jardine had said.

'Broken up?'

'Yes. I need hardly tell you, Colonel, that we live in a troubled world where things flare up suddenly and die down again. That is a situation in which a person holding a stockpile of useable weapons—'

'Not major pieces of artillery?' he interrupted.

Jardine shook his head: he was going to have enough trouble getting guns across a desert; wheeled cannon were out of the question. 'I would be interested in what one man can carry, really.'

'I fear that would affect the price.'

'By driving it down, Colonel, I think. Right now the market is not buoyant for what you are seeking to dispose of . . .'

'That, Herr Jardine, is guesswork. I have not said yet the government are keen to sell it.'

'Soup,' he replied, glad of time to think, for in his last statement Dimitrescu had put heavy emphasis on the word 'government'. Was that deliberate or accidental? If the former, what was he trying to say? Whatever it was, Jardine knew he would have to pick up on it by inference: this fellow was too shrewd to ever say anything definite to someone he had only just met. He had to dip a toe in the water, in between dipping his spoon in his soup.

'Would I be required to request an indication of policy from a minister?'

'I think not necessary – I feel you can safely deal with me.'

That either meant he was powerful enough to act independently or he was offering to work on his own behalf, and if that were the case, the price would head for the floor. Paying a government was one thing, lining the pockets of a high-placed thief quite another. If Jardine had been trading normally he would have stopped the conversation there, but he was acutely aware that time was not on his side, so he would have to push matters, yet such haste had to avoid selling the pass. His next dip was really a plunge, followed by another mouthful of his fish soup.

'Perhaps I should come to the Ministry for discussions.' No reply came, just a cold stare that did not waver as he supped. 'This soup is delicious, is it not?'

Dimitrescu did not say a word until he finished, sitting back in his chair and flapping his linen napkin. 'I am to understand you would wish to stockpile these arms, that is, if they were available for disposal?'

'That is my intention.'

'Perhaps they could be kept in their present locations and only released from the armouries when required.'

That was very much like a price negotiation, which, if true, had jumped matters on even quicker than Jardine was prepared for; if the Rumanian held the keys to the goods the payments would be his to set at the time they were required, no doubt after a hefty down payment.

'After all, securing warehousing is so expensive.'

Reel him in, Jardine, reel him in. 'An interesting point, Colonel, which would require much examination.'

'While I must take an accurate inventory of what it is possible to dispose of, and when.'

Time for a bit of cold water. 'And I would be required to consult with my principal to get his view.'

That did not please him; he was near to being brusque. 'You are not here with the power of decision?'

'Let us say, Colonel, that my advice is central, but it would never do to wound the *amour propre* of the person with the money needed to complete, now sitting in a Swiss bank.'

'That would be where the transaction took place?'

'Contracts could be signed in Bucharest and the monies released on my cognisance.'

'Let us leave that all aside, Herr Jardine, and get to know each other better. Enough has been said tonight to encourage me to believe you are a serious person, and given I have much to ponder, I fear to say more in case it is potentially misleading. I suggest, however, we commit to meet tomorrow, where I will be happy to return your generosity, for there are better places to eat and drink in Budapest than these grand hotels.'

'Very kind.'

'Tell me, Herr Jardine, are you a married man?'

# CHAPTER EIGHT

'He's as slippery as a barrel of eels and I think he plans to ply me with food, drink and loose women tomorrow evening.'

'Time to swap places, old fruit,' Lanchester joked.

'What about me?' Vince asked. 'Don't I get a sniff?'

'Find your own,' Jardine replied as he went to his jacket and pulled out the paper Monty Redfern had given him, which he waved before the others. 'Given I don't trust the bugger, I think it is best if I try and find out something about him. I was given a number to call by a Jewish friend in London and there's no time like the present.'

'Is he Jewish too?' Jardine nodded. 'Then don't call him from the room, Cal. I had a meeting with a banker today. He spent half the time railing about the Jews, as well as telling me how wonderful the Iron Guard was and how they would soon rid the country of what I think he called a pestilence. It might be worse than Germany.'

'Christ,' Vince exclaimed. 'I might as well 'ave stayed fightin' Mosley.'

'I'll call from the lobby.'

That was still busy, the Rumanians keeping the kind of late hours that would have pleased a Spaniard. The phone was on a desk by the reception and Jardine was just about to go to it when a fellow in a grey suit, not terribly well cut, turned his face away just a mite too quickly, bringing up the hackles. Still he went to the phone, but instead of asking for an outside line he called Vince's room.

'I am in the lobby, Vince, and I fear not alone. I will go out for a bit of a walk, old son, and I need a second eye. I will wait in the lobby, then take point.'

There was enough of the soldier still in Vince to pick up on what he was saying: 'second eye' was an expression they had used in Iraq when a man going out needed cover. 'Taking point', another one, was self-explanatory.

'Gotcha, guv. Two ticks and I'll use the stairs.'

Jardine positioned himself looking towards the lifts and staircase so he would see Vince appear, thankfully unseen by the man that needed to be checked out: his eyeline was angled. There was always a chance he was wrong, that the fellow looking away, as he had, was coincidence. When Vince appeared on the first landing, Jardine headed for the double doors at the entrance, nodding to the uniformed flunkey who held it open for him and ignoring the look of the top-hatted doorman, who wondered if he wanted a motor taxi or a *trăsură*. Shaking his head he went past the deep rows of diners sitting in the outside restaurant and out to the plaza on which the hotel stood.

The night was warm, even slightly muggy, and the streets were busy with promenading couples, the women dressed up to the nines and the menfolk in clothing that announced good tailoring, the impression very like that of the Italian nightly *passeggiata*. All along the boulevard there were cafés, even open shops, and every building was lit up, giving the place an air of prosperity, not that it was complete.

Beggars were ubiquitous, overweight women swathed in shawls held forth emaciated babies, uttering a constant low-volume plea, gaunt-looking men sitting in doorways with their hands held out making a similar sound. Jardine did no more than an uneven circuit, spotting several places that should have a phone, probably a public one, before coming back to the hotel like the bored tourist he was seeking to portray. Back in his suite, Vince joined him.

'You're being tailed; one geezer is all I could see.'

'Dimitrescu.'

'Has to be, dun it?' Vince made a fist. 'You want I should see him off?'

'No, there's no point, but I want you to go up to Mr Lanchester's room and say from now on he's to stay off my floor. You can take messages back and forth if need be.'

'What about that call you was gonna make, guv?'

'I saw a few places. Any idea what the phones take?'

Vince pulled out the coins from his pocket, bani and lei notes, left over from the purchases they had made that day. As usual for a pair who did not know the currency there was a mass of it.

'Help yourself.'

'I'd like to speak to Israel Goldfarbeen, if I may.' The English was a long shot – he had forgotten to ask Monty if the contact spoke it – as was the idea of hearing a reply, the café he was in being so busy he needed a finger in one ear.

'You are speaking to him.' The voice was deep, the speech careful and slow.

'I am a friend of Monty Redfern, from London, he gave me your number.'

'Montague Rötefarn, the *alter bok*, how is he?'

Not having the least idea what an *'alter bok'* was, he replied, 'In rude good health, sir, and my name is Jardine. I am a stranger in Bucharest and he advised me that you could help me.'

The reply was jovial. 'Mr Hardeen, I am stranger in this country and I have lived here all my life.'

'I'm in search of advice. Would it be possible to meet?'

'If a *bohmer* like Montague sent you, how can I refuse?' Which left Jardine wondering where to find a Yiddish dictionary. 'You got a pen?'

'I have.'

'What am I saying, "pen"? You get a *trăsură*, you say the Yiddish theatre. The driver will spit at you, the *ganef*, but he will want the fare, so spit back. My house is on the left of the theatre. You'll see the lit window. Just knock.' He then demanded to know from where he was coming. 'But don't pay more than thirty bani.'

'Tomorrow?'

'Now, if you like.'

Jardine looked at his watch. 'It's after eleven.'

'In this *sheise* country that is midday. Come now and drink with me. I want to hear about Montague.'

He and Vince were in one of the few motor taxis not long after, having handed over a ten-lei note to the top-hatted doorman for the service of lifting his finger, Vince being sure the tail had no wheels. 'He's probably on the blower now, guv, telling his boss.'

'As long as his boss doesn't know where we're going.'

The taxi took them from the Athénée Palace to another grand hotel, the Francez, where Jardine paid the driver off, engaging the aid – after a bit of a wait and for another ten-lei note – of a second top-hatted doorman to get another taxi. Vince, having observed others do the same, insisted that when he died and came back, a hotel doorman was the job he wanted.

'Talk about easy green.'

'You have to buy that job, Vince.'

'I'll borrow the money off you. The way the berks that use these places give tips, I'll pay you back in a week.'

The ride was not long because Bucharest was not large, and the driver did not spit, which was just as well because Vince would probably have clouted him, but he did look as though someone had just shot his cat as Jardine paid him off.

'Cheery sod,' was the Londoner's opinion.

The door opened a split second after Jardine knocked, and before him was a giant of a man in a collarless shirt, with big shoulders, protruding belly, a round smiling face and a thick red beard. 'So rich you use motor cars, already. Enter, enter.'

Going through the door Jardine touched the mezuzah, and told Vince to do so too, which got him an approving nod. The room they entered had a fire in the grate, even though it was a warm night, which was thankfully dying.

'You Jewish, Mr Hardeen?'

'It's Jardine and no, pure Gentile, but I have been to Palestine.'

The hands went up. *'Dos gefelt mir.'* The confusion on Jardine's face being obvious, he added, 'You don't speak Yiddish; why would you?'

'No.'

'And you have been to *Eretz Yisrael*, I should be so lucky.'

He looked past Jardine to Vince, who was introduced, and then a bottle of wine was produced, three glasses poured, toasts proposed and seen off, all in genial good humour. Goldfarbeen asked about Monty Rötefarn, an '*eizel*' for changing his name to the English, and they talked about him for a while, which made Jardine realise how little he really knew about his Jewish friend.

Goldfarbeen, as a young man, had gone to London to study theatre, met and befriended Monty before he was rich, and here he was the theatre administrator, the man who raised and spent the money to keep the place going, some of it sent from Hampstead. An hour passed and the fire died completely before Jardine looked at his watch. He needed to move things on.

'So, Mr Hardeen, what can I do to aid you?'

Geniality evaporated the more Goldfarbeen heard, and Jardine was pretty open, only leaving out for where the weapons were destined. By the time his visitor was finished he was shaking his massive head.

'You have picked a bad man to do business with.'

'You know him?'

'Bucharest is like a village, my friend, and everyone gossips.'

'I don't care if he's bad, as long as the business is completed.'

'Dimitrescu is an anti-Semite, but that matters not, nine out of ten of the people of Rumania are that, but I would not trust him and I would advise you to do the same.'

'He don't trust him,' Vince growled.

Goldfarbeen's beard was on his ample chest and he was thinking.

111

'Would I be allowed to ask about and see what is in the wind?' Jardine was about to say 'discreetly', but he sensed that was superfluous. 'This is a country split in two, Mr Hardeen, and for every one of the far right there is one on the near right and they make it their business to spy on each other.'

'No one on the left?'

'None with power, but the closest are the liberals, who would skin Dimitrescu in acid.'

'Very liberal.'

The great belly shook as he laughed. 'This is not England, my friend. Here they think and act like Turks.'

'They was right bastards,' Vince spat. 'We saw some of what they did in Mesopotamia, didn't we, guv?' Jardine nodded. 'Every place you walk you's treading on bones. Made us look like saints.'

'What do you think you will find out?'

'A great deal, Mr Hardeen, half of it nonsense, but once I have sorted out fantasy from fact, I will pass on what I hear and you may decide what to do with it. Now I get my coat and walk you back to where you can get a *trăsură*.'

'Just tell us; we can go alone.'

'No, my friend, for out there, lurking in the dark, are the Roma, the double curse of Rumania, people who will cut your throat just for your shoes.'

Coat on, Goldfarbeen picked up a large stick with a knob at one end; it was not to aid his walking.

Jardine saw Peter Lanchester set off for Constanta – he was taking an early morning train – where he was to meet up with a representative of one of the people who had set this whole enterprise in motion;

Peter had not said the supporter was in shipping, he did not have to. Whoever represented them in Rumania had received a telegram from London, and it had been sent before they departed. It had informed them of the imminent arrival of an English-flagged freighter that was to wait there for a cargo: Lanchester was going down to check things out.

Having barely finished breakfast in a deserted dining room, Jardine finally realised the bellhop, who was bearing aloft a note and calling out for attention, was using a scrambled version of his name. It was from Goldfarbeen, though he had used only his initials, and it posed a simple question. Would he know why a message had been sent to Berlin triggered by his name? He was out of the hotel looking for a phone in seconds and to hell with his watcher.

'I made a few calls.'

'You must have been up all night.'

'Who sleeps, Mr Hardeen? I am cursed because I cannot, so better to do something than toss and turn and get my wife's elbow in the belly. First, I spoke to one member of the Peasants' Party, who said there was something up, and he put me on to another contact who recognised your name.'

Jardine was wondering how, given Goldfarbeen's pronunciation.

'That set bells ringing like I am the patriarch, already, so I thought I would spread a little money around, promised you understand, which is the quickest way to get things done in this *sheise* country.'

'I'll pay you back.'

'Montague will set it straight. I went to a fellow who is in military intelligence, like they have such a quality in Rumania, who tells me a certain colonel asked them yesterday to find out about you, Mr Hardeen. He tells me you are an interesting man, but what is important is he found out you are wanted in Germany for something which happened in Hamburg.'

'I know what that is.'

'I hope the man you murdered was German, the bastards.' Jardine was about to correct this statement, but what was the point? 'That colonel is very friendly with the Germans and he has sent them a message last night to say you are in Bucharest. It was also he who did the business you told me of last night, the little package you say is coming from Germany. He will have an interest in that. I think your English expression is a finger in the pie.'

'You must have good sources.'

'I have a lot of people who hate other people, and even more people who live higher than they can afford who would betray their mother.'

'Would my man have me arrested and hand me over?'

'I thought about that before calling you, and if you will take the opinion of an old Jew, he is a man who loves money and is known to be greedy. He likes fast cars, expensive women and the casino. If he is going to hand you over it will be for payment. When you think what to do, keep that in mind.'

'I need to know if arrest is possible.'

'Don't worry, I will find for you, but who is going to pay to have you thrown in jail? If you don't hear from me, call me back before you meet with your colonel again.'

'Let's hope I have time for that.'

'If you do not, you will know beforehand.'

With a silent blessing to Monty Redfern, Jardine walked back to the hotel, called Vince's room to wake him up and sat down to think. What he had to work out was worrying, the safest thing being to get out of Rumania right away, taking Vince, and either trying to contact Lanchester to take a boat or leaving him a letter at reception, which he would pick up when he got back. Mulling over what Goldfarbeen was telling him he might have time to do something, and it all hinged on one fact: would Dimitrescu find out he knew of the message to Berlin?

'So he has sent a message to Berlin,' Jardine said, rhetorically, to a bleary-eyed Vince Castellano, a surprisingly late riser. 'Who to?'

'Can I order some bleedin' breakfast?'

'That arrives where?' The response was a shrug: Vince had never been a morning person. 'If he is buying arms it is from the War Ministry. They have to tell someone else, who then has to act on it.'

'If you say so, guv.'

'Vince, when you have filled your face, I want you to go out and buy some rations, you know the kind of stuff, things that don't go off. Take them to the car and leave them there, then come back here.'

'What you going to do, guv?'

'I am going to send a veiled warning to Peter Lanchester, then do a Sherlock Holmes, old son, and follow a masterly policy of inactivity. If you come back to or get a message saying I have bought tickets for a boxing match, head back for the car.'

Dimitrescu was waiting in a Maybach Zeppelin outside the hotel, the chauffeur opening the door for his passenger. 'So, Herr Jardine, what kind of day have you had?'

*As if you don't know, you bastard!* He had spent the day like any tourist would, visiting the Royal Palace to watch the guard change, an art gallery that was interesting for its lack of old masters – countries that conquered had most of those – and its plethora of more modern works which showed a rich vein of local artistic endeavour.

The Orthodox cathedral to look at the icons was an obvious attraction, as was gazing at the statuary, especially the one of King Carol the First on the rearing horse. Generally he went tootling about, stopping every so often at one of the numerous outdoor cafés, which the berk tailing him dare not enter, going inside to a phone to keep in touch with Goldfarbeen, who reassured him he was still safe, and Vince, to report that as the case.

'You live in a very interesting city, Colonel, fascinating, in fact. I shall be recommending to some of my friends it is a place they should visit.'

'It pleases me that you say so. We have high hopes that after so many years of turmoil Rumania will take its rightful place amongst the nations of Europe.' It was easy to smile at such hyperbolic nonsense, but tempting to respond with the truth, which was less flattering: despite the glitter, there was more poverty in this place than wealth. 'You will be pleased to know that I have made certain enquiries regarding your interests and the results have come back as very positive.'

'Where are we off to?' Jardine asked, with the very real anxiety that by getting in this car he was taking a hell of a risk: this swine could take him straight to the cells.

'What I think to be the best restaurant in the city, where I will, if you will permit me, introduce you to the cuisine of my country.'

'Splendid.'

With only the light from street lamps coming into the back of the car, it was surprising to observe a twinkle in the eyes of Dimitrescu. 'There are, of course, many other attractions.'

Eat your heart out, Peter Lanchester, Jardine thought.

* * *

116

The restaurant was more like some kind of club, in a basement, with a small dance floor, the colouring predominately purple and the women universally dark and sultry, two of the most beautiful coming with the champagne – real and the last foreign thing he tasted that night. The food was excellent, a sour soup called *ciorbä* and *ostropel* duck. The Rumanian wines were robust and had unpronounceable names – but then so did his female companion, who let him know almost immediately with a searching hand what the last part of his night was going to be like.

'Business, Colonel?'

'Not tonight, Herr Jardine, tonight we take pleasure. Tomorrow we will talk business, and maybe come to an arrangement beneficial to us both. You are my guest and I intend that your stay in my country should be memorable.'

Occasionally he caught Dimitrescu looking at him, in between trying to hold a conversation with a girl with flashing eyes, long ringlets in her hair, a dress cut so low and occasionally revealing it was impossible to maintain eye contact, and a tongue that made constant promises of pleasure to come. Those occasional observations were sobering, or was he just imagining that the colonel was looking at him in a way a fox might look at a chicken?

'Please, Herr Jardine,' Dimitrescu said, as he dropped him and his 'gift' off at the Athénée Palace. 'If she asks you for money, do not give her any more than the needs of gratitude. She has already been paid.'

As it transpired, Jardine was very generous indeed, which was only fitting given she was so very much that first. His only worry was her screaming, which was loud enough to have him hope the walls of his suite were thick enough to leave the other guests in peace.

# CHAPTER NINE

'Peter, you should move out to another hotel. This one might not be safe if it all goes tits up.'

'You are so sure of your Yid?' The apology was immediate. 'Sorry, old boy, habits of a lifetime.'

'Are you sure we have a boat?'

'Piece of cake, and the captain is Turkish. I had a look at the engines, which, to my untutored eye, appeared to be in fine shape, and so clean, which is more than I can say for the port. If you think things are tough at home, you should see the docks at Constanta. Dire everywhere, except for the oil terminal.'

'Which makes it doubly strange the Rumanian Government are buying weapons. If the main port is in bad shape the country can't be making the kind of money needed for such a purchase, even if they do have oil to sell.'

'Then you of all people should know what that means, Cal,'

Lanchester replied, rubbing finger and thumb together. 'It wouldn't be the first time the guiding principle of an arms deal is personal profit.'

'Anyway, pack your bags, check out and go to the Hotel Francez. Let me know your room number as soon as you're checked in. Then I'll send Vince over.'

'No chance of my being entertained by your Rumanian colonel, is there? I do think I deserve equal treatment.'

'None.'

'Dirty, lucky sod.'

Jardine left Lanchester's room, and him packing, with caution, making sure the floor manager was not about, or the cleaners. As soon as he got back to his suite, he found a note under his door with the simple message, *I.G. Call*. As usual, when he left the hotel he picked up the man tasked to report his movements, Jardine registering that if it was always the same poor sod in the grey, badly cut suit, only able to trail him on foot, then Dimitrescu was not overburdened with resources, while his man was severely lacking in his wardrobe. Wondering what was being reported back, it was amusing to think it was that the target was addicted to coffee.

'Herr Hardeen, I have some news for you and I think we should meet.'

'At your house?'

'No, come to the Great Synagogue, I will meet you there.'

It was double motor taxis again, this time bouncing off a third five-star hotel, the Grand Hotel du Boulevard, and a sour response when his second cab was directed to the *Große Synagoge*, which left Jardine thinking that compared to Germany this place was truly rabid; God help the Jews if Hitler's kind of fascism took hold here. As he entered, to the sound of some gentle Hebrew chanting, he had to remind himself not to remove his hat.

Goldfarbeen was waiting for him and took him to a quiet corner and sat him down, in case, as he put it, 'The rabbi sees a *goyim* in his house of worship.'

'First, I am near certain you have some time. A message has come back from Berlin to Dimitrescu, telling him they want you and they will send an escort to take you back to Germany. He sent a reply insisting they wait until he says it is time to come.'

'For what reason?'

For the first time the old man looked cross, like what-does-it-matter irritated. 'Also, he has ordered, this very morning, the small weapon armouries cleared out into railway wagons, as the guns he has bought are on their way from Germany by freight train.'

There was a twinkle in the older man's eyes now, which begged a question. 'What are you thinking?'

'I am thinking, Herr Hardeen, that Dimitrescu is going to sell you those guns in the railway wagons.'

'That's not all you are thinking.'

'You must let your mind work like a Rumanian.'

'Better you do that.'

'How would you pay him?'

Jardine explained the transaction, which would be between banks, one in Zurich and whichever one Dimitrescu designated in Bucharest.

'Something tells me it won't be the National Bank,' Goldfarbeen pronounced.

'It should be.'

That got a shrug, which with his shoulders was impressive. 'Here is what I think he will do. The transaction will be between a bank of his choice and yours.' Jardine was about to say it would be hard to keep that a secret, but he suspected Goldfarbeen would say 'this is Rumania'.

'He will do everything to make it look kosher and that is why he has asked his German friends to wait. As soon as you have made the payment he will find a reason to detain you, just long enough for a train to come from Berlin with the men who want to take you back.'

'You're saying he'll have me arrested.'

'No, Herr Hardeen, he does not want you screaming "cheat" from the cells.'

'Quicker to kill me, then.'

'Which would not please his German friends, who it seems want you very badly, and – who knows? – they might even pay to get you. I told you he was greedy.'

'How much of this can you keep on top of?' Jardine had to clarify that: it was too colloquial for Goldfarbeen.

'If I spend enough money, I will know everything.'

'Can you find out when that armaments train from Germany will arrive?' Seeing the question in his eyes, he added, 'I think the people who want to escort me back might come at the same time, perhaps they won't wait even if he has told them to. A German will not like taking orders from a man like Dimitrescu.'

The old man thought for a while, then nodded. 'There are a few Communists in this country. Some are Jews, of course, but there are others who work in the mines, docks and the railways. Maybe even they like money.'

'They might act out of conviction.'

'I am not sure I would trust conviction, Mr Hardeen.'

'Spend what you need and I will pay you back, or I'll get Monty to do it when I get back to London.'

'My friend, I would like to do it out of my own pockets, just to stick a finger up Hitler's arse, but my pockets are not that deep.'

'Herr Jardine, I have been trying to contact you.' The voice became jocular. 'I had a fear my little gift brought on such exhaustion and you were still asleep.'

Cheeky sod: that was a dig at his manhood. 'I was at the British embassy, just to let them know I am here.'

The voice became tense: it was not a place any arms dealer should go near. 'The British embassy?'

'Social call, really, sort of good manners. The last thing I need is them becoming aware a fellow countryman is in town and wondering why I am here. Better to call in and spin them a yarn.'

'So you still wish to do business?'

'Most certainly.'

'Then if you go downstairs in, say, twenty minutes you will find my car waiting for you. Oh, and by the way, I would appreciate details of your banking facilities, without which we cannot proceed.'

'Of course.'

First he phoned Lanchester, who just acknowledged the message, then Vince Castellano. 'We're on.'

'Is it safe, guv?'

'Not for long, Vince, not for long.'

'Take your shooter.'

'I will.'

In warm weather it was impossible to carry a gun without it showing, so he used the attaché case he had bought in Brussels, which had a side pocket near the inside top into which he could slip the Colt in such a way that it could be extracted quickly. With the time he had, once he had also put in some papers, only the bank details being really needed, Jardine sat in a chair with the case slightly open by his side and practised pulling it out, slipping off the safety and aiming it, feeling absurdly like a poor man's Tom Mix.

The car was waiting as promised and he got in with a confident smile, hardly noticing Vince, who was writing down the number. He did not see him jump into the motor taxi he had standing by and, in Italian with gestures, order it to follow the limousine – not hard, since it was the kind of car to be driven at a stately pace. It soon became clear it was heading away from the district that housed the official buildings, the Royal Palace and the ministries. To Cal Jardine it made no difference, and in his mind he toyed with that absurd expression used by Sherlock Holmes: 'The game's afoot.'

It was a bank but in not the least bit a grand one. Jardine did not even bother to look at the signage to see what it said: Vince would take care of that and make more sense of it than he. He was escorted in by the driver to find Dimitrescu waiting for him, then led into a small office furnished in poor-imitation art deco. The colonel took a seat behind a desk, clear of anything except for a single folder and a push bell, with Jardine sitting opposite, his first act, as he put down his case, to slip the catch.

'As you will appreciate, Herr Jardine, discretion is all in such transactions.'

'Of course.'

'Hence the need to meet in an out-of-the-way banking facility like this one. First of all, I have considered our previous conversation and

I wish to establish if your aim is to purchase everything you think you can sell on and take it out of Rumania.'

'It is.'

'Might I ask how?'

'By truck to Varna.' Dimitrescu lost his genial air then, and his expression came close to a scowl: just the mention of a Bulgarian port was enough to raise his national hackles. 'I would ask as part of our transaction that you clear us through customs on the Rumanian-Bulgarian border.'

'Why Varna?'

'To divulge that would be to open up a path that might lead to excessive disclosure, Colonel, and really, once the transaction is complete, and I say this with no ill intent, your interest in what happens to the goods is at an end.'

'You will appreciate that any weaponry going to that country raises concerns. The Bulgarians are not good neighbours and to this I cannot agree.'

Jardine made a show of thinking deeply, hand on chin. In reality he was amused: he had just said that to guy the bastard, to see how far he would go, and he knew he could insist. Greed would overcome patriotism.

'You would prefer Constanta?'

'Most certainly.'

The response was a shrug of supposed indifference. 'My ship can dock anywhere. I will send instructions to move to Constanta and we will load there.'

'Good!' The folder was slipped across the table. 'Here is a list of what we have. It is probably best if I leave you in peace to consider what you want and don't want. I take it you have a pen?'

'Of course,' Jardine replied, pulling a Mont Blanc Meisterstück from his inside pocket. He was with a man who knew quality when he saw it, evident in his look of admiration, with the owner playing another joke. 'Bought it in Hamburg. Damn fine pen.'

'Hamburg,' Dimitrescu replied, his facial skin a trifle tight. 'I do not know it.'

'Neither do I, really, just paid a short visit. Bit windy for my taste.'

'I will leave you to it.' Jardine thanked him, then promised himself no more guying: the bugger might join the dots. 'You have details of your bank?'

That was passed over and Dimitrescu exited. Opening the folder he perused the list, and it was obvious his colonel was telling the truth about this, at least. It was a real hotchpotch of weapons: French, Russian, some old Austrian pre-Great War pieces, but there were Maxim guns and, in reality, a rifle was a rifle; they had not changed much in fifty years, except the Mannlichers had clips while most were bolt action. There were French 6.5 mm Daudeteaus and M75s, plus eighty-odd Lee-Enfields. Also listed were mortars that he wanted, and some small-calibre field guns, which he struck off, but in the main the list conformed to what Zaharoff had shown him.

The fountain pen was used to put a price beside each set of items, including the required ammunition, the whole totted up to a low total which he knew Dimitrescu would try to negotiate upwards, opening with an outrageous value, this being a country where bargaining was part of the fabric. So the arguments would be, unless he cut them short, long and boring. Sure he had the means to curtail matters, he rang the bell and his man re-entered with his bank details, which were handed back before he resumed his seat.

'I have had the manager send a telegram to Zurich, if that is acceptable, just to check the account exists.'

'Essential I would say, wouldn't you?'

'So?' he asked, nodding to the folder, once again closed, assuming there was no need to wait for a reply.

'I think we can very much do business, Colonel Dimitrescu.' Then Jardine made a big play of looking around the office. 'But I think when we do, the price I pay should reflect the unusual nature of our surroundings, don't you?'

'I have already explained—'

Jardine cut him off, but with some gentility. 'Please, Colonel, I am a man of the world and as long as I get that which I seek I have no other concerns. I will deal with you in good faith, but I think it is obvious you are acting . . . how shall I say it? . . . at the very limits of your authority, perhaps.'

He was not one to surrender too easily. 'I am acting as the representative of my nation.'

'I was good enough to give to you the details of my banking facility. Would you be good enough to respond?'

'It is too early for such a thing.'

Jardine was thinking, *good try, old cock, but not good enough.* Time for a little bit of a lie, so that Dimitrescu started operating to his timetable instead of the other way round. 'As I told you, I called at the British embassy this morning. I established they are happy to arrange for me to see the Minister of War.'

'You mentioned these weapons?'

'Of course not. I said I was trying to sell some British products, and they were keen to aid me. A forged business card does wonders. Now, do we do business, or do I accept their offer?'

'You are living very dangerously, Herr Jardine.'

'I think we both are.'

'It does not seem to occur to you that I am acting on the instructions of that very same minister.'

'Then you have nothing to fear in me meeting him.' Jardine leant forward. 'Come, Colonel, I have no interest in what you are up to or who stands to gain from it, I am merely keen to get what I want for as little as I am required to pay, so that I can increase the profit I make when I sell it. It is business.'

Dimitrescu opened the folder and looked down the notes Jardine had made. There was no need to enquire if he had got to the total: his hiss of anger was too audible.

'An opening gambit, Colonel, but it has a purpose and that is to tell you I expect to pay a good price, but not an unreasonable one.'

Dimitrescu did not hesitate: he came back with a figure three times that on the paper before him and they were off, back and forth, edging closer until they seemed close to a deal on one just above twice what Jardine had proposed, a point from which he refused to budge. But then, neither would the colonel, and that was when Jardine recalled Goldfarbeen saying the weapons had been loaded onto railway wagons.

'I'll tell you what, Colonel, I will agree that price if you get my weapons to Constanta.'

Dimitrescu was quick to agree, unaware the man he was negotiating with knew such transportation was, to him, probably cost-free; time to close him out.

'Naturally, the weapons being on the dockside, ready to be loaded, would represent the completion of the transaction. I am sure your bank has a branch in the country's main port.'

* * *

'Dimitrescu wants the money more than he wants to do the Germans a favour and he won't move till that's in his bank. We complete the deal, he tells them to come and nail me, and by the time they get here I will be in the middle of the Black Sea, we will have our weapons and, I can tell you, at a price a lot less than I expected to pay. It's a good deal, and you don't have to get involved except in the money transfer, and you can do that from here.'

'Your show, old boy,' Lanchester said. 'No point in hiring a dog . . .'

'Don't you dare finish that sentence!'

'Heel, boy,' Lanchester joked. 'I'd best get word to London that matters are coming to a head.'

'You don't want to meet Dimitrescu, anyway.'

'It wasn't him I wanted to meet, it was those dark-haired floozies you told me about.'

'I missed out on that an' all,' Vince cut in.

'It is our misfortune, Vince, to be in cahoots with a selfish bastard. So what's the process, Cal?'

'We need speed, so the transfer will have to be by telephone, telegrams will take too long, which means you have to set up a line to Switzerland from this hotel and keep it open.'

'Can you do that?' Vince asked.

Lanchester shrugged. 'Grand luxury hotel, they should be used to that sort of thing.'

'I will phone reception from Constanta on another line with a coded message, you process the funds, I will insist he is on to his bank in the same way, and as soon as all is complete I put a gun to his head and tell him if he tries to stop me leaving with the weapons his brains will be all over the wall. Simple, really.'

'I can spot one or two flaws.'

'So can I, but I will have Vince with me. They don't know about him and he will have your Colt Automatic.'

'I've only ever fired a rifle and a machine gun.'

'It's easy, Vince,' Lanchester said.

'Must be,' Vince retorted, 'if a bleedin' officer can do it.'

Jardine responded, 'You just point it and pull the trigger, like James Cagney in *The Public Enemy*.'

'What's the timing?' asked Lanchester.

'Dimitrescu is calling in the morning, Peter. I'll tell you then.' Jardine pulled a card out of his pocket. 'This is the place he and I went to last night. Why don't you take Vince there and have a night on the firm?'

'You?'

'Whacked, Peter.'

'And don't we know why. Anything else we might need to have a romantic evening?'

'Cotton wool.'

Cal Jardine stopped at the bar of the Athénée Palace to have a drink, before dinner and an early night. That a stranger spoke to him in a hotel bar, on hearing him order from a multilingual barman, was not anything to remark upon, nor even that the man was clearly German and wanted someone to talk to over a drink; after all, they did much business in Rumania. Besides, as he said, he was keen to try out his English, which he feared was becoming rusty, evidenced by his accent and grammatical errors when he spoke it.

There is a certain air about some men, and for a businessman in machine tools, Herr Reisner, with his firm handshake, seemed very fit. When Jardine deliberately laid a hand on his upper arm as they got up to go into dinner, it was clear the fellow had hard biceps. He also had scars in certain places on his face and cheeks, nothing too obvious, but the little mementoes that come from action; Jardine had seen enough of those in his own shaving mirror, and there was also a similarity in the skin: he was a man accustomed to the outdoors.

His hair was blond, the eyes – a startling blue – were rarely concealed by a blink, while they had at the corners the kind of lines that came from peering at a strong sun. In the none-too-taxing enquiries he made about his presence in Bucharest and his business, the replies were just a shade too slow in coming, as if he had a flimsy cover story, while every time he asked Jardine about his reasons for being in Bucharest, there was just the slightest trace, a tightening of the upper jaw, that indicated those replies were being measured against another narrative.

Dinner over, Jardine politely declined a late-night stroll or a nightcap, pleading a long and tiring day, and went back to his room, his first act to lock his door and jam a chair against it. Then he rang Lanchester's hotel and Vince's room, leaving a simple code they would understand and no German should. It took time for the receptionist to get the letters down when he spelt it out and he made the man read it back.

'That's right. We've been bowled a googly.'

Then he went to bed with the Colt under his pillow, caring not one jot that the oil on the gun would stain the linen of his sheets. What would the chambermaid think, having changed them that morning after his night of passion?

# CHAPTER TEN

Aware that he might be indulging in an overreaction, Jardine was at the reception desk while the cleaners were still trying to dust the lobby and the day staff had not yet come on duty: if you want to find out anything in a hotel, those who work overnight are much more malleable than the more stuffy daytime people and his question, in truth, was seemingly harmless. A twenty-lei note and a hint he was a potential business competitor established that Herr Reisner had checked in late the day before. As soon as office hours came into play he phoned the German embassy and asked for the same person, to be told no one of that name occupied a position there, which eliminated one possibility.

There was no need to bribe the night-time receptionist to keep hush what he had been asked: if Reisner was genuine, he would not enquire; if he was what Jardine thought he might be, a member of the SS Intelligence Branch, either resident in Bucharest or sent from

Berlin, he did not need to. It was not surprising they met at breakfast – being guests in the same place it was natural – nor was there anything untoward in the way the German greeted him and made a polite and silent gesture that asked permission to share his table.

In daylight, over the kind of food one has in the morning, jams and hot rolls, it was easier for Jardine to study his hands, for they tell you much about what a person might do in his life. A fellow who occupies a desk and uses his pen as a weapon should, in the main, have soft hands. Reisner's were not excessively large but the knuckles were prominent, the skin covering them showing some evidence of scarring as if, many times in his life, he had used them in physical conflict; in short, the man was a fighter.

'You have busy day ahead again, Herr Jardine?'

'Not as taxing as yesterday, but enough to be going on with. And you?'

Reisner smiled, showing perfectly even and white teeth, his answer, once more a millisecond delayed. 'Mostly telephone, make contacts I hope call on.'

Not a good answer: you did not come all the way to Rumania to make those calls; you wrote beforehand and only expended money on travel when you had firm commitments to talk.

'I, too, have many calls to make,' Jardine said, draining his coffee cup, 'so if you will forgive me . . .'

'Perhaps tonight dinner?' came the reply. 'Not hotel . . . somewhere other perhaps? I told many good eating places in Bucharest.'

'What's your room number, Herr Reisner?'

This time the pause was way too long, while the eyes flickered, as though divulgence was unwise. '*Drei, fünf, eins.*'

Tempted to muck him about by asking for a translation, Jardine decided not to bother. 'I shall call you later and let you know if I am free.'

Vince always took his breakfast in his room and later than Jardine, more so on this morning having had a late night, an evening out his one-time CO had to enquire about, having been required to get him out of bed to answer the door. A quick glance at the state of his linen showed only the crumbs of toast.

'It was way too pricey, guv, and that was the food. The women were out of sight. God only knows how much your colonel shelled out on you.'

'You got my message?' Vince nodded, but showed no evidence of understanding until it was explained to him, and that from a man who lived within shouting distance of the Oval. 'I need you to ride shotgun again, but this time ignore Dimitrescu's dolt and see if there's anyone else too interested.'

'Nazi bastards,' Vince replied, thumbing his oft-broken nose and shimmying a straight left and a right hook. 'Be nice to land one on the sods.'

'They won't be goose-stepping, Vince. If they are around they won't look much different to anyone else, and it occurs to me there are so many fascists in the place already, half of them probably funded by the German Foreign Office, that my Reisner bloke would not have needed to bring anyone with him.'

The phone call he made to Lanchester from his exterior café got a more positive response: he had understood the message. 'That guy you asked in Berlin about me, any chance of getting on the blower and seeing if he can pick up a whisper?'

'Worth a try, though I think we'll end up spending more money on international phone calls than—'

'Don't say it, Peter.'

'I was about to say those ladies of the night Vince and I turned down. Christ, they were expensive, and I always thought when one went abroad such things were cheaper.'

'Since I am completely in ignorance of the price at home I am not able to comment.'

'Stop being pious, Cal, and send Vince over later.'

Exiting the café, he had an agreed signal with Vince: if he was reading a paper, it was back to the Athénée Palace for a report; all clear and it would be under his arm, so he could phone Goldfarbeen and get a taxi to meet him. They both assumed that the bad grey suit was a given. Vince was reading.

'He was right behind the berk we've had since the off. Big shoulders and heavyweight muscles, 'cause his suit jacket was real tight on his biceps, hands like hams and square head under his titfer, as well, but that's what you expect with Huns.'

'I must introduce you to some German women.'

'Whenever you like, guv, I'm game.'

'There's one called Gretl I think you'd like.'

'Don't get the idea I'm fussy, but what about this new bloke?'

'If he was following me, that means Dimitrescu does not know he is here. In contact he would not have to, he could just ask.'

'Good or bad?'

'Ask me another.'

'What's goin' to win the three-thirty at Kempton Park?'

'All I know is it's getting messier, Vince.'

'Might be towel time – like throw it in, guv.'

There was no fear in that statement, just the option anyone but an idiot might take. 'Not yet, I've got to go and see Goldfarbeen, usual drill.'

'What if our new chum follows you in a cab?'

Jardine wrote down and passed over Goldfarbeen's number. 'Call him and say not to show up.'

'You never did tell me what coins the phones take.'

One phone call and two taxis later Jardine entered the synagogue once more, to be greeted by a man with good news and, of more immediate concern to him, a troubled stomach, over which he constantly rubbed his hands, an act that only demonstrated how massive it was.

'My wife's cooking is so good, Herr Hardeen, if we had time I would let you taste it and you would never leave Rumania. I ate too much of it last night.' That was followed by an attempt at a burp, not wholly successful. 'It will surprise you how much I eat.'

'I cannot believe that,' Jardine responded, with a glance at the offending belly.

'I should shed a few kilos, no?'

'I heard a Yiddish expression in Germany once, that a man should eat like a bird and shit like a horse, then he will be thin.'

Goldfarbeen laughed, which he started loudly but had to cut quickly: they were in a house of worship. 'Me, I eat like a horse and today I shit like a bird, but I have hopes that later—'

'The Berlin train?'

'Will arrive at the Chitila Marshalling Yard tonight at around ten.'

*Have I got time to get my weapons on the way to Constanta and be out of Bucharest before . . . ?* Jardine paused his self-questioning thoughts and decided to share another thought with his indigestive Jew. 'My problem is, I think the SS are already here, or at least a couple of them.'

'You have done the business with the pig?'

'I have.'

'And who are these Germans?' Jardine's explanation was brief.

'As I said, I didn't think they'd wait.'

'You are in a bad place, my friend.'

That got a wry smile. 'I have been in a lot of bad places in my life, and something tells me if we do this thing I will be heading for another one. It's what I do.'

'For love or to run away?'

'I have no time for philosophy, but maybe one day, in the future, we can sit at your table, eat your wife's wonderful cooking and talk of what drives me to crave danger.'

Goldfarbeen held out his hand. 'A day to look forward to, Meester Hardeen.'

'I want you to try something.' Goldfarbeen looked curious. 'Say Jardine.'

Four failed attempts later he gave up, passed over an excessive amount of money and said farewell.


'You best read this, guv,' Vince said, passing over a piece of paper from Peter Lanchester. 'I can't read the important bit. He said the bloke in Berlin has come up trumps.'

'I'll read it out to you, Vince; it's about the fellow who spoke to me in the bar. His name is *Obersturmbannführer* Gottlieb Resnick. Kept the same initials, which shows sense.'

'Why's everything in German so bleedin' long?'

'The verb is at the end of the sentence.'

'Forget I asked.'

'At least we know where we are now.'

'Shit creek?' Vince enquired.

'Hang on to your paddle, I have to make a phone call.'

\* \* \*

136

'Once again I find you out and about, Herr Jardine,' said Dimitrescu. The call was to the colonel, not from him; Jardine had come back to the Rumanian's message and the number to ring was not the ministry where he worked. 'You are a man who never stays still, I think.'

'I learnt in the war, Colonel, that was the best way to get yourself killed.'

'I, too, fought in that war, Herr Jardine, so we have something in common. However, such talk is for another time; I have some good news for you. The weapons I have had loaded onto railway wagons.'

'Not trucks?' Jardine asked, disingenuously.

'How many trucks would that take? No, rail freight is better and I have had them shunted from the armoury to the railway marshalling yards, where they can depart at your convenience.'

Jardine had to keep reminding himself that Dimitrescu did not know the Germans were already here; in fact, the poor sod probably believed, in his arrogance, they would obey his injunction not to come to Bucharest until he alerted them, but the sooner he was out of here the less the risk.

'Could they be moved today?'

The reply had to wait while he thought about it. 'I doubt there is time to arrange that at such short notice, but tomorrow.'

'Simple enough for a man of your standing, I would have thought, Colonel,' Jardine replied, just to push him, because he was probably telling the truth. Dimitrescu off balance was better than him comfortable.

He tried not to growl but failed. 'Not even I can move mountains, or put trains carrying a hazardous cargo on a busy track at a moment's notice.'

'Tomorrow, then, and it might be best if I have a look before they leave Bucharest.'

The why never came: there was no need to point out that he would hate to get to Constanta and find the weapons were not in the cars; as a way of saying he did not trust him, it was very pointed, yet not outrageous in what was a clandestine trade.

'I will send my car for you, phone ahead to the manager of the yard to get you admitted, and meet you there. By the time you arrive I hope I will have arranged movement to Constanta.'

This time he took Vince, partly because of the presence of the SS, but just as much to send a message he was not alone, that he had assistance the Rumanian was unaware of, which was part of his policy of creating doubts: keep your adversary thinking – and he now saw the colonel as that. Dimitrescu would wonder if the fellow with him, obviously handy, with a boxer's face, quick movements and light on his feet, was the only muscle Jardine had along.

No introductions were made and Vince played the part of bodyguard to perfection, always alert and stony-faced, never allowing himself to be manoeuvred into a position where he could not react to a threat. It was amusing to see the colonel's driver doing the same; they were like a pair of suspicious ferrets.

The marshalling yards were extensive, as suited the central hub of the national rail network, row upon row of rail wagons and oval-shaped oil bowsers in no sort of order that Jardine could discern. There had to be method: the people who oversaw this would have ways of locating and moving what had to be where to the place it was supposed to be, which could be anywhere in the countries bordering Rumania and beyond, especially the oil tankers, which carried the one booming part of the country's economy, the crude oil from the Ploesti fields to the north.

His line of half a dozen wagons was apart from everything else, highly inflammable oil especially, at the very furthest point from any buildings or other freight containers – a sound idea, since they contained ammunition and thus the risk, small but too dangerous to discount in a yard full of oil, of an explosion, while ahead of and behind them the track was clear.

'As you will see from these plates on each car, where they are to go to is already designated.'

Jardine peered at the flat pieces of metal slotted into grooves in the side of the wagons, each with bold writing on, a number and a destination. 'As it's in your language I will have to take your word for it.'

Dimitrescu scoffed. 'Come, Herr Jardine, even you can read the name Constanta!' Satisfied with a nodded response, he asked if Jardine wanted to see in them all.

'I will look in one, but I will be happy with an open cover on the rest.'

Each carriage tarpaulin was secured with a padlocked chain running through metal eyeholes. Just getting onto a railway wagon is not easy without a platform, so the handholds on the side were essential. Since everything was boxed, he chose a few at random, had them opened, handled a few of the items, worked the bolts on a number of the rifles and checked the firing pins were in place, requiring a cloth to clean himself afterward, the weapons being well greased.

'What time will the train leave tomorrow?'

'Before four in the morning, and it should be in Constanta by around five o'clock in the afternoon.'

'A hundred and fifty miles, give or take?' Dimitrescu looked confused, he was working in kilometres. 'That is slow progress.'

'It has to be set in amongst the normal daily schedule, and these yards are on the wrong side of the city, so it is the best I can do.'

'Too late to load my ship that day, really.'

'Unfortunately yes, I imagine.'

There is a look people employ when they are telling you what Vince would call a 'porky'. It's a little too engaged for what they are saying, a bit too keen that you should agree, and Dimitrescu had it on his face now. The slowness of the train journey suited him.

'Still,' Jardine replied breezily, 'that will give us ample time to conclude the transfer of funds, and I think another night in Bucharest would be preferable to staying in Constanta. I will make my way there early in the morning.'

'You will be travelling by . . . ?'

'Train, how else?'

He shrugged. 'I would offer you my car, but there is a ceremony I must attend.'

'I understand, Colonel, but the train will be fine.'

Throughout the yard, freight was being moved. As they were walking back, a rather imperious fellow in uniform stopped them crossing a track in front of a line of wagons, Jardine indicating to an irritated Dimitrescu that it was of no matter. With the colonel furiously looking at his watch, the official checked off the last of the wagons on a manifest he had on his clipboard, then walked past them with the superior air a functionary adopts when going about his duties before watching eyes.

There was a steam engine huffing and puffing a little way off and he blew a whistle before going to a long metal lever, which he hauled hard on to change the points, this as the engine was backing up, its wheels screeching as it went through on to the correct line. It slid up to the line of wagons, made noisy and juddering contact with the hydraulic buffers, then a footplateman jumped down to make the necessary connections. The clipboard was passed up to the driver, who scribbled a signature and got a nod, no doubt permission to set off.

Dimitrescu, his dignity deeply offended, started abusing the freight dispatcher and the fellow responded with a stream of invective. Jardine and Vince were witness to an example of Rumanian democracy in action as they indulged in a furious and expletive-splattered exchange, with Vince gleefully translating what he was sure were the swear words.

Back at the Athénée Palace, Dimitrescu got out of the car and, having given over the address of the bank in Constanta, shook hands with firm resolve. 'We will meet there, say at ten of the clock. Till the day after tomorrow.'

Jardine waved him off and went inside, but only long enough for him to get out of sight, fretting when Vince said he needed a pee. That taken care of it was off to the café and the phone, back on to Goldfarbeen and the double-taxi ride again. He had one very important question to ask the Jew and, security be damned, he would have to ring him at the hotel with the response.

When he returned, he ran straight into 'Reisner' by the reception desk and apologised for the need to turn him down for dinner; Vince, following him in, was sharp enough to walk straight past the pair as though Jardine was a stranger.

'I am departing very early in the morning, Herr Reisner, for Kladno. Some business has presented itself and I must prepare my proposals.' Then he called to the desk clerk. 'Please make up my bill for the morning and I will require an early taxi to take me to the Gara de Nord.'

'Such a pity, I looking forward to trying more English.'

'Then let us hope there is another time, Herr Reisner.'

The smile was not in the eyes, they were narrow and had a trace of a glint, it was just the teeth. 'Perhaps, Herr Jardine, perhaps.'

By standing still, Jardine almost forced the German to go towards the lift, and as soon as he disappeared he went to talk to the concierge. In a first-class hotel he is a very important man and a well-paid one – it is another job you buy, not one you are given. He has to be the soul of discretion and the provider of goods and services of all natures to the well-heeled clients. He is also a fellow accustomed to strange requests; his job not to question but to provide, and often, even if what is requested might be on the borders of illegality, he will merely smile, accept the request and pocket the excessive payment he expects for compliance.

Back in his suite Jardine was all business. 'Vince, I am going to pack my bags and you do the same. Then go down, check out and clear your bill. I will come to your room later with my bags. You'd better eat, and phone Lanchester and tell him to do the same, so he's ready to check out too. When my call comes from Goldfarbeen you will take both your luggage and mine out of here and collect him. I will go to the car and meet you there.'

When Vince departed he called down to reception for a local road map and asked the time of the Prague train. The city, being built late in the last century, was dissected with long, straight roads, very much like Berlin, so working out his route was easier than expected. To keep up appearances he dressed for an early dinner and went down to the restaurant, making straight for the table of

'Reisner', who was eating at a German, not a Rumanian hour.

'You have decided not to dine out after all, Herr Reisner? That gives you one last chance to test your English.'

'You are your tasks finished so soon?'

'I have some time in the morning, having got the time of the train wrong.'

'I wondered when you said you leaving early morning, to go to Kladno you must Prague pass through, which is, of course, on the line to Berlin.'

'Silly of me; now, why don't I buy us a very good bottle of Sekt?'

'Is something to celebrate?'

'I am sure, when I get to my destination, I am going to do some very good and profitable business.'

A signal brought over the sommelier and the wine was ordered. They had only just looked, sniffed and sipped, when the German said, 'Is that boy calling your name?'

'So he is; excuse me, I am expecting a telephone call.'

That he took at reception and Goldfarbeen supplied the answer to the question he had asked, which made perfect sense. Next, he called Vince on the internal phone and told him to be prepared to get moving, ran up to his room, grabbed his cases and took them to Vince's room, before dashing back to join his SS man, smiling broadly.

'Matters are proceeding splendidly, Herr Reisner. Now, shall we order some food?'

The man's expression was so stiff it was waxwork-like. Cal Jardine then played a game he enjoyed; he loved nothing more than to take the rise out of an opponent. The way he talked to the German was such fun, for the SS man had to play along with his string of invention, he had no choice.

'Time for my slumbers, I think. You know the word "slumber", Herr Reisner?'

'No.'

'Another word for sleep; busy day tomorrow, so I must bid you *gute Nacht.*'

The grin was rigid still: he knew he was being guyed. 'Perhaps, Herr Jardine, we should say *auf Wiedersehen.*'

The reply was cheery. 'Yes, let's do that.'

Out of sight of the dining room, at reception, he paid his bill, then went back to the concierge desk to collect the package of items he had requested and to ask the man who ran it to take care of the tips he would not have time to disburse in the morning: chambermaids, the floor manager and the maître d' in the restaurant. Naturally, the concierge was included, and generously, his discretion being essential. It was bad form to do otherwise, just as it was bad form to leave such an establishment without taking care of various staff, those who had seen to his needs.

There was one other task: a pair of stamped and addressed envelopes, which were handed over, with instructions that they should be posted the following evening.

# CHAPTER ELEVEN

The only items left in his suite were his trench coat, his trilby and Colt Automatic. Those gathered, he slipped out and along to the service stairs, the door to which was opened and closed silently given there was always someone present on the floor of such prestigious accommodation, housing the really wealthy clients, who, when they desired attention, wanted it in seconds.

The stairs took him down to the basement and out onto a loading bay, quiet at this time of night, staffed only by a single bored individual in a small bothy of an office. Jardine gave him a wave and put his finger to his lips, hoping the fellow would assume, seeing him dressed for dinner, he was perhaps an errant husband sneaking out, not an unknown event in such establishments.

The alleyway was full of refuse bins, stinking in the warm weather, and he stayed close to those as he made his way to the junction with the well-lit boulevard that led into the vast plaza on which the hotel stood. He was not stupid enough to assume that 'Reisner' believed him; it was best to operate on the reverse and take precautions accordingly. His coat he put over one shoulder, which with his hat tipped to one side hid most of his face, then he went straight across the wide road, careful to avoid any screech of car brakes, it being a busy thoroughfare, and once on the opposite pavement he made his way round the counter corner to the other side of the plaza, where he hailed a *trăsură*.

That he paid off a street away. Lanchester and Vince were sitting in the car, puffing away, so it was full of smoke. Jardine's first act was to open the door and leave it so, letting the fug escape, as Peter Lanchester made what he thought was an important announcement. 'I have just realised, old boy, seeing where the steering wheel is, that these blighters drive on the wrong side of the road.'

'Then, Peter, it's a wonder you haven't been run over.'

'I hope you don't expect me to drive, for if you do, I have to tell you, you are taking your life in your hands.' Jardine had a moment of disbelief before he burst out laughing, soon followed by Vince, with Peter shouting, 'What's so bloody funny?'

'Nothing, I'll drive. Now, put those gaspers out before I choke.'

He passed the package he had taken from the concierge over to Vince. 'Torch, wire cutters and twine.'

'Are we to be enlightened as to the purpose?' Lanchester enquired.

'I'm designing a midnight garden, Peter, for the Chelsea Flower Show.'

The response was typically Peter Lanchester and flippant. 'Too late in the year, don't you know, but then you are such a prole, Cal, and are probably unaware of that.'

'Nothin' amiss wi' the proletariat, Mr Lanchester.'

'I could take issue with you, Vince, but I fear we might be too busy.'

'Did it start OK?'

'First time, guv. I'll get back on the handle.'

Two swings of the starting handle and the engine was running – not purring, but fairly even with only the occasional misfire. Everyone aboard, the map open on Lanchester's lap, Jardine double-declutched into gear and took off, soon establishing that, whatever else it was, this motor was no racer.

'I hope we are not pursued by the forces of law and order, Cal: this bugger would not outrun them if they are on bicycles.'

'Just read the map, Peter.'

At night the marshalling yards were brightly lit by arc lamps, and not just the working areas; the perimeter fencing was illuminated as well, and it took some time, driving round, to find a place where they could both park and force an entry, and also that would give them sight of the freight wagons they had visited earlier that day. Vince volunteered to do the fence cutting while Jardine kept the engine running, with Lanchester in the back so Vince could dive, if need be, into the car for a hurried getaway.

'I am becoming accustomed to this sort of endeavour, Cal, it seems to go with being in your company.'

Aware it was just the man being jocular, as a way of steadying everyone's nerves, Jardine replied in the same vein. 'You sound like you'd rather be a desk-wallah, Peter.'

'I desire nothing more than to be a desk man, old chap, with a warm fire, an ashtray to hand, not too much work and, of course, a secretary with no morality and legs up to her armpits.'

Vince signalled he had made a gap big enough to get through and Jardine killed the engine, got out with the starting handle and located it ready. He and Vince changed into the overalls and flat caps they had bought as a general disguise in the flea market, the ex-boxer with his knife handy and Jardine ensuring he could easily get to his Colt, this while Vince cut a couple of lengths of twine. As Jardine had explained, if the perimeter was patrolled, and it might be, then an obvious gap would not be missed, one joined by twine might, with the additional benefit that if they had to make a hurried exit, it would not much impede them.

'Peter, the first sign of trouble, let fly with your gun and shoot to kill if you must.'

There was no need for further explanation as Lanchester handed over the torch. Easing through Vince's gap, Jardine did the lacing-up with the twine and they headed away from the fence into the interior, passing through pools of light, then areas of relative darkness, making for the wagons containing the cargo of weapons, walking upright and with confidence. If they were spotted creeping it would arouse more suspicion than two people acting normally.

'Bit like old times, guv,' said Vince as they stepped across empty steel rails. 'Night patrols.'

'No Arabs,' Jardine said as he flashed the torch at his watch, which showed half past ten.

'That's a blessing.'

Approaching the wagons they had to be careful: there had been no guards earlier in the day but that might not apply now. Fully expecting to be challenged – Jardine's pistol grip was once more as warm as the holding hand – it said something about this part of the world and its lax attitudes that he was not. Looking towards the distant gate and the main buildings, which included offices and what he had supposed earlier that day to be a rest room and canteen for the railway workers, he was sure he saw the outline of a lorry that looked to be military, but there was no one by his carriages.

'Let's do it, Vince.'

Slowly and quietly they took the destination plates out of their slots, then went to the other side of the wagons so only their legs were visible from the gate side.

'No chance of me having a fag, is there, guv?'

'How can you be a boxer and smoke, Vince?'

'I'm an ex-boxer, or ain't you spotted that? How long?'

'Depends on whether we are working to German time or Rumanian time.'

'What's the odds?'

'One is punctual to the second, the other not even to the day. Let's move up and down: two pairs of legs doing nothing might get someone asking what we're doing.'

Like a pair of sentries they marched to and fro in a silence broken by an occasional shouted voice and some activity going on around some of the petrol bowsers. There was some distant screeching and clanging as an engine backed up to a set of carriages – passenger trains used this yard too – and they were dragged out, no doubt heading south towards the Gara de Nord, the main Bucharest station.

'Can you hear it?' Jardine whispered, looking north.

The slow puffing was unmistakeable, that chuff chuff of a steam engine moving slowly, then the distinctive sound of it easing through various sets of points. Ducking under the train, Jardine saw the single central light that lit up the track, as well as the glow of the fires heating the boilers reflected on the cab roof. The train pulled slowly towards them; someone was pulling on a points lever quite far off and the train came on to a track that ran parallel to the one on which stood Dimitrescu's freight. The men watching it arrive were holding their breath, eased for Jardine when he heard a shout in German: it was the right train.

'How in the name of Christ did you know it was going to be stopped here?'

'Easy, Vince,' Jardine replied, which was a lie: it had been a hope rather than a certainty. 'Our wagons are where they are, well away from anything else, because they have a dangerous cargo.' He had to raise his voice to finish: the sound of the train – engine and screeching wheels – was loud. 'So does this one. Where else are they going to park it when it is not due to be pulled to the armoury till tomorrow? Those were the questions I needed to ask Israel Goldfarbeen.'

There was an escort, a platoon of soldiers who jumped down from a passenger carriage and were lined up by a shouting officer, who, spotting Vince and Jardine, demanded to know where was the party who had been sent to take over the duty of guarding the weapons. Jardine replied, in what he hoped was a Rumanian accent, that he thought they were in the canteen, this as another quartet alighted, men in long leather coats and big fedoras. The army officer barked an order at what had to be his NCO, and then marched off towards the office block and main gate.

'Now, guv,' Vince whispered.

Jardine was eyeing the clutch of what he was sure were Gestapo; could they possibly recognise him dressed as he was? The choice was simple, to do what he had come for or cut and run, which was not his style. 'Better now than never.'

Casually they approached the German train and removed the plates saying 'Bucharest', replacing them with those saying 'Constanta', while the German plates went back into the vacated slots on Dimitrescu's wagons. That completed, they wandered off, Vince whistling tunelessly, as behind them the engine which had brought in the wagons was uncoupled and moved off. They got to their gap in the fence unchallenged and slipped through, retying their twine, to sit in the car and watch, while behind them in the distance, the German officer, who it was hoped knew nothing about freight trains, punctiliously handed over to a set of Rumanian army guards who ought to be equally ignorant.

'You can have a ciggie now, Vince, but open the bloody window, and don't throw your fag ends out: we don't want them finding stubs saying "Craven A" in the morning.'

To say that waiting for hours, as they had to, was agony came under the heading of understatement. The guess was that if their ploy was discovered it would be put down to the inefficiency, possibly even the malice, of a Communist railway worker. If it was not discovered, it was housey-housey, a full card, all the numbers and the jackpot!

Work went on right through the night, trains moving and arriving, so the engine designated to take their weapons to Constanta was not spotted right away, only becoming an object of interest when it got close, all three getting out to stand by the fence and watch. They could see the puffs of smoke lit up by the arc lamps, yet it was impossible to tell, from a distance, which set of freight wagons it had backed up to. Breath was held as a steady jet of steam and smoke was ejected from its funnel, indicating it was beginning to pull, that turning to yelps of delight as the set of wagons that had pulled in earlier were now being towed out.

'Time we made for Constanta, I think.'

'Bit bloody rich, Cal, fetching the Gestapo in another country, don't you think? Cause a diplomatic incident, I shouldn't wonder.'

They had been discussing the possibility of them turning up here in Constanta, but Jardine thought that unlikely until Dimitrescu alerted them. 'He will come with enough bods to take me, because he will want to hand me over as a present, and he will only do that when he is certain his money is in the bank.'

'If we get away with this he's going to come a right cropper.'

'He might, but it would not surprise me if he manages to shift the blame. Slippery buggers have a habit of doing that.'

'You going to enlighten him?'

'No, Peter, let him think it was the Communists or his political opponents that did the dirty. Right now we have to locate your contact, then get him to find some dockers to work overtime.'

The Constanta agent, a man named Antonescu, had so little English it was a wonder a non-linguist like Lanchester had managed to deal with him, but, like most of his fellow countrymen, he did speak German, so the task of asking for his help fell to Jardine, who found him a pleasure to deal with, he being brisk, businesslike and eager to please. First he sent a messenger to the Turkish captain to be ready to load cargo. MS *Tarvita*, displacing three and a half thousand tons, was tied up at the quayside. She had been hired by a British shipping line, one that Lanchester declined to name when asked.

Lanchester had a little surprise for Cal Jardine, one he had kept quiet about, but an act that served to show he was not just a gofer on this job. He had got Antonescu to bespeak a cargo of grain, enough to provide a visible cover for the amount of goods *Tarvita* was going to be transporting. His ship's manifest would say the whole cargo was that, a product produced in abundance round the Black Sea, and he had independently decided the captain should also state the vessel's destination as the island of Madagascar.

Jardine enquired about how difficult it would be getting out through the Sea of Marmara into the Med, the response from Antonescu a rubbed finger and thumb; the captain being Turkish would bribe the customs inspectors, with further elucidation indicating it would not be expensive as they were not landing goods on Turkish soil.

Asked about finding stevedores to load late in the day also proved easy: with the port run down they were in need of work. Antonescu sent for one of the men who led the union, not forgetting to add, with no great pleasure, that the man was a rabid Communist and troublemaker.

Captain Erdogan arrived to be introduced – not easy, as there was another language barrier, given his English was eccentric – then to be told by Antonescu that they would be loading immediately a train arrived and to get his holds open, which had Jardine referring to the conversation Lanchester must have had with him on his first visit.

'Ask awkward questions, Cal? No, he did not. Something tells me this is not the first time our Mr Antonescu has indulged in moving contraband. Whoever found him for us did well.'

'I can't help wondering how you dealt with him.'

'It was murder, given I dare not use an interpreter.'

Respect for Peter Lanchester was rising; Jardine had always known he was not an idiot, but he was showing signs of being a very smart operator too. Reverting to German he asked Antonescu what the dock workers liked to drink and where to get hold of it, money being produced and handed over for the procurement of a large quantity of booze, to include food as well as music.

Jardine and Vince were at the rail freight yard when the train pulled in – Lanchester having gone off to do a bit of prearranged business. Again Antonescu proved an asset: he instructed the local railway manager that it was to be sent straight on through to the quayside for loading, though the engine driver required to be squared with an extra payment for him and his footplateman for what they insisted were extra duties.

The dockers, three dozen in number, had been assembled, and as soon as the canvas covers were removed from the wagons the crates of weapons were loaded by crane onto the ship. Trucks full of grain sacks came alongside within the hour and they, too, were loaded on and laid over as cover, bottles of the fiery local brandy produced on completion.

Unseen by Jardine, Vince and Peter Lanchester, a late-afternoon ceremony was taking place at the main arsenal buildings, located not far from the headquarters of the Rumanian army. The line of wagons had been pulled in by a train bedecked with the flags of two nations: the red, white and black swastikas of Nazi Germany vying with the blue, yellow and red tricolour of Rumania. King Carol II was present, his mistress Magda Lupescu too, as well as generals, admirals and ministers, and, of course, Colonel Ion Dimitrescu.

The German ambassador represented Hitler, while the officers and men who had escorted the train south provided an honour guard from the *Wehrmacht*. Speeches were made, bits of paper made up as scrolls exchanged and a band played the national anthem, followed by 'Deutschland über Alles' and the 'Horst Wessel Lied', before the dignitaries climbed into their cars and went off to the Royal Palace to make toasts and dine in the splendidly decorated staterooms.

A snatch squad, four members of the Gestapo, were no

longer sitting outside the Athénée Palace in a car, while, inside, *Obersturmbannführer* Gottlieb Resnick paced the lobby, for the time of the train to Prague had long passed and he had discovered his bird had flown. They were at the Ministry of War, not well staffed given what was happening elsewhere, demanding that an urgent message be sent to the Royal Palace for Colonel Dimitrescu to return to his office, a message he received and, being angry that the Germans had jumped the gun against his wishes, one he ignored.

The next message he got made him move: at the arsenal they had just examined the markings on the first packing cases, and on opening them had found what they contained.

The lengths to which officialdom will go to avoid embarrassment knows no bounds; Dimitrescu had to tell his minister, who, after going white and downing his drink in one go, ordered him to solve the problem before anyone else, like the king and the prime minster, found out. Now it was not about money, it was about saving face as well as quite possibly his skin, and the least number of his fellow countrymen involved the better. Thus the notion of sending a message ahead to the authorities in Constanta to impound the train risked too much exposure: questions would be asked as to why.

But he had to hand a party of Germans he could use and no need to tell them why he wanted their help. Speeding back to his office he gathered up Resnick and his party of five, the man who had tailed Jardine being the fifth, and they set off for Constanta at high speed, on a journey down a good highway that should take no more than three hours. As long as he got to that cargo before it was loaded he would be saved and the Germans could shoot Jardine if they so wished.

It was dark long before the last of the grain was loaded under arc lights, at which point Jardine took his dock workers to an empty warehouse he had found, where both food and drink in abundance had been laid out on trestle tables. Before indulging, each man was invited up to receive a very generous payout for their services and then it was a time for toasts.

Thanking them he could not do in German: these men were at the very minimum militant socialists, with a visceral hatred of fascists, so Vince was given the task, this done in a stumbling combination of Italian and Rumanian followed by a toast, which turned into not just one, but dozens, often with linked arms.

Jardine felt he would be in need of hollow legs, drinking water as often as he could to remain sober and not always getting away with it. Then the band arrived, a group of lively fiddlers, and the merriment increased in a part of the world where men dancing together was a commonplace.

The dock workers were soon drunk, while on board the MS *Tarvita* the captain had covered his holds, got his engines started and his crew alerted to weigh, which he did as soon as permission came from the unsuspecting harbour master. The ship exited the actual port through a narrow entrance too easy to close, anchoring in the outer roads of the Black Sea, the motor boat sent back in for the passengers.

A fretting, furious Dimitrescu arrived with his Germans – they were told to stay in the car – while the railway manager was dragged from his home and threatened with death unless he told the colonel the whereabouts of the wagons. Dimitrescu's heart nearly stopped when he was told they had been passed straight through to the quayside for loading. Back in the car they raced to the docks to find the named ship gone.

The noise of the fiddlers in the warehouse was audible on a warm night with the doors open and, leaving the car, all seven of the new arrivals walked towards the sound, to see before them flat-capped men drinking and spinning as they danced, clearly either drunk or well on the way. So dense was the crowd it took time to catch sight of Jardine at the back; they did not see either Vince or Peter Lanchester, who had detached themselves from the dancing much earlier and taken up station on either side of the doorway, out of sight.

'Jardine!' Dimitrescu yelled; it did not silence the music but it did interrupt the flow. It was the man he had shouted at, approaching the players and holding up his hand, who brought the fiddling to a stop.

'Colonel Dimitrescu, how pleasant to see you, and of course you too, Herr Reisner.'

There was a temptation to call him by his real name and rank; it had to be suppressed: he was bound to wonder how Jardine had acquired it and it was sound policy never to give anything away that you did not have to. The SS man produced a pistol and his subordinates were in the act of doing the same when Lanchester shouted out for them to stay still, aiming his Colt at the head of the leading German.

'Seven against one, Herr Jardine, not good odds, I think. You are a criminal and I have come to take you back to Germany where you will beg to be called a piece of shit.'

'If you try, you will die for certain, for my friend is a very good shot. The next person to get a bullet, I suspect within a split second, will be you, Colonel.'

'You think you will get away with this?'

'Vince, tell our Rumanian friends what this lot are trying to do.'

That took time, longer for a group well oiled, but the growling started when the word 'Germans' was used, and grew as Vince told them the fascists had come to arrest the man who had paid them all that money and provided the drink, the food and entertainment. It became loud shouting and the workers began to close in on Dimitrescu and the Germans, forcing them to back away.

'You see, Colonel, you will have to shoot a lot of people and use Germans to do it. I wonder how that will be considered in the higher offices of the state. Herr Reisner could be had up for murder if he uses that gun, and I should think the police here are no less brutal than they are in Germany. Perhaps he will beg to be called a piece of shit.'

Jardine addressed the SS man directly. 'I suggest, *mein Herr*, that you leave the Colonel and I to talk, for I have something interesting to tell him. Alternatively, your men can pull out their weapons, but you will certainly die and I think my friends here, who are drunk enough to do violence, will tear everyone else to pieces even if they are armed.'

'Go, *Herr Obersturmbannführer.*'

That got raised eyebrows from Jardine. 'A Lieutenant Colonel, I am flattered.'

'No.'

'Do as I say,' Dimitrescu hissed. 'You are in my country.'

It made sense: Dimitrescu was in enough trouble as it was; a massacre of innocents by foreign policemen would not help. Reisner backed off, not because he was asked to, but because he knew he would die if he did not, Jardine speaking as soon as he was out of earshot.

'There is a letter at the British embassy, which will be copied to various people if anything happens to me: for instance, if I am detained by a ship of your navy. I will be out of your territorial waters within a few hours in any case, and I will make a point of sailing down the coast of Bulgaria where you dare not come close or you might start a war. If I even see a Rumanian warship on the horizon, I will send a radio message, which will trigger the release of my letter. That details everything we have talked about, the price you demanded and for what, where our business took place and also with certain embellishments.'

'It won't be believed.'

'I'm afraid it will be. You see, the money – not the full amount I grant you, but a substantial payment – is already in your bank account, Colonel, paid in by my colleague this very day, so it will look as though you deliberately betrayed your country and sold me the consignment from Germany instead of the redundant weapons. These are the embellishments I mentioned. Where we met as well, that little bank well away from your ministry. I doubt the man who runs it will sacrifice his life for yours. Do yourself a favour, blame the Opposition, blame someone else, but don't blame me, or the British Government. If you do, the contents of that communication will be made public.'

'You think you are clever?'

'You now sound like something from a cheap thriller, but the answer is not that I am clever, it is that I have won. Now, my new friends are going to escort me and my colleagues to a motor boat, which will take us out to our ship.'

He threw his arms out and shouted for the music to play again, kissed every dock worker he could get close to and headed out of the warehouse door surrounded by a crowd of happy drunks, shouting abuse at the disconsolate Germans, who were given a shouted parting shot.

'Who needs guns when you have such friends!'

Dimitrescu was glaring at him and Jardine was sure he could see his mind working out how to get that letter from the British embassy in time to do something about his dilemma. That glare got him a responsive grin and a wink: the second letter, carrying the same information, had gone to Israel Goldfarbeen, with a suggestion he show it to the political opposition, sent for the very simple reason that he had no faith in the diplomats of his own country to do the right thing.

# CHAPTER TWELVE

The main port city of British Somaliland was a bloody awful place to get to and no charming spot when you did, the only blessing being that, sitting on the Gulf of Aden, there was a wind slightly less hot than the normal air temperature, which could rise in the high summer to over fifty degrees.

Jardine had departed the ship at Istanbul, taking a train to Athens to pick up an Imperial Airways flight that went via Aden to Rhodesia and South Africa, then the regular boat across from Aden, having sent a telegram ahead to alert the man from the Colonial Office of his impending arrival.

To call Berbera a port in the modern sense was risible: it had a tiny harbour, and any ship of size calling would have been obliged to anchor offshore, while behind that the buildings were sparse, low, mostly mud-built and painted white. That, combined with the sandy nature of the soil, made the landscape blinding to the eye.

The hat Jardine now wore was a white panama; the man waiting to meet him on the quayside was in the ubiquitous pith helmet and shorts of the cartoons, and he had a clipped tone to his voice that made him sound, as well as look, like the archetypal district officer.

'Conrad Mason, Mr Jardine,' a greeting that came with a rather feeble handshake. 'Welcome to British Somaliland.'

Behind Jardine the boat, more a sort of ferry, was being loaded with live animals, cattle, sheep and goats destined for the dinner tables of Aden; being herded by irate owners, that was a noisy affair. Not far from where Mason stood was a dust-covered grey Hillman with a local driver, tall, slim, barefoot, in crisp whites and a red fez, which made Jardine wonder, for he was sweating profusely, how the native managed to look so smart and dry.

'We are up in the hills at this time of year,' Mason said. 'It's too hot in this place, so if you give your luggage to my driver we will be off.'

'Cooler, is it, in the hills?' he asked, instructing by sign language the porter who had brought ashore his luggage to hand over his one suitcase.

Mason grinned. 'Only marginally so, but any relief is welcome.'

The inside of the car was hotter than the exterior till they got moving, while the breeze through the open windows was baking when they did, the two passengers engaging in the kind of small talk which seemed so out of place. 'Did you have a pleasant journey?'; 'How were the India Office wallahs in Aden, helpful I hope?'; 'How was London the last time you were there?' The questions were banal, but then so were Jardine's replies.

Hat off, Mason was a rather bland-looking fellow, sandy-haired, that cut very short for obvious reasons, his unlined face tanned in that way which comes from reflected sunlight rather than direct exposure, a sort of pale-beige colour, in contrast to his forearms and legs, which were a deep-brown hue. Jardine guessed him to be about thirty years of age, and given his location, not very well connected in the service: whoever was governor, British Somaliland was not a top posting, and flyblown Berbera was below that in the Colonial Office pecking order.

General chat, as they bounced along a far-from-perfect road, explained that not much happened in this part of Africa, which Jardine took to mean it was seen as unimportant. It was one of those places Britannia occupied as much to prevent others from doing so as against any strategic imperative.

There was the control of the slave trade to Arabia, still active, and the fertility of the grazing land, which, thanks to biannual rains, fed Aden and removed the need for that enclave to rely on its own hostile Yemeni hinterlands. Added to that was the protection of the ancient caravan routes to the interior, carried out by the British-led Somali Camel Corps, based in Hargeisa.

The hill settlement was not large, a series of scattered bungalows, each with a servant on the veranda pulling a string to move the interior punkah, for the air was still hot, though not as baking as the coast. To be under the sun was to be broiled, so it was a relief just to get to the indoor shade, where he was introduced to Mason's wife. There was nothing soft about her handshake: it was both firm and energetic, backed up by a very toothy grin, which could not be called a smile, the teeth were too large, and to that was added a sort of endless bobbing of the body.

Margery Mason, 'M' for short, was a big woman, much more so than her husband, and that was in her bones, as well as a head topped by a mass of tight curls. The voice, when she spoke, had that hearty tone Jardine associated with fox-hunting folk, and she was dressed in a shapeless, floral garment that did nothing to delineate a figure, if indeed she had one. When she asked him if he wanted something cool to drink, it was following by a sort of braying sound.

'Cool is relative, is it not, M?'

'Golly, yes, Conrad,' she replied. 'No ice here, I'm afraid. Our refrigerator is on the coast and there's no power up here; the contents are fetched up in a box every morning by Sulli, our driver. The ice melts almost as soon as it is opened. Still, the lemonade will be refreshing.'

'Thank you.'

'Do you wish a shower and to change into a fresh shirt?'

'That would be nice.'

'Banda,' she cried, unnecessary since the servant was only a few feet away. 'Show Mr Jardine to his room.'

The person who came forward was young, with the even features and mid-brown face of the local Somalis, while he moved with a lithe grace that seemed common to the people. Idly looking out of the car window on the way, Jardine had seen women with baskets on their heads walking, their slender hips swaying in the most alluring way. Yet there was also something in the look the Banda gave this new guest, direct, enquiring, that seemed somewhat out of place: it was too bold.

'When you are changed,' Mason said, 'you can join me in my study.'

'Man talk,' brayed his wife, making a sort of chuffing sound as amusement set her large teeth playing a tattoo on her lower lip.

If the lemonade was not chilled it did still manage to be refreshing, though Jardine had made sure there was enough left over: it would be poor manners to drink them out of house and home when everything had to be fetched up from the coast.

'Fear not, Sulli has to make another journey to get the food for supper. Can't keep it up here, rots in no time. Now, Mr Jardine, to business.' Mason sat forward in his basket-weave chair and joined his hands before his knees. 'While I will do everything in my power to facilitate your endeavours, my actual participation has to be limited. I cannot have them finding out in Hargeisa what you are up to.'

'I understand, Mr Mason, and I will try to do nothing which jeopardises your position here, which I appreciate is delicate.'

'Good, it's not much of one, but I like it.'

Jardine had to stop himself expressing surprise: if he had been stuck here, he would be lobbying hard for a move and asking his guest if he knew of anyone who could help him get a better posting. He was also tempted to ask what motivated Mason to go against the official line of non-intervention, but that was a given: the man had his own reasons and would probably be embarrassed if asked to enumerate them.

'We will have some guests tonight to dinner, and a couple of our military chaps who will fill you in on what the Eyeties are up to, and pretty comprehensive it will be. I am obliged also to entertain a pair of American visitors whom the Governor General stopped from entering Ethiopia through Hargeisa.'

'The military, they have good intelligence?'

'They do. We are not much loved here, but compared to the Italians, our neighbours to the south, we are considered saintly. Most of what you will hear comes from their capital of Mogadishu and the waters off Massawa, reports of the build-up of supplies in both Eritrea and Italian Somaliland.'

'Why are the Italians so hated?'

'Usual thing: brutal repression in the past, settlements – a surprising number of people have come from Italy to make their homes here, and naturally they want the best land to grow crops or as pasture for their animals. Forced eviction has been common in the past, with the odd poor native slung from the nearest tree if he dared to protest.'

'And we don't do that?'

Mason grinned. 'Britain imposes a very light touch in our part of Somalia now.'

'Not always the case, Mr Mason.'

The colonial man nodded to acknowledge that. 'That is what happens when you give the military its head, Mr Jardine.'

Mason was referring to the way this territory had been pacified. Britannia originally held the coast but not the interior: this was the homeland of what the British yellow press had named the 'Mad Mullah', really Abdullah Hassan, the leader of the Dervish State. He had held the colonisers at bay for two decades and had even defeated what was then called the Somali Camel Constabulary in a pitched battle before the Great War.

That conflict left him in peace, but as soon as it was over the army came in and now they had what Cal Jardine had so railed against in Iraq: aircraft and the ability to bomb civilians at will, and even then it took trickery to defeat the 'Mad Mullah'. He had been lured by the military command into a promise of talks, assured of an official visit by some worthy from London, to discuss some kind of settlement.

What he got, having gathered his family and followers at his own capital city, was a massacre. Unopposed by anything other than rifle fire, British planes had bombed the mud-built city and indiscriminately killed hundreds of both warriors and civilians. Hassan had been forced to flee and his twenty-year fight for independence – the British press called it his rebellion – was over.

'We civvies are very much in control now,' Mason continued. 'We let the people do very much what they want, as long as it's legal, and few of our fellow countrymen seem to want to settle here. If they do, and seek to buy land, we make sure they pay a fair price – not something the Italians are prone to. Certainly they have sought to mend their ways with agriculture and recruitment in their armed forces. When they do invade Abyssinia, the colonial recruits will be at the forefront.'

'They will invade?'

'As soon as the weather cools, I fear.'

'I was told in London arrangements had been made to transport what I am bringing overland.'

'Tell me when your goods will be here, what they comprise of, and I will send a message at once.'

'Where do I land them?'

'Tell me, Mr Jardine, how much do you know about the slave trade and an old port called Ziela?'

By the time he changed for dinner Cal Jardine knew a great deal about slaving, the most telling fact that it still happened, despite the best efforts of the various colonial powers to stop it. All around in this part of the world there were people disinclined to work: they would much rather have someone else do it for them, and if such people could be unpaid slaves so much the better, very much so in the Arabian Peninsula.

He had seen the beauty of many of the Somalis for himself, and they were prized for that quality and often sold as wives or catamites.

For the more menial tasks, no part of the interior – remote areas of Abyssinia and Southern Sudan – was safe from raids by bands of armed men who made their living from transporting those they kidnapped to the markets of Oman, Saudi Arabia and the various lands of the emirs along the Persian Gulf. But fearing interference from the British, they had stopped using a port that had, for centuries, provided their route out.

It was not just slavery that had declined: the port of Zeila, at one time bustling and important, was now a decaying backwater thanks to the rise of Djibouti, the capital of French Somaliland just to the north. Zeila had been a port for sailing boats; the French had made a proper harbour for large ships at Djibouti, just like the Italians had done further north at Massawa. The British, with the wonderful natural harbour of Aden so close, had no plans to improve Berbera.

His shirts had been washed, starched and ironed while he had been talking to Mason and his other clothing had been pressed. Now, with the sun gone and the heat of the day rising into a clear sky, the atmosphere was becoming tolerable and the time came to dress for dinner. As he put in his shirt studs he wondered at the progress of the *Tarvita*: where would she have got to now? Had that been managed without difficulty? Certainly they had got through the Bosphorus with ease, and by now they ought to be approaching the Suez Canal.

Jardine was hungry, having had little to eat since arriving, some dates and nuts brought in to the study by one of Mason's many serving boys, it being the practice to wait till the sun went down to have a proper meal. The whole bungalow was now full of the smell of good cooking, of spices and roast meat which he had seen turning on a spit above glowing wood outdoors. Also he had heard vehicles arriving, he assumed the soldiers, as well as two American voices, one rather strident and female, the other a deep male one, both bouncing off the braying enthusiasm of M. Bow tie knotted, he put on his dinner jacket and made his way to meet them.

'Ah, Jardine,' cried Mason, 'come and be introduced to my other guests. This is Miss Corrie Littleton, from Boston, and our other American guest, Tyler Alverson, who, I believe, hails originally from California. And, of course, our two defenders of this part of the colony, Captain Peydon and our naval representative, Lieutenant Grace, who has kindly brought with him some of his Plymouth Gin.'

'My God, it packs a punch,' said Alverson. 'Even with ice.'

'Hundred per cent proof,' Grace replied, grabbing the lapel of his dark-blue dress mess jacket like a lawyer.

M brayed. 'Our American friend has brought a load of ice up from Berbera, ha ha! Insists he can't drink gin without it.'

'A touch of bitters is all I need,' insisted the navy man, a rather vacuous-looking fellow. 'Be thought a pansy if I asked for ice in the wardroom, what?'

It was interesting to see Peydon react to that: for some reason the captain was angry with his naval chum. Red of face already, and with pronounced cheeks, he went a sort of scarlet shade that was as near as damn it to the colour of his army mess jacket and his voice was a growl.

'Each to his own, I say.'

'You would be better off not drinking it at all,' insisted Miss Littleton.

She was young, slim, quite tall for a woman and looked slightly mannish with her bobbed blonde hair. Added to that she had the kind of cracked voice that sounded like a permanent bad throat.

'It is bad for your body and your brain, indeed it is nothing but a social ill which—'

'More lemonade?' asked Mason, her words and his gesture underlining the fact that she was a teetotaller, the interjection seeming to spare them a lecture on temperance. Her voice had a strangely orotund accent too, seemingly elongating each word in what sounded like a parody of the King's English.

Her host indicated to one of his houseboys and a jug was brought forward. 'And you, Jardine, what will you have, old chap?'

'I think a pink gin would be the ticket, with, if Mr Alverson can spare it, some of his ice.'

'What do we have here,' drawled the American, his face amused, 'a cultured Englishman?'

'Scotsman, Mr Alverson, which removes any hope of my being civilised.'

'Hear, hear,' cackled M, who then suddenly realised she was praising the wrong thing. 'Oh dear, most dreadfully sorry.'

Mason was mixing his drink, throwing the Angostura Bitters around the glass before tipping it out, then pouring the gin. 'Mr Jardine is here on a little errand for HMG, to pick our brains about the ice cream vendors next door.'

'Really?' asked Alverson, with a slightly arch look.

'Yes, I am going to closet him with our military might for a bit so they can brief him.'

'Can I sit in?'

'Why ever would you want to do that?' cawed M. 'Dreadful bore.'

That got raised eyebrows from the servicemen, with Mason adding, 'Really, my dear, you can be so tactless.'

M looked a touch broken by that, her voice for once small and meek. 'I can, can't I?'

At least she got female support. 'Well, I agree with you, Mrs Mason, it's boys talk and . . . well, war and all that.'

Alverson spoke up with a tone of deep irony. 'And you, Corrie Littleton, you must be the only admirer of Sparta who does not like war.'

'I am an admirer of the women of Sparta, Tyler. As for the men of Sparta, well we know *all* about them.'

Peydon nearly choked on his drink and he began coughing, Mason went pink under his tan and Alverson said, 'Well, being a newspaperman, I am interested.'

'Sorry,' Mason responded. 'No can do, can't have you spilling the beans on what we know.'

'Might queer our pitch,' said Lieutenant Grace.

That had the captain barking at him. 'Shall we go to the study?'

Mason addressed their backs. 'Call the boys if you want any more to drink.'

'Damned odd,' Peydon said quietly, as he closed the door behind Grace, 'Mason inviting a reporter like that.'

'Odd the chap is here at all,' Grace added.

'Gentlemen, to business, I think. Mr Mason's guest list is his affair.'

'Quite right, Mr Jardine,' Peydon said, pulling out from his pocket a tightly folded paper. Opening it showed it was a rough-drawn map outlining, in very neat but tiny handwriting, the position of the Italian forces, which consisted of one division, the 29th *Peloritana* – their numbers, seven thousand effectives, and equipment, three thousand mules and sixty light trucks – the extent of their supply dumps, and even the names of the senior officers serving under their commander, General Graziani.

'This, I have to say, Captain, is damned good.'

That made the soldier's chest expand, an act which pushed out a pair of not-very-special medals. 'Thank you, sir, we try our best.'

'There's nothing in the naval line that matches this,' cut in Grace gloomily. 'Although my proper area of operations is the Gulf of Aden, I can and do patrol up the Red Sea. We talk to the dhows coming out of Massawa and they are only too happy to pass on snippets of information. Eyeties have been at it for so long we have had a chance to list the whole kit and caboodle up there too.'

The soldier then added, with not a little pride, 'We sneak across the border on our camels and get chapter and verse about what's happening on the Italian part of the Abyssinian border.' Now he looked sly, if still pleased with himself. 'They are not much on patrolling, the Eyeties, so I usually take a few of my boys right forward and get a dekko of what they are up to through my binoculars.'

'No sign of movement?'

Peydon made a dismissive snuffling sound not too dissimilar to Mason's wife. 'Plenty signs of frustration, more like, and Grace and I pick up the same stuff. Apparently all the talk in the bars is of the need to replace their commanding officer, De Bono. They were ready to go before the small rains came, but they sat on their arses because he insisted they lacked enough equipment.'

There was a dual purpose to this short meeting: first, of course, a briefing on what these two knew, but more importantly to get them out of his way so he could operate with safety. Mason wanted no part of seeking to keep them occupied, for if anything went wrong, like Jardine being intercepted, he would take the blame. Grace had the only naval vessel, an armed patrol boat, this side of the Gulf of Aden, his official task to guard the coastline, look out for smugglers and slavers, while protecting the fishermen and local traders from piracy.

Peydon had two British NCOs and a clerk, but his soldiers were askaris, locally recruited camel-riding Somalis, and, if he was doing his job properly, he would be out on the caravan routes that led to the interior preventing robbery and slaving, the very places Jardine needed him to be kept clear of. Mason had given him the public puff of being sent specially from London and implied, without actually saying so, that he had the power to request them to act at his instructions.

'I don't want to go back to London without the most up-to-date picture.'

'Are we going to intervene, sir?'

'Not up to me, Lieutenant Grace, but I do know that it would be folly to even consider it on a false premise.' He waved Peydon's map. 'I just need to know if this is still accurate.'

'I can go up the Red Sea anytime I like, almost to the end of the Suez Canal, if I wish, but I would need to refuel in Aden before I did so and my superior officer there could kybosh the trip.'

Jardine was close to saying 'damn' then: if that naval officer had any brains he would ask who the hell he was. Peydon saved the day by a bit of inter-service scoffing. 'Well, I shall do as I damn well please and say nothing to Hargeisa. Those buggers in Aden are Indian army and I am not, so I will not tell them a damn thing either.'

'The navy is of a piece, Archie, there's no division between India and home, and quite apart from the base commander, there is the Captain of HMS *Enterprise* to consider, as well as officers from vessels other than the cruiser.'

'Yes, but if you go blabbing they will poke their oar in, Charlie.

This is a colony and it is not run from Delhi, but London. In defending it that is where your instructions should come from. Your bloody superior spends all his time drinking with those sepoy-bashers and he is bound to let slip anything you tell him. You don't need his approval anyway, do you?'

'Strictly speaking, no.'

'Next thing you know you'll be asking for ice in your drink.'

'Steady on, Archie!' Grace exclaimed, a mite too excessively to Jardine's mind.

'Well!' Peydon replied, like a disappointed parent.

Jardine suspected that, stuck in this hole of a posting, Peydon enjoyed his little excursions to spy on the Italians and he was being a bit disingenuous about not needing permission to do so. When he was engaged in such escapades he was not carrying out his proper duties, and it did not matter how news of that got back to the powers that be, he would get at least a rap across the knuckles if it was exposed, and quite possibly, given the fear in Whitehall of upsetting Mussolini, be subject to a severe reprimand.

'I have to refuel anyway,' Grace conceded, 'and the Aden command has no idea of where I go and what I do. I doubt my superior ever reads my logs.'

'Stout fellow,' cried Peydon.

'Shall we rejoin the others?' Jardine said. 'I think we have been absent long enough.'

# CHAPTER THIRTEEN

It was interesting to monitor the undercurrents of the Masons' dinner, in particular the fact that the two Americans did not conform to what was expected at such a board by Jardine's fellow Britons. It was an observation he had made many times in his life, that the further you got away from the core of Empire, the more rigid became the adherence to what was considered good form: dressing properly for dinner, eating and drinking, at least in public, with circumspection and, most of all, never saying anything contentious.

Most voluble was Corrie Littleton – dressed in shirt and slacks – who had a trenchant opinion on everything, the more relaxed, loose-suited and middle-aged Alverson being quietly funny with sharp observations that ran counter to the way the conversation was going, which Jardine put down to their occupations: she an academic historian and he a newspaperman. It was only much later he realised they represented two strands of a complex nation, strident East Coast versus laconic West.

Thinking of how to describe her, and she was attractive, Jardine took refuge in the expression 'rangy'. In some senses she shared the loose body movements of the locals, that is if you excepted her face in argument, which was rigid of jaw when listening – usually in disagreement and impatience to counter – while being highly animated in making her points which, right now, were on her speciality subject, classical Greece, and quite specifically, Sparta.

The similarity was from the shoulders down: expressive arms and hands, a fluid upper body in a shirt through which her pert breasts were visible, given she did not seem to be wearing a brassiere – Lieutenant Grace could barely take his eyes off them – and a tight backside that seemed to have minimal contact with her chair when pressing home an argument.

Alverson was a man who could sit bolt upright and appear to be lounging, his drawling voice hiding the speed of thought and observation that allowed him to amuse. It was as if, to him, human life was moving at the wrong pace, slightly too quickly, and was in need of a gentle application of the brakes. He wore his knowledge of the world lightly and he seemed to have been witness to quite a deal of it – Manchuria was mentioned, as well as Japan and the Balkans – and he clearly had some knowledge of South America, a knowledge Jardine shared but decided to keep to himself.

Captain Archie Peydon was a type Jardine had messed with often: bluff, opinionated with a small 'o' and Conservative with a large 'C', a career soldier in a peacetime army going nowhere fast. Aside from his views he had half a dozen well-worn anecdotes which, judging by the flash of boredom on the face of his host, he trotted out at every dinner he attended.

His naval counterpart was young and strikingly naive for a

seagoing man who must surely, in his service life, have visited a few steamy fleshpots around the globe: Jardine's memories of Portsmouth were alone quite hairy. If he had, it had not coloured him with sophistication, and, of course, Margery Mason kept putting her foot in it, and large feet they were.

They were well attended to by four servants, all young and handsome Somalis, and it was while watching them go about their tasks that something became evident, that provided by Conrad Mason. While ever the attentive host, seemingly listening to his guests with focus, his eyes kept flicking away to the moving boys as they silently flitted around on their bare feet with that grace Jardine had already noted.

It was not just the look in the eye in these rapid inspections, but the slight parting and wetting of the lips which told Jardine that to Mason these youngsters were possibly more than houseboys, which made clear the reaction to a couple of earlier remarks made by the disingenuous naval lieutenant.

'The women of Sparta were not like the supine creatures who we have around us today,' Corrie Littleton insisted. 'At the beck and call of their menfolk; they ran their own lives—'

'You know,' Jardine gently interrupted, 'I've never understood the use of the word "platonic" just to mean a non-carnal human relationship.'

'Golly gosh,' exclaimed M, while Peydon harrumphed and Grace blushed, but only after several seconds, when he had figured out what was being alluded to.

'Sure,' Alverson said, 'the guy wrote a blueprint for the likes of Mussolini and Hitler.'

'Not when it comes to the rights of women, he didn't.'

'Corrie, honey, you have such an unbiased world view.'

'But that's you men all over, able to read a classical text and only take out the bits that suit you.'

'Like the Bible, really,' said Mason, 'full of stoning and damning and striking down dead for things we think nothing of today.'

'Which your local episcopalian guy still preaches to the savages, I hear.'

'They are not savages, Tyler!'

'They don't do irony in Boston,' Alverson responded, as an aside to the whole table. 'But it is still permissible, I believe, to call an Irishman a barbarian. Your holy man is not too fond of you, Mr Mason.'

'Thinks I don't give him the support he needs to turn all the Somalis into good Anglicans.'

'Shall we be toasting the king?' Peydon interjected, in a crude attempt to change the subject.

Mason nodded and made a sign his servants obviously understood, since they came to fill up the wine glasses. Corrie Littleton, still on lemonade, was about to protest, her bottom well off her chair, when Alverson cut her off. 'When in Rome, honey.'

'Shoot Mussolini,' Grace responded, adding a silly grin.

'You gotta appreciate, Mr Mason,' Alverson said, with a lopsided grin, 'that having kicked out one King George we are not too keen on toasting another.'

The response was dry and came with a wry smile. 'We are drinking to his health, Mr Alverson, not to his territorial ambitions. Captain Peydon?'

'The king,' he croaked as he rose, everyone doing likewise.

'I do not see you passing your wine over the water, Mr Jardine.'

'I'm Scottish, but not rabidly so.'

'What the hell are you two talking about?' Corrie Littleton demanded.

'You tell her, Mr Alverson.'

'Well, way back, the Limeys . . . sorry, force of habit . . . the Brits fell out over who should have the keys to the palace and they got rid of the guys called Stuarts.'

'Kings of Scotland and England,' Mason added, getting for his trouble an arch look from someone who had studied history.

'So, for some Scots folk, their king is exiled across the water. Caused quite a stir in 1745. Bonnie Prince Charlie . . .'

'I know all this, especially that particular guy. Kinda romantic, don't you think?'

'Odd, Miss Littleton,' Jardine said. 'Everyone has that opinion and everyone sees a romantic loser. No one ever asks what would have happened if he had won.'

'Inclined to the bottle by all account, Bonnie Prince Charlie,' grumbled Peydon.

Jardine held up his glass, smiling. 'A national affliction, perhaps.'

'An international curse,' Corrie Littleton snapped, taking a deep drink of lemonade as if that proved her point.

'A worldwide one, Corrie,' Alverson replied, for once in serious mien. 'We drink bourbon, the Japs drink sake and the Chinese glug rice wine. Getting drunk for most folk sure beats the hell out of a clear view of this lousy world.'

'I say, Mr Alverson!' M exclaimed.

Alverson reverted to his amused drawl. 'Sorry, Mrs Mason, we colonials are a little short on sophistication.'

'Of course you are, poor dears,' she replied, her cut-glass voice full of sympathetic understanding.

'Speak for yourself, buster,' came the Bostonian response, given with such gusto that Grace's eyes were glued to the front of her dress.

'A perfect example of my point,' drawled her fellow American.

About to protest, Corrie Littleton was cut off by Mason. 'You have been in Japan, Mr Alverson?'

'I have, and to go back several conversations, they have definitely taken Plato to heart.'

The talk became general on the subject of racial superiority, which was, according to the American, innate in the Japanese, while the Chinese could never comprehend the inability of others to acknowledge their vastly superior civilisation. Hitler and his master race theories were derided, while Mussolini's posturing provided much amusement.

'Racial superiority is not something,' Jardine proffered, 'to which we British are immune.'

Peydon, more red-faced than previously, due to alcohol, looked deeply offended: he was a mother-of-parliaments, British-fair-play sort of chap, who would not hesitate to stick his polished size tens up the backside of one of his Somali recruits, nor think twice about slipping in some extra leave and a bit of a money present to one who had family problems, unable to see the difference between paternalism and equality.

'And it is a stance I fear we Americans are only too ready to share,' Alverson said.

'Did you not kill off all your own savages, Mr Alverson?' asked M, in her cawing voice.

'Not personally, ma'am.'

'I was not accusing *you*,' she insisted, quite missing the irony.

'We're pretty damn overbearing in our own backyard.'

'Don't you have gardens in America?'

'I was referring, Mrs Mason, to the lands south of the Panama Canal.'

Jardine wondered why the laconic American was looking so pointedly at him, so he responded. 'Don't you mean the Rio Grande?'

'I stand corrected.'

'M?' Mason said, with a slight lift of the brow.

'Quite; time for we ladies to withdraw.'

'What for?'

'To let the men have their cigars and tell risqué stories, Miss Littleton.'

'I like a cigar, and if there are any filthy stories around, count me in.'

'Truly,' Jardine joked, in a reference to the tune played by the British troops who surrendered at Yorktown, 'the world turned upside down.'

That interjection, by the girl from Boston, put paid to any passing round the port and telling jokes: she stayed put and so did Margery Mason. Peydon told a story of being out on exercises in Egypt and setting up a small supply dump – food, petrol and the like – which the troops slept round.

'They woke up in the morning to find everything gone, with no one, including the pickets doing two-on-four-off guard duty, hearing a thing.'

Jardine topped that by telling of a time in Iraq when the locals, in the course of one night, dismantled and stole a small steam engine from the inside of a camp with only one guarded main gate and with mobile patrols on the perimeter fence.

'And they did not drive it out either: the rails went through that main gate, so they must have taken it to bits. When it comes to theft the Arabs are peerless.'

Corrie Littleton was on a mission to persuade her mother to leave Abyssinia. Engaged in writing a treatise on comparative religions, Littleton *mère* was in the old Ethiopian capital of Gondar, digging around in the archives for connections to Judaism and Christianity. She also knew that in nearby Aksum, the fabled home of the Queen of Sheba, was supposed to reside the Ark of the Covenant. The trouble was, for her daughter, that Ethiopia was, right now, for non-natives, a hard place to get into.

'If the guineas are going to invade, it's not a good place for Mother to be.'

'For "guineas" read "Italians",' Alverson explained.

'Gangsters,' cried Grace, as though it were an accolade. 'Little Caesar.'

'And what, Mr Alverson, are your reasons for being hereabouts?'

'Chasing stories, Mr Jardine, which is what I do. I wanted to get into Abyssinia without going through the normal channels or to where everyone is being sent.' Responding to a raised eyebrow, he added, 'Right now there are correspondents from all over the world sitting in Addis Ababa drinking on their employer's tab and filing nothing of interest. They ask to go up to the north where the Italians are massed and they are told no; they ask to have a look-see at the borderlands with Italian Somaliland, same answer. So, I decided on a little wandering in the hope of having something to tell my readers back home, but your Limey governor stopped me.'

'And your newspaper is?'

'Syndicated, Mr Jardine. I am reporting for half the papers in the States.'

'Which grants you a rather large budget, I am given to understand,' Mason remarked.

'It does, but that has yet to translate into any hard news. The Ethiopians are sitting on everything, because they think if we report on the Italian military we will also report on them.'

'A reasonable assumption?' asked Jardine.

'It is, but they are not really helping their cause. This is David versus Goliath, and the more that is stated the better the chance of some of the Western powers ganging up to stop Mussolini.'

'You're in the know, Mr Jardine,' said Grace. 'Any chance of that?'

'I think you overrate my position, Lieutenant.'

'Just what is your position, Mr Jardine?' Alverson asked, with his deceptive drawl. There was nothing indolent about his look now.

'No shop talk, Mr Alverson,' Mason said quickly. 'It is a rule we British tend towards imposing on our guests. Time for coffee, I think. Tell me, Miss Littleton, why are you here in our bailiwick if you need to get to Ethiopia to find your mother?'

'Well, I figure you will be less stuffy than the French.'

'No problem in that regard,' boomed Peydon. 'Damned Frogs, begging your pardon Mrs Mason, and, of course, you, young lady.'

'They would not let me cross the border,' she continued in that rather fetching cracked voice, giving the captain a look that wondered what was wrong with the odd damnation. 'And there is no point, no point at all, in trying to get into Abyssinia through Eritrea.' She rolled her eyes then. 'The Italians won't even take a bribe, my God, so worried are they that little old me might tell the world about their silly dispositions.'

'And you hope to make your way from here?'

'I do.'

Mason pulled a face. 'I think I might have to disappoint you as well. The governor has instructions from Whitehall to keep the border sealed, as, no doubt, Mr Alverson has already informed you. Odd, you two fellow countrymen ending up here at the same time.'

'Country folk will do, Mr Mason. I am not a man.'

That got a look that rendered the statement questionable. 'Where will you go now, Mr Alverson?'

It was a delight to Jardine the way the American responded: he very likely had a plan but he was not about to let on. 'Mr Mason, I will go to Aden, if I go anywhere.'

'Thank you, Mason, for a splendid evening,' said the army captain, standing up. 'But reveille is at six and I have to be sharp eyes or the men won't polish their boots.'

'But they are barefoot, Captain Peydon,' said his hostess, on her face a look that could only be described as gormless.

'Figure of speech, Mrs M.'

'Oh!'

It was a signal for the break-up of the evening and, in truth, Jardine was pleased: he had been travelling and was bushed. On top of that, he needed to make a quick trip up the coast to Zeila and have a look before Grace headed that way in his patrol boat. Everyone was on their feet now, saying their goodbyes, not that they were going far, only to one of the other hilltop bungalows. Jardine was therefore a little surprised when Alverson got in between him and the other guests and spoke to him softly.

'I wonder if we could have a little stroll, clear the head before hitting the sack?' Jardine picked up immediately it was not so much a request as a requirement, which made him wary. 'There's a couple of things I think we could talk about to advantage.'

'Whose advantage?'

'Let's start with mutual.'

'I'm pretty tired.'

'If I said "Chaco War", would that give you a boost?'

'You coming, Tyler?' Corrie Littleton called, which had Jardine give him an enquiring look.

'When she turned up here I offered her a room,' he said softly, before calling back, 'I'm going to take some air, honey, and Mr Jardine is going to join me, I hope.'

'Certainly,' Jardine responded.

'Maybe I should join you,' she said. Alverson swung round slowly; he did not say anything, but whatever he imparted had to be in the look, as her face altered, showing doubt bordering on hurt. 'Maybe not, I'm worn out.'

Mason touched Jardine's arm. 'Before you go to your slumbers, there's something I need you to do. In my study.'

Jardine nodded, then passing the boys clearing up, he said goodnight to M and went out onto the veranda with Alverson. The night was cool and would get more so as the clear sky sucked the heat up into the atmosphere, but right now it was pleasant. Alverson walked away from the house, taking his time in lighting a cigar so that they were out of earshot before he spoke.

'First thing I'd like to say, Mr Jardine, is that I am no peace lover, but then nor am I too fond of war, having seen the consequences from time to time.'

'In Paraguay?'

'And Bolivia – I covered both sides. I also know that there was a

League of Nations arms embargo, though that proved to be pretty porous.'

'It might be advantageous to get to the point, Mr Alverson.'

That got a smile, which was picked up by the moon and starlight, because there was no anger in Jardine's voice: it was even and controlled.

'Let's just say your name rings a bell, shall we, and it occurs that, since we are on the edge of a country with another of these League embargoes in place, it might turn out to be just as porous.'

'And if it was, what would you do about it?'

'Why, take advantage, Mr Jardine, what else? I am looking for a story.'

'I might not be one.'

'And I might be Al Jolson without make-up. Let me level with you. I want not just to get into Abyssinia, but to get to where the action is.'

'And you think I can take you there?'

'I am guessing you can. I could get back to Addis, and quick as that through the Sudan.' He clicked his fingers and drew deeply on his cigar. 'But sitting on my ass drinking whisky is not my style. You are a man who runs guns and I picked up on what you did in South America.'

'I could be acting on behalf of the British Government.'

'You're not, and the way Mason changed the subject was like semaphore. All I am asking is to come along with whatever it is you are up to, at my own risk and on my own dollar.'

'What do I get out of it?'

'Good company.'

Jardine laughed. Alverson would not say he might blow the gaff on the whole thing, but he could with one telegram, and it was not malice. He was a reporter and they reported, while no appeal to his better nature was likely to cut much ice.

'Let me think about it. I'll talk to you in the morning.'

'Suits me,' came the reply. Alverson knew 'yes' when he heard it.

Mason was, as he said, in his study, the only jarring note that one of his boys was there too.

'Don't worry about Rani, he speaks little English.' He pointed to his desk, on which lay a piece of paper with the Colonial Office crest, really the British crown with the necessary departmental embellishments.

'I have forged for you a set of orders from London, instructions to me to give you every cooperation. It has at the bottom the name of one of the undersecretaries who is a new appointment, so I would not know his signature. Please sign it in his name so that, should things go wrong, I am covered. I have no desire to lose my post.'

Mason could not help looking at his boy and that said everything. He was a homosexual, probably with a preference for the young, and out here he was safe to indulge his tastes, with the added advantage that his paramours were damned attractive and, given his position, no doubt numerous. It had been in those fleeting glances at the dinner table and, once realised, in the man's gestures, which were slightly fastidious.

It was possible that his proclivities were the spur to make him act as he was doing, sympathy for the natives overriding his sense of duty to his office. Jardine was not bothered, nor was he in the least bit disgusted: what people did in the privacy of their own bedroom was no concern of his.

What revolted him was hating people for their colour or their bloodline, torturing them and depriving them of the right to a decent life because of their race. The Jews of Hamburg, with their mordant humour, would loudly proclaim their thanks to the Lord they were not homosexual, Gypsies, Communists or mad, for life would be intolerable: the Nazi state hated them more than Semites.

'Of course,' he said, looked at the name, picked up the pen and signed with a flourish.

The noise that woke him was slight, but a life of danger makes any such disturbance a matter of concern, doubly so given he was in what should be a safe place. There was a zephyr of breeze as his mosquito net was pulled aside and the bed dropped as another body got in. About to hit out, he was stopped as a hand searched for his cock, the untoward thought that it might be Mason unavoidable. Yet his own hand touching flesh, looking for the throat, brushed a breast, and that told him the body was female and a vision of Corrie Littleton filled his mind at the same time as blood filled his tugged-at penis.

That outstretched hand, the size of the mammary, plus a sort of snuffling sound gave him the first intimation he was mistaken, that and the sheer force with which he was dragged into full body contact. Part of his mind was telling him to resist, to insist Margery Mason get out of his bed, but her incessant tugging and the fact that an erect cock had no conscience overrode his scruples. Their coupling was swift, grunting, and for her, judging by her rising then choked-off whimpering, deeply satisfying.

Cal Jardine could not deny he was pleasured too, but when she was gone and he lay back to go to sleep, he also felt like a Boy Scout who had performed his good deed for the day.

# CHAPTER FOURTEEN

The choke point for the MS *Tarvita* was Port Said, where there was a British garrison guarding the entrance to the Suez Canal. That was the means by which Mussolini had reinforced his troops in Eritrea and Somaliland, and was still supplying them, given the colonies the Italians occupied could not easily feed his armies. Howls of protest in the democracies from those opposed to Italy fell on deaf ears; Britain could have choked off the whole Abyssinian operation by one simple stroke: the banning of military equipment from using the canal.

Vince was enjoying himself, using the deck as a mobile running track, finding things on the ship to use as weights, teaching boxing to some of the hands, who were of a dozen nationalities; whatever it was, he was outdoors. Having started off a bright pink in the Black Sea and itching from sunburn, that soon changed; he had been in the Middle East before, and given his Italian bloodline he soon began to turn brown, seeming to get palpably darker by the day.

Peter Lanchester stayed out of the sun as much as he could, spending his time in the shade trying to read Marcel Proust, an endeavour he had promised himself he would undertake as soon as he had time. There was nothing for them to do on the boat – the captain sailed her, he had a woman to cook for them and plenty of supplies, while the crew were pleasant fellows who tried very hard to speak with both him and Vince in fractured English.

Both could only wonder at how Cal Jardine was doing, but given they had no way of knowing, it was not a thing to fret on. Sailing on a sound vessel with reasonable accommodation across a blue Mediterranean Sea in midsummer, it was best to treat it as what it was: a cruise. With the coast of Egypt on the horizon, that came to an end, and the tension increased as the twin minarets of the Grand Fouad Mosque became clear, piercing the sky across from the muggy sky of Port Said.

In the end it was a formality: the canal was under British oversight but it was a commercial enterprise and profit was the primary concern, not the seeking of contraband. From Istanbul Lanchester had organised the payment of the necessary tonnage dues to the Suez Canal Company, and this was a British cargo being moved in a hired foreign bottom, in other words, commonplace and not worth a search. Soon Lanchester was back to *A la Recherche du Temps Perdu* and Vince was back to his running, boxing and browning, this time with desert sand on either side of the vessel instead of sparkling sea.

Zeila made Berbera look like a sort of paradise: if it had been a major port once there was scant evidence of it now. A scruffy town of dilapidated buildings, surrounded by a low mud wall, it reeked of no sanitation and loss, the only boats plying any sort of trade a few Arab dhows, while most were tied up in harbour or dragged out of the water altogether on to the beach, some of them now too rotten to take to the water.

The outer roads, a mile and a half offshore, so slight was the fall of the seabed, were empty. There was an official resident here, a bachelor, but no troops or other Europeans. He had gone home on sick leave, hardly surprising given the flyblown quality of the place. Being here on one's own would be nothing less than soul-destroying.

It had been with some trepidation that Jardine had emerged to take breakfast, after his usual morning exercises and a long and satisfying shower. He found Mason already up and at his desk, which, rather worryingly, left him with the wife and dreading a repeat of what had happened in the hours of darkness. Her attitude was remarkable: there was not the slightest hint of what she had done the night before, no change in either her awkward behaviour or her proneness to inappropriate remarks; the subject was not even alluded to in a look.

That left Jardine wondering if she was a sleepwalker – it was possible, but in the end he decided, with her husband in another bed probably every night and with a different companion, she, with an appetite to be sated, took her pleasure where she could find it, with the caveat that she would avoid congress with a native for fear of scandal.

That word gave him pause – if Whitehall found out what Conrad Mason was doing they would drum him out of the Colonial Service, yet it seemed that many people knew. Peydon, for one, was certainly aware, hence his reaction to gormless Grace, and was that the real reason for his troubled relationship with the local Anglican divine?

Those were thoughts to be put aside. He had come to Zeila by boat, sailing up the coast in a hired dhow, no problem now he knew that Grace had sailed for Aden at first light, so he and his patrol boat were well past the place. Peydon was busy at his barracks organising his trip into the desert; Jardine had passed by to hear much frustrated shouting and the honking of camels.

By his calculation, if everything had gone well, his weapons would be in the Suez Canal only a few days' sailing away. His task was to organise the unloading, which would have to be into boats, probably those dhows rotting in the harbour.

Mason, having taken over the sick fellow's duties, had given him the name of a contact, Jamal Cabdille Xasan, a local worthy who had once been prosperous but had suffered the same fate as the place in which he resided. If there was one decent dwelling in the town it was his, but that only became apparent once Jardine was through the doors and into the cool and columned courtyard. Having introduced himself, Xasan sent for a man to interpret their conversation.

Jardine knew 'Jamal' meant 'beautiful' in Arabic and never was it more inaccurately applied. Xasan had a hooked nose, drooping black eyes, rotting teeth in a sour, turned-down mouth, bad breath and a manner that reeked of a life of double-dealing. Mason was sure he was still involved in the slave trade, now something much interdicted by all the colonial powers. Whatever, he was the fellow who, for a price, could secure the men and boats Jardine needed to get his goods ashore, so for a visitor who knew he would need hours to negotiate with him, he could breathe fire for all he cared.

It was a lengthy and tedious business, but unavoidable, fuelled by endless cups of sweet tea, for there was not a Muslim born who did not see it as a bounden duty to bargain for hours, and Xasan was both a hard man to read and one difficult to beat down. It was late in the afternoon when the terms were finally struck and a down payment made, plus a 'gift' to the interpreter.

He could have sailed back to Berbera easily and landed in darkness – it was another clear, starry night – but Jardine decided, discretion being the better part of valour, he would sleep on the boat. There were any number of places to anchor along a near-deserted shore, and the men transporting him were adept fisherfolk who caught a couple of flathead mullet to be cooked over a brazier hung on the vessel's side. With those same fellows keeping a look out for sharks he had a dawn dip in the sea as well.

Once back at the bungalow he was informed by Mason that a message had gone off to the Ethiopians at Dire Dawa to speed a camel caravan to Zeila; if it arrived early and had to wait, it was not a problem, given there was a set of wells just inland at Tashoka. Jardine had no notion how it had been sent or to whom, nor was he about to ask.

It was enough that it had been done; it was the kind of thing he did not need to know, and information like that, inadvertently spread, could jeopardise the messenger as well as the means of communication. So far, apart from Alverson, everything had gone swimmingly. He should have known it was too good to continue; when the problem arose it came in trousers and a shirt and was female.

'You guys think you are smart, but when I see Tyler Alverson making ready to ship out and he is not telling me where he is going, and this is after you two had a cosy midnight talk, I begin to smell something.'

'I can't imagine what you think it is, Miss Littleton.'

'There's only one place Tyler wants to go and it is not Aden, so when he informs me that's where he is headed I know he is lying.'

'I am not privy to where he wants to go or is headed, I have my own concerns.'

'You know, Jardine, the folks round here are real friendly, and when I saw you come in on a dhow this morning—'

'You were in Berbera, not here?'

'Sure I was, and when you disappeared I went and had a little word.'

'They don't know anything.'

'They know more than you think and they took you to a place called Zeila where you met some guy and—'

'Don't tell me,' he interrupted, 'you paid them to talk?'

'Naw, I undid a couple of buttons on my shirt. They were so keen to see what a white woman had inside they would have denied Mohammed.'

'God knows why,' Jardine replied with an infuriated growl, 'you'd hardly fill an egg cup.'

His attempt to divert her with an insult failed utterly, she just grinned and wiggled her tight bottom. 'Some guys like their ladies a little on the slender side. Now, I will tell you what I think: Tyler wants to get into a part of Abyssinia that the locals are keeping him out of and I figure he has engaged you to get him there, which is why you went to Zeila, which I am told is a shithole.'

'Fishing trip.'

'My ass.'

'I've met stevedores who swear less than you.'

'And I have met liars in academia who would leave you for dead. I need to get to Gondar or Aksum and drag my dear mother out of there. I have sent her cables by the dozen saying it is dangerous, but either they don't get through or she is not listening.'

'Neither are you. It is bloody dangerous.'

'You don't remember, I am a Spartan woman.'

'What the hell does that mean?'

'It means I can read and write, it means I can shoot a rifle or a pistol, and if you can find a bow and arrow I will knock an apple off your goddamned head. It means I can ride a horse bareback and go without food, climb mountains and herd cattle.'

'I read somewhere those Spartan women were happy to be seen prancing around in the nude.'

'There I draw the line.'

'You might have just blown your best chance of persuading me.'

'And I thought you were a decent guy.'

'When it comes to lust, honey, there's no such thing.' The drawling interruption identified the speaker. 'They also shared their charms with more than one man to beget children. You now have a chance to get me on your side, Corrie.'

'How much did you hear, Tyler?'

'Enough.'

'So, Jardine, what's it to be?' Corrie Littleton asked.

'When did I cease to be a "Mr" and become someone you address like a servant?'

'I'll call you "sir" if it will help,' the girl said.

'Wrong Jardine – that's my cousin.'

'You got a first name?'

'Yes, my friends call me Cal, you can call me Mister Jardine.'

'I have to tell you I am desperate. The only way I will get my mother out of there is if I drag her by the hair. I know nothing about armies . . .'

'Except classical ones,' Alverson suggested, with a slight smirk.

The remark got Tyler Alverson a glare, one that softened when she looked back at Jardine.

'I know where she is, right in the path of Mussolini's soldiers and on the road to Addis.'

Jardine had read up on places like Gondar and Aksum, both at one time home to Ethiopian royalty going back to antiquity. In Gondar each succeeding king or queen seemed to feel the need to build a place or fortress of their own, so there were multiple buildings of real historical interest, not to mention a source of national pride, and that might be a place the present ruler would be determined to fight for. It was almost as if Corrie Littleton read his mind.

'Haile Selassie will try to defend Aksum and Gondar for sure, and I have heard enough about those Blackshirt bastards to know they will not respect the old royal palaces. They'll blow them to hell if they need to and kill anyone who gets in their way. If you had ever met my mother you would know she will try to stop them with her bare hands.'

'Now I know where you get it from.'

'I'm desperate, Mr Jardine, really desperate.'

'I don't know what's the matter with me,' he sighed, 'and you would not credit the number of people who tell me I've got a stone instead of a heart.'

She ran at him then and jumped into his arms, bestowing a smacking kiss on his cheek. Jardine was shocked; Tyler Alverson was laughing.

There is nothing worse than waiting, except waiting with other people who are, like you, keeping a secret. Everything you say, every gesture you make, seems to allude to that which you are trying to hide. Conversations are started and broken off, and all the while there was the worry for Jardine, who had settled in his own mind on the additions to his party, that Lieutenant Grace would return in his boat or Peydon would reappear from the desert, either of which would put the mockers on everything.

Grace was sailing the Red Sea, unaware of the nature of one ship he was passing, flying a red duster. His own white ensign pennant seemed to be of excessive interest to a couple of folk on the deck, one of whom waved, an act that was responded to by a rating, earning the sailor a reprimand and a reminder that he was not on holiday. He had spoken to several of the traders who plied this sea route and used Massawa as their home harbour; there was still no sign of an Italian advance. That rendered him crestfallen: he would really have nothing to report.

Out in the wilderness, on the Abyssinian border with Italian Somaliland, Archie Peydon was in his element. He was a Boy Scout turned soldier, unsuited to the routine of the task he now had, on a detached duty training native troops and camels in a backwater where nothing was ever going to happen, with an occasional visit from his CO, a Royal Marine of all bloody things, to tell him he was all wrong in the way he went about his duties.

The man craved action, prayed for a war, even one of the so-called police actions would do, just to relieve his boredom. Heaven knew that Britannia, with her commitments, had a bit of a conflict going on somewhere all the time.

Lying in scrub, with squatting camels and his askaris in the wadi behind him, he watched the Italians through his binoculars as they went about their duties in a desultory fashion. Nothing had changed since his last excursion to this spot, one no enemy would ever have got near to if he had been in command: there would have been an outpost on this spot for certain. It would have been no use pointing out to Peydon that the men he was watching were not his enemies: anyone not of the same nationality as he, Jocks, Taffs and Paddies excluded, was, in his mind, a foe.

It would be depressing to go back to this Jardine fellow and tell him the situation was unaltered. In his mind he had carried a vision of racing his camel force back into Berbera with exciting news, the kind of act that might get a mention to enhance his hitherto dull career. But it was not to be and so he slid back down the slope and signalled to his men to get themselves back on board their grunting beasts.

'Mr Jardine.' The knocking on the door was insistent and it was Mason's voice, which had him out of his bed and dragging the chair from under the door handle, put there to avoid a repeat visit from the man's wife, then opening it a crack. 'I have received a radio message from a Mr Lanchester, saying the ship is in Aden.'

'How long will our caravan take to get to Zeila?'

'Dire Dawa is near the Ethiopian border, which is about one hundred and fifty miles of travel, as they need to move from oasis to oasis. That would normally take about ten days, but given what you are bringing, I would say they would push hard to do it in eight as long as they are not stopped and questioned.'

He and Mason had already discussed the risk of interception, which came down to the small chance of them encountering patrolling units of the Somali Camel Corps, who would wonder at a caravan coming out of Ethiopia by a little-used route carrying nothing. The main body of the corps was based in Hargeisa, which they would skirt round, and there were small units like Peydon's at certain strategic points, as well as a reserve. But with the Italian build-up, Mason's opinion was that the force would need to stay concentrated, while to call up reserves would cost money the governor did not have to spare.

Jardine's next requirement was to get to Aden and aboard the *Tarvita*, and have it sail to the anchorage off Zeila, which would require some subterfuge. Also, he needed a local with knowledge of the coastline, because the only available Admiralty charts would be on board Grace's patrol boat, not that it would have been wise to ask for them. The men who had transported him before, as well as their dhow, were pressed into service. The crossing also depended on a favourable wind and that was not forthcoming.

They sailed slowly back up the coastline, with Jardine going ashore at Zeila to ensure all the arrangements were in place. He also had to hand over to Xasan a second instalment of the agreed payment so he could actually gather the required men and boats. Then it was a journey in open sea straight across a wide part of the gulf to Aden, beating up tack on tack into a contrary wind, this to avoid the chance of being intercepted by the French, finally turning north close the Yemeni shore.

Two frustrating days passed before they sighted the high mountains that enclosed the huge natural harbour of Aden, the feature that made it so important, and several hours before they could get alongside the *Tarvita*, which was anchored well off Steamer Point, rocking on a swell which made a nightmare out of climbing the rope ladder dropped over the side.

'You make a bloody awful pirate, Cal,' said Lanchester as he finally made the deck. 'No Blackbeard you, what? Perhaps we should have winched you aboard.'

'A hello would be nice, Peter. Had any trouble?'

'Have you ever tried to read Proust, old boy?' A confused Jardine shook his head. 'Thought not, or you wouldn't ask.'

'Vince, what is he talking about?'

'Beats me, guv.'

'Had a customs chappie aboard,' Lanchester added, 'but it's the same old story: they're not terribly interested if you are on your way to another port, and you have no idea how much confusion can be caused by him trying to understand the captain's Turkish form of English.'

'Do we need permission to get under way?'

'Dues are paid but we should tell the harbour master, it seems.'

'Well we are not going to. Tonight we will get the captain to darken the ship and head straight out to sea and we need to keep the dhow I came in within sight.'

'Not me, old boy,' Lanchester said, 'this is where I bail out.'

'Where's your sense of adventure?'

'All used up, Cal.' Lanchester dropped his flippant tone. 'Listen, old chap, if you do get the goods into the right hands, get out right away. That was the job, to deliver, and once the weapons are handed over, your involvement is finished.'

'Why do you think it necessary to say that?'

'I know you, that's why.' He turned to Vince. 'I am relying on you to make sure he does what I have just said.'

'Thanks a bunch, Mr Lanchester.'

'How long will it take to get the stuff into Ethiopia, Cal?'

'A week, maybe ten days after it is landed.'

'And have you thought about how you are going to get yourself out?'

'Peter, you worry about you and let me worry about me.'

That made Lanchester frown, but he clearly realised there was little point in saying more. 'Vince, oblige me by getting the captain to warm up his motor launch while I go and pack.'

'You're not going to believe this, Peter, but I am actually going to miss your company.'

'Get in touch when you get back to London.'

'Will do.'

Lanchester's last act was to pass over a large sum of Austrian thalers, the preferred currency in Ethiopia and Somalia, which went into Jardine's belt. They saw him over the side within half an hour, heading for the shore and the offices of the passenger line that ran ships to and from India, which, as he had said, might give him time to see off Proust.

# CHAPTER FIFTEEN

Mindful of Captain Peydon's story of his disappearing supply dump, Jardine was disinclined to unload the cargo until the Ethiopians arrived with their camels – he was not prepared to pile up a fortune in weapons on a Somali beach where they could be pilfered, for he suspected when it came to being light-fingered these people would not be far behind the Arabs, and a man like Cabdille Xasan would not stop them; if anything, he would encourage such a thing and seek to profit from the theft. What followed was two days of he and Vince sitting fretting offshore until Mason arrived by dhow to say the caravan was now at the wells of Tashoka.

Their leader was brought into Zeila, where the motor launch was waiting in the harbour to take him out to the *Tarvita*, and the introductions were made. She lay three miles out to sea: the captain had insisted they stay well offshore until unloading was imminent to give him some sea room in case of bad weather.

The Ethiopian was a tall man and not young, an elegant, grey-haired fellow called *Ras* Kassa Meghoum; the title equated to something like a prince or a duke. He was dressed in an embroidered garment that went to below his knees, his shoulders covered by a short red cloak. His skin was unlined and he moved with that Horn of Africa grace, which also applied to the way he spoke and acted, making it difficult to guess his age.

More importantly, he had the welcome gift of being able to communicate easily: he had learnt some English as a young man and perfected it in the two years he served as an ambassador in London, seeking to gain for his county the one thing they prized above all others, barring independance – access to the sea.

Jardine took a liking to him on first acquaintance; he had an honesty about him that was endearing, almost his first remark being that Britain had let down an old and trusted friend, though he was quick to accept what those present were doing went some way to make amends, as were the private backers who had provided the funds.

'What I have managed to bring is not even a fraction, sir, of what you need,' Jardine said. 'No more than a symbolic contribution to show you that not all of my countrymen share the views of our government.'

'And it is welcome, Mr Jardine. It is good that we know we still have friends in Britain. I am bound to ask who they are.'

'And I am duty-bound to refuse to answer, sir,' Jardine replied, covering for the fact that he did not really know.

It was with sonorous respect that *Ras* Kassa responded. 'An offering is all the greater when the giver seeks no praise.'

'Time to get them ashore, sir.'

The *ras* had brought a hundred camels to Zeila, as well as a hundred warriors who would escort the caravan back to Ethiopian soil, but when Jardine suggested, for the sake of increased speed, they might help unload, he refused for two reasons. First, their dignity as Shewan warriors would be offended, and secondly, because of the trouble it might cause with the local Somalis, given they despised each other – which reminded Jardine of what had been said to him by Geoffrey Amherst about the tribal nature of this part of the world.

Getting the ship as close inshore as possible was paramount: the lesser the distance, the quicker the goods would be landed, and that was tricky – running aground was not an option when the only tug they could send for would have to come from Aden. First they got labourers into the holds to shift the sacks of grain – they formed the final part of the payment to Cabdille Xasan – then they had to be got ashore and safely stored, with the ugly old sod counting in and weighing every bag.

When it came to the weapons and boxes of ammunition Vince took care of the loading end with Peter Lanchester's very obvious Colt pistol in his belt. Jardine, likewise armed, escorted each consignment to shore and saw it handed over to *Ras* Kassa. Camels were being led to the shoreline in strings of ten at a time to have panniers strapped on under his supervision, then taken back to the wells to be unloaded, given they would be rested there overnight.

It was slow going and hard work under a hot sun, so when, escorted by Mason, Tyler Alverson and Corrie Littleton arrived and issued cheerful greetings, they got the sharper end of Jardine's tongue and were told to stay out of the way.

It was near to night when they got to the last crates, and once Vince's baggage was on board the time came for he and Jardine to say farewell, which included rewarding the captain and spreading a few gratuities to the crew and the cook. The Suez Canal tonnage fees for the return were paid, as well as the cost of refuelling at Port Said.

Such a parting, especially for Vince, was not without a degree of sentiment, for this lot had not only accepted the risk but had behaved with real credit, so cheerful waves and cries of good luck in several languages marked the final parting.

There was trouble with Xasan, not that it came as a surprise, given the look of the man and his previous hard bargaining: Jardine expected he would demand extra payment, citing a list of imagined tasks over and above those previously agreed. He had to be bought off, though not without an argument.

If the ugly old bugger had not been told what the cargo was beforehand, it took no genius, given the presence of Ethiopians, even if he had no way of deciphering the German markings, to work out what the wooden crates contained. The border with French Somalia was not far off, and any talk of this contraband in the bazaars and tea shops of Djibouti could easily reach Italian ears, not much further up the coast.

The two Americans had bought a pair of donkeys, which were now burdened by a serious amount of baggage, not least Alverson's typewriter and camera tripod. The American set up his Leica on that so he could take a photograph as a memento of Zeila and the story he would write, once the weapons were safely delivered, without, of course, using any names.

Vince was introduced and, easily identified as an ex-boxer, he found an immediate soulmate in the middle-aged newspaperman. The two of them were soon locked in what seemed like a competition to name the greatest number of famous pugilists, which lasted all the way to the wells, not, in truth, more than a mile distant, an oasis of verdant green in what was a barren landscape of sand and coastal scrub.

The weapons were in a pile surrounded by the squatting camels and their drovers, while *Ras* Kassa's warriors formed a circular guard around the encampment, several of them armed with ancient rifles, most with spears, some with bows and arrows.

They were tall willowy men in very white *shammas,* a sort of paletot garment that was wrapped round the body with a part thrown over the shoulder, all lean muscle and supple movement. In a sense, it was Jardine's first look at what made up the bulk of the Ethiopian army, though it was too soon to make a judgement on their discipline or ability; but if the weaponry was standard, then they were in for a hard fight.

The *ras* had set up a tent and it was to that Mason took them, with Jardine wondering what Kassa would say about the two Americans tagging along, a worry soon laid to rest: the Ethiopian was delighted when he found out Alverson was a reporter. He thought telling the world about Italian intentions a good thing, that it was a badly mistaken notion to keep correspondents from abroad away from the front lines. With Corrie Littleton he was such a perfect gentleman that she was immediately smitten.

Soon food was cooking on spits – they were strong on meat in this part of the world – while one of the drovers was crouched over a large flat stone, that too on burning wood, cooking great roundels of unleavened bread. While they were eating, more tents were put up, one for the Caucasian men, plus another small one for Corrie Littleton, as *Ras* Kassa, already photographed, answered a stream of questions posed by Alverson. Jardine did not interject: the American was asking the questions he would have put himself.

'We have pulled back our forces fifty miles on the Eritrean front to avoid giving our enemies the excuse of an incident. Also, it is near desert, so crossing it will weaken them, for the road they have built ends at the border and they must drive their vehicles across bad open country. The infantry, too, will suffer before they meet our fighters.'

Alverson next asked what the force levels were, a question, when it came to the Italians, Jardine answered from memory, a feat that much impressed his host. The reverse was not the case: the way *Ras* Kassa boasted of an Ethiopian army of over a million men rang a little false. Jardine was in no position to argue, he just thought the claim smacked of exaggeration, or perhaps to be kinder, wishful thinking, rather than the truth.

'What about tanks and aircraft, *Ras*?' Jardine asked.

For the first time the gentlemanly Ethiopian looked irritated, only a flash across the face but enough to tell Jardine the question was unwelcome; his army had a few First World War tanks and, according to what was known, less than thirty aircraft, against an enemy who numbered those assets in the hundreds.

'We will beat them even if they do have many of these things, for God is on our side, and I am bound to ask again why the democratic nations do not send us such weapons.'

That, in effect, killed the conversation stone dead, moving it to more general topics and, after a hard day, it was time for everyone to sleep, barring those set to guard the encampment.

At dawn the trio formed to say goodbye to Conrad Mason, a man who had risked his career in aiding this enterprise, as well as turning a blind eye to the wishes of the two Americans, though he waited until the Ethiopians finished their prayers so he could have a quiet talk with *Ras* Kassa.

The last act, just before he mounted the horse that would take him back to Berbera, was a quiet word with Cal Jardine, who, while insisting his own influence was nil, intimated he knew certain people – he was thinking of Peter Lanchester and perhaps even Monty Redfern – who might be able to put in a word and get the man a better posting.

Mason was not looking at him as he made the offer, seemingly intent on the drovers carrying out their ritual morning task of combing their camels for their moulting hair, a saleable commodity once enough was gathered.

'No thanks, Jardine. Odd as it seems, I am rather fond of this part of the world, don't you know?'

He was no longer looking away, indeed the stare that accompanied those words was direct and challenging, as if Mason was daring him to allude to the real reason he was happy to remain in Somaliland; it was an invitation declined, but Jardine was determined to test the colonial officer as well, even if, in his heart, he knew it to be both unwise and potentially a cause of trouble.

'Give my regards and thanks to your wife, for everything.'

'Ah yes, Margery,' Mason said absent-mindedly, as if she were a distant person suddenly recalled. 'She is not the finest hostess in the world, but she does her best.'

'On the contrary, I found her very accommodating.'

The last word hung in the air, but Mason was not to be drawn, though it was noticeable his farewell handshake was a little firmer. Jardine was tempted to add that, while Mason was content to stay here, he doubted if that applied to her, but he put such a comment aside too, on the very good grounds that it was really none of his business: you never knew the secrets of a marriage – God only knew how that applied to him – and it was something best to steer clear of.

Mason's departure combined with the arrival of a troop of women leading camels, which set up one of those vocal matches between their beasts and the Ethiopian animals, who voiced their resentment at the intrusion while the Somalis' camels responded in kind. It seemed they had come to fetch water, Zeila having none, so every drop had to be carried in on a daily basis and no doubt sold, a thriving and everlasting business. Though the visitors could not understand what was being said, it was apparent the Ethiopian fighting men were making lewd suggestions to these women, offers that were being rudely rejected.

'I noticed some of your men are armed,' Jardine said, as, with the water ladies gone, he rejoined *Ras* Kassa. 'How safe are we travelling back to your homeland?'

'Less safe than coming, Mr Jardine, given we will have much worth stealing and we will need to go by a different route to that by which caravans normally travel to and from the coast.'

Seeing an explanation was required he carried on speaking.

'We are, as you know, landlocked, and since our easiest routes to the sea have been blocked by our enemies we must trade through the only major port left to us. With Massawa and Mogadishu in Italian hands that only leaves Djibouti, and not everything goes by rail – the ancient methods are very much still in use. Normally our caravans travel by a more southerly route that would take us through your British capital of Hargeisa, where we enjoy protection from your Camel Corps, but that, for obvious reasons, given what we are carrying, is not open to us.'

'So the route we will use is?'

'The one by which we came here, an old slavers' route along the border with French Somaliland.'

'Dangerous.'

'The French are only really interested in Djibouti, and inland is not fertile, it is barren, waterless and hot, which allows the local Somali tribesmen who live by selling salt to be lawless if they choose, but we are numerous, so we should be safe.'

'Nevertheless, I think it would be an idea to issue some modern weapons here and now and make sure your men know how to use them. Those ancient pieces are not likely to be accurate and there are, in truth, not many of them.'

'You say that before you have seen these men use them.'

'I'm sure they are good shots. They will be even more deadly with more modern arms.'

That exchange left a question hanging in the air. Now the guns were off the ship, who was in charge of getting them to where they were needed? It was all very well for Cal Jardine to see his task as delivery to the source of the conflict, but all he had was himself, Vince and his military experience; *Ras* Kassa had a hundred warriors, albeit poorly armed, and was close to his home turf. If the old man insisted on taking charge he would not get an argument: they were, after all, on the same side.

*Ras* Kassa waved at the pile of crates. 'Mr Jardine, they are yours to do with as you wish.'

Appreciating the courtesy, there was only one reply. 'Not so, *Ras*. My task may be to get them to Addis Ababa but even here they are the property of your emperor, and since you represent him . . .'

The smile was as slow as the nod. 'Then I think your suggestion a good one.'

'Then select ten of your men – we do not have time to work with them all.'

'Ah, the jealousies that will cause.'

Jardine grinned: that would happen with any group of young warriors. 'We'll do ten a day, tell them.'

'You know, Vince,' Jardine said, as he leant over what should be a box of rifles with a jemmy in his hand, 'I have just had a notion it might have been us who were diddled. These boxes might be full of nothing but stones.'

'Not to worry, guv, everyone keeps telling me this here fight we're heading for is between David and Goliath, so that might be no bad thing.'

'Did you bring a catapult?'

'I knew I'd forgotten something.'

The act of opening a box got everyone's attention and a crowd had gathered by the time Jardine had wrenched it open to reveal the top layer of Karabiner 98s, heavily greased on the metal parts, the whole layered by oiled paper, with another tier underneath. The first task was to get them cleaned, prior to opening a box of M88 ammunition.

Jardine set up a rough target on a tree trunk and personally tested each weapon, filling the oasis with the sound of single gunshots, adjusting the sights as he went. He then handed the rifles over to the selected warriors and had them aim and fire in dumb show before allowing them one bullet each, with he and Vince supervising the way they held and aimed them to contain the recoil: broken shoulders were not a good idea.

He knew that *Ras* Kassa was dying to get his hands on one of them, but his dignity and quite possibly his rank forbade him to ask. Jardine was teasing him, for amongst the cases was a much better weapon for a man who ranked as a high aristocrat; if no one else could read the case markings he could, and the second box he opened contained, according to the lettering, M35 sub-machine guns.

These were weapons he had heard of but never seen, the very latest kit issued to the German army, but a gun is a gun – this one the successor to several previous versions – and once you have learnt how to take apart and reassemble one, you pretty much know how to do them all.

Equally well-greased on the metal parts, the first one he prepared and assembled himself, a task that he had not undertaken since Palestine days. Vince did not have to be asked: he just got on with opening a box of 9 mm bullets and slotting them into a magazine. Jardine set it to single shot to adjust the sights, then fired off a burst that removed several branches of a palm tree. Happy it was working properly, he reloaded it with a second magazine and presented it to a beaming *Ras* Kassa.

'A weapon that befits your rank, sir.'

'Does that come under the heading of sweet talk?' Corrie Littleton asked, in a voice sugary but false, as the *ras* went to test his weapon.

'Always be nice to the natives, something you Americans never quite got hold of.'

'Like you Limeys did?' Alverson demanded. 'Remind me to a have a word with Mahatma Ghandi.'

'Spare us the pieties, buster,' Corrie Littleton said, 'when do I get a weapon?'

'Can you use one?'

'Try me.'

Jardine nodded and fetched a rifle, checked the bolt to make sure the chamber was clear and handed it over. He knew immediately that this was a woman who had handled guns: she made sure the muzzle was pointed safely up in the air, then worked the bolt before asking, 'Do I get a stripper clip?' There was a moment then when Jardine had to make sense of that; not long, for he realised she meant a speed loader.

'Maybe, when we find out if we have any and where they are; right now stick to a single shot.'

Corrie Littleton, having loaded the weapon, stepped up and took aim, screwing the stock into the crook of her shoulder, with a slight twist on her left leading hand, the twin acts that seated the weapon properly and allowed her to cope with the recoil. All around the men had stopped and were watching her, feet planted for balance, leaning very slightly forward. Squinting along the barrel her pull on the trigger was controlled and she put her shot about six inches from the middle of the target.

'Damn, I'm out of practice.'

'That should stop anyone creeping into your tent, honey,' Alverson said.

'Who would want to?' Jardine replied, which got him a good sight of her tongue. 'I have to get some more weapons ready, but it's time to load up.'

Such a thing was easier said than done, camels being awkward beasts, much given to biting even the men they knew well. They were not in the least willing to cooperate as their double panniers were lashed onto their backs, before being tied together in lines of ten, which would be fronted by a lead male and rider.

Moving between them, wary of being kicked or bitten, which many of them tried to do, Cal Jardine carried two flat pieces of wood, taken from the one now broken-up wooden crate. Beside each loaded camel he stopped, then cracked the two pieces of wood close to their ears.

If they jumped away, he walked on; for those that seemed indifferent, he had a word with the drover who would lead them.

'What are you up to, guv?'

'I wondered if we might rustle up a couple of zamburaks, Vince.'

'As long as you don't want me to work one of them! I don't want to mount a camel, never mind one with a machine gun on its hump.'

'We probably won't have time. For now we have to get moving, so get your head and mouth covered.'

The need for that was obvious once they emerged from the shade of the oasis trees: a great cloud of dust kicked up by the camels' hooves. That was picked up and blown about by a wind that came off the now-invisible Indian Ocean. *Ras* Kassa, sitting on a donkey, his feet near to touching the ground, led the two Americans, likewise mounted, to the front of the line where they were able to stay ahead of the beasts of burden, while their warrior escort lined up on both sides.

Wrapped in the kind of desert gear they had not worn since Iraq, a turban round both head and mouth and square kitbags on their backs, Jardine and Vince walked ahead of the whole caravan, M36s slung over their shoulders and their eyes scanning the landscape for possible threats. The sun beat down, which meant frequent trips to the female camel bearing the water skins, though care was taken: this was not the worst they would face, and the habit of conservation of liquid was a good one to employ.

The men leading the camel strings seemed to be asleep, gently rocking on the backs of their animals, and it was only if you got close you could hear them singing softly to themselves, dirges that probably went back to ancient times. Jardine was thinking that his fellow Britons would see this, a camel caravan, as romantic; he knew better – it was stinking because they stank, and even with a covered mouth he was spitting dust and cursing the annoying cloud of flies around his head. He also ruminated on another hazard, the sheer danger of the landscape itself, this being a place where a scratch from a thorn bush could give you fatal blood poisoning, as could the bite from any number of insects.

'You used to the outdoors?' he asked Corrie Littleton, as she left off a conversation she was having with Vince and came trotting alongside him – he asked her not to get in front and obscure his view.

'Some, but not desert. Where I come from it's woods, big cats and bears.'

'And snakes?' That got a nod. 'Well, the desert is full of them too, and they are just as hard to spot. You are going to want to relieve yourself and that is not something you will do in full view.'

'You're damn right.'

'Then be careful if you seek cover. That's where the biters are, scorpions, too, and if there is shade, those reptiles I mentioned.'

'Seems to me you should be telling Tyler, he's the city feller.'

'Don't worry, I will, when, as we Brits say, he wants to go about his occasions.'

'If you mean he needs to shit, say so, I'm no shrinking violet and when I relieve myself, I piss.'

'More a cactus plant, I think, and a very prickly one.'

'How did you get involved in this, Jardine?'

'If you insist on using that name, I'd rather you called me Cal.'

'OK, but does calling you Cal get an answer?'

'What difference does it make?'

'I'm curious. What makes a guy like you take risks, and for what?'

'It's not the pay.'

'Vince says you're a bit of an adventurer, which is kind of quaint, but he won't say much more, except when he was in the military you were his officer.'

'Just one of them, and he was a good soldier, Vince; bit prone to the drink, but no one better to have alongside you when trouble blew up.'

'He said the same sort of thing about you, in fact he insisted you were the best company commander he's ever known.'

'I'm glad he's sticking to the script.'

'So why not stay in the army?'

'If you'd ever been in the British army you would know the answer to that, and I don't suppose your own is much different. Military service in peacetime is a sort of purgatory. There's never enough of the right equipment, your superiors are generally idiots, your peers are not much better, life is guaranteed to be boring and promotion is so slow you can die before you ever get to the level of making a difference.'

'Don't know much about it. No one in my family has been a soldier since the Civil War.'

'So where did you learn to shoot?'

'Pa loved hunting and he used to take me out with him. If you go out into the forests of America, being able to shoot is a must. Ever met a grizzly bear?'

'I met you.'

'Very funny! Trouble with grizzly bears in the woods is you can't see them, and if they are hungry and have cubs to feed, you are lunch, so you keep a sharp eye out for droppings and keep your weapon loaded and the safety off, 'cause there's no time if they come at you.'

Looking at Jardine she saw his eyes were narrowed, his binoculars were up and he was looking ahead with concentration; he had not been listening to her.

'What's up?'

'Nothing, most likely, but you see those hills up ahead? A couple of what looked like horsemen just appeared out of one of the folds, then disappeared again very quickly before I could get my field glasses on them. It was the mounts I saw, really.'

'Danger?'

'Might be. I'd have been happier if they had decided to just come on and say hello.'

# CHAPTER SIXTEEN

Jardine was searching ahead and up, sweeping his field glasses around to see if he could catch another sight of those two men. The hills seemed to fold in on each other, red earth, rocks, gnarled bushes and stunted trees blunting the outline, the larger ones rising, he guessed, to something well over a thousand feet, those lower down creating the defile which they would have to make their way through.

'Fire a shot in the air.'

'Why?'

'Makes an interesting noise?'

'And tells them we have spotted them.'

She did as he asked, the sound of the shot reverberating off the hills where he had seen the riders.

'That's a warning, because I don't think we can avoid going through that track up ahead, which is where I would be if I wanted to rob a part of this caravan.' He called over to Vince. 'Did you see them?'

'Just a flash and so did the old gent.'

Jardine moved to talk to *Ras* Kassa who was now sitting on his donkey with his machine pistol cradled in his lap. Having stopped the caravan, he too was peering at the hills ahead.

'What I saw troubles me, Mr Jardine.' There was no fear in the statement; in fact there was some doubt if it was an emotion to which he would be subject. 'There are two tribes in this region, Afars and Issas, both nomadic animal herders and salt traders who would ride a donkey at best. It is unusual they made no attempt to make talk with us, which is also not common.'

'Are the tribes to be trusted?' Jardine asked.

'The climate is harsh, the soil not good and the poor have their needs.'

It took no great genius to see that anyone trying to eke a living out of such a landscape would have to struggle to survive. Loaded camels were a tempting target and the problem was obvious. All you had to do was look at a string of camels nearly a mile in length and wonder, even with the amount of warriors available, how it was going to be defended from opportunistic raiders trying to cut out a couple. That was true now, out in the open; how much more was it the case on a winding valley track, where losing sight of parts of the caravan was a certainty?

Jardine suggested that when this route had been in full use, knowing the local tribes could turn to theft, the slavers, rather than travel with any more mouths to feed and carry more water than necessary, might have paid tribute to pass through freely.

'That is very possible.'

The guarded response made Jardine wonder just how open the older man was being about a trade that had gone on for thousands of years and was not ended yet: he seemed to know this route well enough. Ethiopian emperors paid lip service to the notion of stopping the slave trade but they had not succeeded, and it was interesting to speculate how much they gained from it themselves. Such a lucrative trade could buy influence at the highest level, and even if imperial edicts forbade it, the local satraps in such a large, wild and inhospitable land could pretty much ignore them.

'Could we do that– pay to be left alone?'

'That, Mr Jardine, would require someone to make a demand, and those fellows showed no sign of even wishing to approach us.'

'So how do you assess what has just happened?'

'Not good. We have to get through those hills ahead of us.'

'You're sure there is no other way?'

'Not one that absolutely avoids the risk of these weapons being discovered.'

Their destination for the day was another oasis on the far side of those hills, a very necessary source of water, which meant anyone observing them, if they knew the country, would have a precise knowledge of where such a large caravan was headed. This was not a part of the world in which you could just deviate; the route existed precisely because of the availability of each aquifer-fed waterhole. There were no rivers and to turn aside was to risk everything.

What lay before them was a natural obstacle through which those plying the route must pass, which made it the perfect place for an ambuscade, and the presence of unknown riders was bound to cause alarm. They might be entirely innocent, they might just be a couple of tribesmen more afraid than brave, but they could also represent a larger group for whom they had been scouting; it was best to assume the worst.

'How far to the oasis from here?'

'Four miles, perhaps six.'

That imprecise number underlined something Mason had said in his study: many parts of this land had never been properly mapped and he had none of this route. Sense dictated that the hills be reconnoitred before they passed through, yet that would take time. While no expert on camels, Jardine knew that, loaded as they were, it would not be a lack of water so much as a need for respite that would affect them. Resting here for an hour might mean they had to continue to travel into the hours of darkness, but better that than they lose some of them to exhaustion.

'So what's the decision?' asked Tyler Alverson, who had been listening to the exchange.

'Mr Jardine, I think you should take some of my men up the hillsides to see what they can find.'

'I agree, but how will they understand me?'

'Use your hands, Mr Jardine, they are Shewan warriors and they will obey you, while I will concentrate on the caravan and rest the camels until you return.'

'Any chance of getting out of the sun, *Ras*?' asked Alverson, covered in a layer of dust stuck to those places where he had sweated heavily in his bush clothing.

A series of rapid commands followed, detaching some of the white-shrouded warriors, all with spears, none of those with the new rifles, while still others were unloading part of a tent to erect an awning. Jardine and Vince divested themselves of their kitbags and led away their scouting party as the awning was being erected and the caravan condensed into a defensible mass, with *Ras* Kassa putting the riflemen out to the fore.

'Two horsemen, boss, an' all this?' said Vince.

'From what I know of this part of the world, which I admit is not a lot, people are pretty outgoing, yet they saw us and didn't come to parley to ask our purpose. A caravan headed towards the interior, clearly with loaded camels, has to be unusual, so if you are not curious, what are you?'

'They might have been going somewhere.'

'They might, Vince, but we can't risk it.'

Eyes flicking, weapon at the ready, he led the way towards the first part of the defile, not much of one, as the hills on either side were not high. The trail, which up until now had been wide, like the course of a dry river bed – odd, given there were no rivers in this part of the Somaliland – narrowed to the width of two or three men, and every sound was magnified, mostly the scraping of European boots on the hard earth, because the Shewan were barefoot.

Two high mounds cut off sight of the hillsides at the entrance. Jardine stopped behind them and signalled with five fingers and pointed left, which sent the correct number of silent warriors upwards on that side, while he led the rest in the opposite direction, to where he had seen those riders, fanning them out, pleased that no orders were required for them to do what was needed: to look at the ground for signs of human or equine traffic. They had not gone far when the first shot ricocheted off the rocks.

If these Shewan were brave and intelligent enough to obey sign language, they were also foolhardy. It took shouts accompanied by furious arm waving to get them to take cover, instead of brandishing their spears and uttering threats. The last man to get down, on the opposite side of the ravine, too slow by far, spun away as another shot, from what was a fusillade, took him in the shoulder. Another nearly bought one by trying to go to his aid, the folly of that underlined when a third grabbed his arm and hauled him down; the wounded man would have to wait.

'That's a lot of firepower, guv,' said Vince from behind his rock.

'It is,' Jardine replied, looking around for a way of getting a bit higher so he could see what it was they faced. 'Did you get a chance to count?'

'No, it was volley fire.'

'One round, then stopped, Vince, what does that tell us?'

'Trained men.'

'We need those riflemen up here, they're no good where they are.'

'Right,' Vince replied, slithering backwards.

Jardine had to signal hard again for his spearmen to keep their heads down and stay put on both sides of the ravine, but he also had to keep in place those facing them: against spears they could just walk forward and kill. He raised himself just enough to fire off half a magazine, the sound of that, and the way the bullets hit rock, echoing around the folds of those hills, surprised that no return fire came his way.

In a contact with an enemy, and this was very much that, you filter a mass of little things through your mind without any conscious application, like Vince had discerned as quickly as Jardine that a single, coordinated volley meant men who have been trained to obey commands: tribesmen, wherever they came from, were not normally so disciplined. Nor, up against spearmen, had they abandoned their cover to come forward and remove the approaching threat.

It had been the men he had sent up the left-hand hills who had spooked them, because they had been approaching a point where their chosen position would have become visible, and they had not

223

melted away to avoid discovery but stayed to fight for possession of the ground. So they had positions they were content to hold, the conclusion obvious: this was an attempt to block the passage through the hills, not bandits trying to steal the camels and what they carried, and he was bound to wonder who would embark on that.

'Bloody hell,' Jardine said to himself, as that led to the only possible deduction. 'Italians.'

Those thoughts had to be checked against other possibilities. Renegade Ethiopians? Highly unlikely to be that, or *Ras* Kassa would have mentioned it. The French? He had no real idea if he was right now in British territory or part of French Somaliland, but if it was the latter and they wanted to stop the passage of weaponry, they would not have taken up a blocking position, kept out of sight, and opened fire. They would have come out into the open and, no doubt, they would have been told, by some sneering Foreign Legion officer, they could not pass through to the next oasis and must turn back.

In the few seconds these thoughts were being filtered it was also apparent that only in catching a fleeting sight of those two mounted men had the caravan been saved from getting into real trouble. Had they come on, unaware that they faced any threat at all, and been caught in those defiles, there would have been a massacre. But if they were Italian troops, what they were doing made a certain kind of sense, though there was no logic in them being here at all unless . . .

'Someone, somewhere, has done the dirty on us.'

Filtering names through his mind only one made sense! Jamal Cabdille Xasan. Mason was a certain no and so was his wife, while people like Peydon and Grace, even if they had been aware, would not have told the Eyeties. But that ugly old sod might have, and he would have done it for money, which the Italians would spread around willingly for information. As he had already surmised, in arranging for a contraband cargo to be offloaded, and being paid handsomely, it did not take too deductive a brain to figure out what it might be and where in the end it was headed.

Yet the Italians could have just informed the British Governor General with a telegram and he would have ordered Mason to stop any arms coming ashore, an instruction the district officer could not have dared to disobey. Another way to interdict the unloading would have been to send an Italian gunboat down the coast and force the landing of the cargo to cease. What lay in front of him, if he had figured it out correctly, made no sense at all!

Jardine ducked automatically at another volley of rifle fire, thanking God there was no sign of a machine gun, a weapon that could take out the whole of *Ras* Kassa's warrior escort in a single sweep. The shots cracking overhead and not striking rocks told him they were aimed at the Ethiopian riflemen now coming up from defending the caravan, with the *ras* leading – not Vince – two of his warriors carrying a box of rifle ammunition. He got his men into cover as soon as they made the rocks at the head of the defile, only coming on himself, ducking through various bits of cover with ease, to get to Jardine, his first act to hand over a couple of spare, filled magazines.

'Your man is looking for a mortar as well as a crate of hand grenades.'

'Clever Vince,' Jardine replied, then explained his thinking to the *ras*. 'Right now, all they have to do is hold their position and we are obliged to attack as the only means of shifting them.'

'So they must be pushed aside.'

'Tell your spearmen to retire and to keep their bloody heads down.'

*Ras* Kassa smiled. '"Bloody" is a word I have not heard for some time, Mr Jardine.'

'I think you will have occasion to hear it more than once today, because this is not going to be easy.'

'What was your rank in the army?'

'Captain, why?'

'Then I shall, from now on, call you by that title. Mister seems not appropriate in the situation we are in.'

Cupping his hands he called out, in a high-pitched voice at odds with his normal even bass, a series of commands that had his spearmen retiring, crawling backwards on their bellies to keep from getting shot at, though not one bullet came their way.

'Some of them must have presented a target,' Jardine said, 'yet no shots, so I don't think our johnny up ahead is too well blessed with ammo. Either that, or he wants to save it for killing us.'

Crawling a few feet, till he could find a gap through which to fire, Jardine set his weapon to single shot and slowly, deliberately, sent bullets into the hills above his head, aiming for a thick bush or a prominent rock, quickly changing the magazine to a fresh one. Still no response, which underlined their discipline, which was not good news; worse, he had not seen any true indication of their precise position and he needed to bring forward those riflemen cowering behind them. Right now they were in no danger: due to elevation, the enemy did not have fire control at the point at which the trail opened up to the flatlands.

'*Ras* Kassa, how comfortable are you about firing off that gun?'

'I pray to God for the chance.'

'Half the magazine, rapid fire, no more, you to the left, me to the right, your riflemen to move to join us as soon as we open up.' The *ras* was just about to comply when Jardine stopped him. 'If they are Italians up ahead, they might be askaris, and if they are, will they understand what you shout to your men?'

'Only if they know Shewan, Captain Jardine, and since there are fifty different tongues in my homeland alone I cannot think a Somali will know what I am saying.'

'Tell them what they are to do, but not to move until we begin firing.'

Again came that high-pitched calling, with Jardine waiting to see if it provoked a response. Lacking that, after a decent wait, he nodded and got to one knee, firing as soon he had sight of the positions he hoped the enemy occupied, the *ras* beside him doing likewise, though to Jardine, exposing himself too much.

'Down,' he shouted, as this time the riflemen up ahead did respond, firing at will, which at least allowed him to sneak a look and fix their positions using the muzzle flashes and smoke. One side of the ravine elevated enough to give them cover firing down, making it hard for anyone below to return shot in an effective way. Numbers he tried to guess by individual discharges but it could only be an estimate.

Choice? Stay put and wait for Vince to bring up a mortar, which he would have had to unpack and prepare. He would also have to find the panniers with the ammunition, which could take ages given his lack of German. Option two, seek to winkle out the men who tried to ambush them with no clear idea of their numbers, leading warriors who were certain to be less well trained in the use of weapons than those they were facing.

The sun on his back was baking and enervating, but that also applied to his opponents, who would think, if he failed to come forward, they had the upper hand. Unconscious thoughts came to him again.

Whoever is in command up there has no idea of what weapons we are carrying; in fact, if he wanted to take the time, Jardine could unpack two machine guns and spray the whole hillside at will, mixing it with multiple mortar fire, deadly in rocky terrain. So whoever he was, good sense said that as soon as the first mortar shell landed amongst them he should get out quick unless he had the means to respond in kind.

'More orders, *Ras*: keeping as much cover as they can, get your chaps to move forward as far as I do. I want to see if he has any more firepower than rifles, and if he has, we need to withdraw.'

'Can we not just charge them?'

'You could lose half your men, maybe all of them.'

'Men get killed in war,' *Ras* Kassa replied callously.

'Not when I can help it,' Jardine snapped, pointing to the hill opposite. 'There's a wounded man over there too; we have to get him out to where he can be looked at.'

'My friend,' the Ethiopian leader said gravely, 'he will wait, because he will know he has to, and die if he must without complaint. God will care for him as he cares for us all.'

Jardine declined to respond to that. 'Twenty-feet advance, no more. Make sure they know that and get them to pick their cover fast. If they go on, they are at risk from hand grenades as well as bullets.'

He had no idea if the *ras* passed on that message in its entirety and there was nothing he could do about his ignorance. What he did know was that if the bugger in front of him had a mortar, this was the time to use it. Wait till your enemy is in the open and coming from a known position. Range it to drop in front of that point and it will be right in amongst them, causing carnage.

The tactics of whoever was in command up ahead were not great: he had fired off his rifles at too extended a range. He should have let those searching come on until he was sighted, so they were closer, better targets, more likely to be either killed or wounded with much further to go to get back to safety, a retreat compounded by the need to care for their casualties.

Would they take those now? Would these Ethiopian warriors do what was required? It was galling not to be able to effectively communicate exactly what he wanted, and Jardine promised that one of his first tasks after this would be to learn some basic universal words that everyone could understand – even with fifty languages, there had to be some commonality or nothing would ever get done.

There was no shout: that would only alert the opposition a second in advance. The signal for everyone was his actions, and he stood to set off a short burst, not really aimed, given half his attention was on looking for his next bit of cover. When he moved, he had to worry about keeping his footing on loose, rock-filled earth. Twenty feet does not sound like much, but when you are running uphill exposed to gunfire it turns into an eternity.

There was no thought of potential pain as he threw himself behind a second boulder just as bullets pinged off the crest. *Ras* Kassa was beside him a second later, plucking at his red cloak where a bullet had torn it, which made Jardine wonder why the old sod was still wearing something so easy to see.

'I guess from the fire we have received we are facing about platoon strength – under thirty effectives. I suspect our enemy has nothing other than what he has employed, which would have been sufficient if he had caught us unawares, and I think he has no idea of what

229

we can counter with. He set himself the task of closing the path to the next oasis and making it so bloody to get through we would withdraw. When that failed he fell back on the hope of denying us the trail. I think if we press him he will retire.'

'Then let us do that.'

'Wait for the mortar, *Ras*.'

# CHAPTER SEVENTEEN

In good cover, at no seeming risk and with time to think, Jardine was not impressed with the opposition, or at least not with whoever was in command. First he had allowed his presence to become known; second, he had taken no action following on from the single gunshot fired by Corrie Littleton, which surely indicated an awareness of the threat. He had adopted the fixed tactic of the ambush so that his relative strength would count for more.

Yet if the need was to block the trail, he would have been better to have sealed off the point of entry where, with rifles effective at long range and over a field of fire with no cover, provided he had water – and he had an oasis, albeit a distant one, at his back – he could have sat there for ever while inviting the warriors from the caravan to attack him over open ground.

Another option was to radically alter his dispositions in a set of ravines and a folding gully that obviously extended a long way, by seeking a better, more camouflaged position from which to launch an initial attack, then using a series of short, sharp engagements allied to partial pullbacks to draw his enemy into the kind of sapping and continuous losses necessary to clear the route, which would remain blocked, with the caravan stuck and thirsty for an indefinite amount of time. If that could be extended long enough, they would have to head back for the coast and the job would be done.

Now he was staying put when falling back was a sounder tactic, given the amount of cover available on these boulder-strewn, scrub-covered hillsides, that being the best way to confuse the opposition. All this thinking was predicated on them being Italian, or at least local Somali recruits led by one or more officers of Mussolini's army, who did not seem too blessed with brains.

The aim was blockage, yet he had elected for carnage, which, while no doubt satisfying, rendered complex what should have been simple. He was now in a firefight with a force greater than his own, in terrain that made them, in effect, equal, albeit the man in command would think they, in the defensive position, had the upper hand.

'He knew we were coming by this route,' *Ras* Kassa said.

'You came this way with a hundred empty camels and the same number of Shewan warriors, so there is a very high chance you were seen. Word was picked up about the landing of a cargo at Zeila, where this slave route ends. What would an Ethiopian caravan be on its way to collect with an invasion imminent? Sherlock Holmes it's not.'

'Ah, the great detective; I had his stories read to me.'

'*Ras*, we need half your men to get higher up the hillside unseen, the rest to keep up a slow rate of fire to pin the enemy and keep him thinking we are stuck. I want us above them when that mortar comes into play, ready to inflict casualties when they break cover.'

'And if they do not?'

'Then we'll mortar them till they do.'

'We are running out of daylight, Captain Jardine, would it not be better just to attack?'

'Once we have shifted this lot we can go on in starlight, or, if we must, the caravan can camp where they are overnight.' Jardine looked the older man right in the eye. 'This is your show, not mine, but I am advising you that exposing your men will get many of them killed, and it is not a course I would recommend.'

'And if darkness comes and our enemies are still before us?'

'Then I expect him to withdraw, but I would wait until dawn to find out.'

'My men are good fighters in the dark.'

'I don't doubt it, *Ras*, but if they are askaris holding the ground before us, they will be that too. Of course, if you order an attack, I am not going to interfere, these are your men.'

'I will wait till darkness falls, but when that happens, Captain Jardine, I suspect I will have more fighting knowledge than you, and it is I who will personally lead my men using nothing but knives. We will clear the way by stealth.'

'Your decision.'

The scrabbling sound to their rear showed a Shewan with a skin of water, for which Jardine especially was grateful; he also brought a message for his *ras*.

'Your man has set up the mortar on flat ground and needs someone to range for him.'

That was not going to be easy from where he was, and damned difficult if he moved: thanks to those mounds at the entrance, the higher he went the less Vince could see of him; sending messages back and forth was too slow and he was too far away to hear a shout. Mortar fire was most effective when it was quick and continuous, while it was also true it was not the most accurate weapon in creation, that oddly adding to its effect: you never knew where the next incoming round was going to land.

'I need your red cloak, *Ras*, or part of it,' Jardine said, unwrapping his own white headdress. 'And a stick long enough to signal. The message that should go back to Vince is up fifty for white, drop fifty for red, multiply by times shown, bang on with both, and I still need your men getting elevation to pour in volley fire when they break cover.'

The red cloak came off to be handed over, though finding a stick long enough was harder: not much grew to a height in this barren place. How the *ras* managed to convey that message to his men he did not know, he could only hope it was done accurately. The sun was dropping and, at the speed it does near the equator, the intense heat easing with it.

Up ahead the enemy commander must be feeling content: his tactics would seem to be producing the intended result, if not in the anticipated manner. The caravan was static, as were those attacking his position, and he could anticipate no change the next day.

Jardine was worried that the sun would disappear before they were ready, because he could not range-find for Vince in the dark, and if they did get some rounds off they were not going to have much time to dislodge the enemy. Finally ready, he raised both colours to tell Vince to commence firing, an act that proved his opponent, whatever else he had, exercised control over his men: there was no useless firing at a flapping cloth.

He was too far off to hear the odd plop a mortar round makes when it is dropped for detonation, but he could imagine Vince, having dropped the shell, sticking his fingers in his ears and ducking to get clear, then he heard the 'whoosh' it made as it passed overhead, which required him to time the point at which he must expose himself to observe the fall. Vince had to be careful, had to fire at near maximum range, afraid of being too short and dropping a round on his own side, but in his caution he was excessive.

Set as it was and at low elevation, the round landed way beyond the target, so far that it was a guess how much it had to be reduced, with Jardine jabbing up the red cloak three times, on the last attracting fire, which at least showed how alarmed the enemy was at the introduction of the weapon.

Frustration followed as Vince made the necessary adjustment, sacrificing length of range for increased elevation in a weapon that was short on that anyway, five to six hundred yards being about the limits of effectiveness for a 50 mm model. The second round showed Jardine had overdone his signals: it landed between the enemy position and him, which made very dangerous his looking out from cover to observe, and it was only just in time that he got his head back to avoid a fusillade of dislodged stones and earth.

The white flag went up, with Jardine wondering if those ahead would think he was trying to surrender; what came next disabused them if they thought that. It seemed to Jardine to be right on the button and he raised both signals to a torrent of enemy rifle fire.

Vince was profligate, firing off ten rounds inside two minutes, a measure of drift due to spinning and a bit of breeze ensuring none of the high-explosive shells landed in the same place, and that was how long it took to break the defence, brought home to Jardine as *Ras* Kassa's men opened fire from above him, pouring rifle rounds into an enemy forced to make themselves a target in order to retreat.

Both the signals went up again to tell Vince to cease fire, and if the remainder of the Ethiopian warriors did not understand what he shouted out, they knew to follow him once he stood up and rushed forward, his weapon burping in short three-round bursts. Even with the noise of guns going off he could hear the Shewan war cries; high, controlled keening screams designed to strike fear into an enemy heart. Magazine empty, Jardine stopped to reload, which let those following him pass. By the time he made the enemy position it was overrun, and lacking bayonets or more ammunition, rifle butts were raining down on the heads of what were, by their greenish uniforms, Italian askaris.

Not being understood now was again a problem: he wanted people to interrogate, he needed information on how much was known about the caravan and the weapons he was carrying, but all his commands to halt the killing were ignored. He actually had to stand over one wounded man and protect him from what was a massacre as the Shewan clubbed their enemies to death.

The light was going now, the sun hitting the edge of the earth, but enough was left to show the broken, blood-covered body of an Italian officer, a lieutenant by his rank badges. He had been hit by mortar fire and there would be no questioning him.

And then it was over, the bodies were being stripped, the knives were out to mutilate them, and he was shouting at *Ras* Kassa to stop the mayhem and not having much effect. The older man's eyes were afire with as much bloodlust as those he led and he had thrown his head back to start calling out in that high-pitched voice what Jardine could only think was a victory chant.

Between Jardine's spread legs was a man whimpering in terror, and more than once he was obliged to deflect a Shewan who wanted to kill him.

Alverson brought his camera up to view the field of conflict at dawn, as below the caravan was being loaded, prior to moving on. There were few trees of any height but one bore the body of the Italian officer, though the American only knew what it was because Jardine had told him. Hanging by its feet, the naked cadaver swung above a dark patch of earth, which had been a pool of black blood where it had drained from the myriad cuts inflicted on the dead body.

Overnight, hyenas had torn at the head and torso, turning it to a bloody pulp with bones exposed where their massive jaws had crunched and stripped them of flesh, but they had been given so many bodies to feed on they had not finished the task. Now, with the morning heating up, the site was beginning to attract flies in the hundreds, soon to be thousands. What was left would be picked at by carrion throughout the day and the sun would do its work, so that by the time night came again only bones would be left.

He trained the lens of his Leica on what had been a battlefield. If there had been emotion for such a sight, the man had seen too much to be affected by it now; it was news and his job was to show the world what war really meant.

'Jesus Christ!'

'Corrie, what the hell are you doing here?'

'I had to come and look.'

'Did you?' She nodded, her hand to her mouth. 'Happy now?'

'Is this what this war is going to be like?'

'Honey, this is what all wars are like.'

'They should be buried, not just left.'

Tyler Alverson sighed. 'They don't care anymore and neither do the *ras* and his boys.'

'What do you think happened to that Somali kid after Jardine finished questioning him?'

'Take it to the limits of your imagination, Corrie, then go a little further.'

'Why didn't Jardine intervene?'

'Why didn't I? Why didn't you?' Alverson asked as he clicked the camera. 'Because you don't; you just accept these people have their ways, and if the tables were turned the same would happen, and the best thing to do is pray, when it's you, you're already dead.'

'They're savages.'

'Who, when I left, were saying their prayers to a God they have worshipped for two thousand years.'

'Will they print those at home?'

'No. These are for the exhibition I will hold one day, photographs at which our fellow Americans will look with deep fascination. That is if I can find somebody to develop the damned things.' Looking over her shoulder Alverson jerked his head. 'Caravan's moving, time to rejoin them.'


'His name was Alberto Soradino and he commanded the garrison at Assab, which is on the southern border of Italian and French Somaliland. Soradino was a lieutenant in the 3rd Bersaglieri Regiment, stuck in a dead-end spot, and I should think going mad, while up north all his regimental friends were getting ready for a glorious invasion.'

Jardine passed over his wallet, which Corrie Littleton took off him.

'There's a photograph in there, I think of his mother.'

'God!'

'No good asking for his help, is there? Alberto believed in him and look where it got him.'

'What will she be told, his mother?'

'Missing in action, presumed dead.'

'No body?' she asked, handing back the wallet, which Jardine put in his kitbag.

'No, but if I get a chance I will somehow see this gets to Italy. I met too many people after the Great War who still hoped their presumed dead would show up one day. The really important thing is, as far as the man I questioned knew, he acted without telling his superiors, setting off to cross French territory as soon as he got wind of this caravan. Just breaching the border is grounds for a court martial, never mind setting off on a wild goose chase without telling anyone and leaving his mortar and machine gun sections behind. Alberto was searching for glory and he was not the brightest star in the firmament.'

'You can't say that about a man you don't know.'

'I can about a man I fought, and look what *Ras* Kassa is riding now.'

'So he's riding the poor bastard's horse, so what?'

The Ethiopian leader was also sporting the Italian lieutenant's hat, decorated with black capercaillie feathers.

'Look where we are, in the middle of a waterless wilderness, and he's on his horse like he's Caesar! This is not horse terrain, because a horse needs eight gallons of water a day and feed. Do you know how much eight gallons of water weighs?'

'Do you?'

'A lot, and some poor bastard has to carry it.'

'That was the second horse, the pack animal, the one they roasted and we ate last night. It doesn't make him stupid.'

'Alberto gets news about a shipment being unloaded at Zeila and information comes in, I am guessing here, of a caravan with unloaded camels seen heading along the old slave route, or maybe he just figured out it was the only way the return could be made. He does not pass this news up the chain of command. Instead Alberto mounts his trusty steed, lines up his askaris and heads out into the wilds. To get here, he crossed a border he should not, dreaming that on the return he would be able to tell his superiors how he magnificently stopped weapons getting into enemy territory; he may even have hoped to have them to show, with prisoners as well. He can feel the medals on his chest, he can imagine old fatso Mussolini shaking his hand.'

Jardine's voice had been rising as he spoke, getting more and more irritated, the narrowness of the trail and the closeness of the enclosing hillsides amplifying it.

'Why are you so upset? You won.'

'I'm upset because he got thirty men killed, which was probably his entire rifle platoon. That photograph of his mother, who thought her darling son was the best thing on God's earth, distresses me. I'm upset because there will be Somali widows who will never know what became of their husbands, and children who will never know what happened to their father. I'm upset that Alberto was an idiot and even more upset he had to cross our path.'

'I think you are in the wrong game, buster.'

'Maybe you're right.'

'He's always like that, miss,' Vince said. 'We call it the "black dog", an' it was made a lot harder by the way they took out that wounded geezer he was questioning to have a bit of sport.'

'Folk think soldiers are made of stone, honey,' Alverson added, 'and they ain't.'

'Is he married, Vince?'

'Down, girl,' Alverson barked.

'It's only a question.'

'One you'll have to ask the guv, miss. I don't talk about things he don't want talked about.'

'So he is married. Any kids?'

'Honey, you should have been a reporter like me.'

'Jaundiced, cynical, overweight, drinks too much, smokes cigars and can photograph mutilated bodies without turning a hair.'

'I can't wait till you get to my bad points.'

'Oasis,' cried Vince, pointing ahead to the first hint of greenery, glad to get off the subject.

The Ethiopians were sat in a wide circle, those with rifles cleaning their weapons, while the camels, who had now been let loose to forage, crunched at the tough thorny foliage that surrounded an aquifer-fed waterhole. The ammunition was on the inside of the pile of crates, those around it protecting it from the fires they had lit as much to ward off animals as to keep them warm, for if they needed water, so did the wildlife.

Jardine and Vince, having set the task of cleaning and oiling in motion, had reconnoitred the waterhole, staying well away from the mud-churned area where animals fed: water buffalo, wild asses, antelopes, and sometimes, no doubt, elephants. Some of these being prey, at night there would be lions and hyenas, which worried Vince.

'These people we are with live here; if they are not frightened we shouldn't be either.'

'I'm more used to mice and the occasional rat, guv, and the biggest cat I've seen is a neighbour's moggie.'

'People pay good money for this. A night on the savannah and big beasts to hunt during the day.'

'That,' Vince replied emphatically, 'do not make them sensible.'

'Snakes are more of a problem, mind. Sometimes they like to snuggle up to a warm body at night.'

'Thanks for that, I'll sleep much easier now.'

'Then you won't mind being awake half the night, will you?'

'Not sentry duty, guv?'

'I'm only joking. *Ras* Kassa's men can do the sentinel job and we can sleep undisturbed.'

Tyler Alverson had purchased half a dozen oil lamps – he had given one to Jardine – and the remainder were illuminating his tent and that of Corrie Littleton, where they had set up flimsy metal and canvas beds. The Ethiopians were round the fire saying evening prayers again, they being a pious lot, and all around the sounds of the African night were emerging: deep-throated toads, barking creatures and laughing hyenas – seemingly magnified by the vastness of the landscape. When the first lion roared – there would always be a pride close to a waterhole – the Ethiopians looked engrossed.

'Have you ever killed a lion, Captain Jardine?' *Ras* Kassa enquired. 'I did as a young man, with nothing but a spear, which elevated me among my tribe. It is the aim of every one of our warriors to do the same.'

Jardine had a vision of the warriors and half his camel drovers rushing about trying to spear a lion. 'Tell them they will have to put it aside, we have more important things to worry about.'

It was not Jardine's place to set the pickets but he did look over the arrangements and was satisfied. He and Vince, by the limited light from their lantern, laid out their bedrolls on the weapon crates, wondering if in doing so they were being watched. Not that they had seen or heard anything, but people who were born into this kind of land could move about with an assurance denied to Europeans, and that applied as much to their drovers as anyone out in the bush-like landscape. If there were nomads about they might seek to sneak inside the ring of sentinels, perhaps just to steal what they could, perhaps to see what there was worth stealing.

'As long as they don't have knives, guv. It always worried me in Mesopotamia that some Arab would slit my throat in the night.'

'You still got that sod of a knife you bought in Brussels?'

'I have.'

'Well, sleep with it by your side.'

'What about you?'

Jardine raised his sub-machine gun. 'For anything that wakes me up.'

'Christ, I hope you're not upset by snoring.'

'Mind if I join you, gentlemen?'

Visually all they could see was a silhouette and the end of a glowing cigar; it was the deep voice and drawl that identified Tyler Alverson.

'This club is not exclusive,' Jardine replied. 'Anyone can join.'

'Good, I brought us a little nightcap.' As he moved into the circle of light the proffered square bottle of Johnnie Walker Scotch Whisky became visible, the golden liquid picking up the lantern glow. 'Your national drink, Jardine.'

Drinking whisky in the middle of Africa was not the same as at home – water that had been in a flask all day and warm did nothing for the purity of flavour – but it was welcome nonetheless.

'I was wondering,' the American said, after a quick toast, 'what you guys are planning to do after this little job is completed.'

'Goin' home, I hope,' Vince Castellano said.

'Not your style, Jardine, from what I recall. Strikes me you are the kinda guy that gets involved in a fracas like this one.' Met with a non-committal look on Jardine's face and a 'here we go again' look on that of Vince, Alverson continued, 'I have always found that having along a man who knows his way around a battlefield is a real help when it comes to understanding what is going on.'

'From what I have gathered you have been round a few yourself.'

'With nothing but a camera.'

'What are you going to do?'

'Get to where the action is – what else, it's my job? – and that means a trip to the Eritrean borderlands. I have promised Corrie Littleton that I will help her get to where her mother is doing her stuff, but after that I need to make sense of the campaign. I was wondering if a tour of the probable battle area might interest you?'

'It's a thought.'

'Guv!' Vince protested.

'Good,' the American said, unscrewing the bottle cap again.

Vince Castellano had no idea of how close he came to dying that night: with his well-hit boxer's nose and full of Alverson's whisky, he was noisy enough with his snores to frighten off any curious lions, which gave Cal Jardine a disturbed night.

# CHAPTER EIGHTEEN

General Emilio De Bono had procrastinated as much as possible before advancing into Ethiopia: a man his age could remember the Battle of Adowa. Indeed, as he was selfishly inclined to remind people, the news of that defeat and massacre of Italian forces had gone a long way to ruining his thirtieth birthday celebrations; the effect on his fellow countrymen – in essence a sense of deep national mourning – seemed to be of less moment.

Benito Mussolini was on his back, demanding action, seeming to forget his position as a senior member of the Fascist Grand Council, the body that had appointed him to his dictatorship. Bad weather, the lesser period of rains, had provided one excuse, but there had been many others: lack of equipment, the need to train his troops, the preparation of weapons for desert warfare, all designed to put off the moment when he must send his soldiers into a battle in which the outcome was far from certain.

The home front was, as usual, bellicose and full of confidence. It was all very well for those in Rome to insist he had such technical and numerical superiority he could not fail; in 1896 the government of Prime Minister Crespi – indeed the whole of Europe – had assumed something similar, quite putting aside how ferocious and numerous these Abyssinian warriors could be and how determined they were not to become a subject colony like the rest of Africa. It was Italian soldiers who had paid the blood price for the last exercise in imperial hubris; what he feared now was a repeat, with his head on the block as the man responsible for the catastrophe.

His comprehensive plan for a cautious advance, the careful taking of positions followed by lengthy consolidation – the building of good roads and fortification added to husbandry in the area of losses – had been swept aside as too feeble for a Fascist state that believed willpower alone was sufficient to overcome opposition. Mussolini and the Italian people wanted a war of tempo, a swift campaign, which would reflect the glory of a nation descended from the all-conquering Caesars.

In the end it was not the impatient telegrams from Il Duce that moved him but the look in the eyes of his inferior officers and aides, which had started off showing understanding for his problems, then moved to frustration at his reluctance to act decisively. Now he observed an air of pity that challenged the very notion of his being in any sense a proper military commander.

It was with a wrinkled and shaking hand that the seventy-year-old general, white of hair, weak of eye and bereft of resolve, signed the order that would send his troops across the Mareb river the next morning. Then he went to the new cathedral of Asmara to confess his sins and ask for God's help, which should be forthcoming in a noble endeavour designed to tame the savage and put an end to heretical barbarism.

Every night round the fires and food, on the way from the coast, Cal Jardine had listened to tales extolling the greatness of Ethiopia: of a two-thousand-year-old empire fluctuating in size but never overcome, of a race of warriors of such numbers and prowess that not even modern weapons could defeat them. The religion that sustained their belief in themselves came from Jerusalem and it was to that city they ascribed the purity of their faith, brought to ancient Aksum by Menelik, the son of the legendary Solomon and Sheba, bearing with him the Ark of the Covenant, the chest which contained the tablets given to Moses by God.

'So you see, Captain Jardine,' *Ras* Kassa Meghoum had intoned, 'we cannot be beaten, for we have God on our side.'

In response he regaled the *ras* and his American guests with the tactics necessary to fight a more powerful enemy, not only citing his own experiences in Iraq, but alluding to the campaign fought in Ireland by the late Michael Collins as a prime example of the effect of insurgent tactics. Naturally, the military opinions of Geoffrey Amherst had been well aired but they were wasted on *Ras* Kassa.

'Our Lion of Judah will not be in favour of what you have called a war of attrition, Captain Jardine. He will seek to win a great victory like Adowa and every Ethiopian warrior will support him.'

'Every one, *Ras*?'

That was not a subject they discussed much; if it came up at all, everyone had adhered to the fiction that Haile Selassie was totally secure on his imperial throne. Jardine threw a rock into that still pool and the ripples of his words soon became evident in the older man's features.

'There are those who think themselves better suited to the title he holds than he, that is true, but they are tiny in number. He commands the loyalty of most of the nobility and they will follow where he leads.'

'And his own vanity?'

'That is an inflexible word to employ, Captain.'

'*Ras* Kassa, I do not know the emperor but I have made some study of the history of your country and you have told me more. Tewodoros killed himself rather than let my fellow countryman, General Napier, take him prisoner. Menelik was advised to avoid battle and went against that advice; in short, his victory at Adowa was close to a fluke. Haile Selassie is heir to those two and many more and I worry he will seek to emulate one or the other. Nations have myths – God knows, the land of my birth has them in spades – and it is not just populations that are goaded by them. Rulers, too, are seduced.'

'You know this?' The *ras* had replied as though it was a fiction.

'I was told by a man with a very fine mind and a keen eye for history.'

'Odd – so few Europeans know anything about our history.'

'But he was right, was he not?'

'Menelik trusted in God, and God provided, for he was King of Kings and so is Haile Selassie.'

Jardine wondered how much *Ras* Kassa knew of the intentions of his emperor and the field commanders, suspecting that to be more than he had ever let on, for, when gently questioned by Tyler Alverson, he had shown great skill, once he had imparted what he wanted to tell, in being politely evasive not only about that, but his own future role in the conflict.

248

This caused Jardine no disquiet: such things were not really of any concern to an outsider, though it had frustrated the American who, with his journalistic eagerness, could not see he would be the last person to be told of any upcoming Ethiopian movements; he was wanted as a mouthpiece for one side, not as a neutral observer.

*Ras* Kassa was inclined to close any discussion with a statement like, 'You will see, Captain Jardine, and so will you, Mr Alverson, the Italians will regret what they do as they did forty years ago.'

The news of the invasion reached the caravan when they were a day's travel from the city of Harar, so high and hard a place to get to they had intended to bypass it. The information was delivered, as had been that of the Ancient Greek victory at Marathon, by a barefoot runner, who, having imparted the information to *Ras* Kassa, went on his way to tell the warriors of village after village, probably all the way to the eastern border.

Weary and filthy after ten days of travel, the caravan was rushed up steep gradients to the provincial capital, the well-being of the camels of less vital moment than that what they carried should be made available to the defending army. *Ras* Kassa then commandeered every motor lorry in Harar to get the weapons to the railhead of Dire Dawa.

That was the junction on the Djibouti-Addis Ababa rail line where control of the traffic passed from the French, who had constructed it, to the Ethiopians, who depended on it, so the guns could be quickly freighted to the northern front, where they could be of most use. Given it would take a very powerful man to get them on to the trains and through Addis, *Ras* Kassa would travel with them.

The whole country had been awaiting the invasion but it had not been totally mobilised to withstand it: the Imperial Ethiopian Army, when fully up to strength, was made up mostly of farmer-warriors. It was these the Italians would have to overcome, and they had been tilling their fields and tending their flocks before the call to arms came.

In essence, once the lorries were loaded and on their way, Cal Jardine's job was over and he had telegraphed Peter Lanchester in code to tell him so. Delivery had been made and it was time for the Ethiopian leader to depart, an invitation to join him and receive the personal thanks of the Lion of Judah for his efforts declined. He said his farewells outside the palace of the Provincial Governor, where the engine of *Ras* Meghoum's vehicle was already running.

As well as the load the lorry carried, some of the warriors who had escorted them from the coast were hanging onto the sides, their rifles slung over the shoulders; it was going to be a rough and slow journey but it was very noticeable how much trouble they had taken to wash their *shammas*: all were brilliantly white again, as they had been when first Jardine clapped eyes on them. As a uniform colour in a modern war it was stupid.

'Captain Jardine, I cannot thank you enough and neither can my country, and not only for the weapons you have brought. You have turned my personal following into a body of men who can stand comparison with the regular troops of the Imperial Army.'

Reacting to those words involved a degree of dissimulation: the *ras* was talking rubbish. The men of whom he spoke were enthusiastic, not competent, while he had learnt too few words in their language to turn them into anything else. He had been training them in batches, each morning while the camels were being loaded, though without the opportunity to do much more, like giving them lessons in the

250

most basic tenets of infantry tactics. If all were now comfortable with a modern pattern rifle, there had been no time to move on to the more potent weapons of machine guns and 50 mm mortars.

'You will leave Ethiopia?'

'Not yet,' Cal Jardine said, before adding, with a degree of dissimulation, 'I have undertaken to help Miss Littleton rescue her mother, whom we hope is in Gondar, but she fears might be in Aksum.'

'She will be in grave danger now the Italians have begun to invade, if she is there. I hope you do not have to employ the weapons which you have taken.'

'So do I, *Ras*,' Jardine replied, his hand running over the stock of his M32. Vince had his too, as well as enough ammunition for a decent engagement, and they still had their pistols. 'Though I think the Italians would be very unwise to harm an elderly American matron.'

'If they do, they will blame us and say it was done by the savages. The pity is, many will believe them.'

'Would you have time to issue me with a safe conduct, sir, a message to the army commanders in the north to say I am a friend of your nation?'

'That is a small request, Captain Jardine. Wait here.'

The *ras* re-entered the governor's palace and was gone for some ten minutes, while all the while the lorry driver wasted precious fuel. Tempted to order him to switch off, Cal Jardine had to stop himself: it was not his place to give commands to these men. The *ras* reappeared with the requested *laissez passer*, signed by him, then embossed with a seal, and handed it over.

'I have requested in the name of the emperor that you be given all assistance and that you are allowed to go where you wish. I have also added that you are a military man whose advice might be of use should you find yourself in an area of conflict.'

'Thank you, sir.'

The final handshake was firm, the cloud of dust as the lorry drove off thick and choking, but not enough to stop the keening war cries of the Shewan warriors. They had barely departed when the next sound emerged, a klaxon-like braying of a car horn, designed to clear the crowded roadway.

'Bloody Ada, a Roller!' cried Vince.

The familiar stainless steel grille, topped with the eagle, the huge headlamps at either side, emerged from a throng of locals to pull up beside them. Behind the wheel was Tyler Alverson, waving over the windscreen of a silver Rolls-Royce Phantom Coupé. Corrie Littleton was in the passenger seat and there was a great deal of luggage strapped to the rear.

'Where in the name of sweet Jesus did you get this?' Jardine demanded.

'A French coffee dealer had it,' Alverson replied with a lopsided grin. 'Thinks business will not be so good right now, so was keen to cash in, especially since Kassa commandeered his lorry, and every donkey in Harar is on the way to war, which leaves him no way of getting his coffee to the railhead even if it is harvested. My guess is he's planning to skeddadle to Djibouti till he sees which way the wind blows.'

'You bought it?'

'With dollars, which speak louder to a Frenchman than thalers, Jardine. You coming?'

'Vince?'

'I ain't never been in a Roller, guv, but I suppose you have.'

'Weddings and funerals, Vince, that's all.'

'Both to be avoided,' said Corrie Littleton.

'Don't build up your hopes of the former,' Jardine replied, as he slung his kitbag into the back seat, Vince doing the same, both piled on top of the luggage already loaded. 'Now, are you going to get out so Vince and I can get in?'

Both seated in the back, albeit cramped, it was Vince who called out to Tyler Alverson in a parody of a cut-glass upper-class accent that sounded very like Peter Lanchester. 'Chop-chop, James, let's get a move on, there's a good chap.'

The route they needed to take led through the modern town of Dire Dawa, up into the highlands and Addis Ababa, but that was a place Tyler Alverson wanted to slip through on the very good grounds that, identified as a reporter, he could be held back from the front – he had no idea if that sanction was still in place – so it was Jardine who drove when they approached the capital, Vince in the passenger seat with his weapon prominent to keep trouble at bay, while the two Americans slunk down in the rear.

At night they set up tents and slept by the roadside, up with the lark and back on their way. The roads were crowded – thousands of the men and women of Ethiopia moving to repel the invaders – growing even more dense as more and more farmer-warriors and their wives and daughters joined the throng on the highway that led from Addis, down past Lake Tana, to the lines on the northern front.

The quartet was now part of a staggering mass movement of human bodies and animals, and not just donkeys. Oxen, either herded or pulling laden carts, mingled with sheep and goats, while spearmen dressed in that loose, white and ubiquitous cloak of the Ethiopian peasant bore, along with their weapons, baskets containing live fowl; their women carried water pots and bales of fodder high on their heads.

This was an army that carried its supplies on its back and they were cheerful, waving as they responded to the klaxon of the Rolls-Royce, and moving aside to let them through in what was, of necessity, a slow progress, even if the road was downhill the whole way. If he could not understand what was being said, Cal Jardine knew they were looking forward to the fight, but, given there were so few guns, it was the lack of weaponry that bothered him.

'Spears, bows and arrows, Vince! I don't know whether to be impressed or depressed.' Jardine said this as yet another man close by the running board jabbed his spear in the air and treated the farangs to a stream of incomprehensible but happy anticipation. 'How many of these poor sods will see their fields again?'

'You tried to tell them, guv,' Vince replied. 'Don't go getting upset because they won't listen.'

It took the best part of three days to get to Gondar, where they heard De Bono's forces had occupied the battlefield site of Adowa, though not by any kind of victory: the pullback from the border had let the Italians come on unopposed. The one person less comforted, once she found her mother was not in Gondar, was Corrie Littleton, something quickly established given the lady was well known.

She had spent much time in the Gondar forts and talking to local scholars but she had gone on to Aksum precisely because it was the next place the invaders would try to take, and she apparently wanted to make sure they respected the historical sites containing obelisks and ancient stelae, as well as any ancient documents.

Corrie Littleton did not have to say that was typical of her mother: the impression created by anyone who had met her was of a formidable matron who seemed to have no fear of taking on the entire invading army. There was no doubt she was in some danger, that made worse when it emerged the commander of the army of Tigray, *Ras* Seyoum, the man tasked with repelling De Bono, had no intention of defending the ancient capital city either.

'We can't just go charging up to the front lines without permission, quite apart from the fact that it's bloody dangerous.'

If the tiled interior of the building in which they were accommodated, the only decent hotel in Gondar, was cool, she was not. 'To hell with you, Jardine, I'll get Tyler to let me take the car and I'll go on my own.'

'I said permission, idiot, which means you ask.'

'Did my mother bother with that?'

'Do be quiet,' Jardine sighed, waving the pass from *Ras* Kassa, 'while I go and be nice to the chaps at the local army headquarters.'

Her face lost its angry glare. 'Sorry, Jardine, I'm worried.'

'Wish me luck.'

'That, and thanks.'

The local commander was a captain in a regular part of the Imperial Army, occupying a large house outside the walls of the old medieval city. The guards in their green uniforms were smart and punctilious in giving him a salute, while inside Jardine recognised that this was a building that could be quickly turned into an operational military HQ. There were numerous phones, unusual in this part of the world, desks and wall maps, which he spent some time studying while waiting to be seen. Naturally they were bereft of any military dispositions.

The captain had 'staff' written all over him; he reminded Cal Jardine of the kind of nattily dressed sods who had come up from Brigade HQ in 1918 to purse their lips at the lack of progress, before returning from the dirty trenches to some comfortable château to eat and drink of the best France had to offer. This captain was handsome, smooth, his uniform pressed and creased in all the right places, and that was allied to an air of superiority that might have hinted at high birth in a force led by aristocratic commanders; he also, fortunately, spoke good French.

When he saw who had written and signed the pass Jardine produced, his arrogance evaporated. He became positively fawning and also very forthcoming about the Italian positions, according to what intelligence he possessed, so powerful was *Ras* Kassa Meghoum's name. De Bono was advancing with caution, and some of his equipment, as well as the less professional Arditi units, were causing concern in what was harsh terrain, so he had halted to consolidate; they could not be expected in Aksum for several days.

He was also not an idiot: he had been educated at the French School in Addis, hence his facility with the language, and he had learnt more than that. Before he issued written instructions to the guard posts on the road south to let Jardine and his companions pass, he also demanded, and got, the request to proceed in writing, so that he could not be held responsible for any unfortunate outcomes. Emerging to meet Vince, Jardine was smiling.

'Don't go thinking these chaps are all primitive, Vince. The bloke I've just been with is as sharp as a tack. Now let's find Alverson, because he will most definitely want to come too.'

That proved quite a task and involved a search of the city and lots of sign language as they sought to describe an American in a pale-linen suit and a big straw hat, quite possibly chomping on a cigar. They were in receipt of many pointed directions, which either by omission or commission led nowhere. Eventually they found him by the walls of the dome-turreted castle of Fasiledes, deep in conversation with a disreputable-looking fellow who reminded Jardine of the treacherous Xasan of Zeila. Seeing them approach, Alverson waved to them to stay back and wait. It was Vince who spotted and pointed out that money was being exchanged.

'What is he up to, guv?'

'Maybe he'll tell us,' Jardine replied, as Alverson detached himself and came to join them.

'Now, that is one creepy bastard.'

'So why are you doing business with him?'

'To get my story out, Jardine, that's why. No point in getting the low-down if I can't tell the world. That sonofabitch is my way out with the news, and boy, did it take time to find him.'

Mutual explanations were exchanged as they made their way back to the hotel. It seemed Alverson's sonofabitch was either a smuggler or maybe even a slaver. Whatever, he had a route over the Sudanese border by which the American could send out his reports to be telegraphed back to the US, thus avoiding the local censors.

'All those lushes in Addis will get is what the Ethiopians want to tell them. My aim is to get the truth out and be ahead of the game.' Then he smiled and rubbed his finger and thumb together. 'No matter where you go in the world, gentlemen, there are people who will do what you want for a little grease, or in his case, Austrian thalers.'

'You trust him? He looked like a real crook to me.'

'I'm no patsy, brother. I have paid him some upfront money, but he only gets the real dough by return when he has sent in my copy.

And as for him being a crook, don't tell me you've never done a deal with a guy like that.'

'It's possible.'

'Definite, more like,' Vince hooted.

Cal Jardine smiled. 'You ever been to Hamburg, Alverson?'

'Nope.'

'Maybe I'll tell you a story sometime, a good one. Now let's stock up on some supplies, a full tank of juice, and get going before Corrie Littleton blows a gasket.'


At checkpoint after checkpoint on the rough road their papers were examined and, passed through each time, they drove on into the gathering gloom, until the great headlamps of the Rolls were all they had to light up a road still thronged with fighters; moving in the dark, this close to an enemy with air power, was sensible.

They dropped in numbers, until eventually the road was deserted, so they knew they must be passing through the front lines of the Ethiopian army; somewhere out in the darkness on either side were thousands upon thousands of silent warriors, and ahead of them, in the distance, a potent and well-equipped enemy.

# CHAPTER NINETEEN

Entering a place like Aksum in darkness was not a good idea, regardless of what Jardine had been told about the slow Italian advance. They spent the last hours of darkness near a military checkpoint, and it was only when daylight came that they saw they had stopped beside the ruins of what looked to have been an extensive palace. Interested as Corrie Littleton was – it was likely to be the one-time palace of the Queen of Sheba – ruins could wait; Jardine had his field glasses out, looking over the fertile fields and low hills of the plateau for signs of the Italians, and he was just about to pronounce it safe when they heard the drone of an aircraft overhead.

'Everyone away from the car,' he yelled. 'Now!'

He was cursing himself as he ran: the checkpoint was heavily camouflaged and such an obvious vehicle as the silver Rolls-Royce should have been hidden from view under one of the roadside trees;

he was losing his touch and that was underlined when the aircraft, a biplane, banked and came in low to have a look, showing on its tail the green, yellow and red colours of the Ethiopian air force. Having made one pass, it executed a tight turn to have another.

'Jesus Christ, a Potez 25,' Alverson pronounced. 'How many of those fellas have we seen, Jardine?'

He had a point: the Potez 25 was one of those two-seater biplanes, highly manoeuvrable and infinitely adaptable, that tended to appear in a lot of conflict locations; Jardine had seen them in their homeland of France, in Paraguay, and Alverson admitted he had come across them in China. The Potez 25 was a real workhorse used for everything: light bombing, as a nippy fighter, as well as a good reconnaissance plane, though, a product of the twenties, it was sadly out of date now.

The aircraft was coming in very low and it was only the dying note of the engine that indicated it was going to land. The party on the ground watched as the wings swayed slightly, the Potez losing airspeed till its wheels touched down on the surface of the road, billowing dust mixing with a trace of smoke as the brakes were applied, the engine dropping down to a steady throb as it taxied close to them, then no more than the whisper of a dying propeller as the power was switched off.

The pilot clambered out onto the wing, then jumped to the ground, whipping off his leather flying helmet as he walked towards them to reveal a mass of blond curls over an absurdly handsome face, graced with a wide smile. His eyes, which turned out to be green close to, flicked over the quartet but settled immediately on Corrie Littleton, and there was no doubting the nature of the look he was giving her, or that those eyes had time to take in her left hand in order to know what to say.

'Bonjour, mademoiselle.'

The pilot effectively cut the three men out of the exchange, then added to their exclusion by taking Corrie's hand and lifting it to his lips, without, Jardine noticed, much in the way of resistance.

'Hi,' she replied feebly, while his lips were still connected to her flesh. 'Nice to meet you.'

'Ah, you are American,' he cried, with that seductive and delicious accent the French were able to give to the English language.

'I sure am,' Corrie said, her own voice, for all it had that habitual crack, carrying no hint of reproach at his obvious gallantry; her stance of militant womanhood seemed to have been put in abeyance. 'Corrine Littleton is the name.'

'An unusual and attractive name it is too.' The pilot, having delivered that over-egged compliment, finally deigned to acknowledge she was not alone. 'And your *amis* are also American?'

'No bloody fear,' said Vince, which got him a look from Alverson, who was quick to reply.

'I am. Tyler Alverson,' he said, holding out his hand.

'If he kisses the back of that, I'm leaving,' Vince added, which got him another hard look.

'You I would suspect to be English by your voice, but such dark skin is—'

Unaware that he was on the edge of an insult, and quite possibly a belt on the nose, for Vince was close to looking like a native now, the pilot was saved by Jardine interrupting and introducing both himself and Vince, explaining that his friend was half-Italian, that information responded to with a raised eyebrow.

'The right half,' Vince snarled. 'You know, the one on your side.'

'And you are?' Jardine enquired.

'Count Henri de Billancourt, monsieur, serving in the air force of His Imperial Majesty, Haile Selassie.'

'Count Henri?' asked Corrie Littleton, in a voice that was not only high but had a trace of simper.

'Not a very large air force,' Jardine interjected, not quite knowing why he felt the need to deflate the man's air of self-importance. 'And, sadly, with out-of-date equipment.'

De Billancourt did not quite bristle, but he let Jardine know he was aware of the diminishing nature of the comment. 'Monsieur, we make up in *élan* what we lack in numbers and modernity.'

'I'm sure you do,' Alverson said, favouring Jardine with an annoying grin. 'Can I ask what you are doing here?'

'Why, I am looking out for the enemy, but when I see such a car on the roadside it tickles my curiosity, so I must come and look.'

'You speak very good English, Count,' said Corrie Littleton, who then added, in a tone of faux fluster, 'Do I call you "Count", or what?'

'Mademoiselle,' the pilot said, in a voice too oily for all three of her companions, who were forced to look away, 'you must call me Henri.'

'How close are the Italians to Aksum?' asked Jardine, in a voice a bit too sharp, and one that got him a narrow-eyed look from those green eyes.

'Only, my mother is there, we think, and I fear for her safety,' explained Corrie Littleton.

'Then perhaps, mademoiselle, you would care to come with me and have a look, to see where those Italian sons-of-whores are.'

'Am I allowed to clock him one, guv?'

'No, Vince,' Jardine replied, aware that what had been said was too colloquial for even this French aristocrat to understand. 'It might be of more use if I come with you, monsieur?'

'*Pourqoi?*' he demanded.

Tempted to reply in French, Jardine stopped himself, either through pique or precaution, he was unsure. The only certainty was that his intervention was not appreciated by Corrie Littleton.

'I am an ex-soldier, Count Henri, and I think I would make a better observer than Miss Littleton. In fact, I am surprised you are flying alone.'

'Airspeed, monsieur, the Italian Fiats are faster than the Potez. However . . .' de Billancourt shrugged. 'I hope you can manage a pair of Vickers machine guns.'

'The captain can,' snapped Vince, 'and better than you think, Froggie.'

After a nod at the rank, the green eyes turned slowly to Vince, who was sure the man's nostrils flared. 'Perhaps you will be good enough to spin the propeller for me?'

For all the courtesy of the way that sounded, this Frenchman was telling Vince he could spot a member of the other ranks. Vince's fists tightened, his shoulders stiffened and his feet moved for the balance needed to deliver a punch.

'If you don't mind, Vince,' Cal Jardine said.

'For you, guv,' Vince replied, slowly relaxing.

Count Henri was already on his way back to his plane. Jardine observed the way he expertly back-jumped onto the lower wing before spinning round and up like a ballet dancer to make his cockpit in one smooth manoeuvre. Jardine needed a hand up from Vince, the rear cockpit not being accessible from the wing, and as he settled in to the cramped space, a leather helmet and a pair of gloves were flicked back into his lap. By the time he had strapped himself in, Vince was on the propeller, and at a signal from de Billancourt he swung hard as the Frenchman pressed the ignition, the engine firing immediately and the exhaust pipes emitting smelly clouds of black smoke and a strong smell of kerosene.

Swinging round into the wind, the engine was gunned and the Potez picked up speed, eventually slipping into the air with a degree of grace that told Jardine whatever else this snooty French bastard might be he was a good pilot. Below, thanks to the recent rains, the landscape was generally green, near-black where the soil had been tilled, broken up by high, conical mounds of pale-brown hills.

Within minutes they were over the town of Aksum, able to see the outlines of the ancient ruins of castles, as well as the obelisks that dotted the landscape. More importantly, for all the pointing fingers, there was no gunfire: the place was not yet taken. De Billancourt continued north-east, gaining altitude, no doubt seeking both safety and the ability to see into the distance, heading for Adowa and the Italian positions.

His hand pointing down was not necessary: Jardine could see clearly the evidence of the enemy positions, most tellingly that they were static, which was odd given that there was no force opposing them. The Italians should be moving, using their mechanised forces to punch into and through any resistance, never mind the odd broken-down vehicle or footsore Blackshirt.

Jardine wondered what Geoffrey Amherst would say if he could see this. Many times in his company he had heard the older man expound his theories on how the next war should be fought: fast-moving tanks supported by trucked infantry, with aircraft acting as flying artillery to soften up resistance, which if it held its ground, should be bypassed and left, as he said, 'to wither on the vine'.

He could hear his voice in his head and imagine the table pounding that accompanied his damnation of the military boneheads of his home country who would not listen to him, while his writings were openly admired by people he called 'the nation's enemies'; he had never been invited to lecture at Sandhurst – most of his invitations to do that came from Hitler's Germany.

De Billancourt was waving his hand; if he was shouting, Jardine could not hear it, but he got the message by the way the Frenchman was casting his eyes around the sky, telling him to look out for enemy fighters, this as he banked to fly along the front lines of the army below, until they were over what looked like a motor park by a series of very large tents. Winking shots showed, even in the sunlight, as ground fire came in their direction, with de Billancourt jinking to put off the gunners, as puffs of black smoke burst all around them.

Jardine had to ignore the anti-aircraft fire: he was looking around the sky above, for, if he was not a pilot, he knew, having drunk with many ex-members of the Royal Flying Corps, which had morphed into the RAF, that the most dangerous type of air attacks came from above, out of the sun.

It was a flash of reflected sunlight that fixed his gaze, a glint as the golden light bounced off an aeroplane windscreen perhaps. He tapped de Billancourt's shoulder and pointed up in the general direction, receiving a nod in return, and once he was sure the Frenchman understood, he spun round to kneel on his seat rather than sit, using a second strap to secure himself in. The twin Vickers were just a double version of a machine gun he had fired many times before, and he checked the belt feed was clear to run before he cocked both. Only then did he look out for an enemy.

The bulky, box-like Fiat CR32 was plain to see now as it flew overhead, seeking to get sun side of the Potez so that he could attack with that glaring orb behind him. In his favour the Italian had speed and two forward-firing machine guns to the Potez's one, but he did not have the swivelling Vickers, which narrowed his secure angles of attack; head-on would be best for safety unless he set out to get the rear gunner first and neutralised him.

That was a sobering thought, but when Vince had reacted to the question about Jardine's ability with the Vickers, he was not just talking about that weapon: the cockney-Italian had seen his old CO shoot everything from objects and animals, including running human beings, and at long range. The only thing unfamiliar on these weapons was the ranging sight, different from those used on the ground.

He had shot game in Scotland as a youth and a man – stags, grouse and pheasants – so the need for deflection aiming was second nature, the requirement to put your bullets where the target was going to be, rather than where it was. Talking to those RFC flyers he also knew that in aerial combat the task was made more difficult, given the lack of any fixed object off which to measure the position and distance to your target.

De Billancourt had not turned for home – he was still flying into the sun – which did surprise his passenger, who had expected, up against a faster and better-armed plane, as well as anti-aircraft guns, he would seek to draw him into a position of potential danger by flying for the Ethiopian lines and losing altitude.

If the Italian pilot followed him down he would be at a greater risk of concentrated ground fire, and massed rifles could be deadly. Jardine had seen aircraft brought down by that in 1918 – his own side and the Germans'. The thought came to his mind that this Frenchman wanted to show off, a potentially suicidal way to behave.

There was no point in worrying: he could not fly the plane, so he just had to rely on the man who was doing so, even if he thought he disliked him; it was another one of those situations where the acceptance of risk went with the territory. The anti-aircraft fire ceased, which meant they were content to leave it to their flyer to see off this pest, and it would not be a good idea to keep blazing away in case they downed their own aircraft.

Glancing over his shoulder he saw that de Billancourt was pointing forward with a flat hand, which he dipped sharply under his other hand – he must have had the joystick clamped between his knees – an act he repeated, leaving his passenger to hope he understood. Then the plane began to jink seriously, left, right, up and down, which told Jardine action was imminent.

Getting as low as he could, Jardine pulled the machine gun handles down so the Vickers barrels were aiming as high as possible, the good thing about that being his own head was lowered, lessening the risk of him being hit. He had to assume the Italian had got to where he wanted to be and then banked to reverse his course and engage; his assumption proved right as bullets began to crack over his head, loud enough to overcome both engine noise and wind.

He felt the judder of the Potez as de Billancourt responded, then the sudden dip as the Frenchman put the plane into a dive, Jardine pulling both his triggers as soon as that happened. The camouflaged body of the Fiat was a huge blur as it shot past at a fractionally higher altitude that seemed very close to his head, and the notion that his man had risked a head-on collision was a fleeting but useless concern. All he was concentrating on now was keeping his Vickers firing as he raised himself to seek to stay on target, sure that bits were flying off the enemy aircraft.

De Billancourt banked as soon as he ceased firing and executed a tight turn to come round on the Italian's tail, which was nothing short of madness. Looking over his shoulder now, Jardine saw the Fiat beginning to climb, and at a rate he suspected the Potez could not match.

What was this bloody idiot of a Frenchman about? The pitch of the engine was now a scream as the plane sought altitude, and a craning Jardine could see the Fiat fighter plane had what he wanted, sufficient height and distance, for he was now banking to come in on a second attack.

As soon as he began to dive, de Billancourt spun his plane to drop like a stone in what turned out to be a race towards ground level. Not only was the Fiat faster, it was heavier, which increased the speed at which it could close. Jardine now saw before him, and rapidly closing, the wisp of the spinning propeller, with the certain knowledge that two machine guns were timed to fire right through the blades, only then realising how cold were the hands holding the handles of the Vickers, almost too cold to function, even in gloves.

Stiff as the fingers were, he knew he had to wait until the Italian opened fire, which he would not do until he was in range, an option open to him but not to a rear machine gunner unfamiliar with the sights, who could only guess by the size of the object he was aiming at. If he fired off too soon it would only waste precious ammo; leave it too late and it was what the Americans called a 'turkey shoot', an almost unmissable target. The first wink came a split second before the gunfire hit the side of his cockpit, which proved the Frenchman was no coward, for he held his course.

The diving, attacking plane now looked like a large bee right before his eyes, the cowls covering its landing wheels in plain sight. Jardine opened up, moving his aim fractionally right, left, up and down to cover as much sky as possible inside a very small arc, and it had the desired effect: it takes a very brave man, or even a fool, to fly into a hail of bullets. He had no idea if he struck home, for de Billancourt hauled on his joystick and took the Potez, which if it was slower was more manoeuvrable, out of the line of fire, and the Italian shot by.

What happened then made Jardine thank the Lord he was strapped in: the blood rushed to his head as de Billancourt executed a tight loop the loop in what felt like a sixpence of airspace. Unbeknown to his passenger, the Frenchman had calculated that with a target no longer in his sights, the enemy plane would rapidly slow its own speed to turn. He was now on its tail again before the heavier Fiat could make that turn; closing significantly, he opened up again with his single forward-firing machine gun.

It wasn't deadly, but it was enough to remove great patches of the covering on the Italian's airframe, bits that flew past Jardine, still facing backwards. Then he was in amongst a trail of smoke, wondering to whom it belonged, the answer coming as the Fiat CR32 came into view with a black trail coming from its fuselage as it headed earthwards.

De Billancourt spun to follow, but the Italian was doing the sensible thing, which Jardine had expected from the Frenchman, heading for his own lines and supporting ground fire; thankfully this daredevil pilot was too shrewd to follow and he banked gently to head south.

The victory roll was just showing off.


The trio and the Rolls had not moved, and it took Jardine a little while to realise how small an amount of time had passed since they had taken off – under twenty minutes by his watch. Taxiing to the same spot as before, the damage to the aircraft was obvious enough to have Vince rushing forward, Tyler Alverson putting his hands to his cheeks and Corrie Littleton hers to her mouth, an act which she reversed when Henri de Billancourt whipped off his helmet and grinned at her with teeth of stunning perfection.

Wondering why he was so stiff – that is, till he realised he was still cold – Cal Jardine clambered out of the cockpit just in time to see the Frenchman slobbering over the female hand again. In perfect idiomatic French, albeit with a faint trace of a Marseilles accent, Callum Jardine loudly informed him that he thought he was a glory-seeking idiot. The response was a look of surprise and amusement, so he reverted to English in order that his companions could understand.

'You're mad to take on an enemy who's got a superior plane.'

'Ah, but *mon ami*, he is not the superior pilot, as you witnessed.'

'That was luck!'

The wagging single digit was infuriating, but not as much as the admonishing schoolmasterly voice. '*Non!* Not luck, but skill. The best man won, as you say in English, and what sort of man would I be to turn down a challenge to a dogfight, eh, and from a miserable Italian?'

'They can kill too,' insisted Vince. 'Even Frenchmen.'

'To be afraid to die, not Henri de Billancourt, monsieur! Henri de Billancourt is not afraid to die. To fear death is a nonsense; to die nobly and in single combat, a gift.'

'While you are so nobly dying, would you mind making sure you are alone?'

'If you were full of fear, I ask forgiveness. I thought you were a soldier.'

'He's full of anger, mate!' Vince spat, handing Jardine his sub-machine gun. 'You might want to use this, guv.'

'Would somebody mind telling me what the hell is going on?' demanded Tyler Alverson.

'I will,' Jardine barked, and he did, aware as he related what he knew, that the admiration in the eyes of Corrie Littleton was increasing, not diminishing, which he found even more annoying, summed up in the words she used.

'How gallant you are.'

'Mademoiselle will not mind if I dedicate my victory to your beauty?'

'I think I'm going to be sick,' Vince croaked.

'*Our* victory,' Jardine snapped.

'Of course,' the count replied with an elegant half-bow. 'I must acknowledge you were a most able associate.'

Alverson laughed, a shoulder-shaking affair. 'I've never heard anyone make that sound like the shoeshine boy before.'

When he took off again, Corrie Littleton watched him go until the Potez was so small it was like a fly on a window, her face when she turned round having on it a beatific look.

'What a guy.'

'What an arsehole,' Jardine spat. 'Now, if you are ready, we can go find your bloody mother.'

'Who rattled his cage?' she demanded of Tyler Alverson.

'You did, honey.'

# CHAPTER TWENTY

Aksum was far from the deserted town Jardine had expected: not only was it still crowded but there was an open-air market in progress, as bustling as if it was peacetime, if you accepted the absence of any younger men: they were all with the army. Female stallholders selling cloth mingled with those who, squatting on the dusty ground, vended from sacks and baskets containing everything a fertile land could produce: flour, spices, peppers, great tubs of garlic, as well as penned livestock and creel-like baskets full of flapping fowl.

'Has anybody told them an army is coming this way?' Vince asked.

'They're stoical, these Ethiopians.'

'Is that a disease, guv?'

'Oddly, Vince, it could be called one.' Jardine was recalling all those tales told by *Ras* Kassa, as well as his unshakeable attitude – one, even if he could not understand the language, that seemed common to the whole nation. 'They are so convinced of their pre-eminence as a civilisation that they cannot imagine being subdued.'

'You mean like the English?' Alverson joked from the driving seat.

'The Scots are best when it comes to that. Now, stop the car so I can ask if there is somewhere to stay.'

'We staying, Jardine?'

'No, but if the lady you call Ma Littleton—'

The interruption from the lady's daughter was swift. 'Don't let her hear you say that, either of you, or she'll kill you.'

'What I was going to say is there can't be too many places for a farang woman to lay her head round here, so your mother is going to be in one of them.'

When the Rolls stopped, curious children surrounded them. They touched the body with a sort of reverence and sent warm smiles in the direction of the occupants. Almost all of them were either beautiful or handsome with gorgeous big eyes and the soft, unblemished skin of their years, which led Jardine to a reflection he had harboured before: part of the Ethiopian sense of themselves as a nation was in that attractiveness of their features and their grace of movement.

Of course, there were ugly people, old crones and bent, aged men, but there had been in those warriors they had passed not only a physical attraction, but a look in the eye that bespoke of folk at harmony with their life and surroundings; in short, though there were bound to be people with whom he could not bond, he definitely liked the Ethiopians in the mass.

In the same manner his enquiries were treated with respect, the way he tilted his head and put his hands to one side as if sleeping understood, that followed by a mime of eating, producing a flood of instructions which were initially confusing, given there was a noisy competition to assist. Eventually, one tall fellow, of fighting age but unfortunately with very swollen lower legs and feet, used his staff to draw a sort of map in the dust, and after a few pointed hand gestures from Jardine he had a good idea he knew where to go.

It was not a hotel but a sort of inn, a two-storey mud-brick building with whitened walls, dark inside, cool, and run by one of the few fat men any of them had seen in this country of lean folk: a jolly round fellow who did not speak a word of any language they knew. But he understood almost immediately who they were looking for and she was indeed accommodated in his establishment.

When they finally came face-to-face with Mother Littleton his gestures indicating something square made sense, for she was indeed formidable and not in the least bit rangy like her daughter. She was big-boned, especially in the shoulders, tall, and added to that she had a booming voice and a seeming lack of any maternal instinct, not that there was much of a filial nature in the response.

'What in the name of the devil incarnate are you doing here, Corrine?'

'No "hello" Mother? No saying "thank you" to me for coming to find and rescue you? No kiss on the cheek?'

'Fiddlesticks. I do not need you to rescue me.'

'Is that so?' her daughter croaked. 'Like there is not over half a million Italian soldiers headed your way?'

'Happy families, guv,' whispered Vince. 'Just like home.'

'And just who are you?' Ma demanded, giving Vince a withering look.

'Just passing, lady.'

'Then pass and be on your way.'

'Just a moment, madam,' Jardine said. 'Your daughter is right, and I do not know if you are aware of it, but what she says about the Italian army is true.'

'Of course I know it's true. Why do you think I am here waiting for them to arrive?'

'You're *waiting* for them?' Corrie Littleton spat. 'In God's name, why?'

'If you had any sense, child, you would not ask.'

'It does not occur to you that Dad is worried for you.'

That got a loud, dismissive sniff. 'So worried he sent you and did not come himself.'

'You are supposed to be researching in Gondar.'

'I have done that and sent masses of stuff home, but where I choose to go and what I choose to do are none of your concern.'

'Yes it damn well is, Mother!'

'Stop!' None of them had ever heard Alverson shout, but he did so now and it had the desired effect. 'Mrs Littleton, would you mind explaining what you have just said?'

'And who are you, sir?'

'He's a reporter, Mother.'

The eyes showed a mixture of anger and surprise as they fixed on her daughter. 'And you mix with such people. How could you?'

'Whadaya mean, "such people"?'

'What he wants to know,' Jardine interjected softly, 'indeed, so do we all, is why you are waiting for the Italians.'

It was hard to know what produced a full and polite response; perhaps it was that, to a Bostonian matron of advanced years, his accent, English gentleman with a hint of a Scottish burr, was more acceptable.

'I am hoping to get to see the Ark of the Covenant.'

'Well, I'm none the wiser,' said a perplexed Vince Castellano.

His cockney accent produced a diametrically opposite reaction. 'That would quite possibly be, fellow, because you are likely to be an ignoramus.'

'Nicest thing anyone's said to me all day, luv.'

'It would help if you told us, Mrs Littleton,' said Jardine. 'We have, after all, come some way to find you.'

'Not at my bidding.'

'Just tell us, Mother,' Corrie Littleton sighed.

'Oh, very well, then,' she responded, her voice then taking on a preachy tone. 'The Ark is reputed to have been brought here by the son of Solomon and Sheba. If it exists at all, and it might be no more than a fable, it is housed here in Aksum, in a special chapel in the Church of St Mary of Zion.'

'So go visit.'

That got her daughter a withering look. 'You cannot! It is guarded by one monk, who is the only man allowed to enter the chapel where it is kept. Before he dies he names a successor, so that line of damned monks are the only folk who know if it is a myth or a fact, and you can ask till you're blue and offer a fortune, but it won't get you inside; and that means, as far as I can gather, not even the damned emperor.'

'That still does not explain why you are waiting for the Italians,' insisted Alverson.

The arch look he got equated him to something untoward on the sole of her shoe, but she did answer, if not with much regard. 'You, too, must be an idiot. The Italians will not be constrained by Ethiopian tradition, will they?'

276

'You think,' Corrie Littleton said softly, 'they will let you have a little look-see?'

'Thank God someone has got some brains round here.'

'And what if they refuse?' Jardine asked.

The reply, 'They would not dare, I am an American', was priceless.

'Lady,' Vince said, 'strikes me you don't know much about the Italians.'

'And I suppose,' she replied, with contemptuous doubt, 'you are going to tell me you do.'

'When it comes to anythin' religious, they are as superstitious as anythin' going.'

'Can't you speak in plain English, man?'

Jardine had never seen Vince so patient, but then, she was a woman of some years, not a bloke, whom he would likely have floored. 'They won't go into that chapel, an' nor will they let anyone else, 'cause they is deeply religious themselves and likely frightened of being struck down dead.'

'Poppycock!'

'Tell her your name and where you were born, Vince.'

'Name's Castellano, lady, an' I was born in a place called Montesarchio, near to Capua, which is where most of my family still lives.'

'Oh!'

'So you see, Mrs Littleton, Vince knows of what he speaks.'

'They won't touch the door of that chapel, lady, in case it sends them straight to hell.'

'You believe that?'

'Not me, lady, them. Personally I think it's all bollocks, if you'll pardon my French.'

'That's not French, is it?'

'Let's say it's Italian, shall we?' Jardine proposed, with a grin.

'Quite apart,' Alverson added, 'of the effect such a sacrilegious act would have on the folk they want to rule.'

'The locals would riot,' Jardine added, 'which is the last thing a fighting army wants at its back.'

'I'm sure,' she replied, though with the first hint of uncertainty, 'they will understand my position.'

'They might,' Alverson said, with some relish, 'but they might also shoot you as a spy.'

Speaking before she could react, Cal Jardine suggested she should depart with them.

'He's right, Mother,' her daughter said.

'Are you mad?' came the response, in a way that made Jardine wonder if she was that. 'Can you imagine what I will have achieved if I can see the Ark and photograph it?'

'This is not another attempt to outshine Daddy, is it?' In order to explain, she included the others. 'He's quite a famous academic.'

'To hell with your father.' Mother Littleton's eyes had taken on a look of boundless vision. 'I'll be world-famous, Corrine, a person of consequence, invited to lecture at the great halls of learning, a guest at the White House—'

'Or,' Alverson interrupted, 'a corpse in an unmarked grave.'

'Corrie,' Jardine said, using her Christian name for the first time, which got a raised eyebrow from mater.

'Please do not use that diminutive, young man, my daughter's name is Corrine.'

'Tyler and I, along with Vince, have a little nosing around to do, but I think we will be getting out of here very soon, because if what

I saw from the air this morning decides to move, the Italian army will be here in hours, there is nothing to stop them. I think it would be sensible to depart tomorrow, certainly the next day; so, Miss Littleton, that is how much time you have to persuade your mother to join us.'

'She'll be wasting her breath.'

'Let us see, shall we?'


'What a cow,' Vince said, as they emerged into sunlight once more.

'She's a Boston Brahmin, Vince.' The look of confusion made Alverson explain the Indian caste system and how the Brahmins were the highest ranked. 'That's what we call those snotty Bostonian bastards who can trace the ancestors back to somewhere in England, and usually to the landed gentry.'

'Some of them were transported criminals.'

'They ended up in Virginia,' Alverson replied, grinning. 'The Boston Brahmins are at the top of the social pile, and that is where folk like Mrs Littleton see themselves.'

'She didn't think much of you, did she?'

'As you so aptly described her, Vince, she is a cow.'

'So, Tyler, what is it you want to do?'

'Get as close to the Italian lines as I can.'

'We won't see much.'

Alverson pointed to one of the high conical hills which overlooked Aksum. 'Maybe from on top of something like that.'

'You prepared to walk up one?'

'For a story, I'd walk through fire, buddy boy.'

'As you wish, but food first. Vince, get the water canteens filled, will you, please, while I go and see if we can hire some donkeys?'

'We're not taking the car?' Alverson asked.

'No point, Tyler: the road runs out just north of here, and by the time we get close it will be too dark to get back, so we'll need bedrolls too.'

The roly-poly owner of the place was only too happy to rustle them up a meal – a dish of spiced peppers stuffed with lamb that was heavy on the garlic too.

'Why worry?' Jardine said to Alverson, as the American waved his hand in front of his mouth. 'You weren't planning to kiss anyone, were you?'

'I'll leave that to you, friend.'

'In your dreams,' came the response; Jardine knew what he was driving at.

'You seen a movie called *It Happened One Night*?'

'I did,' Vince said, as Jardine shook his head. 'It just came over, didn't it? Claudette Colbert an' Clark Gable. She's a peach, but he's a bit fat. They spend the whole film arguin' wiv each other, then fall in love.'

'Life can mirror art, Vince, wouldn't you say?'

'Can we get on?' Cal Jardine insisted.


Even with a saddle there is little comfort in riding a donkey, quite apart from the fact of feeling ridiculous, as anyone of any height, like Jardine and Alverson, had trouble keeping their feet off the ground, while Vince just managed. But they were the perfect animal for the terrain: sturdy, sure-footed on uneven ground and good on the lower slopes of the hill they eventually decided to climb, one that was topped by what looked like a tiny, stone-built monastery.

They had got Alverson out of his suit and into more suitable clothes again, while each now had their bedroll behind the saddle and their kitbags on their back, Vince and Jardine also carrying their weapons. In line they had passed through ploughed fields being tended by working women and old men, again there being no sense of impending invasion, then onto the cultivated terraced hillsides.

These were cut in such a way as to preserve as much as possible of the water that would cascade down the hills in a land that was short on irrigation and subject to torrential rainfall. Once past those, the hill was too steep, meaning the donkeys had to be led, and by the time they got to the summit, sweating profusely and cursing the loose earth underneath, the sun was dipping towards the horizon.

The monastery, with only slits to let in any light, was an ancient structure in a state of some dilapidation, the walls stained with age and the mortar loose or missing on the walls, but the monks were welcoming, if utterly incomprehensible in their greetings. No matter, sign language and a gift of a couple of thalers made sure they had a cell to sleep in and, when they took off their boots, a monk came to wash and dry their feet as an act of Christ-like humility.

'I haven't had this kind of treatment since I was in a Manchurian bordello,' Alverson proclaimed.

'Let's hope you don't get offered the other bits, guv,' Vince joked. 'They're all blokes up here and you can guess what that means.'

'You have a twisted mind, Vince.'

'And a virgin arse. I know about places like these, 'cause the Italian mountains are full of 'em – supposed holy men who seem to spend all their time drinking hooch and rogering each other.'

'And praying for forgiveness for their sins.'

'Sleep, gents,' Jardine said. 'We are up with the lark.'

They were up before that, even, woken by the gentle chanting of the Ethiopian monks, breakfasting on dates and unleavened bread before emerging to overlook, in moon and starlight, the still-dark landscape to the north, with Jardine focusing on the fires and lanterns of the Italian front lines.

'They're up and about early.'

'Let's have a look-see.'

The field glasses were handed over just as the sun tinged the eastern horizon, with Alverson still as he examined the encampment, reciting what he would write in a semi-jocular way . . .

'Your reporter has tramped alongside the peasant defender of Ethiopia, his feet raw from toiling through the rocks and dust of a terrain that would tax the most intrepid explorer. But how can he not follow the example of these sturdy farmer-warriors, who have marched with their out-of-date weaponry to get close to a powerful enemy equipped with the most modern of munitions . . . ?'

'Did I explain to you what "bollocks" means, given you are in good boots?'

'No need, Vince, I am just setting the scene, giving it a bit of colour. To continue: Fearless, I have come close to the lines of the invaders, an army half a million or more strong, to bring to you, my readers, some sense of what these under-equipped . . . dammit,' he said softly. 'I've used "equipped" once already.'

'Does it matter?' Jardine asked.

'Sure does, brother, never use the same word in the same paragraph unless it's a name. Basic journalism.'

'Do go on, I'm fascinated.'

'Was that a yawn I just saw out of the corner of my eye?'

'Don't take it personally.'

Alverson dropped the field glasses and slowly passed them to

Jardine. 'You might want to take this personally, old buddy. I think our friends over yonder are getting ready to pull out.'

Jardine was issuing orders to Vince before he had the binoculars to his eyes. 'Donkeys ready to leave. Get armed, Vince, and fetch my weapon too.'

There was no need to tell Vince to top up the water canteens, that was standard, and he concentrated on looking at the Italian lines. What he could see, as the morning light increased, was numerous khaki-clad soldiers clambering into lorries. Small tankettes were moving through gaps which had only just been created in the line of defensive sandbags he had seen from the air. Behind them, other troops were forming up in what he suspected to be preparatory to an order to march; those he could stay ahead of, it was the trucked infantry and the tracked vehicles that were the problem.

'Your despatch is going to be more exciting than you thought, Tyler; that is, unless they catch us.'

'Will they?'

'Depends on the speed they want to advance, and the ground, which should hold them up some.'

'Ready, guv.'

'Then let's get the bloody hell out of here.'

They went down the hill fast, the donkeys, sure-footed as they were, occasionally splaying their feet at some particularly dangerous spot, forcing Jardine to seek out an alternative route, and all the while they could see less and less of what they would need to avoid until all it became was a dust cloud on the edge of their horizon. On even ground they started to jog, even Alverson, who was far from as fit as Vince and Jardine, their kitbags bouncing against their backs.

It was not tanks and trucks that presented a problem to the

fleeing trio, but the cavalry screen General De Bono had sent out in the hours of darkness to warn him of any potential threat to his measured advance. Thankfully, because of their higher profile, added to the direction of their concentration, Jardine spotted them before they saw him, yet that was not of much use: he could seek cover, but not with donkeys, and together they were at more risk than separate, while to just let the animals go would only create curiosity and most certainly initiate a search.

'Vince,' Jardine called softly, as they crouched down, passing over his sub-machine gun. 'Give me your knife.' That was passed over swiftly and unquestioningly. 'Use the gullies and irrigation ditches to try to stay out of sight. Get Tyler back to Aksum and get the hell out of there with or without the Littletons. Wherever the Ethiopian lines are, get to the rear of them.'

'You, guv?'

'Distraction, Vince; we can't all get away.'

'Hold the phone here—'

Jardine rounded on Alverson then, his voice a furious hiss. 'Do as you're bloody well told. Now get down and crawl for cover.'

Waiting till they were out of sight, he crouched to discard two of the bedrolls, jammed Vince's knife into his own so it was out of sight, then taking the lead ropes of their donkeys, Jardine stood up and began to walk towards the cavalry.

# CHAPTER TWENTY-ONE

He was soon spotted. Closer to the mounted men he could see they were askaris, their shouting communication in their own tongue. Those closest detached themselves to surround him, all jabbering away, while another had gone to fetch an officer, who was not long in arriving on a snorting, pawing charger that could not be less than seventeen hands, the stream of Italian he aimed at Jardine not much more comprehensible than what his excitable native horsemen had been shouting. More important to Jardine, there was no cry of discovery; Vince and Tyler Alverson might just get away.

'Do you speak English?' he enquired.

Receiving a negative response, he tried French, then German, which was the one that worked – not fluently, but many Italians knew some: for centuries a large part of northern Italy had been either connected to, or part of, the Austrian Empire, the Trentino region and Trieste integral till 1919. The stilted interrogation was enough to allow him to establish his own nationality, though he was unsure if the Italian officer quite got a hold of his story as to why he was where he was.

The man fired off a series of rapid orders to two of his men, one of them, by his badges, a junior NCO, who dismounted and stripped him of his Colt Automatic and his kitbag and searched him for more weapons. The officer then informed Jardine he was being taken back to be interrogated at the base camp.

As they had been conversing – if it could be called that – the noise of moving armour had been growing, the sound of tracked vehicles unmistakeable, and the first of the small Carro Veloce 33 tankettes came into view, sending up clouds of dust as it bounced its way across the uneven terrain, the long snout of its machine gun waving to and fro threateningly. That set the horses prancing and his donkeys braying– no equine creature likes to be near the noise of armour – which hurried his departure, the officer leading his men back to what they had been doing before, providing a reconnaissance screen at the very forefront of the advance.

His escort, one of whom now had the donkey lead ropes, gave the tankettes a wide berth, which partly took them out of the dust cloud and allowed Jardine to observe the differing arms of what was moving forward, the big-wheeled trucks in a line, on a track that could not be called a road, trying to avoid the unrepaired potholes caused by the recent rains. They were followed by marching men, heads down, who made no attempt at smartness, their pith helmets pulled low and their mouths covered, each one bearing on his back the heavy equipment – packs, rifles, entrenching tools and a steel helmet – every infantryman must carry into battle.

Then came more and heavier tanks: L640s, and in their wake self-propelled cannon, then horse- and truck-towed artillery, including the anti-aircraft guns that had been aimed at him the previous day – an excessive amount considering the Ethiopian air force consisted of only a couple of dozen planes.

It seemed endless, and Jardine had to remind himself he was only seeing a fraction of a force advancing on a broad front of several miles across. He could not avoid contrasting it with what he had observed on the road south from Addis, thoughts that were far from comfortable. By the time he reached what had been their main encampment he had still not seen this movement decrease.

Now, with his escort dismounted, he was being led through an extensive motor park full of lorries, cars, command vehicles and motorbikes, to a series of large brown-coloured marquees which he assumed, judging by the regimental and command flags flying above them, formed the headquarters of the army. This, too, he had seen from the air; it looked a damn sight more scary now.

Told to wait – even he understood that in Italian – Jardine was rehearsing what he would say; he knew he would have to expand on what he had tried to tell the cavalry officer. An army this size was bound to have an intelligence section, and he expected that someone in that would be enough of an English speaker to fully test his excuses.

Whatever took place inside, the askari cavalryman emerged with two Italian soldiers, both with rifles, and using a series of sharp gestures he was marched off, leaving his donkeys behind, and led to a small empty tent, where, after emptying out his pockets and stripping off his watch, he was put under guard, his few possessions, including his belt, watch and shoelaces, taken away.

How much time passed he did not know, certainly hours, but eventually an Italian NCO came to collect him, with another two rifle-bearing escorts, to take him back to the main marquees. Inside they were divided into compartments, into one of which he was shown, to find an officer, a major, sitting behind a trestle desk on which lay his Colt, magazine removed, his watch, passport, the contents of his kitbag, and what little money he had brought from Aksum; his money belt he had left behind.

To one side at another trestle desk sat a bespectacled private soldier, armed with pens, ink and paper, obviously there to take notes, while before the main desk sat a single folding chair.

The major picked up the passport and opened it. 'Mr Jardine.'

'I am.'

'I am Major d'Agostino of the *Servizio Informazioni Militare*; please be seated.'

Jardine did so, facing the intelligence officer, noting his near-perfect English, while also picking up a slight whiff of cologne – or was it hair oil? – from a very well-barbered fellow. Clean-shaven, the hair was thick, wavy and black, the eyes equally dark in a sallow complexion on a rather severe face: sharp nose, hollow cheeks, plus a downturned mouth over a pointed chin.

'What are you doing in Ethiopia, Mr Jardine?'

Responding with a half-smile, Jardine said, 'As I tried to tell the previous officer, the cavalryman, I am interested in the Christian religion of this country, which I am sure you know goes back, at least they claim it does, over two thousand years. I was visiting Aksum to see the Church of St Mary of Zion, and I also took the opportunity to visit the nearby monasteries in the hope of talking to the monks. I was on my way back from one when I ran into your patrols. I am not sure your cavalry officer understood.'

'Religion?'

'I assume you are aware that the Ark of the Covenant is supposed to reside in Aksum.'

'It does not worry you that you are in a war zone?'

'I am a neutral, it is no concern of mine.'

The major tapped his fingers on the desk in a sort of tattoo. 'Bullets flying around, an army on the march and it does not concern you?'

'You were not marching when I set out and I am sure I have nothing to fear from the Italian army, whom, I have every reason to believe, will respect my nationality."

The passport was lifted to a point before his face and flicked through, page by page. 'You seem to be a well-travelled man, judging by the number of stamps you have gathered.'

'My research takes me to many places.'

These were reeled off by d'Agostino. 'Belgium, France, Austria, Rumania, Turkey, Greece, and these on what is a recently issued document, judging by the date.'

'When you are researching comparative religions it takes you to many places.'

That got a thin smile. 'But not Italy, or perhaps Palestine?'

'I do intend to visit Rome at some time in the future. Palestine, being mandated to my country by the League of Nations, would not justify a stamp.'

'Would I be correct in thinking you came to Ethiopia through British Somaliland?'

'Yes, and again no need for a stamp on my passport when I entered a colony of my country.'

'And you have come to Ethiopia, even though the border is sealed?'

'Yes.'

'But no stamp for entry into this country?'

Jardine tried to look abashed. 'I'm afraid I sneaked into Ethiopia. Bit naughty, but I am only one soul and I did not think my presence would hurt anyone.'

'One soul who has the audacity to defy his government and one studying comparative religions, Mr Jardine? To what purpose would this be put?'

'I hope to write a book one day.'

'Without notes?' the major snapped.

Jardine leant forward and looked at his possessions laid out on the desk. 'They should be there, there was a set of notebooks in my kitbag.'

'Now missing.'

Trying to look perplexed, Jardine said, 'Perhaps I left them at the monastery by mistake.'

'Tell me, Mr Jardine, would this monastery of which you speak be on a nearby hilltop?' Answered with a nod, d'Agostino continued, 'And did that hilltop overlook the encampment in which we are now sitting?'

'It did, but that was not something I have any interest in, or at least, only a passing sort of one.'

'So, if I put it to you that you were spying on the Italian Expeditionary Force, you would deny it?'

'Most certainly,' Jardine insisted, adding an affronted look for good measure.

The major's hand slipped below the level of the desk and emerged with his field glasses, last seen in his kitbag. 'Yet, I am sure, from such a vantage point, you were tempted to employ these, merely from curiosity if nothing else?'

'Just as I am sure you will be aware that a set of binoculars are standard equipment for the traveller in such a barren country as this.'

That got a sneer as the major looked at his weapon. 'As is a Colt Automatic pistol with a fully loaded magazine clip.'

Jardine knew he was in trouble, indeed he had known his story was as leaky as a bucket full of holes, but it was the best he could conjure up, taking his cue from Ma Littleton. Rule one is, whatever the tale you're telling, stick to it, for time is your only asset.

'Major, I can understand your concerns . . .'

The man's eyes flicked sideways and the clerk half-stood as the tent flap to the rear of Jardine swished. Spinning round he was presented with such an unexpected sight his jaw dropped. Dressed in fawn twill jodhpurs, highly polished riding boots, a crisp white blouse and standing in the doorway, was a strikingly beautiful woman with a mass of flowing blonde hair that came down to her shoulders and framed a quite stunning face.

She made Jardine think 'film star' right away, aided by the breeze wafting to his nose a quite distinct but obviously expensive perfume, so delicate was it as a fragrance. He was speedily on his feet as her eyes moved from the major and, with a slightly quizzical expression, fixed on him.

'*Non addesso, cara,*' the intelligence officer said from behind him, in a quite sharp tone.

'I heard you speaking English, Umberto.'

'To this gentleman here.'

'Callum Jardine,' he said, introducing himself quickly and adding a lopsided, self-deprecating grin. 'I seem to have upset the apple cart a bit.'

She smiled in response and it was heart-melting; what was it about

291

her accent that was different? It was almost like a slight impediment. 'And what is an Englishman doing here, I wonder?'

'Seeking to explain his innocence to the Major here.'

'Sit down, Mr Jardine, you are a prisoner not a guest.'

His reply was deliberately flippant. 'In the presence of a lady of such beauty, Major, a lack of courtesy would never serve. If I apologise for my presence, I will not do so for my manners.'

That got, as a response, a delightful, throaty chuckle and parted lips to show the tips of a set of even teeth. She was quite simply stunning and he could not help but let his eyes drop to that crisp white blouse and the very obvious, if not overbearing twin peaks of her bosom. When he looked up again she was still smiling, and that having noted the direction of his gaze.

'How gallant . . .' Jardine had to laugh then, that being the same word Corrie Littleton had said to that oily French bugger, de Billancourt, '. . . for a prisoner.'

Major d'Agostino was beside Jardine now and a sideways glance showed a furious face. But he did not speak, he merely passed by, took the beauty by the arm and led her away from the tent flap, which dropped behind them, insufficient as a screen to cover the exchange which followed: fury from the major, frivolity from the woman, though he understood not one word; it was all in the tone. When d'Agostino came back, still palpably furious, for some reason he felt the need to explain.

'The *Marquesa* wished to go riding and wanted to know if it was safe to do so. I told her she had nothing to fear.'

Jardine was so tempted to guy him – the words were in his head: 'I wish she had gone out riding earlier and I wish I had been captured by her, rather than those askaris.' But they remained

292

there, given he was in too much trouble to risk being glib.

Back behind his desk, d'Agostino rearranged the items on it in a rather fussy way, which Jardine thought he was using as a means to calm himself, for they had not moved. Then he looked up and said, 'You were not tempted to snatch up your weapon in my absence, Mr Jardine?'

'I am not a violent man, Major, I have that gun only for protection. In fact, I dislike firearms.'

'So, you insist you are not a spy, you say you are an innocent traveller who just happens to be in a bad place at a bad time?'

The man was smiling now, but it was thin-lipped and threatening, not humorous, and that gave Jardine a bad feeling. The hand was under the desk again and when it came up and he saw what d'Agostino was holding, his heart sank. It was the wallet of the late Lieutenant Alberto Soradino, which he had forgotten he had in his kitbag.

'Then I am curious, if you are a man not of violence, how you came across this?'

Making sure he did not sound feeble, even if he knew the words to be just that, Jardine replied firmly, 'I found it and, in truth, I had forgotten I had done so.'

'Found it? Might I ask where?' Jardine was about to give a near nonsensical reply when the major slammed the table. 'Please do not treat me as a fool, Mr Jardine.'

'I had no intention of doing so.'

'Then it will not surprise you that on finding this I sent a radio signal back to Asmara, and they informed me that a certain Lieutenant Soradino is missing from his post at Assab, and has been for over two weeks. It seems, without orders and without informing his superiors, he took a contingent of askaris off on some wild goose chase into the country south of the Danakil Depression, where I can tell you, there are no monasteries. Given you have his wallet, you are armed and he has not been heard of since departing Assab, I am forced to assume he might no longer be alive.'

'He must have dropped it.'

The response was larded with sarcasm. 'And along comes an innocent Englishman, out for a stroll in the desert, who just happens to find it. But he does not find the owner to return it, then forgets he had it in the first place. How strange.'

'I must compliment you on your command of English, Major,' Jardine replied, aware that there was not a lot he could say and he needed time to think, because this he had not bargained for. That wallet made his position, precarious to begin with, so much more so.

'Then perhaps since I have no trouble understanding, you would care to enlighten me as to where the lieutenant is, not to mention the men he commanded?'

'I have no idea, but I did tell you I slipped across the border illegally by engaging with a camel caravan doing likewise, a most villainous crew who assured me the border crossing was not guarded.'

'Somalis or Ethiopians?'

'Neither, but they were Muslims.'

'No doubt they enlightened you as to the tenets of the Koran.'

'It was informative to observe them, yes.'

'And was this caravan carrying anything, Mr Jardine?'

He had to be careful: the Italians must have informants in Ethiopia, but how numerous and active they were was to him a mystery. There was one notion worth a try.

'I fear they might have been involved in the slave trade and were returning from the coast, having sent on their despicable consignment to the markets of Arabia.'

'Empty?'

It was like playing poker, seeking in little inflections in the voice and the way his eyes and hands moved to detect if he knew the answer to the question or was just probing.

'The camels were loaded, but with what I do not know.'

'Three days after Soradino went missing, his area commander requested to be sent up a reconnaissance aircraft from our *Regia Aeronautica* to look for him. I take it you know what a vulture is, Mr Jardine? When he saw them in large numbers it was enough to make our pilot curious, so he flew very low over a range of hills and was sure he could see a field of bodies being picked clean by the birds.'

'Perhaps he was mistaken – from the air they could be animals.'

'Fortunately the land to the east is flat, and there he put down his light aircraft to go and investigate, to find he was indeed correct: they are human remains, much scattered, chewed at by other animals and bones bleached by the sun. Yet there are scraps of uniform left and they are, when examined, the same as those worn by the askari levies Lieutenant Soradino commanded.'

'How shocking! What do you think happened?'

The voice became quite terse. 'Soradino was an idiot, a fellow convinced he was a genius when in truth he was a dolt, sent to Assab to fester in a place he could do no harm. Now he is dead and you have the poor fool's wallet, so perhaps you can tell me what to think.'

As the major had been speaking, and he had not raised his voice at all, Jardine had become aware of the scratching of the pen at the other table; a glance sideways showed the soldier-clerk was indeed taking notes, so he must speak English too. Then the youngster looked up and stared at him through his round, steel-rimmed spectacles, though that did not last: he went back to his scribbling as d'Agostino continued.

'What did you plan to do with this wallet, which still has a sum of lire in it, so you are no thief?'

'I had a vague idea to send it back to Italy, but I confess I had not thought that through.'

'So you would like me to believe that you were not involved in those deaths?'

'I was most certainly not.'

'Then it is such a pity, Mr Jardine, that I do not believe you.'

'I take it you do not have the bodies?'

'No.'

'Then all you have is that wallet, Major d'Agostino, and my assertion, truthful even if you do not believe it, that I found it. You have no evidence I was anywhere near this supposed area where you say these bodies were found. Naturally, if you have lost some of your men, I have sympathy, but what I do not have is guilt, and you do not have the evidence to counter what I insist is the truth, which I trust a court will uphold.'

The intelligence man threw back his head and laughed, his sharp nose pointing to the roof of the tent and his body shaking with mirth. 'How English that is, the land of fair play and justice, is it not, Spinetti?'

'It is, sir,' the clerk replied, tonelessly.

'Our lad, Arturo here, studied in London, at your School of Economics and he loves your country very much.' The laughing stopped and the face darkened. 'Which is why he is a private soldier in the army, instead of a *professore* in some university, for, pity of pities, Arturo is not a good son of the new Italy. "Evidence" you say, Mr Jardine, as if there is going to be some kind of trial before a judge. But this is an area under military control and I am, unfortunately for you, both judge and jury. Would you care to hear my verdict?'

'If it will amuse you,' Jardine replied; there was no doubt what it was going to be.

'We are about to take Aksum, and when we do, when our general rides in triumph into the old capital of the country, I will give you to him as a gift. As a spy, you should be shot, but I think you are also a murderer; so, Mr Jardine, we will either hang you in front of General De Bono and the citizens of Aksum, or behead you, to tell them what happens to those who kill Italian officers.'

He turned to the clerk, Arturo, and snapped, 'Make sure you write that clearly. Now call for the guards to take him away.'

# CHAPTER TWENTY-TWO

There was only one consolation for Jardine as he squatted in his empty tent: there was no sign they had caught Vince or Tyler Alverson, so he had a reasonable hope that they had got clear. He had already peered through the tied-up flap of his tent to see an armed guard there, pacing to and fro, wisely a couple of yards away – too far for him to be suddenly grabbed and subdued. Lifting the groundsheet and the bottom of the rear canvas had shown him the soles of another pair of moving sentinel boots, which meant that the sides of the tent were also covered by their criss-cross movement.

From outside came noise and a great deal of it: shouting, the sounds of lorries revving, reversing and driving off in low gear, of motorbikes popping as they departed, and the odd car as well, which he had to assume was the moving of the headquarters. That was a major operation, this being the central directing brain of an army several hundred thousand strong, which would require a vast amount of staff organisation.

Quite apart from the officers who planned every metre of movement, feeding and supply, there would be aides to the general officers, the heads of the various branches, a mass of clerks, telephonists plus radio operators, quartermasters, batmen, mess servants, military police, cooks and at least a headquarters company of infantrymen to provide perimeter security and guards.

When he was finally fetched out, the scene that greeted him was vastly different: the great marquees were gone, as were the vehicles and bikes from the motor pool, leaving only a few tents for the remainder of the pioneer company responsible for ensuring the site was clear and that nothing had been left behind. The men of that unit were now emptying the sandbags – which had formed the forward perimeter defence – into the dugouts of the latrines, filling the air with the smell of human filth. Wild dogs had started to root around the periphery looking for anything edible.

Of more import to Jardine was the escort of four infantrymen and an NCO designated to accompany him to Aksum. Between the encampment and that city, on a near-windless day, the dust hung in the air, the residue of the massive military movement. As they marched, the same peasants he had seen in the fields the day before were out again now, but instead of tending to their crop they were sadly surveying the ruin brought on by the invading army marching over their once-ploughed fields, the only redress to glare at the military police controlling the continuing stream of traffic.

The appearance of the *marquesa* on a white horse came as a real surprise. She looked imperious in a white cloak to keep off the dust, her blonde hair tied back, and she acted like that too, as she galloped over the Ethiopian peasants' land with a total disregard for their presence, hooves kicking up great clods of what had been irrigated earth.

Spotting his party she hauled on her reins and came towards them, stopping before him with the sun at her back, which forced the now-stationary Jardine – his escorting NCO had called a halt and saluted – to narrow his eyes to even see her silhouette, his nose wrinkling, this time at the stable smell of the impatient mount, which was pawing and jagging its head, straining her grip on the reins.

'They make you march like a common criminal?' she asked, again with that slight impediment. Recalling the title d'Agostino had used, it suddenly came to Jardine she was possibly not Italian, but Spanish.

'The major thinks me that.'

'No,' she replied, tugging to keep her horse still. 'He can see you are a soldier, he has told me so.' Then she reprised that throaty chuckle he had heard previously. 'And I have observed you are a gentleman. Were you a soldier?'

'Name, rank and number, *Marquesa*,' he joked, 'is all I am allowed to say.'

'I am not interrogating you.'

'Now that is a damn shame.'

'For a man who is shortly to die you have a surprising lack of anxiety.'

The horse moved with such force she was obliged to let it spin, but she still had the sun at her back.

'We all die at some time. Tell me, *Marquesa*, what is the rest of your title?'

'De Alanatara.'

'Spanish?'

'*Si.*'

'I am curious about your relationship with Major d'Agostino.'

'Who is also the Count of Terni. But now you are interrogating me.'

The NCO, who had hitherto stood silently, now coughed, then barked at his men, not surprising given they were staring with a degree of interest at the *marquesa*, and also not at attention but slouching. Jardine ignored the hint he should shut up and move on.

'Am I allowed to continue doing so?'

'No. I think it best you go to your fate.'

'Does the notion of that fate sadden you, at all?'

'I am not sure.'

'That is something; I would be disappointed if it pleased you.'

'For an Englishman, you are more forward than many I have met.'

'You obviously have met too few Scotsmen.'

'You are Scottish?' Jardine nodded. 'Do they die with more bravery than Englishmen?'

'No. When it comes to that we are the same carefree bunch.'

'I will be interested to see if that is true.'

Her heels moved and she hauled on the reins, the horse breaking into an immediate trot. The NCO, hitherto indifferent, was now obviously cross, because he pushed Jardine to get him moving.

If breaking up an army camp involved much organisation, the relocating of one was just as chaotic. An advance party of staff officers had entered Aksum on the heels of the fighting men to secure the buildings that could be used for what, in the British army, would be called the various GSO branches – the best accommodation, of course, secured for the commanding general, with his chief of staff next, in a pecking order that supposedly designated quality in strict order of rank.

Arturo Spinetti found himself in a two-storey sort of inn, run by a fat fellow of hand-wringing obsequiousness, overseeing the unloading, from a lorry, of the filing cabinets that went everywhere with the department of which he was a part. Major d'Agostino had no hand in the setting up of his branch HQ, he was too busy trying to ensure himself, and who Spinetti thought of as his aristocratic blonde tart, a decent billet in which to eat and sleep, this place not being to his mind of a standard he felt was his due.

There were also two lieutenants of the SIM attached to De Bono's HQ, but they had just told their NCOs to get on with it, before setting off to find out if there was a decent brothel in Aksum. Those non-commissioned officers, a sergeant and two corporals, were more intent on finding a place to drink than actually performing their duties, so, as the only private soldier around, Spinetti had been left to curse the Italian army, Benito Mussolini, the Fascist Grand Council and the Horn of Africa, while, as he saw it, being left holding the *bambino*.

He needed to sort out an office for the major, the best room and coolest, of course, with another for himself close enough to be at the bastard's beck and call. That had to be capacious enough to contain the filing cabinets full of intelligence reports, most of them of no use whatsoever, which would mean an argument with the lieutenants.

They would complain, when it came to an office, he had looked after himself, not them; like d'Agostino they would sleep elsewhere – living above the place of work was not to be tolerated if one wanted a decent night's sleep, a woman as company and the ability to begin work at an hour of one's own choosing.

He had sorted out a shared billet for the NCOs, a secure room for the English prisoner and, last but not least, a place for him to lay his head, and all the while his enforced host was dogging his heels, rubbing his hands with worry and asking in very broken Italian how he was to be paid for the services he was providing.

Jardine, who arrived with his escort, got a dank cellar, a place with a stout door which would have to be secured by a baulk of wood jammed against it in the temporary absence of a lock or a padlock and hasp. Asked to continue guarding him, the escorting NCO furiously refused: his orders were to fetch the prisoner to this place, then rejoin the headquarters company. Spinetti had to beg him for an hour so he could sort out the rest of what was needed, given he feared to leave Jardine without anyone to guard him.

That included the securing and laying of a field telephone as well as a visit to the quartermaster to indent for the supplies to sustain the whole unit, plus one prisoner. There he found such chaos, he was told to make the inn owner feed them for now; a padlock and hasp would be delivered to him when they could find one, a promise he did not believe for one second. Back at the inn, with the escort gone, Spinetti, the least martial of men, was obliged to touch the pistol in his holster to get Jardine some food and drink, then he had to deliver it.

'You lived in London.'

'I studied there, yes,' Spinetti replied, 'and I got a degree.'

He took off his steel-rimmed glasses and wiped them on a handkerchief, his face doleful. 'Not that it has served me much, just to have chosen England over an Italian university is seen as a crime in my country – unpatriotic.'

'Conscripted?' The clerk nodded. 'I wonder if you could do me a favour and ask the owner something.' That got a suspicious look. 'It's a simple question. There was a party of Americans here, I just wonder if they have left.'

The young man, in appearance a studious type, stood thinking. Lean to the point of being spare, he had a pallid face, though not an unattractive one. Spinetti looked gentle and Jardine thought he would smile a lot if his life were not, to him, so rotten.

'Americans?'

'Yes. If they are still here, I need them to know I am a prisoner.'

'I could get into trouble.'

'Call it the wish of a dying man.'

'*Infamita!*' he spat, before looking at Jardine. 'You should be tried by a court, even if it is a military one.'

'If my Americans are still around, maybe I will be.'

Odd that he felt uncomfortable lying to this young fellow; he really wanted to know if Alverson and Vince, as well as the Littletons, had got away, which would be some small solace for what he was about to face.

'Then I will ask.'

'I also need something to sleep on, maybe the bedroll on my donkey?'

'I'll see what I can do.'

Jardine pushed at the door when the clerk left: given he was no soldier he might not have secured it properly, but it would not budge. Looking at the food he had been brought, he surmised the owner to be limited in his culinary skills: it was the same meal he had eaten before going out to spy on the Italians. He had barely got halfway through when the clerk returned carrying, disappointingly, a straw-filled paillasse.

'Your Americans left in a big car, two ladies and two men.'

'Thank you, Arturo.'

The use of his name made him smile. 'Mr Jardine, I am not part of this, I hope you know that.'

'You don't hide it very well.'

That seemed to please him, producing a sly smile.


Major Umberto d'Agostino had been drinking and so had his blonde mistress, though not, it appeared, as much as him, for he was actually unsteady. Spinetti registered he was in his dress uniform, unarmed, having attended a celebratory meal held for the senior officers; she, his guest, was wearing high heels, a loose black dress with two very thin shoulder straps, a set of pearls round her neck and a clutch bag in her hand, while her hair had been expertly dressed by someone; maybe Aksum was not such a backwater after all.

Spinetti, trying to sort out his office, knew from experience the major was a man who liked his wine and brandy; indeed, thanks to his CO's batman he had tasted quite a bit of the personal stores d'Agostino insisted went everywhere he did: not only wine, but whole Parma hams, good olive oil, various kinds of wheat to make good bread and fresh pasta, cheeses which taxed the ingenuity of all to keep them fresh.

He was not alone in this: it seemed every officer in the Italian army wished to have some home comforts along, and to accommodate those, certain things an army might need had been left in Asmara to provide the space. A stern commander would have stopped such actions if he had not been one of the worst culprits himself, and Emilio De Bono had his fawning staff officers to care for him as well – sleek, well-connected aides who saw to it that whatever bed he slept in was comfortable and that he was allowed a proper night's rest, free from his military concerns. Naturally, their own comfort was not ignored.

'The prisoner is secure?'

'I have done my best, sir. The door lock is broken and there are no padlocks in the quartermaster's stores, sir; I asked.'

The major rolled his eyes, the clerk thought for effect, to impress his mistress. 'Spinetti, are you an idiot? Go out and find one. There must be a shop in Aksum which sells them.'

'I cannot find the petty cash tin and that is the reason I cannot pay the owner of this place for the food he has given the prisoner and I.'

'Pay him! Tell him if he asks to be paid he will be shot! And if you find a shop with a padlock and hasp just take it and tell the owner to come and fit it or I'll have his head off too. Now, fetch a lantern and take me to the prisoner.'

'Can I come?' the *marquesa* asked, rubbing d'Agostino's cheek.

'What for?' he demanded, suspiciously.

Spinetti looked away and waited for the explosion: these two had a fiery relationship, especially when the major had been drinking, given the *marquesa* was such a flirt. In an army of Italian officers never shy of showing their gallantry, that led to a great deal of tempestuous dispute, which only exposed the innate jealousy of d'Agostino's nature and the delight his mistress took in playing on that. He hated to see men pay her compliments, and she sought them out on purpose to torment him.

'He's going to die tomorrow, Umberto. Let him see your woman before he goes so he will know what he is giving up. He is, after all, a handsome fellow and, I think,' she dug him in the ribs, then, 'he is quite a man for the ladies.'

'Handsome?' the major barked.

She pouted. 'Not as handsome as you, my sweet.' One strap she slipped off her shoulder, which exposed the rising mound of the top of her breast, making the clerk's blood flow a little stronger: she was stunning even if he thought her a horror. 'But let us torture him a little.'

That appealed and d'Agostino smiled, his head waving slightly. 'Spinetti, take us to the wretch.'

'Sir,' he replied, picking up a lantern as the *marquesa* slipped off her shoes and dropped her clutch bag on the trestle desk.

'Perhaps I will do for him a little Spanish dance.'

'Save that for me, my sweet,' the major growled.

Not a man to miss showing off his authority, Spinetti was loudly lambasted for the gimcrack way the door was secured, a raised voice which meant that when they entered the windowless cellar Jardine was standing up. Unshaven, still with the dust of his march to this place of confinement, it would have been generous to say he was handsome: he looked, given his clothing was grimy too, like a bit of a vagrant, that is if you excluded the way he held himself, which was defiant.

'Come to gloat, have you, Major?'

That made d'Agostino blink: it was as if Jardine had overheard their conversation in the room designated as his office. 'I have come to tell you that you will die tomorrow, as soon as the general has completed his victory parade.'

'Victory? He didn't have to fight anyone. Still, you Italians love comic opera.'

'You dare to insult General De Bono.'

'Take me to him and I'll do it to his face.'

'See, Umberto,' the *marquesa* said, executing a spin that made her dress flare, 'he is a brave man and he is handsome, is he not?'

'Stop that!'

'No, let me dance, let me show our Scotsman—'

'Scotsman!' d'Agostino barked, his dark eyes flitting angrily from her to Jardine. 'Are you a—?'

'Yes he is, he told me.'

'When?'

'Today.'

'You sought him out?'

'Oh,' she replied, her face mock-sad, 'Umberto is jealous.'

'He is not,' d'Agostino hissed.

The mock-sad look went, to be replaced with one that was cross, and the voice mirrored that. 'Then you should be. Maybe you should go and leave me with my gallant Scotsman and I will send him to meet God as a happy man.'

'Stop it, Francesca.'

'What a nice name,' Jardine said; he was enjoying this and it showed.

'Thank you, Scottishman. You see, Umberto, *caro*, he knows how to pay a lady a compliment.'

'How I would love to pay you more than that, *Marquesa*.'

The major went white. 'How dare you. If I had my pistol I would shoot you now like the murdering dog you are.'

Her eyes were wild now. 'Do it, Umberto, get a gun and shoot him.'

'I will accept that gladly for a kiss, *Marquesa*.'

She started to sashay towards Jardine but was dragged rudely back, which had her rounding on her major with spitting fury. In order to avoid her anger d'Agostino lurched towards Jardine, fists clenched, but he stopped when he saw that he was about to get into a fight: far from seeking to withdraw, his prisoner looked as if he was ready to engage, and in the Italian's eyes there was a sudden flash of doubt that told Jardine he expected he would lose.

The risk to his dignity stopped him and he worked to get a sneer in his voice that matched the one on his face. 'Perhaps I will have you flogged to death, or have your skin stripped off with hot pincers. But know this, for the insults you have heaped on me this night your death will be more, much more, painful than even you can imagine.'

He took the *marquesa*'s hand and dragged her out, the lantern in the other, with her pleading that he should not be angry, that it was only a silly game. The sound of their dispute took a long time to fade.

Sitting in the dark, unable to sleep, Jardine spent a long time wondering if he had been wise to bait the man. What price would he pay for his jibes? Noises came, of drunken, singing soldiery, then died away until there was no sound at all, leaving him with his troubled thoughts, and time lost any meaning. The door opening suddenly, and a little light from a tallow wad entering his cellar had him on his feet; had the bastard come back armed?

'Who's there?'

There was no reply and he moved gingerly towards the door, hands ready for a fight, because if he was going it was not about to be quietly. His foot kicked something and he looked down to see his Colt Automatic pistol alongside the loaded clip. Bending down he found his passport and his kitbag, which when he lifted it, by its weight, seemed to have everything he possessed inside. Lifting the canvas he sniffed at it, registering the odour of expensive perfume, and that made him smile. What a clever game the *marquesa* had played!

Why she was doing this he did not know, and there was no denying a tickle to his vanity as he sifted through the possible motives. Whatever, the way was clear in front of him, all he had to do was get out of Aksum. Gingerly, Colt and magazine now combined, he walked up the stairs that led to the ground floor, hearing snoring from one of the rooms he passed. Having been here before, he knew the way out, though the door to the street had to be opened slowly, given it creaked.

Then he was out in the Stygian, moonless night, with not even starlight because of overhead cloud. There would be a curfew in place, that was standard military practice in a newly captured town, but Callum Jardine was in his element. With soft footfall and his senses tingling he moved through the town, silent but for the occasional barking of dogs. If there were patrols out they were far from diligent, for he did not see one. Even then it took hours to get out into open country, where finally he had a line of Italian pickets to get through, which had him crawling on his belly, hoping he did not come across a snake or a nest of scorpions.

Long before Jardine got clear and could stand and walk normally, using pinpricks of light from Aksum to guide him south, Arturo Spinetti had gone into the cellar and sprayed around a great deal of the *marquesa*'s expensive and distinctive fragrance, which he hoped was strong enough to last until the morning, when the bastard of a major would find out his prisoner had escaped.

There would be hell to pay, but of course he, like the three NCOs, had been sound asleep and had heard or seen nothing.

# CHAPTER TWENTY-THREE

'Well, I can sure as hell say this Spanish lady saw something I have missed.'

Corrie Littleton said that with feeling, to a rested, washed and breakfasted escapee, who had endured a long and wearying three-day walk south and was now enjoying a cup of excellent coffee in the lounge of the Gondar hotel.

'Then thank the Lord you have not been looking,' Jardine replied.

'I am looking now, buster, and I am still mystified.'

'Put it down to charm, luv,' Vince Castellano proposed. 'Must have been love at first sight. Italians call it the "thunderbolt".'

The dismissive sound the American girl made riled Jardine, while he was aware that she was not alone in her reaction. Vince had been delighted to see him and had appreciated how close a call it had been, but when Jardine explained how he had got away, who was responsible and why, the bland look of obscured disbelief was too obvious to miss.

Tyler Alverson had only opined with a doubt-filled aside that stranger things had happened in his life, while Ma Littleton, the only one not still present in the hotel – she had gone back to her previous archaeological digs – had been of the view that this Spanish lady was no better than she ought to be.

'I just hope she is not in trouble for it.'

Alverson's slow drawl was filled with irony. 'Now, in a movie, Cal, you would strap on your weapons, put your hat firmly on your head, set your square jaw and, ignoring the pleas of your friends to show some sense, head out on your trusty steed to rescue her, backed by swelling music . . .'

'Not swelling enough to fill that head, Tyler,' Corrie Littleton cracked.

'What are you still doing here?'

'And what business, Jardine, is that of yours?'

'You're annoying me.'

'Then leave.'

'He would if he knew where to go, honey.'

'Nothing stopping us now, guv,' said Vince, backing Alverson up.

'I thought you wanted to report on the war, Tyler?'

'I do, Cal, but I guess I kinda think I dropped you in enough shit for one fight.'

'You shouldn't swear in front of ladies, Mr Alverson,' complained Vince.

'He didn't,' Jardine said, glaring at Corrie Littleton, seeing her tongue again.

The commotion outside distracted them all at the same time, the sound of a number of noisy vehicles arriving at once surprising them all equally. They got to their feet as *Ras* Kassa Meghoum, with several junior military officers on his heels, strode into the hotel lounge, his eyes fixed firmly on one man.

'Captain Jardine, I was told you were here.'

'Can I say I am surprised to see you, sir?'

'My being here is not something I expected either, Captain,' Kassa replied, nodding in turn to the others, 'but my emperor has been betrayed and I have come to shore up an event that should never have happened. Haile Selassie Gugsa, the Lion of Judah's own son-in-law, has deserted to the Italians, which has left a gaping hole in our front lines, the size of which we are uncertain.'

'How important is this Gugsa feller?' Alverson asked, which made the *ras* look at him hard, in a way that indicated he was disinclined to answer. 'You can tell me, sir, or I can find out another way, given, even if it is a secret now, it won't be that for long.'

'It is not something I would want the world to know, Mr Alverson.'

'Then I suggest you figure out a way to shoot every journalist the Italians have with them, and I am reliably told they brought along near two hundred. The Rome papers will spread this story fast and use it to make out the whole of Ethiopia is falling apart.'

'Which it is not!'

'That was my next question, and if that is true, it is a story you have to get out and damn quick. How have the Italians reacted?'

'They are still in Aksum, as far as I am aware, making preparations to move on to Mek'ele.'

'He should have done that days ago,' Jardine said. 'Stopping in Aksum was madness.'

'For De Bono read De Bonehead.'

'I was told you acquired a car, Mr Alverson.'

'I did.'

'Then perhaps you will use it to follow Captain Jardine and I while I go forward to assess the damage.'

'I'll get my kit,' Jardine said, before looking towards a curious-cum-concerned Vince. 'You don't have to come.'

'What? Leave you, guv, the trouble you get yourself into?'

'Can I come?' Corrie Littleton asked.

'Why?' Jardine demanded.

'To annoy you, that's why.'

'Really.'

'Beats sitting on my butt round here.'

'If you're sure you want to, honey,' Alverson drawled, 'there's room in the Rolls.'

'Tyler, it could be dangerous.'

'Good,' Corrie Littleton spat back at Jardine. 'Do I get a gun, *Ras*?'

'Why would you want a gun, Miss Littleton?'

'There's a Spanish broad up north very short on brains who needs to be put out of her misery.' Seeing the confusion on the older man's face, she added, 'I'll explain later.'

They went in convoy, on a road now free of any traffic, apart from a few supply columns that were rapidly shifted by a blaring klaxon, the *ras* in front in a Dodge with Alverson behind, he followed by several of the limited number of trucks in the Ethiopian army. They were carrying the escort, those same Shewan warriors that had accompanied them from the coast, and all armed with a portion of the weapons they had helped bring in. Jardine had asked Vince to go in the open-topped Rolls and keep his eyes peeled for aircraft, while he used the time to quiz *Ras* Kassa about what he thought would happen now.

'For the moment our problem is nothing is happening in the way we anticipated, and that is due to De Bono, for he will not advance except at the pace of a snail. Information is coming in from those in Italy who are sympathetic that Mussolini is losing patience with him and he may be replaced.'

'Would it not be better to hope he remained?'

'No, Captain Jardine, it would not. We must fight these devils, and the longer our forces stay in the field, the greater the strain on our resources and morale. We need our people to see that it is possible to take on the Italians, and soon. Then we need them back on their land growing food.'

What the older man was not saying, and Jardine could understand why, was that the defection of the emperor's own son-in-law was a blow that might have repercussions: Gugsa would not be the only Ethiopian aristocrat with flaky loyalty, while some tribes like the Galla, according to what he had learnt, were outright in opposition, openly supporting the Italians.

The double sound of the klaxon behind indicated to Jardine that Vince had spotted a plane, which led him to suggest that they pull off the road and get out of the vehicles. He had been wondering where the Italian air force was, because if he had been in command of the *Regia Aeronautica* this road would have been shut to traffic in daylight, and it was not.

The Ethiopians did have some anti-aircraft capability but not enough to trouble an Italian air force said to run to nearly a thousand planes. Perhaps they wanted their enemies before them in the mass and had no desire to stop them – foolish to his mind because he had seen what aircraft could do to a marching army, and it was devastating.

'It may be friendly, Captain. I asked for reconnaissance so I could be kept informed.'

So it proved, with a biplane landing on the road before them. Jardine suspected before he knew that it would be de Billancourt and he was disappointed to be proved right, though the information the Frenchman brought was positive. Most of Gugsa's men had stayed loyal and the front seemed secure, which left Alverson with a dilemma: it was a scoop and he wanted that story out before it got back to Addis and became general knowledge, a point he put to a pensive *Ras* Kassa while Corrie Littleton allowed her hand to be drooled over once more, that was until the Frenchman was called over to the *ras*.

'Take Mr Alverson to the headquarters of *Ras* Seyoum and ask, from me, that he be given access to the telegraph line through to the Sudan. Just this once, Mr Alverson, we will do this, for it is important, but it is not something which will happen again, I fear.'

'Thank you, sir,' Alverson replied, before addressing de Billancourt. 'No dogfights, pal, I get airsick.'

'It's goin' to be just you an' me in the Rolls, miss.'

'You can't win them all, Vince,' Jardine said in a voice larded with deep sympathy.

None of them had ever known how powerful *Ras* Kassa Meghoum was, but you did not have to be at the main tactical HQ of the Ethiopian army behind Mek'ele to realise he was a man who had the ear and the trust of the emperor. He was not deferred to in an obsequious way, but the attention paid to his words by the field commanders showed they took what he said seriously. After a conference lasting several hours, from which the people he had fetched along were excluded, he emerged and took Jardine aside.

'I have been asked to take over the remainder of Gugsa's forces and a whole sector of the army, which will be reinforced and brought up to its previous strength. I would consider it an honour if you would agree to become an advisor to my command.'

'You know what my advice would be, as I have told you many times: don't fight, withdraw and harry the enemy.'

'That was strategic advice, which I cannot take, nor would I want to, and besides, the decision resides with my emperor. But we must have a battle soon and I expect the forces I command to be part of that. I would value your tactical advice in such a situation.'

'Do you intend to hold your present positions?'

'We do, and De Bono must come towards us and take a risk, eventually.'

'Might be an idea to goad him by launching some raids.'

'That is what you would suggest?'

'He must have disgruntled inferiors, sir, officers eager to engage with you. All the pressure will not just be coming from Rome, and it is a bad idea to leave him to choose his own time to do whatever he wishes. You said your men were good night fighters, and a few slit throats . . .'

'These men I brought with me are the ones you were training and I know they respect you.'

'You want me to lead them?'

'I am to be in command of forty thousand warriors. It is not something I could do, much as my spirit wishes it.'

'Where are we based?'

'I think it is time, Captain Jardine, that I let you see a map of where the emperor's forces are.'

Accustomed to European quality maps it was sobering to see the paucity of detail on the Ethiopian equivalents, but the main thrust of their approach was obvious. Their forces were in three divisions arced behind Mek'ele, covering the two routes to Addis: the one they had come by, via Gondar and the side of Lake Tana, the second more easterly route passing through Lalibela. One flank was protected by the Simien mountains and the eastern one by the waterless Danakil Depression. If those two features canalised the Italian advance it was still a broad front to defend.

By pulling back from the kind of flat terrain that favoured a mechanised army into more broken country they had blunted the enemy hopes. De Bono, if he wanted to make progress, would have to beat them in the hills and valleys that confined his armour, but which allowed for the lateral movement of foot-bound spearmen. They could not avoid facing tanks, but the Ethiopians could limit their exposure while making life difficult for the Italian artillery. That still left the air force as a problem, and there was no doubt they would suffer from aerial bombing.

Jardine's problem was one of command – there was no way he was going to go forward with completely untrained troops – quite apart from, for him, his lack of language; he needed an interpreter, not necessarily at the point of contact with the enemy, but at all points in between, and especially when it came to outlining his intentions. Such training would not be speedy, weeks would be required, and these were points he put to *Ras* Kassa and they were accepted.

'But let us hope the Italians do not grant you the time.'

'I also need to do some air reconnaissance to look for

opportunities. And since, if we do raid the Italian lines, it will be at night, can we get them to wear black *shammas* instead of white?'

In the end it was the two rulers who decided the next phase, Mussolini by removing De Bono just after he had occupied Mek'ele, promoting him to *Maresciallo d'Italia* to soothe his pride, and replacing him with the reputedly more aggressive Marshal Pietro Badoglio. He certainly seemed more active, using his air force, with many more reconnaissance flights and bombing raids on the supply routes, forcing the Ethiopians off the roads, yet that exposed one of the values of a peasant army: they could operate cross-country.

Likewise Haile Selassie, given a new and untried enemy commander, set his mind on attacking the Italians as quickly as an offensive could be mounted, rank folly to Cal Jardine, but it was unmistakeable the enthusiasm such a notion – not to mention his imperial presence – engendered in the forces under his command, and even he had to accept that in war, with nothing being certain, it might just work.

Not that Haile Selassie was personally impressive, excepting he had the power of his monarchical office. He was a small, rather insignificant man, bearded, and he arrived on his various visits to his troops on a donkey, with even his truncated height leaving his feet perilously close to the ground. If, to Western eyes, it appeared absurd, it did not do so to his subjects, and Tyler Alverson, who had now established himself as a sort of special correspondent, was given permission to report on his arrival and even allowed to send out photographs, scooping the whole tribe of journalists still stuck in Addis Ababa.

Jardine and Vince, having spent weeks in training groups of

319

warriors, were encouraged to speed up their instruction, which meant trying to get some order and tactical nous into what was the usual form of warfare in this part of the world, based on brio and sheer weight of numbers. Proper weapons were so limited they had to be shared – if you left out spears, which every warrior carried and seemed to favour – and communication was slow, since everything had to be translated by a young man called Shalwe, a one-time teacher who knew a fair amount of English.

Any success they had, and that was partial, came by the picking out of those few who showed some appreciation of the need for battlefield control and forming them into cadres in charge of manageable platoons of thirty men, then companies of ninety to a hundred, though care needed to be exercised not to upset tribal superiors in a very hierarchical society.

So, when it came to battalion level, the leaders were aristocrats, one named Yoannis, the other Aswaf, of the level of *fitawrari*, which equated to commander of the vanguard – fitting, given they were assigned a special attacking role at the forefront of *Ras* Kassa's loosely coordinated divisions, while it was made plain to Jardine he was an advisor, not a commander.

He was at least privileged to be allowed access to the Ethiopian plan of attack, through the good offices of *Ras* Kassa, which was certainly ambitious: nothing less than an attempt to separate the various corps, then crush the Italian ground forces and invade Eritrea with the aim of evicting them from that territory. But there was little sense in being an advisor and not giving advice. Thanks to a notion of his, readily agreed to, Yoannis and Aswaf would be right at the spearhead of that attack, and they would have the men who had overseen their training alongside them.

'So let me into the loop, Cal,' Alverson demanded. 'I promise to keep the plans under my hat till it's clear to spill.'

'You have to wait, Tyler, until the offensive is under way.'

'You think it's a secret, you think our Italian friends don't know what's coming?'

'They know there's an offensive coming but they don't know the details.'

'You hope, brother. My guess is that this place leaks plenty, and this new guy is a hotter proposition than De Bonehead.'

'Where's Goody Two Shoes?' Jardine asked, to change the subject.

'Who dat?'

'It's a very old children's story, but in this case it's Corrie Littleton.'

'You have a real down on her, Cal, don't you?'

'I think you've got that the wrong way round.'

'She's a feisty dame, for sure, but she's not a bad person, though I will grant that her mother is a pain in the ass.'

'So where is she?'

'Right now she's helping to set up a field hospital with a Spanish doctor and driving *Ras* Kassa mad asking for supplies and equipment. That French pilot guy is doing his best to get stuff into her.'

'I bet he is.'

'Jealous?'

'In your dreams.'

'If you two cats would stop spitting at each other you might find you could get along.'

'That is what I need to do, Tyler – we move out at dawn, so get your head down.'

'I'll be there.'

'Tyler, I know you've been around some, and in a few hairy places, but this is going to be real bloody. We're attacking prepared positions, sandbagged lines, trenches with machine guns, artillery that is already ranged – and that leaves out planes which will be strafing us all day long.'

'Cal, you're not suggesting I should stay at home?'

'No, just be careful. I just had a vision of you ending up in Corrie Littleton's field hospital, that's all.'

'Hell, I'll be right alongside *Ras* Kassa.'

'Tyler, that old bastard is set on sticking a spear into an Italian arse and twisting it. Being next to him once his blood is up could be the most dangerous place on the battlefield, bar none.'

'Boy, that would be some photograph, Cal.'

All along the Ethiopian front lines, in a chilled pre-dawn, a mass of movement was under way, close to two hundred thousand men pressing forward like pale white ghosts in three separate armies. Any observer looking into their eyes would not have seen fear, for it was not present. They might have seen excitement and anticipation; they would most certainly have heard the soft sound of prayers from deeply religious warriors. As the first hint of light touched the eastern sky the Italian artillery opened fire, dropping shells in front of their lines, for they did indeed know what was coming. Soon there would be bombers and fighters overhead.

With Vince Castellano at his side, Cal Jardine had moved out in the hours of darkness. They were just behind Yoannis and Aswaf, the leaders of the men they had trained, moving towards their chosen objective, the Dembeguina Pass: a narrow, heavily defended defile that was a critical part of the Italian defences.

The aim was to get behind the Italians holding the head of the pass and, acting in conjunction with the local assault, drive a wedge into the Italian positions which, exploited, could threaten the whole security of their line, which would draw in more troops to hold it and thus create weaknesses elsewhere that the rest of the army could take advantage of.

Jardine was troubled: Pietro Badoglio had tempted the army of Haile Selassie into the kind of battle that should have been fought in reverse. He knew from bitter experience the cost of attacking prepared positions, yet he could also feel that excitement, like his blood was coursing through his veins at a faster pace, which half-pleased him and half-appalled him: was it right that a man, any man, should seemingly so love war that he actively sought it out?

# CHAPTER TWENTY-FOUR

Tyler Alverson was now in possession of a powerful pair of binoculars so he could see when *Ras* Kassa Meghoum's forward elements hit the Italian line at first light. They did so with such force and in such numbers that the enemy were forced away from their natural line of retreat north-east, falling back instead into the confines of the Dembeguina Pass, through which they could rejoin their compatriots. What Alverson could not see was that which lay behind them, the two thousand men led by the two *fitawraris* Yoannis and Aswaf, sent by the *ras* on the suggestion of Cal Jardine to cover just such an eventuality.

The Italian commander, Major Angelo Critini, was a bit of a ruffian but a good soldier, if not a popular one amongst his fellow officers, given he was inclined to remind them that their duties extended beyond the needs of their personal comforts and that, if they failed to care for their men, their men could hardly be expected to care for them. This was not news most of his peers wished to hear, nor did his superiors care much for such reminders, moving him to the position of senior major in a battalion of Eritrean askaris, seen as something of a push aside in the snobbish army of which he was a member.

Critini had two reasons to be happy: first, his colonel, a cavalryman, was absent having his crippling haemorrhoids seen to in Italy. Secondly, he was a fighter, and he knew that when it came to combat, the askaris would be in the forefront: there were going to be casualties and the high command would rather sacrifice native troops than the boys from home.

A professional soldier, Critini had fought his first serious engagement in the Great War as a newly commissioned lieutenant at the battle of Caporetto, where the Italian army, poorly led and bled white by twelve repeated and futile assaults on the Austrian lines of the River Isonzo, was nearly destroyed by an unexpected combination of battle-hardened Germans released from the Eastern Front by the collapse of imperial Russia, backing up the more feeble Austrians, an attack that had led to a confused, bloody and costly retreat.

He was in retreat now from his prepared positions before a set of hills, but, even if the sheer numbers of those who had begun the assault had forced him away from his natural route of disengagement, he was not worried. Seeing the mass of warriors he faced, who seemed indifferent to risk, and to avoid being outflanked before he could retire into the pass, he sent forward the six Carro Veloce L3/35 tanks he commanded to slow the enemy advance with machine-gun fire and retired behind their twin 8 mm guns in good order.

It was only then he discovered he had been out-thought: lying on the hillsides of the pass through which he intended to retire were elements of the enemy he had no idea were present; they had got behind him during the night by crossing the high hills on foot, and they now sent down a withering fire from two machine guns onto his battalion, that followed by sporadic but steady rifle fire.

Unbeknown to Critini, they did not all have rifles, for if they had, assailed by two thousand of them, he would have suffered an immediate and near-total massacre. He was spared that because he faced a force armed mostly with spears and bows, something he realised as arrows began to drop in amongst his forward elements and the dozens of mules carrying his supplies.

The commands he then issued were crisp and orderly, something Cal Jardine watched with appreciation through his field glasses. He did not know the man in charge, but his actions told anyone with a military brain the fellow knew his job. He did not panic, nor did he allow his troops to. Critini, himself on horseback, immediately ordered his men and animals forward into what seemed like a maelstrom, accepting the casualties he suffered in both areas as unavoidable to get them to a point where, with decent cover, the terrain favoured him.

Dismounted, he then calmly formed them up in a hedgehog defence, which would be hard to break through, and, stripping his remaining mules, set up his own machine guns to rake the hillsides. He also managed to salvage a number of mortars. Jardine immediately requested Yoannis's machine guns to cease fire in order to conserve their very limited ammunition, which produced a pout on the face of the nearest *fitawrari*: he disliked having an advisor along and he was not in the least affected by a mortar round landing nearby, which severely wounded some of his men.

Drawing a heavy sword, Yoannis shouted, through Shalwe, the interpreter, 'We attack now and kill them all.'

'I advise against that.'

Jardine guessed as the words were translated he was wasting his breath: the light in the Ethiopian leader's eyes was one of wild excitement, and all around him the men he led, indifferent to the casualties among them, were keening in anticipation of what they expected to do. Many, like their leader, were brandishing swords, while Yoannis was waving his weapon and shouting to his fellow *fitawrari*, Aswaf, across the narrow pass, to join in the slaughter.

'He is saying they are beaten,' Shalwe said, and it looked as though the young interpreter believed it too.

'Tell Yoannis they are not and they have machine guns and more mortar rounds. If he tries to overwhelm them many will die.'

'You won't stop them, guv,' Vince said quietly in his ear. 'They are too worked up.'

Jardine never got a chance to answer that because all around him the *shamma*-clad warriors were on their feet and being led out of their excellent cover in a wild charge down the hillside, presenting, in their white garments, tempting targets. They were attacking troops who had years of training, not weeks, and it showed immediately as the controlled volley fire began to decimate the attackers.

The Italian machine guns raked the hillsides in a slow and deadly progression, the mortar-fire range dropping also, a steady rate of shells bursting in amongst the rushing warriors. It was not all one-sided, for defenders were falling to rifle fire: Jardine saw one Italian officer go down; he was – as was required in such a circumstance – bravely standing up to control his men, making him an easy target, yet it had to be luck, given the discharges were wild.

Critini saw one lieutenant drop just before he took a bullet in the soft muscle of his upper left arm, which felled him, thankfully and quickly aware that it had missed the bone. He was back on his feet within two seconds, seeing clearly that his defence was holding and that the furious Ethiopian charge was faltering in the face of everything already employed, now backed up by the machine guns of his tanks, which were in the middle of his position and had manoeuvred into a circle to cover all the approaches.

Jardine was cursing the folly of what he saw, yet there was a glimmer of a positive, something that told him the instructions he and Vince had tried to impart were not entirely wasted. On the other side of the pass Aswaf had not engaged in a wild charge, but instead sent out his riflemen to make their way slowly down the hillside, seeking cover from boulders as they went, their aim to pick off individual targets, particularly the Italian officers, easy to spot in their distinctive uniforms. It was they who were inflicting the most damage.

Yoannis, now stuck lower down, clearly realised the folly of his attack and was signalling to fall back using cover. Was it a tribute to training that he was so quickly obeyed? Jardine did not know, he was only grateful to see the casualty count drop away as men got behind boulders or crawled through scrub back to their starting positions.

The Italians had been chased into the pass by other forces, yet none of their fire was aimed in the direction from which they had come, a condition Jardine had insisted upon when the plan had been outlined. He was advising hard to control warriors and he did not want to have to worry about shooting those on his own side coming in pursuit. If the pass was cleared, that was the time for a good part of the main body to advance.

Corrie Littleton was no doctor, but she was one of nature's organisers and that, with the first casualties pouring into her aid station, was just as important as wielding a surgical knife. The Spanish doctor and his nurses were working flat-out, but thanks to the American, the only cases that got to his operating table were those that would benefit from immediate treatment. Having been violently sick when the first wounded came in with torn bodies and hanging-off limbs, she was now working on a stomach long empty to assess each case.

Those close to death were left, as were the men with wounds that left them ambulant; it was the in-betweens that were given priority, and Corrie Littleton had lost any guilt for the fact that her decision-making might be flawed: the numbers as well as the extent of wounds from artillery fire were too great for such concerns, because the main attack of *Ras* Kassa's forces, taking place to the east of the Dembeguina Pass, had run into a solid Italian defence.

In soft ground the Italians had dug trenches, on rocky surfaces they had built lines of sandbags interspersed with redoubts, both types of defence backed by machine guns and mortars aided by tactical and long-range artillery. Fanatical bravery, and the Ethiopians had that in excess, was another reason for the high casualty numbers, and what was being seen by Corrie Littleton was only a fraction of the losses the Imperial Army was suffering.

Tyler Alverson stood on the high outcrop from which *Ras* Kassa Meghoum was trying to control his part of the battle, watching the stream of messages coming in from staff officers in the green uniforms of the regular forces, but even with powerful glasses he could see nothing much, so great was the smoke and dust being created by gunfire and explosive shells.

Every so often an Italian fighter would strafe their position, the few anti-aircraft weapons they possessed seeking to dissuade them, which meant a leap into the previously prepared dugouts, but what they feared most was not long in coming into play: the Italian bombers.

Not a single projectile was dropped on their position, but dozens of the Savoia-Marchetti trimotors ranged across the rear areas of the advancing forces, covered overhead by numerous fighters to ward off any attempts to interfere in the destruction of the thousands of men waiting their turn to go into the battle raging before them. When the bombers departed, their escorts dived in to rake the area with gunfire, yet even under such an aerial assault the Ethiopian forces did not buckle.

'Can you not advance through the Dembeguina Pass, *Ras?*' Alverson asked.

The old man shook his head. 'Not until we hear it is clear. Your friend Jardine was adamant that we would end up shooting at each other. Word will come when they are successful.'

'Would I be allowed to go and see?'

'You are a free spirit, Mr Alverson, you may go where you wish, but I will detail someone to escort you.'

That journey took Tyler Alverson past the casualty clearing station where he encountered a blood-covered Corrie Littleton racing to and fro between the wounded cases lying and sitting all around her tents, shouting to orderlies to take this one and that, while a constant stream of new cases were carried or staggered in. He was about to try and talk to her when he heard the screaming engine of an aeroplane and he looked up to see the silhouette in the sky of a Fiat fighter.

His shout to her to get down took a second to register, so that she was still standing when the first of a line of bullets hit the ground. She did dive to her right, which saved her life, but the run of gunfire hit the comatose bodies of those already wounded until the firing ceased as the Fiat screamed overhead, with Corrie Littleton up, yelling and shaking her fist at a bastard who had ignored the huge red crosses on the tent roofs.

Alverson saw that same bastard bank for another run and shouted a fresh warning, but so intent was the Italian fighter pilot on what he was doing that he had ignored the first rule of aerial combat – keep your eyes open and look around you at all times. The Potez 25 came from above, with the eastern sun at its back, its machine gun a stuttering, muted tattoo at the distance from which the two Americans could hear it.

The Italian fighter seemed to stagger almost, as though its engine had lost power, then it banked as smoke began to pour out from the cockpit area. So fast was it moving that only imagination could picture what was happening to that pilot, but what was obvious was the way the Ethiopian was following him down as he lost altitude, firing short bursts into the burning enemy.

The explosion of the Fiat hitting the earth made the ground around them shake, but the aircraft noise did not diminish. The Potez came flashing low overhead, slightly banked, and the pilot had taken off his flying helmet. Even at a hundred and twenty miles an hour the waving hand, the blond hair and, Alverson was sure, the gleaming teeth of Count Henri de Billancourt were plain to see.

Corrie Littleton was screeching her thanks and jumping up and down as the Frenchman came over for a victory roll, but as soon as he disappeared she went back to her tasks. Tyler Alverson got no more than a look, and a grim one at that.

The site the Italian commander had chosen was, as long as his ammunition and water lasted, in a reasonably good place. The rate of fire on both sides had dropped – to be expected, since to just keep going was a useless expenditure of ammunition – but Critini kept up sporadic mortar fire at a conserving rate, given it was his most effective deterrent weapon. He also wasted no time in seeking to get away a small party of his most fleet-footed *askaris* to test out an escape route.

Jardine and Vince grabbed rifles from a couple of the returning tribesmen and sought to pick them off, while the machine guns were employed from both sides of the pass. Dodging from boulder to boulder, or seeking shelter behind the scrub that covered the valley floor, made them hard targets, but to cheers, one by one they were brought down, aided by intelligent fire from Aswan's men opposite.

'*Fitawrari* Yoannis wishes to know what will happen now,' Shalwe asked, pointing to the man in question, who had got back to safety but seemed to want to stay well away from the professional soldier advising him.

The reply was angry. 'Tell him to look.'

The Carro Veloce CV35s were using their tracks to turn in tight circles, noses pointing north, while some of the askaris were levering a large rock out of the way that blocked the exit route.

'This is no time to be snooty, is it?' Vince said. 'He knows he's cocked up, guv, an' he wants your help.'

'That's a boot up the arse you owe me, Vince,' Jardine replied after a pause, for his friend was right.

'I'd settle for a pint of Bass.'

'I'll let you have a sip of water.'

'Right now that will taste as sweet as best bitter.'

A skin was called for and they both drank from it, refreshed even if it was body temperature warm.

'OK. They are going to try and break out with those tanks, but if you look at the valley floor I think they will have a tough time of it.'

'Too many boulders.'

'Not just that, Vince, it's bloody uneven. At best they will be slow, so I want you to stay here with half a dozen rifles, and once the tanks are out, keep up a steady fire on the Italian perimeter to stop the infantry following. Use the machine guns if you have to, but we are short on ammo for those. I am going to take Yoannis and most of his men further up the pass. Shalwe, tell *Fitawrari* Yoannis that we need some grenades and his men are to do what I do. And tell him as well, don't fire off rifles, it will be a waste of bullets.'

Jardine crawled away to the sound of tanks moving, their engines, lacking silencers, roaring, a sound that echoed and was magnified as it bounced off the faces of the surrounding hills. Slowly, in single file, they emerged from the defensive perimeter and it was obvious what Jardine had said was true.

Tanks were good over rough ground but this was more than that: it was horrendous for such small armoured vehicles powered by not very strong engines, with boulders forcing the drivers to try and take routes that were too steep even for their tracks, and that was before one side dropped into the depressions unseen by a driver peering through a narrow, metal-armoured slit, which gave him no sideways vision.

Regardless of Jardine's instructions, some of Yoannis's warriors were wasting ammo on the tank armour, but that, pinging on the side and exaggerated in what must be a baking hellhole of an interior, was enough to keep those driver slits closed. They were well away from the main Italian position now, and behind them they could hear the steady crack of rifle fire as the men with Vince kept up enough of a threat to ensure that infantry did not support the tanks.

It only took one to break down and get into trouble to show what would happen. Tank Number Three got stuck, and regardless of how hard it revved and bucked to and fro, stuck it stayed. Those to the rear tried to go round it and that meant a second tank ended up in difficulty, though it looked as though the driver was about to reverse and extricate himself, this while those to his rear stopped to see if he could manage it, for if he could not, they must reverse.

Now it was Cal Jardine on his feet and waving, as he plunged down the hillside, firing off single shots from his sub-machine gun, more for effect than to kill. With no turret to swing, the CV35s were sitting ducks from the rear, their machine guns only able to fire forward in a constrained arc, which he avoided by coming in behind them. He was yelling as hard as he could to draw the attention of those he was leading, as he dragged a pin out of a grenade and jammed it into the track of the rear tank, diving under the spitting machine guns to get out of the way of the blast.

The explosion sounded tremendous, but it was the clanking sound of a destroyed metal track that was music to Cal Jardine's ears. Now his sword-wielding warriors were on top of the tank, beating with the flat of their blades on the armour, while one sought to lever open the hatch to drop in a grenade, another jabbing his weapon through the driving slit. The Italian gunner should have kept up his fire, if only to aid those ahead of him, but either he or the driver panicked and the hatch swung open, with two hands coming out as the first one tried to surrender.

He was grabbed by the hands of his enemies and dragged onto the side of the tank, where one yanked at his hair while another caught hold of his feet, then the sword came flashing down to take his head off in one sweep, with his driver being lugged into daylight just in time to see his mate die. His screams seemed as ear-splitting as the explosion of that grenade, but they were stopped as he too was decapitated. Jardine was shouting as loud as he could to let him be and take him prisoner; it was wasted breath.

One by one they moved up the line of tanks and each crew suffered the same fate, which sickened a man who knew that to seek to interfere was to risk the same himself. These warriors had their blood up and for them this primitive form of retribution was the norm, not some exception. Someone must have had the means to light a fire, for first one tank burst into flames, then another, with Jardine now yelling for them to get clear before the ammunition went up. By the time they left, all six tanks were ablaze.

Down the pass Vince could see the smoke and he knew that the Italian commander would see it too, so he called on his riflemen to cease fire; those askaris were going nowhere. Yet even he, and he considered himself immune, nearly puked when some of Yoannis's warriors came loping along carrying Italian heads, which they threw in a blood-dripping arc into the enemy defences.

# CHAPTER TWENTY-FIVE

D own below, Major Critini, arm now in a sling, was on his radio, a piece of equipment not functioning well because of the high surrounding hills, seeking aid from headquarters to extricate the remainder of his battalion from the Dembeguina Pass, aware merely by the garbled replies that his messages were not being fully understood. His remaining officers, two lieutenants being wounded, had reported to him that casualty numbers were high, supplies of ammunition adequate, and water supplies were worrying, given they were trapped in a spot that intensified the heat of the sun.

He was thanking God, and he was a deeply religious man, that he was in command of native troops, for when it came to forbearance they were streets ahead of his fellow Italians. Those tankers' heads, thrown in amongst European soldiers, might have induced panic; in his Eritreans it got a response of loud whistles, which he hoped his enemies understood to be derision.

He had been attacked at dawn and his withdrawal had occupied no more than two hours, so he knew there would be no shade for a long time, but his men were used to the heat and being thirsty; his officers, being Italian, less so. He told them to get some kind of shelter constructed where they could take turns in getting out of the sun, and to drink small amounts frequently; they would be no good to him woolly and confused with dehydration.

Up above him Cal Jardine was seeking him out through his field glasses – decapitate the enemy and they are more easily overcome – but Critini was too wily a bird to expose himself to either another wound or death. Visible, though, was the long sliver of the antenna of his radio, sticking up above a rock and waving slightly in the gentle breeze. Then it disappeared, indicating the transmission was over, which had Jardine cursing his lack of mortars.

Calling over Shalwe he sent him to Yoannis with a request, one that was answered in the shape of four warriors younger than most of their fellows. In fact, they looked to be hardly meaningfully into their teens, but they had the eagerness and gaiety of youth added to their natural warrior spirit, and once it was made plain what was wanted they seemed to vie to be the one to do it alone. What Jardine was asking for was potentially suicidal and he wanted them to be gifted what safety was possible by numbers: as long as one succeeded, that would suffice.

It is one of the burdens of command that you accept some of your men might die and Jardine had no time for the nonsense spouted by others that you should never ask your men to do what you would not do yourself. Yes, in extreme circumstances, you must share the same risks, but in battle proper command is vital; only idiots threw their lives away with the kind of foolhardy bravery that left their men leaderless.

It took time to explain to these youths what he wanted, and he had to make sure they knew how to use a grenade and how to time the gap between pulling the pin, throwing it and making certain they were not caught by the blast. Most of all, he stressed they had time and they should take it – the last thing he wanted was a stupid rush that would result in utter failure.

'Think you are hunting the lion,' he had Shalwe tell them, pleased at the eager nods such an allusion received: they knew a thing like that required stealth and that was the easiest way of explaining to them the need for that now.

The hardest thing to do was to persuade them to relinquish their *shammas*: it seemed to be seen as a mark of shame to discard it, but Jardine had already observed how the white garment made every man he was with an easy target if they exposed themselves; divested of those, in just loincloths and with their coffee-coloured skin, the boys blended more with their surroundings. He was tempted to tell them not to smile either: they had very good white teeth, as well as a ready propensity to show them.

For those on the hillsides water and ammunition were plentiful, given the mouth of the pass was under the control of the Ethiopians. Food came too, though less welcome was Tyler Alverson, his Leica camera round his neck. He arrived, with an escorting regular officer and a pair of bearers carrying his tripod as well as a kitbag, in such a useless fashion he drew fire from below. He then went on to complain the Italians were too far away and too well camouflaged by nature to get a good picture.

'Well, forgive me,' Jardine responded. 'I'll just nip down and ask them to stand up and come closer.'

'Pity they chucked away all those heads,' Vince remarked. 'That would have made for a good snap.'

That was explained to Alverson, who, if he was fazed by the thought of it, did not let on. 'No prisoners, eh?' Jardine just shook his head. 'You know what that means? The Italians won't take any either.'

'What makes you think they would have anyway, Tyler? How are our boys doing, Vince?'

'They're stuck and need some help.'

Jardine got onto one knee and spayed a whole magazine into the enemy position, aware, through his peripheral vision, that his boys used that wisely. The defenders' heads being kept down, they had taken the opportunity to dart forward, but one exposed himself too long, bullets pinging around him as Jardine changed his magazine. It was Vince who saved him, firing off five rounds rapidly.

Having concentrated on what they could see, the askaris missed one of the others. He was close to his target and threw, as Alverson later described it in print, like a World Series pitcher. The grenade hit the top of the rocks behind which the radio was situated, but the bounce took it on. By the time the operator moved it was too late for him, he was blown away like a thrown sack of spuds, but more important, the Italians were now very likely without communications, so they could no longer keep their Divisional HQ aware of their situation.

'Captain Jardine,' Shalwe shouted from beside a chest-heaving, sweating messenger. 'More tanks, bigger tanks are coming.'

'Take charge here again, Vince – same drill. Shalwe, tell Yoannis to get half his men following and you come too.' Jardine was moving before he realised Alverson was on his heels. 'Where do you think you're going?'

'I gotta see this.'

'See what?'

'Whatever it is you're planning.'

'I don't have a plan, I'm reacting.'

'And I thought you were a military genius.'

'Take my advice, Tyler, if you ever come across one, stay clear – they tend to get themselves killed.'

'Can I come with you?'

'On your head be it.'

Even in his elevated position, Jardine could not move without attracting rifle fire, but being dressed in khaki clothing he at least blended with the surrounding features. Not Alverson in his white linen suit, which got him a string of loud curses. But it was not his fault, really: the two bearers he had brought along just saw their job as following wherever Alverson led. What they did not do was see any need to crawl like the man they were serving, and they had stood up to tag along. It was almost as if the Italian commander guessed such activity was important: he used his mortars again, which he had being doing sparingly to conserve rounds, the first projectile bursting too close for comfort and showering both Jardine and the American with bits of rock, one of which cut Jardine's cheek.

'You're bleeding,' Alverson said.

'And you are a bleeding nuisance.'

'Don't hold back, bud, tell me what you really think.'

Dabbing at his dust-covered cheek, Jardine had to laugh. 'Why do you do this, Tyler, risk getting yourself killed?'

'I could ask you the same question.'

'So we're both stupid.'

'And then some, brother.'

'Tell those bloody bearers of yours to keep their heads down.'

'You speak the lingo?' Jardine's head shake was superfluous. 'No, neither do I, but I can tell you this, those guys can run, so we won't lose them.'

Jardine was up and off like a greyhound out of trap 6, which left Alverson struggling to follow, so he waved his bearers forward and they showed a nice turn of speed as they swept past him, with him crawling in their wake to a point where he could stand up and walk.

'So what we got?' he gasped.

'Tanks, probably Fiat 3000s.'

'That bad?'

'They have turrets, Tyler.'

'Explain.'

'The tanks we destroyed before only had forward-firing machine guns. Turreted tanks, and these have 37 mm cannon, can bombard the hills, both sides. They have good power sources too, and can get over obstacles those little CV35s had to try and get round. We can't stop them the same way and I doubt we can do it without incurring losses.'

'And if they get through, our friend back there gets clear?'

'Yes, and worse, the pass is useless to *Ras* Kassa's forces, not that I think it's as good an opportunity as he does.' Seeing the need to say more, Jardine added, 'Anyone with a brain will have already sealed the other end with artillery and machine guns.'

'Which they are struggling to overcome elsewhere.' As they moved, Alverson explained what he had already witnessed, adding the work Corrie Littleton was doing. 'She is one resilient dame.'

'I never doubted that, Tyler.'

Given that terse response, it seemed churlish to add what had happened with de Billancourt; that could wait.

'Hear that?' Jardine asked.

Alverson had to listen for a while before he picked up what was being alluded to, the growling sound of tank engines. Jardine had broken into a run again, though at less than the previous pace, while behind them came a stream of Yoannis's warriors, with Jardine shouting out to Shalwe to tell them not to show themselves until he could assess the situation. It made no odds: the sound of cannons being fired was the next thing he heard as the Italian tanks put rounds into the hillsides just for safety.

Jardine stopped and called forward Shalwe, telling him to pass on the message to take cover and do nothing. 'And tell Yoannis I will personally put a bullet in him this time if he does not do as I ask.'

If the young interpreter nodded, it was not with the kind of emphasis which implied he was going to accurately pass on that message: whatever, the *fitawrari* would either obey or see his men suffer, because the cannons on the Fiat 3000s could be deadly, either through direct contact or through ricocheting rock splinters, and the Ethiopians had nothing that could lay a finger on them. The last thing Jardine wanted was for Yoannis to try to really engage, for if he did that nothing would be achieved but dead warriors. Also, if they were coming, there had to be significant infantry support.

The sound now was of four roaring tank engines and regular cannon fire. Looking out from behind cover, Jardine saw the more powerful Fiats either push boulders aside or, because they were vertically sprung, just go over them, the front of the tank rising to a seemingly impossible angle, protruding out from the obstacle being crossed, until the nose dropped with a bone-jarring crunch onto the angled front track.

Using his field glasses he could see the pass behind them, and, by some way too far back to be of effective support, the Italian infantry

342

making their way cautiously down the central track. Somebody should have been out of the upper turret of one of the Fiats so they could set their pace to the foot soldiers, but no one was.

With the tank drivers again only able to see forward, that separation presented opportunity. He had to get his head down as another shell hit a nearby boulder, breaking off a good portion of it to fly in all directions, spattering against rock faces all around the places where Yoannis's men had sought cover; at least the sod was doing what Jardine suggested, no doubt chastened by his earlier mistakes.

'So what now, Horatio?'

'You still here, Tyler?'

'Am I, and composing news of your stunning victory in my head.'

'Hold the front page.'

Jardine had to get on his belly to get back to Shalwe, and his message was plain: wait. Then it was back to his position to keep an eye on the Italian infantry support, which, if anything, was moving even slower than he had previously observed. Looking down into the pass, he was now level with the back end of the last of the four tanks, not that such a thing made for safety: the turret was swinging round so that it could fire to its rear if a target presented itself.

'You know, Tyler, if I was Badoglio, I would shoot whoever is in command of that infantry.'

'What infantry?'

'Use your binoculars. They're way down the pass, too far away to do the job they have been given. Which opens the way for us to do the necessary.'

'Which is?'

'Stopping those tanks.'

'Should we throw stones at them or is it to be spears?'

'Maybe,' Jardine replied enigmatically.

'You are a military genius, should I get away from you?' Seeing Jardine grin, he added, 'Even I know you can't stop tanks with rifles, and your guys have precious few of those.'

'You might want to tell your readers armour is only good for exploitation, Tyler. It takes boots to secure ground, and that idiot coming down the pass has left his mates in trouble.'

'I await this trouble with interest.'

'What's the bet we can beat the tanks without even using rifles?'

'I'll put ten dollars on that being impossible.'

'Taken, but make it thalers.' Then Jardine shouted, 'Shalwe, to me!'

The interpreter scrabbled over and Jardine outlined his latest suggestions: the first carried back to Yoannis, the evidence that they were accepted clear, as those warriors with rifles went past Jardine at a crouch, heading to cut off the infantry he suspected would not be hard to interdict. Shalwe was then told to send someone back to their main position for grenades.

By now, the last tank was well away from them – not out of cannon range, but that could not be helped. Jardine hand-signalled to Yoannis that it was time, and the remaining warriors came to join Jardine, their spears at the ready. He took one, shoved the long hardwood haft under a big rock, lifted, strained and pushed, sending it down to the valley floor, turning to see eager nods.

He had no need to tell them which boulders to lever – the biggest ones they thought they could shift. Several spears were jammed under one rock after another, which saw them begin to shift on a hillside that in the first place held them only precariously; such boulders had, at some time, come to rest where they were from a point higher up the hills. There were others further below, and as soon as one got moving, the odd spear shaft breaking in the process, they hit those, sending into the pass a cascade of rocks in a thunderous roaring and increasing avalanche.

The turret hatch on the last tank swung open, so great was the sound even in a noise-filled compartment, while from the north came the sound of the rifle fire Jardine hoped would hold the infantry long enough for him to achieve his goal, and still the boulders were being levered, bounding down the slope to create a wall of increasing size, filling and blocking the valley floor.

The tanks must have had some kind of radio contact, because their progress stopped abruptly and the rearmost tank began to reverse to a point where it could easily turn round, with its cannon firing towards the straining and now obvious warriors as fast as the loader could manage, though at a range which made accuracy difficult. That was a policy repeated by its consorts: the idea of being trapped did not appeal.

'Ten thalers you owe me, Tyler.'

'Not yet, Cal. Let's see what our friends do.'

Now it was a bit of a race: boulders were still being dislodged and the wall below was growing, but at some point the firepower of those cannon would reverse the advantage and the Ethiopians would begin to take serious casualties. Jardine was relieved to see the now-lead tank had stopped and was waiting for his fellows to make their turn: they would come back down the pass as a unit to maximise their firepower; another error, in his view, given time was their enemy too.

'Best pull back, Tyler, and get out of here. It's going to get very hairy.'

'You staying?'

'I have to keep observing.'

'I'm staying too, I have a wager on this.'

Another shout from Jardine brought Shalwe, and the advice was for Yoannis to get his men under any deep cover they could find, a suggestion driven home by the increasing number of shells coming their way. The Italian gunners knew which side the rocks were coming from, and where, so, stationary, they had concentrated their fire and taken more time over their aiming. As soon as they saw the cascade had been stopped, they began to move.

With clanking tracks they made their way towards what was now a serious obstacle, dozens of boulders piled on top of each other. The lead gunner had stopped firing at human flesh and was using his ammunition to blast the barrier, seeking to break it up, not with much success. Unable to observe for the incoming fire, Jardine was now counting shots, because there must be a limit to the shells a light tank could carry and the Italians were being profligate, firing off round after round, with the now-redundant drivers raking the hills with machine guns as well – pointless, given they had no targets to aim at.

The firing diminished and Jardine heard the one-engine note change to a scream, so he risked looking out. The lead tank was climbing the face of his boulder wall, again its nose pointing nearly vertical, tracks scrabbling on the looser rocks and failing to grip. Whoever was in command had a brain: he sent a second tank to get on its backside to aid its traction, which helped and it made the top of the barrier, with Jardine's heart sinking at the thought it was going to make it.

Having made the crest it balanced there precariously for a few seconds, before edging forward till it seemed impossible it could remain on an even keel, so far were its tracks sticking out. Then the nose dropped again with that sickening thud, but this time the forward tracks hit at such an angle they could get no traction and, in slow motion, the Fiat 3000 gently flipped over to drop on its turret and roll onto its side, rocking till it came to rest. The men inside must be seriously injured, but that was less important than that the rest of the tanks were trapped!

It was a waiting game then, cat and mouse, seeking to get the remaining tanks to use up their ammunition as the Italians were presented with seeming targets, which caused them to fire off wildly, until first one stopped and then the other two. They then tried to abandon their vehicles, the lower two-door forward hatches opening and the two-man crews jumping out. What greeted them was a wall of spear-carrying warriors charging downhill, screaming like banshees and totally indifferent to the fire from the Italian pistols.

One by one the tankers went down, to be slain by spear points before, like their compatriots earlier, their heads were cut off and their tanks set alight. The billowing black smoke told the story: through his field glasses Jardine watched as the Italian infantry slowly and deliberately withdrew.

Major Critini saw the smoke too, but he did not despair, for he had under his command good soldiers; trained, unlike those they faced. His men fought all day, but with commendable caution in terms of both life and the expenditure of ammunition. As the sun faded in the west, creating deep shadows, he abandoned any equipment he could not carry and began a fighting withdrawal up the pass, his troops showing admirable discipline under heavy attack, using bayonet charges where necessary to clear the way. That he lost half his remaining men on the way was a price worth paying, the alternative being to stay where he had been and lose them all.

Cal Jardine was not part of the pursuit. He, Vince and Alverson scrabbled down to the position the Eritreans had held on to all day in the heat, to look at the equipment left behind, much of it still strapped to the slaughtered mules. There was the shattered radio; the operator's body, like those of the other casualties, had been laid in neat rows and covered with tent canvas. They were still there when the first elements of the rest of *Ras* Kassa's forces began to pour through the Dembeguina Pass to seek to turn the flank of the Italian line and force them to retreat.

# CHAPTER TWENTY-SIX

The northern exit of the Dembeguina Pass was, as Jardine suspected, sealed off by artillery and well-sited machine guns, and to these were added regular infantry counter-attacks. Yet even backed by bombers and strafing fighters, so great was the pressure from the peasant army, and so reckless were they for their own safety all along the front, that the pressure began to infect the enemy high command, while what the world was to call the Ethiopian Christmas Offensive left little doubt regarding what they were seeking to achieve: nothing less than the destruction of the entire Italian position in the Horn of Africa.

The right- and left-wing armies, as planned, were fighting to get between the two Italian corps that had so recently invested Mek'ele and Aksum, the aim to cut them off, leaving them to be crushed by the Ethiopian centre while the two wings began an assault to the north, into Eritrea, which, if successful, might win them more than a second Adowa, with incalculable consequences in Rome.

Marshal Badoglio was forced to order a tactical withdrawal centred on Aksum, to shorten both his lines and his communications, aware that back in his homeland voices were being raised against the whole enterprise in Abyssinia, not least that of the man he had replaced. Such criticism was impacting on the reputation of Benito Mussolini himself, which brought forth a threat to remove Badoglio as well.

The cable he sent to save his skin was carefully worded to appeal to Il Duce's vanity, while subtly underlining the truth: if the invasion of Abyssinia faltered or even failed, ultimate responsibility rested with the politicians as well as the army commanders, and the price for both would be high.

He had to be careful, the dictator was not a leader he had originally endorsed in 1922. Indeed, for his doubts he had spent a number of years being sidelined for his lack of zealous support for the new dispensation, and it had taken subtle manoeuvring from his many Masonic and army friends to get back into the fold; in short, he was not entirely trusted.

It was necessary to employ flattery, of course, to speak of the glory of Italy, a once-broken country raised by Mussolini to stand as equal to any in Europe. He acknowledged him as the successor to the great dictators of ancient times – Cincinnatus, Sulla and, of course, Julius Caesar – pointing out that such heroic figures had not flinched from extreme measures to subdue their enemies. Yet, sadly, the present-day sons of Italy were paying a high price – a slight massaging to heighten the casualty figures aided him here – for the adherence to sensibilities that had only come to other colonial powers *after* they had secured their conquests.

He had at his disposal not only the means to arrest Emperor Haile Selassie's attempts to halt the march of history, but to throw him back and utterly destroy him, as well as his armies. He also reminded his political master that any finer feelings were required to be suppressed, for they were misplaced, given he had before him enemies who could lay no claim to being civilised. Was it not the mission of the Italian people, as it had been of the other European powers, to bring the vital gift of their culture to Ethiopia and its savage tribes?

Benito Mussolini would know of what he spoke, and being the great man he was, his loyal supporter Pietro Badoglio was sure he would not recoil from what was required, would not allow the hollow and hypocritical opprobrium of the feeble democracies, of socialists, of noble, savage-loving hypocrites, or even the combined voice of the League of Nations to deflect him.

The affirmative reply came back in days and Badoglio immediately sent to Asmara for the equipment necessary to protect his own troops from the decisive weapon, then called in his air force and artillery commanders to discuss how the knockout blow he envisaged could be delivered – one that would save the Italian campaign and his position.

Cal Jardine wanted to train the Ethiopians to do a bit of trench raiding, working on the same principle now as had been applied during the Great War: if you wanted to know the state of enemy morale and perhaps, if you were lucky, their immediate intentions, you infiltrated their lines and took prisoners, a point he had made to *Ras* Kassa, who came close to scoffing at the notion. He seemed content that, should his own warriors undertake such tasks, the slitting of Italian throats was satisfactory, reasoning that the average Italian soldier was as ignorant as any of his own men.

He was beginning to be contemptuous of his enemies; like most of his fellow leaders, and not excepting the emperor himself, the success of their offensive had gone to his head: all they could see was victory while Cal Jardine could observe none of the telltale signs of imminent collapse. There were no great captures of either bodies of troops or masses of equipment, which meant the enemy before them was not beaten but holding its own.

True, the Italians had been forced to give ground, but the opinion that they had not yet lost the battle was far from welcome: native flexibility would triumph over European efficiency and they held to that opinion; if anything it was reinforced, when, with the Ethiopian Christmas Offensive effectively halted, the enemy forces sought to renew their advance south. The fighting became punch and counterpunch, like two inflexible boxers, with only local gains on both sides, quickly reversed.

Try as they did, the Italians could not break through the masses of fanatical warriors; indeed, out from their trenches and sandbagged lines they were losing a higher proportion of their men and equipment compared to when they were purely on the defensive, adding to their woes, which was amazing given the differing levels of not just equipment but command capability both sides possessed.

The Ethiopians operated from rough-and-ready headquarters and the comparison with what Jardine had seen when captured was unavoidable: runners were used instead of field telephones and radio antennae, there were few vehicles and no smart guards, headquarters company or Pioneer Corps, just a mass of warriors squatting around in no sort of discernible order.

Nor did they have field kitchens; later they, and the survivors of a counter-attack now in progress, would be cooking over charcoal that had been carried to this place, not by a wheeled transport arm, but by donkeys or on human shoulders and heads – men, and in some cases women, who responded to an instruction to move this way or that by a series of shouted commands, acting more like a herd than an army.

He and Tyler Alverson were watching the latest foray when he mentioned the raiding problem to the American. The position they occupied, close to the Ethiopian commanders, was on a high elevation, while in front was spread the flat, rocky plateau on which the battle, a diversionary effort against a Fascist Blackshirt Division, was being blunted.

The main activity was taking place further east, the idea of this assault being to draw off artillery and air support from that more telling Italian thrust, which required that lives be sacrificed for that limited objective in a fashion reminiscent of the old Western Front; that it was not succeeding was evident by the deep droning sound of approaching aircraft.

'Seems to me they're reading their own news stories,' Alverson replied. 'You should see the shit they are sending out through their official information channels. They're claiming a Blackshirt division was completely destroyed by a female battalion. According to their news bureau dozens of Italian planes have been brought down, this or that place taken by assault, when, in fact, the Italians pulled out and let them have it.'

'While the truth is not getting out?'

'Not by anything approaching an independent voice.'

'What about the correspondents stuck in Addis?'

'They have taken up knitting as a protest at being kept away from the front.' Alverson laughed at the shocked response, then added, with a sarcastic drawl, 'But they have not, I am told, given up drinking.'

'You're at the front.'

'I am blessed, Cal,' Alverson acknowledged, nodding towards the clutch of Ethiopian commanders. 'But getting the truth out is not easy and I am walking a tightrope. Our friends over yonder think the way to sway world opinion in their favour is to out-lie the Italians. Any hints that the truth might serve them better is not well received, and my main aim is to protect my access.'

'So you're peddling the lies?'

'Not all of them, there are ways to report that let the folks reading the exaggerations see something between the lines.'

'It must be costing a fortune to get your stuff to the Sudan.'

'Thank the Lord it's not my dough. But what about you? Still don't think our friends can win?'

'Tyler, they are doing a damn sight better than I ever dreamt was possible, but I still think they would do more damage if they let the enemy come to them. They see the loss of ground as some kind of disgrace, the failure of a sacred trust. A good field commander gives ground in order to entice his enemy on to the position on which he wants to fight, he chooses the battleground that suits his forces and tactical abilities.'

'Which is what they did at the outset.'

'Precisely! Look what happens when the Italians are out from their prepared positions and into open country. That's where native numbers really count, and the more mountainous it gets the better. What they are doing now is sacrifice to no purpose, and proportionately, our friends, as you call them, are losing more men. There's a point where an attack or even contesting the battle area ceases to have any merit, and they are weeks past that.'

It had been a long time since they had discussed the proposition

Peter Lanchester had originally outlined to Cal Jardine: that trapping Mussolini in an unwinnable war might bring him and the idea of Fascism triumphant down and alter the face of European politics, heading inexorably for another murderous war.

'I'm not too impressed with Mussolini's boys.'

'Their high command is useless and so are a lot of the field commanders, but some of the line officers are as good as any in the world. Just don't blame the boots. Most of them don't want to be here, if you leave out the Blackshirts, all fired up with their specious ideology. But the ordinary soldiers, give or take some regulars, would rather be at home eating polenta.'

'You sound sorry for them.'

'If you're going to have to fight as a bit of cannon fodder, Tyler, then let it be at least for something you care about.'

The sound of aircraft overhead made them look skywards, not least because there was no response from the anti-aircraft batteries which protected *Ras* Kassa's base camp; they were silent and that meant the planes were friendly. There was precious little to worry about in any case – a brace of the quick-firing, spider-like 20 mm Oerlikons, coupled with bigger, longer-range 75 mm Schneiders – but it was enough, it seemed, to deter the Italian fliers. The Ethiopians saw this as cowardice; to Jardine it made sense: why risk your skin when there was an abundance of unprotected targets well away from the guns?

The flight of four Potez 25s which passed low overhead, was, Cal Jardine suspected, a high proportion of what was left of the Ethiopian air force. There had only been six of that model to start with. Facing a superior enemy it was thus rarely exposed, but now they had come into action at a time when they had the potential to inflict some real harm, which indicated forward intelligence, an asset which had been sadly lacking thus far in a tentative campaign.

A flight of a dozen Italian Savoia-Marchetti 73 tri-motors, the ones heard droning earlier, had just begun their bombing run, which of necessity lowered their speed, aiming to hit the attacking Ethiopian infantry, so a biplane fighter which normally could not match the bombers might, by nipping into action when they were already engaged, even up the odds.

Would the SM73s abort their run, given their lateral-firing machine guns could not be used when bombing? The Ethiopian planes were making just enough altitude to get above and behind them – sensible, because that also took out of play the forward-firing defences. The greatest problem was a four-aircraft fighter screen overhead, and this meant, in terms of odds, what the biplanes were about was exceedingly risky; in terms of time, it was a severely limited opportunity.

Whoever commanded the Italians was not going to be deterred: he kept them on their original flight path and the first stick of bombs began to emerge from the bays. Within less than a minute from sighting the biplanes, the leading pair of Potez 25s engaged the front SM73, the other pair going after number two in the bombing line, the crunch of ground explosions mixing with the rattle of the Vickers, much muted by being aerial.

'Fighter screen coming in,' Alverson said, his field glasses raised high into the sunlit sky.

'This could be a massacre,' Jardine grunted.

The Fiat CR30s were dropping fast, the commander of the Italian bombers relying on them to allow him to release his stick; clearly he was prepared to risk damage to deliver. For the attacking biplanes, hitting something vital on a much larger plane made of plywood was a chancy affair, though from the ground it was possible to see bits of wood flying off the fuselages of the two bombers being attacked. But it could not last: with the Italian fighters coming in fast, the Ethiopian pilots broke off and ran, the Fiats on their tail and closing, with the rear-firing machine gunners seeking to keep them at bay.

'Got it!' Jardine cried, for to him the air attack made little sense. The Potez 25s were too lightly armed and slow to have any real hope of downing a bomber. 'They want to suck them into a pursuit.'

It had to have been planned in advance, for the anti-aircraft guns were manned and ready, with their barrels pointed forty-five degrees north. The Fiats, closing, had opened up on four aircraft losing the little height they had to get maximum speed heading for the safety of their own lines.

As soon as they were out of the target area, the quick-firing Oerlikons opened up on the lead Italian fighters, firing at a rate of 450 rounds per minute. Three of the pursuit planes immediately spun away and began a fast climb, but one fighter pilot obviously had only a kill as an object, for he flew through the ground fire, which now included machine guns and rifles, intent on destroying one enemy.

He had picked out his target and he stuck to its tail, guns blazing, now no longer the popping sound of distant aerial bullets, but the harsh crack of projectiles so close, people were ducking their heads. The bullets ripped through the doped canvas of the slower biplane, but the pursuing fighter was taking hits too, one of which must have been on the pilot, for the nose of the Fiat suddenly dropped, bringing it down to skim overhead and plough into the ground well to the rear of the Ethiopian positions, exploding in a great ball of orange fire and black smoke, which produced massed cheering for the whole encampment.

'Our boy is in trouble, I think,' Alverson said.

He was pointing to the biplane which had been the object of the Fiat's foolhardy pursuit, now turning to make a forced landing on the flattest piece of ground it could find, which was near the casualty clearing station where Corrie Littleton laboured. Jardine was already moving towards the spot, with the American shouting he would catch up: hard running was not his style.

The loose and curly blond hair told him who the pilot was before Jardine got really close, while the inert body on the ground was enough to indicate who had suffered in the attack: the observer-gunner was either seriously wounded or dead, while Henri de Billancourt, on his knees, was covered in blood, he having dragged the man out.

Jardine was angered by the sight, even as he knew, deep down, he had no right to be: in combat you took risks and sometimes people got killed. Pointing the finger was generally useless unless someone had been outright stupid. Had the whole thing been de Billancourt's idea? Unfairly, he was thinking it was typical of the man, yet on balance it had been successful: a modern Italian fighter had been destroyed and its pilot killed, which was an exceedingly rare outcome in this war.

They had got a stretcher to the observer-gunner, while someone was doing first aid, and by the time Jardine could see he was an Ethiopian they were lifting him on to it, with the seemingly unaffected Frenchman taking a handle. Jardine grabbed another and they made as much speed as they could to the medical tents, crossing paths with Alverson and his ubiquitous camera, always slung round his neck, snapping away at what was really, if you excepted the flying overalls, a commonplace picture.

Corrie Littleton was at her usual task; the present attack had been blunted by the usual methods of mass artillery, backed up by machine guns firing on fixed arcs, while the bombing and strafing aircraft were now free to roam at will once more, inflicting death and destruction on men falling back. The casualties were being brought in on makeshift stretchers, while out on the battlefield there would be many dead and wounded, remaining there until darkness fell. As soon as she saw the Frenchman she rushed over, no doubt, Jardine suspected, to see if the blood on his overalls was his, to be greeted with a smile.

'I think this fellow,' Jardine growled, nodding to the man on the stretcher, 'needs your attention.'

The American girl was quick then; a few weeks spent dealing with the effects of war had taught her much in a short space of time. Her examination was precise, professional almost, and she addressed Henri de Billancourt, not Jardine, her head shaking as she did so.

'With these wounds I doubt he can be saved, and there are people here who will benefit more from attention than he. The doctor can only deal with those cases that warrant his time. I'm sorry.'

'That's pretty harsh, Corrie,' Alverson said, as the stretcher was laid on the ground.

The reply was weary and resigned. 'It stops being that, Tyler, after the first few hundred cases.'

'I must look to my aircraft,' said de Billancourt, before turning to walk away.

The fact that he was not as indifferent as he at first appeared was evident in the stiffness of his gait, which had in it an attitude that Cal Jardine recognised from the times he had seen men of his own killed in situations where to show your feelings was not permitted; that made him castigate himself for being a bit of a bastard.

The casualty clearing station was within walking distance of where Alverson, Jardine and Vince had a tent, one to which the American girl came to take what little release she allowed herself. Vince Castellano being an expert scrounger, they ate well, he having the depth of Alverson's pocket as an aid, as well as what was left in Jardine's money belt.

Whatever things this peasant army lacked, an active black market in little luxuries was not one of them, while those who supplied their needs also provided the route by which Alverson got out his despatches – both those approved by the censors and his own less cheerleading account – back to Gondar for transmission on to the Sudan, his Rolls-Royce now acting as a temporary ambulance.

A rather morose and uncommunicative Henri de Billancourt was there when she arrived – his plane was damaged and he was waiting for people to arrive from his base and fix it, and it was a testimony to the pressure she was putting herself under that, this time, she barely acknowledged the Frenchman, instead more interested in the bottle Alverson was holding out. It was also an indication of how low de Billancourt was feeling that he did not seem to care.

'Whisky, Tyler, for the love of God.'

'Makes life tolerable, honey.'

Corrie Littleton had ceased to be rangy and was now thin, while her face had that drawn look which comes from continuous exhaustion brought on by relentless toil. If Jardine admired her spirit, and he did, he was not inclined to show it much: they still sparred like two fighting cocks, much to Alverson's continued amusement and Vince's rising irritation. She had taken to occasionally calling him 'Doc Savage' after some ridiculous American comic book hero.

'I am told, Mademoiselle Corrine,' de Billancourt said, when he finally roused himself, no doubt aided by alcohol, 'you will go out tonight with stretcher parties to look for anyone still alive?'

'I have to.'

'Very dangerous, I think, and very brave.'

'She doesn't have to,' Jardine said, 'she chooses to.'

'Maybe I misnamed you: Doc Savage wouldn't hesitate to keep me company, especially him being a medical man.'

'Give that a rest, will you?'

'You should black up if you're going out, miss,' Vince said. 'There's not likely to be a lot of light tonight, what with the cloud cover that's come over, but they will be putting up star shells.'

'It's bad for my complexion, Vince.'

'A bullet's worse.'

'What the hell do you care, Jardine?'

'Odd as it seems, idiot, I do, but don't think it's because you're a female, not that it's certain.'

'Anybody suggested you go to charm school, buster?'

'God help me if you ever went to one.'

'Ah!' de Billancourt sighed, with a wry and irritating smile, 'it is sad when friends fall out, is it not?'

'At least I have you for a friend, Henri.'

'Maybe we should get out of here, Vince,' Jardine sighed. 'There are some Italians whose company I prefer.'

'Those shitty bastards!' she responded angrily, before realising what she had said. 'Sorry, Vince.'

'No offence taken, miss, but I'm a bit like the guv here. I wish you would put a sock in it.'

Her reaction was a startled 'Oh!' – clearly, being put down by Vince mattered.

Seeing Jardine grinning, Vince added, 'An' that goes for you too, guv. It would be much better if you just admitted you fancied her and stopped all the bollocks.'

In the embarrassed silence that followed, the Frenchman, who had now drunk a fair amount of whisky, became more animated, his dancing eyes searching the surrounding faces: Alverson's grin, Vince's irritation and the crabbed looks being exchanged between Jardine and the girl. A sort of dawning seemed to appear in his expression, for Vince's words did not need to be clearly understood in an atmosphere so crackling with obvious tension. Finally he spoke, looking directly at Cal Jardine.

'When my aircraft is repaired, which it will be by tomorrow, *Ras Kassa* has asked me to do a reconnaissance sweep again.'

'So?'

'*Mon ami*, I do not have an observer and I need someone trained to fire my Vickers.'

Then de Billancourt came out with a full smile, for the first time that night, and aimed it right at Corrie Littleton, while Jardine heard himself saying, 'You found one.'

Everyone knew what had just happened: a gauntlet had just been thrown down and Tyler Alverson was not the only one to speak. 'Game on, boys.' Vince Castellano was the other. 'They'll be bloody well jousting next.'

'Have I missed something?' Corrie Littleton asked.

# CHAPTER TWENTY-SEVEN

The aircraft mechanics, a mixed bag of Frenchmen, Germans and Ethiopians, had travelled down from de Billancourt's airfield as soon as they were alerted to the need for repairs, bringing with them on a flatbed truck a complete set of spares, a generator and arc lights by which they could work, as well as a drum of fuel.

The Potez, which was not as badly damaged as first appeared, was serviceable again before dawn, the holes in the canvas covered, several broken struts, a wheel and damaged instruments replaced, the whole covered in a camouflaged sheet before the prospect of a dawn raid by Italian fighters.

Even if that did not materialise, they had to wait till mid-morning to take off on a less-than-perfect strip: it required a party of warriors to clear away a number of rocks. Initially, once airborne, de Billancourt turned south, wishing to test out the repairs before heading for enemy airspace.

There would be standing patrols of Italian fighters up and flying, but, even as numerous as they were, they had a lot of sky to cover along a potential front line stretching hundreds of miles, while a good proportion of their strength had to be diverted to the Somali border, the scene of another hard-fought battle in which the peasant army was pushing back the Italians who had invaded.

Aeroplanes are noisy: you can hear them coming from a long way off and the higher they are, the easier it is to both hear and spot them. The ground-skimming tactic that de Billancourt employed once he did turn north was to avoid a too-rapid alert of an Italian defence line that would have been stood to at first light and kept there in anticipation of another assault, while his relative speed was another safeguard.

At low altitude the aircraft would come upon the Blackshirt infantry unsighted and at speed, cutting down their ability to react. So low were they that Jardine reckoned a pair of scissors would be handy – he could have cut some enemy hair, and it was possible the undercart took off some steel helmets. But it did protect them from ground fire, which was wild and inaccurate. From above and in open country, de Billancourt was relying on his camouflage and the hope that any Italian fighters were at distance enough to make him invisible against the broken ground below.

*Ras* Kassa wanted to know if the Italians were moving forces to face him on the Ethiopian left wing, which led Jardine to suspect, though he had not been told, that things were not progressing as hoped in the main assault further east, and no doubt the counterpart commander of the right wing was asking the same question.

Without metalled roads in very rough country the Italians would only move in daylight over that which their engineers had provided

– a dusty bulldozed track that would not survive the rains when they came – with the added safety of their air superiority to protect them. Even then they could not do so quickly; any build-up should be evident, which would obviate the need to remain over enemy air space for a long period.

The column was not immediately visible but the dust they were sending up was plain for miles, rising on the warm air currents, especially as the Potez was still flying frighteningly low, skimming through slight depressions to stay hidden and near to touching the scrub-covered ground in more open areas. Jardine spent as much time looking at the mounds he was sure de Billancourt was going to plough into as he did searching the sky for enemy fighters, thinking the risk from the former was probably greater than from the latter: the fixed undercarriage was often so close to the earth he feared it might be ripped off by an unseen boulder or tree.

For all his concerns, it was the only safe way to fly and had to be accepted: altitude increased danger, and it takes more than sharp eyes from above to spot a camouflaged aircraft against a same-coloured backdrop over up to a mile – it takes luck. Also, if de Billancourt was an arrogant bastard and a daredevil sod, he was also a damned-good pilot, so Jardine concentrated on keeping his breakfast coffee in his gut as the Potez jinked, rose, swooped and occasionally dropped at a rate that left his stomach under his chin.

The Frenchman was making for the billowing dust, even though that would likewise be visible to, and might attract the attention of, Italian pilots, working on the assumption of there being so few Ethiopian planes they were a rare problem on the front lines and non-existent behind them. So, unless a radio message had been sent from the point of crossing to say that one had entered this particular rear area, it was not something the enemy would expect or look out for with too much zeal.

After a last check of the sky, Jardine got himself into position to use his Vickers; he had no need to be told what was required: having been on the receiving end of aerial gunfire he knew what the pilot would do. Through the dust de Billancourt could now see a line of ten trucks making their way along a rough roadway created by their engineers to get supplies up to the front-line forces. Unprotected on the assumption such a thing was seen as unnecessary, they paid the price as he banked to fly up their line.

Jardine had no need to depress his weapons, the angle of the plane did that for him, and he began his primary burst just before they came level with the lead vehicle, aiming for the driver, then raking the canvas covering in the hope it was carrying infantry. There was no return fire at all; all the drivers did was swing their steering wheels in an attempt to lessen the impact – pretty futile given that Jardine only had to lift or drop his muzzles to compensate.

To the rear of the last truck the Potez swooped up, then made a tight turn so de Billancourt could run down the line of trucks, still close enough to form one because, on both sides of the engineers' roadway, the ground was so broken that to seek to pull off was to invite disaster. The Frenchman was now strafing through his propeller, and as they flew by, Jardine could see that some drivers were abandoning their trucks and running for cover, while others were seeking to accelerate out of trouble.

One was ablaze, while another had left the road, either through terror or wounding, and tipped onto its side. Obviously, whatever they were carrying, it was not troops, given no bodies were either emerging or being flung clear, and while it had to be a pleasure to do what he was about, de Billancourt was also conscious of the need to preserve ammunition for his own defence.

He did one more non-firing run, getting not even a rifle bullet in response, before banking away, heading for some low hills in the distance, this while Jardine observed the remaining trucks re-forming and continuing on their way at as much speed as they could muster; if there was anyone hurt, they were not hanging about to find out.

Facing forward again and curious, Jardine tapped the Frenchman and indicated downwards with his hand, the response a drop in the aircraft speed as de Billancourt acknowledged the message; he was flying a plane that could land anywhere and very likely he, too, was wondering the same as his temporary observer-gunner: what were those trucks carrying if not troops?

It wasn't ammunition, since no explosions were coming from the burning truck now sending a plume of black smoke skywards. What was it? If they landed, some information might be gleaned from the contents.

It was necessary to stay behind those low hills and jink about for a while to let the remaining trucks get clear, but after a short while they re-emerged to see the plume of smoke still rising, now to a point that made watching the sky paramount: if they could see it miles away, an Italian fighter scouting at higher altitude could see it as well, so there was a degree of caution in the approach. Finally thinking it safe, de Billancourt lined up on the roadway and brought the bouncing Potez in to land past the blazing truck, so that Jardine could provide cover in case they were shot at.

There was one inert body on the road but no sign of movement. The plane was taken far enough away to provide room for an emergency take-off, before the Frenchman spun it round and, with a feathering propeller, bumped along the less-than-even surface, taking them closer to the wrecked truck before turning back again to face the way he had come. Jardine was ready to jump out, his pistol in one hand, but he took a last searching look skywards before he executed it: if he was out of the plane and an enemy appeared, any pilot – and quite rightly – would take off, even if he could not get back aboard in time.

His feet had only just hit the ground when two very sad-eyed and dust-covered Italian soldiers emerged from behind the rolled-over truck, with their hands in the air. Searching and failing to see any weapons, he heard them both babbling away in what he took to be a plea to surrender.

A wave of his Colt had them on their knees, while behind him, even with an idling aircraft engine, he could hear de Billancourt laughing, albeit the Frenchman had his pistol out and aimed at the two men who were now looking skywards but praying.

Ignoring them, Jardine pushed past to the turned-over truck, to examine the boxes which had been thrown out, one of which had broken open, scattering its contents. There were no rifles or pistols, which he had half-expected, nor was it food.

The item Jardine picked up was something he had not seen for a long time; still the mere sight of it made him shudder and that made him climb into the truck. There he saw that all the containers were like the one he had found split open.

Back out again, he picked one of the items up; he took it back to the two kneeling Italians, a pair of badly uniformed unshaven louts who could only be drivers, and conscripted ones at that, both with that look in their eye that told him they were sure they were going to die.

He held up the gas mask and used the few Italian words he hoped would make sense, all from a trio of operas, wishing Vince was here now, because to get this wrong was not a good idea. Pointing hard at the mask, he barked his question.

'*Maschera! Tutti camion maschera?*'

The eager nods chilled him instead of pleasing him.

'*Cappa impermeable,*' one of the drivers shouted in a desperate tone, he too pointing after the trucks, before gesturing something covering his body.

Gas masks and capes! He tried to calculate the number of these things that truck convoy must have been carrying and what it meant. Walking over to de Billancourt he showed the gas mask to him and the effect on the Frenchman was equally profound. He was also sharp enough to state an obvious act, which had not occurred to Jardine.

'Gather up as many as you can, *mon ami*. We can fill the cockpits around us.'

That got the two drivers working, carrying gas masks under the threat of Jardine's pistol and dropping the entire contents of the broken container into the cockpits. They had to leave room to fly and fight, but Jardine's last act was to search one Italian and find some matches. He then unscrewed the turned-over lorry's fuel tank cover and let some petrol spill out onto another mask till it was soaked. This was then stuffed into the pipe and lit, before running for the plane, its engine note already at a higher pitch.

The two drivers were running away as they took off and, with the flames taking rapid hold, the lorry went up with a whoosh as the wheels lifted and de Billancourt took them once more into the air.

* * *

'This does not mean they even have brought such a thing to Ethiopia, Captain Jardine,' *Ras* Kassa insisted, holding up one of the masks. 'Or if they have it, they would be so insensitive to world opinion as to use it.'

'Sir, the first thing you must make sure of when using mustard gas as a weapon is that your own troops are protected, and I would remind you that the Italians used it against the rebellious tribesmen in Libya. As for world opinion, that is something they have been happy to ignore up till now. It's over a month since the League of Nations condemned the invasion of your country and what has changed? Nothing.'

'The emperor will not make peace, will not see his country torn apart to salve the conscience of France and Britain.'

'It shames me that they should even suggest it.'

*Ras* Kassa was referring to a sell-out plan cooked up by the two democracies, or rather the British foreign minister, Samuel Hoare and the French premier, Pierre Laval, to give the most fertile bits of Abyssinia to the Italians, with the sop of a corridor to the Red Sea for the Ethiopians. Leaked to the press, it had been roundly denounced by the public, while the two governments had bowed to the resultant pressure, forcing the politicians who had proposed it to resign.

'Sir, it is not my intention to argue with you, that is not my place, but I suggest you have not seen the effect of this weapon . . .'

'And you have?'

'The effect, yes, on the men who faced it on the Western Front, but I have never experienced it myself.'

*Ras* Kassa held up the mask Jardine had shown him, one of the number he and the Frenchman had brought back, enough to protect his command but not his warriors. Others had gone to the casualty station doctor, the two Americans, Vince, and naturally one each for the men who had come across them, this at the insistence of the Ethiopian leader.

'Perhaps it would have been better if you had brought us these and protective capes rather than guns.'

'Can they be got anyway, perhaps by an appeal to the democracies? Surely they will not embargo those.'

'In the quantity and time required, even for just the fighting men? I think not, and I fear, if you are right, my people are going to suffer a great deal. The only way to stop that is a complete victory over the Italian forces and, as I think you have already come to suspect, that is not happening as we hoped.'

'I wondered if you were deluding yourself.'

'No, Captain Jardine, but sadly, it is necessary to delude the nation and keep up the hopes of my people. The Italian corps we hoped to trap have evaded encirclement and are now part of a continuous defensive line of some strength.'

'You won't break through?'

'Only if there is a miracle, and much as I love and respect my God, that I cannot see happening. However, we must try, and the invasion of Somaliland is progressing well.'

'The cost, sir?'

'How will this come, if it comes?' the *ras* asked, holding up the mask again, unwilling to respond to Jardine's question.

'Ground canisters on the right wind were the normal method of delivery, but I believe the Italians used artillery shells in their North African provinces.'

Jardine was sure he could see the *ras* trying to calculate the potential effect; artillery argued it would be local and it was a gas

371

that dispersed reasonably quickly, which might mean the effect would be contained. Conscious that he was inclined to think the man callous in his view of human life, he also had to remind himself that he was not responsible for the alternatives.

Reports of what the Italians had done in their Libyan provinces did not provide a happy prospect for Ethiopia: mass deportations, murderous concentration camps in which thousands of rebellious tribesmen and their families had perished, as well as summary executions. When it came to mass killing, the Fascist generals had what Vince would call 'form', and there was no reason to suppose they would not employ the same methods here.

Yet there was no way the front-line troops could be kept safe from the effects of mustard gas burning; rarely fatal, it was, however, totally incapacitating on exposed eyes and skin, while it was almost as if, in the *shamma*, the Ethiopian peasant army had come up with a garment providing less protection than even an army uniform, and that was useless.

'Ask Mr Alverson to come and see me, Captain Jardine. This, whatever the other leaders say, is a story that must be got out to the world and quickly, without embellishment.'


What had not been calculated for was the use of science to improve delivery, and it was the troops pushing back the Italians in Somalia who were the first to suffer from a cloud of mustard gas dropped on them from the air, a much more effective way to deploy the instrument of terror than had previously been known. From advancing with gusto, the troops of the eastern front were first stopped, then thrown into headlong retreat, unable to face what they said was the terrible rain that burnt and killed.

For weeks the Italians had been preparing a second offensive on the main northern front – Badoglio had been reinforced with more regular troops. It was also obvious by the increased air activity and the relentless bombing of Addis Ababa – as well as the road to the front – to interdict both men and supplies, and it was a fair assumption that having used gas once, they would do so again.

How much the spear- and bow-carrying warriors knew of what was coming Cal Jardine did not know; what he was aware of did not bring peace of mind. There was to be no withdrawal by the imperial armies to the high mountains, but at least they had given up useless assaults and were now waiting to be attacked. What reconnaissance could be undertaken showed the steady build-up of armoured units at the front, and the lines of attack could be in little doubt.

Finally, under pressure from his field commanders, Haile Selassie had ordered his troops pulled back from where the blows would fall, and allowed them to disperse to save lives. Yet it was only half a cake to Cal Jardine, given he also hoped the emperor would allow them a flexible ability to respond in the counter-attacks he was already envisaging.

As they had dispersed, so had Corrie Littleton: she was now in a new field hospital well back from the front, nearer Gondar, while Alverson was toing and froing to there, now he had his Rolls back. Cal Jardine and Vince Castellano stayed with *Ras* Kassa's forward HQ, now leading a very tightly controlled group of a dozen young warriors in raiding, striking the Italian lines in different places and gathering intelligence.

They had, of course, to bow to the wishes of the *ras*: the job of their natives was to instil fear into their enemies by slitting the throats

373

of the Italians, men who never left their front lines to raid themselves, while their British leaders sought prisoners who could be brought back for interrogation; to stop them being subsequently tortured and killed they were being passed back to Addis, ostensibly as presents for the emperor.

'They might still pull it off, Tyler,' Jardine insisted, when they got together for a meal – on a night of a full moon and a clear starlit sky, raiding was out of the question. 'Scattered troops make them hard to find and bomb, and he has taken steps to keep secret where they are going to be concentrated.'

'I'm no soldier, but as soon as Fatso's boys attack they will have to concentrate, and in the open, yes?'

Jardine nodded. 'That's when they will get to see what Badoglio intends.'

'You know, I don't like the odds, guv.' Vince insisted, having made no secret of his view that, even owning a mask, and now with an impermeable cape as well, he did not fancy mustard gas.

'If he looks like he's winning he'll hold off, I think.' There was no need to add what would come were the Italian assault to be held up.

'Nightcap before I hit the sack?' Alverson suggested, proffering yet more whisky. 'I'm going back up to Gondar in the morning. I'm running out of film and my slaver has been asked to bring some in.'

'I'm for that,' Vince said, nodding to the bottle, 'it'll help me get a good night's sleep.'

'Don't kid me, Vince,' Jardine joked. 'You love being up all night.'

'Depends what I'm up, guv.'

There was no proper night's sleep: the Italian artillery barrage started before dawn and it was ferocious, churning up the ground in front of their positions, sending earth and rocks skywards but killing few men – their enemies were no longer there. Virtually all that had been left out front, to fool the air reconnaissance the Italians relied on, were *shammas* supported by triangular sticks, backed up by a piquet; as a barrage it was mostly wasted.

By the time the sun came up Cal Jardine and Vince had been out observing for an hour, finally able to use field glasses to assess what was coming, though given the rate and density of shell there could be little doubt. They also knew exactly when the enemy were going to move, as the barrage lifted and crept forward. *Ras* Kassa Meghoum had been up as long as them, and they could see the vehicles he had kept back getting ready to pull out.

'Time to go, guys,' Alverson said from behind them. 'Your carriage again awaits.'

The plan was sound: to once more let the Italians advance into a vacuum. By the time the Ethiopians engaged, the enemy would have begun to suffer the common gremlins of war – tanks no longer operable and broken into packets, troops in distended formation instead of tight brigades – merely because such discipline in an advance was difficult regardless of which nation was undertaking it, and the Italians had already shown they were not the best. Also, the concentration of the artillery when on the move could not be anything like what they were sending over now.

'You two got a death wish?'

'He has,' Vince replied, nodding at Jardine.

'Not bad gunnery,' was the reply from Jardine, as they watched the churning of the ground move forward at a steady pace. 'Mind, they've had a long time to get the ranges.'

'I take it you want to be the last one here, Cal.'

Cars, including the Dodge of *Ras* Kassa, were behind them now; the warriors with whom they had so recently worked and the old man's bodyguard were going too, and at a fast pace. 'No. I was just living in the past for a bit.'

'Present suits me better, old buddy.'

'Me too, Tyler.'

They left as the creeping barrage inched up to the now abandoned site of the Ethiopian HQ, not looking back; whatever was going to happen in this war was going to be decided in the next few weeks, or maybe even days.

# CHAPTER TWENTY-EIGHT

Not long after they reached the new HQ, halfway to Gondar, they heard the news and it was uniformly bad. On the main battlefront around Mek'ele, through the use of mustard gas, the Italians had completely unhinged Ethiopian resistance and the eighty-thousand-strong army of *Ras* Mulugeta. To call the act indiscriminate did not even begin to describe the damage inflicted. Discharged from special sprayers in the bomb bays of the Italian bombers, they flew in almost continuous formations that avoided the respite of temporary dispersal.

They had inundated the forces – which had concentrated, seeking to encircle them – inflicting terrible burns and causing a great number of warrior fatalities. Their actions, carried out over an ever-widening area as Mulugeta's army fell back, also mutilated women and children and completely destroyed the livestock – sheep, goats and cattle, on which the survivors depended – while poisoning the very waters that irrigated their land and gave them a chance of life.

There was no news blackout on this; indeed, Emperor Haile Selassie sent out his own condemnation communiqué to the nations of the world, but the world, horrified as it might be, was not listening, or at least those that held the power and ability to act against Italy held their tongues. Lesser countries brought forward motions to condemn the use of gas to the floor of the League of Nations Chamber in Geneva, but if they got a resolution that was all it was: words.

Worse followed: a broken army trying to withdraw was at the mercy of a relentless pursuit, forced to abandon the best they had in equipment, and that was not much – a clutch of old tanks and artillery pieces, rifles, machine guns and ammunition – while being harried by every weapon in the Italian armoury. Gas-burnt bodies, unable to move, were mashed to pulp under tank tracks, groups seeking to make a stand were pulverised by field artillery or massed machine gun fire and conventional bombs, while any accumulation of warriors which even showed the ability to hold back the enemy advance was gassed into submission and further retreat.

'I don't know whether to tell the truth or lie, Cal.'

Sat at his typewriter, in a tent close to the newly set up casualty station, Tyler Alverson had lost his air of distance to what was happening; he was not a man given to tears, but he was close now and he was angry too, in that frustrating way of someone who would love to have the power of decision, but lacked even the ability to persuade. He was also in possession of information that had come to him only by accident.

The Ethiopians, while condemning the use of mustard gas, were, quite naturally, seeking to play down both the rout of their forces and the level of their casualties, but the international doctors with the divisions around Mek'ele, retreating ahead of the army they served, had thought it only fair to alert their as yet unburdened colleagues with some idea of what they would face in the event they sustained the same level of defeat: an overwhelming number of casualties, too many to even begin to treat.

'If these figures are true, then that's what you should send out,' Jardine said. 'It helps make the case.'

'Six thousand dead, twelve thousand wounded, *Ras* Mulugeta killed, his army a rabble, and that does not even begin to mention the effect on the civilians.'

'How do they live wiv this back home, guv?' asked a dejected Vince. 'I just don't get it.'

'What you've got to ask yourself, Vince,' said Corrie Littleton from just outside the tent flap, 'is how are we going to deal with it when it comes our way?'

'Which it surely must,' Jardine agreed.

'What does Kassa say?' she asked.

Cal Jardine responded with a wry smile. 'Right now he's not saying much to me.'

'Me neither,' Alverson said, 'which is pretty mean, considering.'

'Considering what, Tyler? He doesn't owe us anything.'

The journalist looked at his fellow American, now sat down out of tiredness. 'Honey, take a look in a mirror and you will see something of what he owes. You should have gone home with your mother.'

That had come as a relief to all: finally convinced she would never get to see the Ark of the Covenant, Ma Littleton had taken the train to Djibouti through Addis Ababa, the idea that her daughter should go with her, brushed aside. Corrie Littleton insisted she was needed and had not stopped working tirelessly at her self-appointed task.

'Tyler's right, you should rest,' Jardine said.

'That's all I need, sympathy from Doc Savage, national hero.'

The reply came without rancour. 'Well, if the war's changed, you haven't.'

'That's not fair, miss.'

'I know, Vince,' she replied in a weary voice. 'Sorry, Jardine.'

'Now I'm really at a loss. A bitch I can cope with.'

The slightest hint of a drone, the signal of approaching aircraft, magnified by their position in a deep, high-sided and narrow valley, killed her sarcastic response. Always a signal for danger, it had taken on an even more deadly meaning now. There was no time to find out if it was friend or foe, it was into the uncomfortable masks and the impermeable cloaks, which might not be protection enough, and that had Corrie Littleton running back to her casualty station where hers, despite numerous warnings, had been left.

It was a false alarm, it being a friendly plane flying over to drop written despatches, the best way to communicate between two armies in the rough mountain country they now occupied: quite apart from the unreliability of the sets, when someone like Haile Selassie Gugsa had gone over to the Italians, radio communication not in code was dangerous. Gas mask off and outside the tent Jardine watched the sudden increase in activity, messages being sent off to the varying commanders; whatever had come had warned of trouble. The man coming towards him only underlined that: *Ras* Kassa wanted to see him.

For all their lack of intelligence gathering, a lot of information on what Badoglio was up to came into the various Ethiopian headquarters, merely through the fact that, behind his lines lay a mass of fellow countrymen, while the front, regardless of Italian efforts, was too extended and porous to close. So they knew of the roads being built, of the increasing numbers of their enemies related to the falling numbers of defenders, of the stockpiles of artillery shells and the certainty of an upcoming Italian offensive. On the situation maps it was all there to be studied.

There were three armies left in the field after the destruction of the one facing Mek'ele: forty thousand men under *Ras* Kassa, another, some thirty thousand strong, under *Ras* Seyoum, and the same on the eastern flank. The first two were spread out through the kind of terrain in which Geoffrey Amherst had advised that they fight: fast-flowing rivers, deep ravines and thick forest, spreading west from the road to Gondar.

'I have been given permission from the emperor to withdraw, Captain Jardine.'

'If it were not for the gas, sir, I would advise against that, but—'

The older man smiled even as he interrupted. 'That, I think, is the first time you have said it is even possible to make a stand.'

'Maybe you can,' Jardine replied, wanting to be positive. 'The terrain is perfect for defence, and provided you don't put large concentrations of men in the open, the gas ceases to be such a potent weapon. The Italians can't sit still, Rome won't let them, and so they have only the option of attack. In such country tanks will be near to useless, the field artillery difficult to move in the mountains, and with the deep forest cover their air force won't know where you are. Not even they have enough bombs to drop them everywhere.'

'And you would advise *Ras* Seyoum to do the same?'

'Definitely.'

'I have just received a despatch telling me that he intends to come out of the mountains and launch an attack northwards to throw back the Italians on Aksum.'

Cal Jardine tried not to shake his head, but he could not resist it. 'Can you override him?'

'Only the King of Kings can do that and he will not interfere.'

'Yet you don't agree with him – *Ras* Seyoum, I mean.'

'I have yet to decide.'

'You should withdraw immediately, sir. If *Ras* Seyoum is defeated, you will be attacked at once with the full enemy strength. With your left flank exposed not even the terrain can save you. Your fellow commander is not being foolish, he's being stupid.'

'But do you not recall telling me that, at Adowa, King Menelik was foolish, or was it stupid?' Jardine knew what was coming. 'But what you do not acknowledge is that the Italians did not expect him to attack for the very reasons he was advised against it, yet in doing that he won a surprise victory. Perhaps *Ras* Seyoum will achieve something similar.'

Their eyes locked, with *Ras* Kassa determined to look as if he meant what he said; the glacial stare more than hinted to Cal Jardine he was trying to convince himself of something he knew to be fundamentally untrue.

'So you will wait?'

'I must, and if he shows any sign of beating the Italian devils I will support him.'

'I take it, by the bustle, the orders for that have already gone out.'

'They have.'

Making his way back to the tent, Jardine was thinking about national myths and the dangers they presented. The Ethiopians had lived off the legend of Adowa for forty years, a whole generation had grown up convinced they were unbeatable, and they were close to right if you took the poison gas out of the mix, while the Italians, or at least the Fascists, prated on about being the new Roman Empire. They were both trapped in national self-deception; men had already died for it and more would follow. He spoke as he entered the tent, and abruptly.

'Tyler, if anyone asks you for the use of your car, say no.'

Surprised as he was, he did not ask the obvious question, given that if the car was required, it would be for a humanitarian need again. 'How, brother?'

'Take out the distributor cap, tell them it's not working; and before you say they will not believe you, ask yourself how many people there are around here who know what a distributor is.'

'What has rattled your cage, tiger?'

'Stupid generals!'

'The car?'

'Might be our only way out.'

What came to be called the Second Battle of Tembien – the title was, as is common, coined by the victors – was nothing short of an unmitigated disaster. *Ras* Seyoum debouched with his entire force onto the plains, an army with more bows and arrows than rifles, no artillery or armour and hardly any machine guns, relying on sheer weight of numbers and the brio of his assault to overwhelm the enemy. The Italians did not need poison gas to blunt that: they had everything they required in conventional arms.

The white-cloaked warriors ran into a hail of shellfire – fighters, bombers and artillery that cut their numbers in half within one hour. Stunned and static, surrounded by the dead and dying, their spirit waned and the retreat began. But now the terrain at their rear became as much of an enemy as the Italians, and any weapons they had possessed which might have given their enemies pause were on the battlefield with the corpses of their fellows.

The Italians streamed into the ravines and valleys in hot pursuit, because the obstacles that would have hampered them in the first instance now became bottlenecks for the Ethiopians. Seeking to get to and cross the Tekezé fords along a single road that canalised the flight, those trying to flee lost all cohesion. Artillery set alight the forested hillsides, for the gunners knew where to aim, and every raging river spewing white water from the surrounding mountains, which would once have taxed the invaders, was now a hazard the defeated could not cross. They became a milling, easy target, doubly so when unable to cross the fords, and forming a heaving, easily spotted mass, they were bombed into a bloody pulp.

Instead of advancing to aid *Ras* Seyoum, the army of *Ras* Kassa was forced into a hurried retreat, seeking and failing to avoid annihilation. Right behind the Dodge of *Ras* Kassa came Alverson's Rolls-Royce, now carrying many of the personal followers of the commander, those that could hanging onto the running boards, avoiding the strafing fighters only by sheer luck, manoeuvring round bomb craters, staying ahead of gas attacks only because of those wheels. Behind them the army of *Ras* Kassa fell apart, dead, collapsed with massive burns to their body, or just dispersed to become useless.

Thousands survived the carnage that ensued, but no one knew how many: they were left only with the claims of the enemy. Those who got away did not join any other army, they went home, their fortitude broken like a dried reed. They had lived the myth and it had either killed them or their spirit. By the time they reached the headquarters of the reserve army, the only men *Ras* Kassa still commanded were his personal bodyguards.

Haile Selassie now took command, gathering all his forces for a final battle, forty years to the day since his predecessor won at Adowa, and he brought with him, to parade before the rest of his warriors, the six battalions of the Imperial Guard, men in smart green uniforms, proper boots, steel helmets, and each with a modern rifle that Cal Jardine suspected were those he had brought into the country, weapons that should have been at the front long ago.

So should the rest of what he had preserved: there was a mobile mortar section, truck-towed 75 mm field guns, twenty in number, the fast-firing, highly mobile French weapon that had been so effective in the Great War as well as an anti-aircraft unit with up-to-date Oerlikons to make sure the King of Kings was protected from the air.

'Where the hell was this lot when we needed them, Vince?'

The bitterness of tone and the fact that it was loudly proclaimed – it had to be, given the cheering – made Tyler Alverson turn to look at Cal Jardine. His eyes were fixed on the tiny, bearded figure of the Emperor of Ethiopia, who, even in ceremonial garb, on a platform that raised him well above the ground, could not even begin to look impressive. Vince said he looked like a doorstop not a figurehead.

'Sittin' in their barracks, guv. Makes you wonder who we've been fighting for – not that ponce of an emperor?'

'You a Bolshevik, Vince?' Alverson asked.

'Not bloody likely.'

'Would these guys have made a difference, Cal?'

'Might have done used wisely, Tyler, it's too late to tell, but I can't see them making much of one now.'

The American just nodded at that; no degree in maths was needed to work out that from the original forces Haile Selassie had fielded – guesses ranged from half- to three-quarters of a million men – he now only had a fraction left, while his enemies were near to their full original strength and had been reinforced. There would be a battle and maybe the Lion of Judah and some of his warriors believed in a miracle; Cal Jardine did not.

What followed did nothing to change that opinion: a week of parades, banquets and ceremonies, at a time when the advancing Italians were defensively vulnerable, threw away what little chance existed, which caused Alverson to opine that what Haile Selassie was doing was mere posturing for the hope of a future: in short, he was prepared to sacrifice anyone and everyone to maintain a tenuous claim to his throne.

By the time the attack was launched, Pietro Badoglio was ready and waiting, and the result was a foregone conclusion: the Ethiopians were routed – but it was what happened in the rear areas that occupied Jardine, Alverson and Vince. The Italian air force, not for the first time, deliberately bombed the field hospital, and one of the casualties was Corrie Littleton.

From their position observing the battle, the trio had seen the aircraft fly over and had heard the crunch of high explosives. It was only when the emperor admitted defeat and broke off the battle that they found out the extent of the damage to a hospital that had yet to start receiving casualties. It was only the needs of her bodily functions that saved Corrie Littleton.

The latrine tent for females had been set well apart from the main treatment tents, the top of which were marked with huge red crosses to tell flyers of their function. It was as if the Italians had used them as aiming points, for there were smashed bodies everywhere, orderlies of both sexes, and nothing left of beds, operating tables or medicines but wreckage around a series of deep craters.

Corrie had been found unconscious and suffering from injuries caused by blast and flying debris, with a broken arm and a gash in her back that had been covered with an antiseptic pad, then bandaged. By the time the trio got to her she was on a stretcher, while streaming past them were the broken elements of the last Ethiopian field army, and gone with them in the general panic and fear of a gas attack were what medical orderlies had survived, including the ones who had treated her.

'You thinking what I'm thinking, Cal?' Alverson asked, as Jardine bent over to examine her; he had seen enough battlefield wounds in his time to realise she was still very much alive but needed help.

'There's no doctors left, guv,' called Vince as he approached from his inspection of the actual hospital tents; there had been two, both Ethiopians. 'They took the full blast, poor sods.'

'The whole thing is falling apart,' the American added. 'And that will include what medical services still exist.'

'Then we have to get her to Addis, Tyler, it's the only place with a properly equipped hospital.'

'Cal. That's where the Italians are going.'

'Where else can we get help?'

'British Somaliland sounds good to me, brother.'

Cal Jardine looked up and nodded, for he knew what Alverson was saying: it was all over bar the shouting. There was nothing left, at least in an organised sense, to stop the Italians now and they would not be kind to those who had aided their enemies. It was time to get out of the country.

'We'd have to go through Addis anyway, it's the only road. We'll just have to hope Badoglio is as cautious as he has been up till now.'

'They're bound to bomb the Addis-to-Gondar road.'

'I know, but unless you can find a plane, we have no choice. Vince, go back into that wreckage and see if you can find any morphine sulphate, bandages, anything we might need – you know what.'

They had to carry Corrie Littleton into the little dusty town of Maychew, which was a slow struggle. Alverson, on the advice of Cal Jardine, had parked the Rolls out of sight, which had been like a harbinger of the coming debacle, on the good grounds that if the army broke, there was no guarantee someone, regardless of the endemic honesty of the locals, would not steal his car.

The loading of their kit was hurried and, with the stretcher lashed across the rear and the three men crowded in the front, they joined the throng of people, warriors, soldiers of the Imperial Guard and fleeing civilians on the crowded road north. Even then they were pushed aside as, from behind them, came the motorised convoy of the emperor.

He, too, was in a Rolls-Royce, a beige coupé. They watched as the Lion of Judah, the King of Kings, the Emperor of Ethiopia, looking like a toy human being, drove by, his gaze unblinking and straight ahead, acknowledging no one to right or left, his face as impassive as it had been before he sent his vastly outnumbered troops into battle. Yet it was the face of a beaten man.

Just how beaten was not long in coming. Badoglio had finished the battle by gassing the survivors who had congregated around a lake, massacring thousands. The road to Addis Ababa was open.

# EPILOGUE

I t took five days to get to Addis, so slow was the road, crowded with refugees – no cheerful warriors now, but people who bore their burdens as a weight heavier than they truly were. Their patient woke up before they parked for the first night to sleep, that only possible when they had stilled her cries of pain with the morphine sulphate, which dulled all her senses. Unable to properly diagnose, apart from the obvious, what Corrie Littleton was suffering from, all three knew that treatment was essential; they could only hope they would get to a proper hospital in time.

Dirty, unshaven, hungry from lack of food and thirsty, with Corrie Littleton going in and out of consciousness, Addis Ababa, when they finally got there, was nothing like it had been before, a thriving African city. It having been severely bombed, and being the place where the wounded warriors made for, they naturally found the hospital full to bursting – the corridors were six deep in wounded and the doctors struggling to cope.

Getting their attention was near to impossible and the notion of her being treated wishful thinking: the place was overwhelmed, medicines were scarce and the wounds of others much more serious. The only thing they established, and it was the badgering American who did it while Jardine argued unsuccessfully with the medical reception, was the presence of a facility at the Imperial Palace.

'We have a bit of juice, Cal, we have to use it,' Alverson insisted.

'He's right, guv, this much they owe us,' said Vince, to back the American up.

'Which means it's down to me to ask?'

'Yup. Of all of us, *Ras* Kassa owes you the most.'

'We don't even know if he's still alive.'

'Then,' Alverson said, 'it's time to find out.'

The roads to the Imperial Palace were blocked off and they had to manoeuvre the car through a throng of supplicants just to get to the line of green-uniformed troops holding them at bay. Later, Tyler Alverson was of the opinion that it was the car that got them through, that Rolls-Royce flying eagle, because, as he put it, 'We looked like shit!' Whatever, the troops made an opening and they entered – once they were away from the keening of those seeking help – an oasis of calm.

The pink-tinged stone-built palace stood in verdant, well-watered gardens; although not of the stature of the European buildings it was modelled on, in a city like Addis it was by far the most imposing dwelling: only the churches outdid it in size. The odd thing was, the place was intact – untouched by the war that had now been raging for five months, in a city that had been repeatedly bombed.

'I'd 'ave made sure this was the first place I went for,' Vince said as they left the empty boulevard and drove through the twin wrought iron gates.

It was Alverson who answered. 'I reckon the Italians are thinking ahead. Why destroy the most comfortable billet in town when you want to lay your weary head there? When Badoglio gets here, you can bet your ass this will be his new home.'

They pulled up in front of the portico to be greeted by an officer Jardine recognised: it was the same French-speaking captain he had met at Gondar when seeking to get to Aksum to find Ma Littleton. Obviously about to ask the purpose of their presence, he was alerted by a groan from Corrie Littleton who, waking yet again, began to writhe from deep pain. With nothing approaching haste the officer walked across the gravel on crunching boots to inspect her, his face showing no emotion.

'She requires treatment, and immediately,' Jardine said.

'The hospital is—'

'I know where it is and I know it's full,' Jardine interrupted, looking around as if to underline the difference between this place and the stinking, crowded charnel house they had just left. 'You have medical facilities here.'

'For the private use of the imperial family and the officials of the government.'

Cal Jardine had been unaware of that fact; Alverson, for all his skill in questioning, had not elicited the information, yet it could not be said to come as a surprise. He had learnt very early on how callous the Ethiopian high-born were about the lower orders and nothing he had seen since altered that view. If there had ever been any doubt, the way they threw them into battle ill-equipped and tactically ignorant would have proved the point.

He had a vision then of the pint-sized emperor as he had driven past them on the Addis to Gondar road, and he wondered whether his lack of response to his broken, retreating followers was really despair at the defeat. Could it be indifference, could it be all he saw was people who were obliged to lay down their lives for his crown and his continuing hold on power? It was a proposition that did nothing for his temper, and his voice was cracked with fury as he responded.

'The imperial family might be better served looking after some of their subjects than themselves. Then maybe they would win a war instead of losing one.'

The man's nostrils flared angrily: he saw an insult to his sovereign and he was not mistaken. Fearing his temper was going to underline an already decided-upon refusal, Jardine suddenly recalled he still carried the pass he had received from *Ras* Kassa. Reaching into his shirt pocket he pulled it out.

'You recognise this, Captain, I am sure.'

'It is no longer valid,' he replied, as Corrie Littleton groaned again.

Opening it, Cal Jardine made a show of examining it. 'I cannot see how – there is no end date. Are you saying the *ras* no longer has any sway?' Hesitation allowed him to press home his point. 'I assume the man who signed this still holds the offices he held when it was written? Or are you saying your country no longer has a government?'

In employing the tone of voice he was using, Cal Jardine was working on instinct, and also on how the man had reacted previously in the face of this pass: this was a staff johnny before him and, in his experience, they were of the type who cared more for their position and prospects than anything else.

If service in the British army had taught him anything it was that the slippery types, the grovellers, unquestioning of even the most absurd orders, were the ones who got to the top. This captain was of that type and would hesitate to question someone of the stature of *Ras* Kassa Meghoum for the very simple fear that it might block his future advancement. The fact that his army was beaten, that in essence it would soon cease to exist, and his country was falling apart around him would probably not come into consideration.

'The pass does not apply here, this is the Imperial Palace.'

It was like playing poker again and there was something in the eyes that made Jardine go straight for an outright bluff. 'Please ask *Ras* Kassa Meghoum to come and tell me that personally.' The man blinked, and encouraged, Jardine added, 'And be assured, I have the means to make him aware of any impediment to his wishes.'

Stood still for several seconds, no doubt weighing the effect of all the alternatives on his own future, the captain suddenly snapped, 'Wait here.' Cal went back to the Rolls, and a patient now moaning continuously, while he went inside.

'How do you know he was here?' Alverson asked.

'Wild guess, brother,' he replied, leaning over Corrie Littleton. Her face was drained of blood, and even if he was not a medic he could see her condition was deteriorating. He brushed a hand across her brow to move aside her unruly hair. 'And if it doesn't work, I don't know what we'll do.'

'Captain Jardine, Mr Alverson.' The deep voice identified the speaker, and just as he turned to respond he caught sight of Vince's face, furious at not being acknowledged. Knowing his friend was capable of saying something offensive, he being no respecter of authority, he spoke quickly. 'And Mr Castellano, *Ras*.'

He was facing him by the time the *ras* added an indifferent, 'Of course,' while behind him came the sound of moaning.

'Miss Littleton is seriously wounded and requires treatment.'

The sound she made and those words brought what appeared to be enlightenment; clearly the captain, who had emerged behind the *ras*, had not told him of the reason his presence was required.

'There is no hope that the hospital will be able to save her.'

'Save her?'

'Yes, sir, if she is not treated she will die.'

The stream of whatever tongue the *ras* was using had soldiers rushing to take the stretcher, and somewhere in there was a reprimand for the captain, judging by the way his facial skin went tight. The eyes, when they flicked towards the source of the rebuke, had Cal Jardine thinking it would be unwise to turn his back on the man.

'Gentlemen, you must too come inside.'

Vince gave the Ethiopian aristocrat a full glare. 'I'll assume that includes me, guv.'


'The emperor and his family will leave the country and seek to gather international support for our cause. He has asked that, with my language skills, I accompany him.'

'By what method?' Alverson asked.

'He dare not fly, Mr Alverson, it is too dangerous with enemy fighters so numerous. He will take the train to Djibouti.'

'On a line which might be bombed,' Jardine said. 'Not to mention the train itself.'

'As would a long convoy of cars and trucks, Captain, and on crowded roads it would move too slowly.'

Washed, fed and watered, they were sitting on a veranda at the rear of the Imperial Palace. Given the birdsong, the flowers, even the buzzing of pollinating bees, it was hard to think they were in the midst of a war. The convoy mentioned was telling: Haile Selassie was not getting out empty-handed. The train would have not only his family on board, but also his followers, his treasury and anything of value he could get away.

It was hard to blame him: he was going into an uncertain exile and if he left anything the Italians would only steal it.

'The French will let him through?'

'That has been arranged.'

About to say something, Jardine stopped himself: Djibouti was likely to leak like a sieve. If the train journey had been arranged, then the Italians would find out about it and send every plane they had to make sure it did not get through – five hundred miles, over three hundred planes, it might be suicidal. Achieve that and they would decapitate the government in exile and make a cakewalk of the takeover. But they must have weighed up the risks; his voicing an opinion would change nothing.

'And you, gentlemen,' the *ras* said, smiling as his eyes moved to include Vince, sitting slightly apart. 'What are your plans?'

'That depends of the health of Miss Littleton,' Jardine replied, which got him a look from his companions, with Vince saying, much to the confusion of their host, 'It Happened One War.' No one, least of all an irritated Cal Jardine, bothered to enlighten him, and in any case, a servant entered to bend over and whisper in his ear.

'Miss Littleton is doing well. The emperor's own doctor has treated her wounds and given her a blood transfusion. Her wound will heal and he has set her arm properly. So, my question.'

'I can do no more here, can I, *Ras*?'

'No, Captain Jardine, but you, Mr Alverson, perhaps.'

'No point, sir: whatever I see and want to report, the Italians will not let me send out.'

That induced a pained expression: up till now none of them had openly referred to the obvious. The Italians would be sitting soon where they were sitting now.

'I could try to get you on the imperial train.'

Thankfully, there was enough doubt in his tone to make a refusal easy for Cal Jardine, and in this he was going to override anything the others might say: he had no notion to travel on a train he was sure would not get through.

'I think we had already decided to make for Hargeisa by car, sir, but we will not do that unless Miss Littleton is well enough to travel.'

'Unless . . .' Alverson added before pausing; he did not need to say more. If the Italians, who had yet to advance, did so, they might have to get out and damned quick, even if it put her at risk.

'It would be interesting to know when the doctor thinks Miss Littleton is up to such a journey.'

That was two weeks away, yet they were in no danger because the Italians did not move with anything like alacrity. On the radio, Vince listened, and translated for the others, as Marshal Badoglio announced what he called 'The March of the Iron Will', which got the soubriquet 'bollocks' from the Londoner, given there was nothing to stop what he called the 'Piedmontese bastard': there was no love lost between the various provinces of old Italy or the people who lived in them. Kassa had got them houses in a palace annexe and there they waited, played cards and talked in between visiting a recovering patient.

'Strikes me, Cal, that we have been together quite a while and yet I know hardly anything about you.'

'Let's leave it that way, shall we?'

'Your father, who was he? Your mother too . . . you don't talk about them.'

'Spanish flu.'

'Sorry,' Alverson replied; that epidemic in 1918 had killed millions.

'So how come you speak French and German so well?'

'My father was an international trader, Tyler. We spent several years in Marseilles and the next stop to make his money was Hamburg. It's simple.'

'And your military service?'

'Is a closed book. Deal the cards.'

Looking at his hand, Alverson said, in a slightly sour tone, 'If your old man was as good at business as you are at poker he must have left you a pile.'

Marshal Pietro Badoglio was furious, but he dared not show it even in front of his most trusted staff. He wanted to curse Il Duce, to say in public what he had always thought of him: that he was a posturing buffoon whose only gift was to appeal to the basest members of Italian society, while people like Badoglio merely tolerated the upstart swine. But that might get back: he could not trust anyone.

In his hand he had an answer to a request he had made to bomb the train he knew Haile Selassie was about to board. His troops were marching in triumph towards the Ethiopian capital, meeting little resistance, which made him the most potent soldier in Italy. True, Graziani had won in the south, but under his overall command. The fat-bellied swine Mussolini, who dared to wear a military uniform to which he was not entitled, had refused a reasonable request. How could he call himself a soldier?

The Imperial Palace showed signs of being stripped, everything of value now loaded on to the train wagons in a special siding. Corrie Littleton was well enough to travel: though weak – she had to be helped to the car and aided to get into the rear seat – Badoglio was on the way and it was time to go. The Rolls was now very clean and highly polished, all marks of its travails removed: it had been under the attention of the emperor's own mechanics and valets.

They had food, water, fuel and their weapons but there was no grand farewell, no sadness, no *Ras* Kassa Meghoum to see them off, only that staff captain who let them depart with a look of deep dislike. The road they travelled was no longer crowded now – the warriors of Ethiopia, at least those who had survived, had gone back to their fields to await the invaders, and their emperor, their King of Kings, their Lion of Judah, was on his way to Djibouti and exile, the ship waiting to take him through the Suez Canal the British cruiser HMS *Enterprise*.

From Aden they went their separate ways, Alverson accompanying Corrie Littleton back to the USA, Jardine and Vince to London, where the boxer found his gym completely refurbished, freshly painted, the window panes whole and new, while any worn equipment had been replaced and the number of youths using the place had doubled.

As the man who had looked after the place for him said, 'You should go away more often, mate.'


Cal Jardine and Peter Lanchester were at the Army & Navy Club, taking luncheon again, talking over what had happened, the former of the opinion that what they had done had been a waste of time. The idea of putting brakes on Mussolini had come to nought, mainly, Jardine insisted, through the appalling and wasteful tactics of most of the Ethiopian commanders, with the caveat that there was no reason why they should alter those to suit the democracies who refused to aid them.

Lanchester was less sure: had they not garnered some goodwill in a spot where in the future it might prove important? 'The Italians have got their empire and the Stresa Front's as dead as a dodo too, old boy.

Adolf Hitler came out in favour of the Italian invasion the moment they went in and Mussolini was grateful. Il Duce is now firmly in the German camp and Britain, France and the League have egg all over their faces. I can tell you, on the QT, that the purse strings have been much loosened and we are seriously going to rearm.'

'So, Peter, the road to war just got a little smoother?'

''Fraid so. Port?'

Walking towards Piccadilly Circus, only half-listening to Peter Lanchester as he outlined the new fighters and bombers being planned, the new tanks and the expansion of the various services, it was impossible for Cal Jardine not to cast his mind back to Addis Ababa and the bomb damage he had seen there, while looking into the faces of the bustling crowds parading along the pavements, some vacuously, others with real purpose, the notion of mustard gas did not bear thinking about.

'Did you hear what I asked, old boy?'

'Sorry, Peter, miles away.'

'I was asking if you are up for anything else we might need, Cal? Naturally, we all hope it does not come to war, but we must prepare and that might mean the odd little commission for a man of your talents.'

Over luncheon, asked the same thing, Jardine thought he might have refused. But out here, and with the thoughts he had just had, that had changed. What he could achieve on his own had to be limited, but from now on he must see himself as a cog in a larger wheel; in short, in a phrase so overworked in the Great War, he had to do his bit.

'As soon as I have settled on somewhere to rent, Peter, I'll send you my phone number.'